SONGSMITH

Tor books by Andre Norton and A.C. Crispin

Gryphon's Eyrie
Songsmith

Tor books by Andre Norton

Caroline (with Enid Cushing)
The Crystal Gryphon
Dare To Go A-Hunting
Elvenbane (with Mercedes Lackey)
Flight in Yiktor
Forerunner
Forerunner: The Second Venture
Grand Masters' Choice (editor)
Here Abide Monsters
House of Shadows (with Phyllis Miller)
Imperial Lady (with Susan Shwartz)
The Jekyll Legacy (with Robert Bloch)
Moon Called
Moon Mirror
The Prince Commands
Ralestone Luck
Sneeze on Sunday (with Grace Allen Hogarth)
Stand and Deliver
Storms of Victory
Wheel of Stars
Wizards' Worlds
Wraiths of Time

THE WITCH WORLD (editor)
Tales of the Witch World 1
Tales of the Witch World 2
Four from the Witch World
Tales of the Witch World 3

MAGIC IN ITHKAR (editor, with Robert Adams)
Magic in Ithkar 1
Magic in Ithkar 2
Magic in Ithkay 3
Magic in Ithkar 4

SONGSMITH

A Witch World Novel

Andre Norton

A. C. Crispin

A Tom Doherty Associates Book

New York

SONGSMITH

Copyright © 1992 by Andre Norton, Ltd., and A. C. Crispin

This book was printed on acid-free paper.

A Tor Book
Published by Tom Doherty Associates, Inc.
49 West 24th Street
New York, N.Y. 10010

Tor® is a registered trademark of Tom Doherty Associates, Inc.

Eydryth's song lyrics were written by Shoshana Hathaway.

Library of Congress Cataloging-in-Publication Data
Norton, Andre.
    Songsmith / Andre Norton and A.C. Crispin.
        p.   cm.
    "A Tom Doherty Associates book."
    ISBN 0-312-85123-5
    I. Crispin, A. C. II. Title.
PS3527.0632S67   1992
813'.52—dc20   92-2965
                                                                              CIP

First edition: May 1992
Printed in the United States of America
0 9 8 7 6 5 5 4 3 2 1

This book is dedicated to Teresa Bigbee, friend and *equestrienne extraordinaire.* If anyone could *really* ride a Keplian, she could!

SONGSMITH

Prologue

*L*ife as a songsmith, a forger and singer of tales, seems to the uninitiated (that is, those who have never tried it) to be a most carefree existence, full of travel, romance and perhaps (only now and then, for spice) a little danger. In truth, it seldom reaches such memorable heights, being mostly work like unto any other.

One listens, one remembers, then one wrestles with words and musical notes to hammer all into a coherent whole, hoping fervently that the finished product will elicit smiles instead of frowns, or, worse, yawns. One learns to count the night's takings from the clinks in the harp case, discerning the clear ring of silver from the thud of bronze and copper or (fortune be praised) the weighty, rare whisper of gold—all by sound alone. One spends nights huddled under the lash of rain, or stinging snow, with perhaps naught but a pocket of sullen fire to hold back the hungry night. One learns to heat brook water and sip it slowly in lieu of real food, trying thus to fool an empty belly. . . .

No, my lords and ladies, gathered here in this age-held citadel to hear the songsmith and sip your wine, the life of a bard is hardly carefree.

There *are* times, though, when the music and the tale are worth it all. Then the tune flows like the ripple of a fine horse's mane, words spring nearly unbidden to the singer's lips. Such a time is now, following the toasts and congratulations that accompany a day of ceremony, high feasting and joy, here in such a lordly keep. Now, after the singing of some of the oldest, best tales, it is time for the birth of a new one . . . a tale that songsmiths will hold in special honor, for reasons soon to be made clear to you.

So . . . an opening chord-sweep, a strum to mimic the sound of wind harrying a cold, early spring mist in the backwater alley of a darkened waterfront, and the new tale opens. . . .

One

*Y*ears of salt spray borne by fierce winds had encrusted the walls guarding the steep lane leading up from the wharves, painting dirty white splotches on the age-blackened stones. The Way of the Empty-Netted Fisher was nearly deserted in the last wan illumination of sunset; only one of its many shadows possessed any substance.

That dark-cloaked, slight figure was already so unsteady from two months at sea that when a bitter cold, salt-tinged blast swept by, it staggered, nearly falling. The hapless wayfarer skidded on the slimy cobbles of the stinking, refuse-covered Way, only saved from a fall by the tall, gryphon-headed quarterstaff that served as a walking aid as well as a weapon. The traveler huddled into the half-shelter of an ancient archway to brace against another gust of wind, long-fingered hands clutching a worn hand-harp case and a much-mended backpack against the icy thrust of the coming storm.

Ahead a dim light beckoned, promising shelter from the wind and soon-to-fall sleet. As the harper neared that flickering beacon, it revealed itself to be a ship's lantern, barely sheltered enough that its flame still lived, hanging outside a hulking, dark-timbered building. Even above the whipping breeze, sounds of tipsy revelry inside were clear.

The traveler eyed the inn with its accompanying tavern warily, realizing that The Dancing Dolphin was no accommodation that anyone with a reasonably well-filled purse would seek out for a meal, much less lodging. Beneath the much-faded lettering on the swinging sign, an improbable greyish shape sported among wildly tossing waves. The harper grimaced, but there was no arguing with the light weight of the purse carefully tucked down inside a sea-stained leather jerkin.

Forcing the door open against a particularly strong wind-bluster, the songsmith stumbled into the taproom. Raucous laughter and shouted arguments made a deafening din. Eyeing the tavern-master, the dark-cloaked traveler picked a cautious way across a floor made nearly as treacherous as the alley outside by slopped wine and greasy, skittering bones.

The tavern-master, a thin, red-nosed man with a balding pate and hair-tufted ears, turned at the tug on his sleeve. "Your pardon, sir," the stranger murmured, indicating the hand-harp case. "Would there be any objection to a few songs by the fire for your customers tonight?"

The tavern-master's eyes were on a level with the harper's as he eyed the stranger; then, abruptly, he nodded. "Not as long as you're willing to pay for your bed and board like anyone else, minstrel."

"Certainly." The stranger shook back the hood of the dark cloak, revealing a mass of curling black hair, cropped short. Small silver hoops winked from both earlobes. "I'll begin—"

"A wench! An' a likely-looking one at that, Mylt! By the Hounds' Teeth, where'd you find 'er?" A hand descended on the traveler's shoulder, jerking her half about to face a heavy-shouldered fisherman with a wind- and ale-reddened face.

His rough handling pulled her dark cloak open, revealing the silver ornament lying pendant on the breast of her laced overjerkin. As the man took in the meaning of that symbol, he stepped back, dropped his hand. "I didn't know—didn't see—" Clumsily, he touched thick fingers to his forehead in apology. "Yer pardon, songsmith. . . ."

The bard graciously inclined her head, her fingers going to the sign of her calling . . . three interlinked circles, each with a flattened, pointed side—stylized finger and thumb picks, for use with a hand-harp. "I'll begin now," she said to the tavern-master, as though the interruption had not occurred.

Carrying her harp case over to the bench by the fire, the songsmith opened it, drawing forth a much-used instrument. It was of old-fashioned design, carved from aged cherry wood, its scrolls and frets enhanced by a silvery blue metal shimmering faintly in the firelight. Resting the harp across her lap, she drew three picks out of the inner pocket of her red tunic, slipping them onto her thumb and first two fingers.

She began tuning the instrument. Hearing the soft strains, the twelve fishermen, eight Sulcar sailors and two grizzled old Falconer marines present in the common room ceased talking and quietly, respectfully, gathered near the fire.

"Draw nigh, sirs!" Mylt the tavern-master loudly urged. "Pay heed to a wandering songsmith who has graciously agreed to provide us with entertainment this stormy eve. Give heed to the Lady—" He hesitated, realizing he'd neglected to ask the bard's name, and she whispered, with a wry smile, "Eydryth of Kar Garudwyn."

". . . the Lady Eydryth of Kar Garudwyn!" Mylt finished with a flourish. A polite silence fell.

Eydryth began playing, a rollicking, toe-tapping tune, limbering her fingers while sizing up her audience. All male, and most of them sailors or fishermen. Sea-songs would go well, then, tales of lost loves, of sweet-voiced sirens and of noble deeds. Perhaps a bawdy one to finish, making them laugh, even as they tossed coins into her harp case. . . .

"Give heed, kind sirs, to a tune taught me aboard the Sulcar

ship *Osprey,"* she said, hoping fervently that the cold dampness of this day's sailing had not thickened her voice. "It
concerns a force of men gathered by one of your legendary
heroes during the Kolder War, one Simon Tregarth. I give you
'The Riving of the Border.' "

Eydryth began singing, softly at first; then, as her voice
warmed up, her contralto rang out, filling the smoke-thick-
ened air with clear, true notes:

> We pledged fair Estcarp's bounds to hold
> We men who ride with Tregarth's band
> That witches might, with knowledge old,
> Avenge the wrongs done in our land.

> Of Falconer blood and elder race
> We ride, united by one will—
> To keep the invaders from this place;
> Send sword and falcon forth to kill!

As she finished the second verse and began the third, the
young woman glanced quickly from face to face. Her audience
was leaning forward, all conversation forgotten. Tension
eased from her as she realized that the people here in the Port
of Eslee were equally susceptible to the "spell" cast by flying
fingers and trained voice as were the folk overseas in High
Hallack or her home in spell-shrouded Arvon. She hoped
they'd be as generous with their coin offerings; it had taken
nearly everything she'd earned on her travels through the
Dales to pay for the long voyage aboard the *Osprey.*

Both fourth and fifth verses went even better. By now the
men were nodding in rhythm to her song. Eydryth finished the
ballad with a last triumphant, clarion strum, and they
thumped their tankards on the board appreciatively. "Another, minstrel! Another!" One of the Sulcar sailors, massive
and fair as were all his race, shouted bull-voiced over the
others, "A Sulcar tune, songsmith! Give us a song for the Sons
of Sul!"

Fortunately, the Sulcar sailors aboard the *Osprey* had

taught her a multitude of songs, since they sang constantly at their work, and their music was easy for trained ears and fingers to master. Eydryth closed her eyes as she strummed, searching for the proper key. . . . There, she had it now.

"Very well, kind sirs. I give you 'The Fall of Sulcarkeep,' which tells the tale of the great hero Magnus Osberic and how he destroyed his own stronghold rather than let it fall into Kolder hands."

The tune this time was in a somber, minor key, as befitted a tragic tale. Eydryth began:

> Wind and flame and earth and wave
> Sulcarkeep, proud Sulcarkeep!
> All sent to dig a trader's grave;
> Sulcarkeep, lost Sulcarkeep!
>
> " 'Tis built to ward," proud Osberic said,
> "Sulcarkeep, strong Sulcarkeep!
> There's none without permission tread
> In Sulcarkeep, fair Sulcarkeep!"

She continued, losing herself in the music. Her tawdry surroundings faded as the song bore her back into that ancient stronghold, transporting her to the fateful night. Eydryth's voice rose into an eerie wail as she described the desperate battle throughout the doomed fortress:

> Yet when the fog stole rank and thick
> On Sulcarkeep, dark Sulcarkeep
> Sent by a Kolder demon-trick
> To Sulcarkeep, cursed Sulcarkeep,
>
> The trader knew his fate was nigh
> In Sulcarkeep, strong Sulcarkeep
> For Death came drifting from the sky
> To Sulcarkeep, doomed Sulcarkeep.
>
> With swinging axe and bloodied sword
> Through Sulcarkeep, vast Sulcarkeep
> They fought the mindless, soulless horde
> Down Sulcarkeep, through Sulcarkeep.

The big sailor's face was saddened and grim now, and Eydryth wondered whether he had lost a father or uncle during
that terror-ridden night. It was almost as though she could *see*
the mighty Osberic in his bear's-head helm, his stained sword
dripping red onto the blood-slicked flags of the ancient stronghold. Her voice soared up into the final sad yet strangely
triumphant verses:

> And when they reached the mighty heart
> Of Sulcarkeep, proud Sulcarkeep
> Then did witchmen and Sulcar part
> In Sulcarkeep, damned Sulcarkeep
>
> "With my own hand shall I lay waste
> My Sulcarkeep, dear Sulcarkeep!"
> Said Osberic, "Now make you haste,
> From Sulcarkeep, lost Sulcarkeep!"
>
> So he unleashed the mighty power
> In Sulcarkeep, proud Sulcarkeep
> That made of stone a flaming flower;
> Ah Sulcarkeep, Ah Sulcarkeep!

When she let the last, ebbing chord die away, there was silence
for a long moment; then, as though just waking from sleep, the
men stirred. The Sulcarman cleared his throat. "Well done,
minstrel. Never have I heard it sung better." A flash of bright
silver spun through the air, landing in the harp case. As
though the sailor's gesture were a floodgate opening, coins
spattered to join the first.

Eydryth nodded graciously, acknowledging their offerings,
then gave them "The Mosswife's Bargain." A lighter mood
prevailed as she spun out the skipping, skirling notes of "The
One-Spell Wizard." After a refreshing swallow of ale from a
tankard ordered by the Sulcarman (even though she was
thirsty, Eydryth dared not drink more—her belly was rumbling with hunger, and she needed a clear head to ferret out
answers to questions she dared not pose too directly), she sang
"Don't Call My Name in Battle." The song was one her father
had taught her, years ago—

Don't think of him, Eydryth told herself firmly, feeling a catch in the back of her throat threatening to ruin the last verse. *After the singing's done, when you've money to journey on,* then *you can call up Jervon's face to mind.* Then *you can think of your foster-parents, the Lady Joisan and her lord, Kerovan.* Then *you can think of Obred, and your chestnut mare Vyar, Hyana and Firdun and Kar Garudwyn itself, may Neave protect those within its walls! But until then, you must sing, and give no hint of what you seek, why you have traveled so far from home. . . .*

Mastering her sorrow, she strummed the opening chords to "Keylor's Rage," feeling weariness threaten to overwhelm and net her like a cloak thrown in battle, muffling, blinding. *Two more songs,* she promised herself. *Only two more, then I can stop and pick up my coins, knowing I've given full measure for what's been paid.*

"And now, kind sirs," she said, a few minutes later, muting the last chord of "Keylor's Rage" with her palm, "a new song, one inspired by the story told me about the Kolder-cursed city of Sippar, on the Island of Gorm. Pay heed an' you will to 'The Haunted City.' "

Eydryth hushed her voice into eerie, thrumming tones, thinking as she did that Sippar—or what was left of it—lay just across the bay, barely a day's sail away. "No children sleep in Sippar now," she began:

> No vessels ride her harbor fair;
> No footstep sounds on street or stair,
> For all lies turned beneath death's plow.
>
> When Kolder to rich Sippar came,
> They drank its life, then stole the cup,
> And when the demon-time was up,
> An empty city cried its blame.
>
> 'Tis said the city twice was slain,
> First with the sword, then with the mind;
> By warfare of an unclean kind
> The unsouled walked its streets again.

Another death did Sippar die,
When Simon Tregarth struck the blow
That laid the power-wielder low,
Then unlife settled with a sigh.

The corpses lay in silent speech,
Slaves from bodies freed at last
To bury with them all that passed;
No more to fight, no more beseech.

No ship now comes to Sippar's quay,
For none will step upon her shore
Though time has shattered every door,
The bravest let her shadows be.

Even as the final words whispered into the silence of The Dancing Dolphin, Eydryth saw her listeners shiver, then sit upright too quickly. The fellow who had accosted her when she'd first entered the tavern actually looked over his shoulder, as though a spectral hand might be descending to rest there.

Can't have them loath to walk into the night, she thought. *Something a bit bawdy will leave them laughing and free with their silver, and I need have no fears about playing something from High Hallack and them not understanding it. . . . A bawdy is a bawdy anywhere. . . .* "Now sirs," she called out, "for the evening's last song, I give you 'The Chambermaid's Dowry.'"

She began the opening notes to the song about the poor young chambermaid who encountered a sailor with designs upon her virtue (though, of course, he protested that he intended honorable marriage). The verses unrolled amid guffaws from the sailors as the pretty maid accepted the sailor's praises of her beauty, along with his many gifts, but through misadventure and misdirection managed to remain chaste—until one day the sailor (determined to succeed at long last) came home from a voyage only to discover that at that very moment the girl was off being married: she'd used for her dowry the gifts he'd given her!

Eydryth was smiling herself as she sang the chorus the last time:

Oh, she was fine, that bonny lass
Like a fair ship upon the sea—
But oh! I rue the day we met
For how that maiden plundered me!

"Thank you, thank you for your attention." She stood and bowed, sipping her ale, as they toasted her, clapping. More coins rang into the harp case. After her listeners had dispersed, Eydryth counted the night's takings. There was plenty to pay for a private room, dinner and breakfast, plus journey funds for several days.

The tavern-keeper showed her to her room, a small, bare loft beneath the overhanging eaves. After stowing away her harp case and pack beneath the wooden bedstead, Eydryth laved her face and hands in the icy water she found waiting in the ewer, then went in search of a late supper.

The tavern was deserted of all but the overnight guests by now, so she had the entire board to herself. At her request, Mylt the tavern-master brought her a late supper. Eydryth was pleasantly surprised by the hot bowl of creamy lobster chowder, vegetable pasty and respectable vintage he set before her, and ate with a good appetite. "My thanks, sir. This is excellent fare."

The little man nodded. "My own recipe. Guests will excuse much in the way of accommodations if the food be good and the beer well chilled. You're welcome to bide another day, songsmith. It's a rare bard who can hold my customers enthralled the way you did tonight."

"Thank you, but no, I must be on my way with the morn," she replied, taking a sip from the goblet of wine. "Tell me," she asked, with studied indifference, "how many days' journey to Es City itself? I've a fancy to see it."

"Walking?" Mylt asked, and at her nod considered for a moment. "At least four, more likely five. 'Tis a full two days on horseback."

"Good roads?"

"Aye, and well-patrolled, too. Koris of Gorm is a just man,

but not one to coddle outlaws, and they stay far off the main roads these days."

"Koris of Gorm . . . Hilder's son," Eydryth said, remembering the history she'd learned aboard the *Osprey.* " 'Tis said that he, for all practical purposes, now rules Estcarp, with his Lady Loyse. And that the witches concern themselves with little but regaining their waning magic."

Mylt lowered his voice, even though the two of them were alone in the taproom. "Even so," he agreed, "but it is not something to speak of loudly. During the Turning many years ago, a goodly number of them died or were left burned-out shells—but there are some that still hold the Power."

"The Turning?" Eydryth ventured.

"When Duke Pagar of Karsten sought to invade from over-mountain, the witches gathered together all their might and magic to shake the spine of the earth itself. The mountains dividing Karsten and Estcarp shook and fell, while thrusting up into other heights. The invaders were wiped out in a single night of destruction, and all the trails to Karsten destroyed."

"It must have been terrible."

"Aye, that's certain. I was little more than a lad, then, but even so, I remember that day. It was as though a shadow lay over the entire land . . . a shadow you couldn't see, only feel. That shadow pressed upon all living things, like a fist that would grind us all into the earth, it weighed so heavy. . . ." The tavern-keeper shivered at the memory.

Eydryth made haste to steer the conversation back to her purpose. "But you said some of the witches still retain their Power?"

"Aye, if the accounts I hear be true. But they have turned away from ruling Estcarp, even as you said. They no longer govern our land; Koris does, he and his Lady Loyse, aided by their friends and battle-companions, the outlander, Lord Simon Tregarth, and his wife, the Lady Jaelithe." The tavern-keeper glanced around him nervously, making sure they were still alone. "Did you know that she used to be one of the witches?"

Eydryth *did* know, but she feigned surprise, eager to learn all she could. *"Really?"*

He raised a hand in a half-pledge. "Truth. Before she was wife, she was witch. After they were wed, she bore her lord children, so theirs was a true marriage—and yet—" He glanced around, then leaned so close she could smell his sour breath, see the blackened pores studding his nose. "—and yet, she still wields the Power! Even though she be no maiden!"

Eydryth summoned an appropriate expression of astonishment, though she was hardly surprised; her own mother, Elys, had not lost *her* Power with her maidenhead, either.

"They say that the other witches have never forgiven the Lady Jaelithe for lying with her lord, and yet not losing her gift. They regard it as a betrayal," Mylt finished.

"Perhaps they envy her," the girl ventured.

The tavern-master chuckled coarsely. "Not the witches of Estcarp, songsmith! To them, the men of this world are something to be barely tolerated, not desired!"

"Tell me, Mylt . . . do the witches ever . . . help people?" Eydryth busied herself scraping the last drops of chowder from her bowl.

" 'Tis said they do, from time to time. Blessing the crops and suchlike, calling storms during dry times, soothing wind and wave to protect ships in their harbors."

"What about smaller magics . . . healing and such?"

"Aye, they do some of that, too. Simples and potions and amulets against fevers . . ." He poured the last of the wine into the songsmith's goblet, then carefully stacked dishes onto the serving tray. "Will you want more, minstrel?"

"Thank you, no," Eydryth said, finishing her wine and rising to take her leave. "Good night."

"A good sleep to you, songsmith."

With a final nod to her host, Eydryth started up the stair to her garret. Her steps were slow; she was so wearied by her long day that even the few sips of Mylt's wine had made her limbs feel as though they were weighted by such brightly colored fishing sinkers as decorated the walls of The Dancing Dolphin. The floor beneath her battered leather boots seemed to move rhythmically; she might still ride the ocean's swells aboard the *Osprey.* When she reached her chamber, the young woman dragged her outer garments off and burrowed beneath the coarse woolen blankets, too tired to search out her night shift.

Sleep was reaching for her with leaden arms when her eyes flew open. *I forgot! But by the Amber Lady, I'm so tired.* . . . She sighed, throwing the bedclothes aside, as she reached for the gryphon-headed quarterstaff lying near to hand on the rough wooden boards. Drawing it to her in the darkness, she fumbled with her other hand for the amulet that she bore around her neck, hidden. The amber and amethyst of its fashioning felt warm and familiar in her hand, as she traced the lines of Gunnora's symbols—a carven sheaf of ripened wheat bound by a heavily laden grapevine.

"Lady," she whispered, "I seek Your help on my quest. I pray that You protect those I love, those who live within the Gryphon's Citadel. Protect Lady Joisan and her lord, Kerovan. Protect their daughter and son, Hyana and Firdun. Most of all, I pray You, protect my father. Help me find someone who can heal him, so that Jervon may be himself again, after all these years. And Lady . . ." Her soft words faltered in the darkness. "Please . . . let me find my mother, the Lady Elys. She has been gone from us so long. . . . Protect her wherever she may be, You who are mindful of those who carry life. . . ."

She grasped the two symbols tightly, wishing for a sign—any sign—that her words were more than empty sounds. But the blue quan-iron eyes of the gryphon did not flare into brightness; the blessed metal had never shone for her. And the amber token of Gunnora was as dark as the night surrounding her. It was always so. . . .

With a tired sigh, Eydryth lay back down, giving herself up to sleep, hoping only that tonight she would be too tired to dream.

The two-wheeled pony cart creaked along the stone-paved road. "Up there with you, Fancy," the young farmer ordered, waving his willow switch at the round rump of the small bay gelding pulling it. "There's Es City in sight, songsmith," he called over his shoulder. "Won't be long now."

Eydryth carefully handed the farmer's wife the sleeping

form of Pris, their tousle-headed little girl, before scrambling
up to peer out of the cart. Even in the full light of the early-
afternoon sun, the approaching city appeared dark with age;
its rounded grey-green towers seeming to crouch atop the
earth as though they had been there since even the land had
been first created. Es was a good-sized city, one obviously
built to serve as fortress as well as capital—a high wall ran
completely around it, enclosing it.

When the farmer's wagon rolled up to the gate, two civil but
well-armed guards scrutinized cart and occupants purpose-
fully. After they had determined that there was nothing hidden
beneath the woven rugs Catkus and Leiona had come to sell,
they waved them through.

As the pony cart lurched over cobbled streets, Eydryth
looked around her wonderingly. Es was the largest municipal-
ity she had ever visited; Dalesfolk were not by nature city-
dwellers, and in all her wanderings across ancient Arvon,
Eydryth had never seen any settlement larger than a village.

Close up, the mossy stone of ancient buildings reared before
her imposingly, the patina of age surrounding them so tangible the young woman wondered—only half-fancifully—
whether it would be felt by an exploring hand. She put out her
fingers as the cart slowed around a precipitous corner in the
narrow street, then drew them back. The stones themselves
seemed to ward off the curious—or was what she sensed real
witchery, a spell designed to protect the city?

"Here we be, minstrel," Catkus announced, drawing rein at
the entrance to the marketplace. "Good fortune go with you
on your travels." The young man touched hand to the ragged
brim of his straw hat in a farewell salute. "Thanks again for
singing little Pris through that bout of colic the other night."

"Thank *you* for the ride and the company," Eydryth returned, scrambling off the cart, then giving a farewell wave to
Catkus, Leiona and Pris.

The young woman had no need to inquire the way to the
Citadel—the witches' stronghold was the most massive building in Es, with a round tower overtopping all of the surrounding structures. She set off through the crowded streets, her

pack and hand-harp slung over her back. As she walked, her eyes were drawn to the people treading the footworn streets—those who called themselves the Old Race.

Tall they were, and of unusually somber mien. They carried themselves proudly, walking straight-backed as any soldier. Their hair was as black as her own, but neither wave nor curl softened the planes of their long, oval, pointed-chinned faces. Eyes that were varying shades of grey were alert in their un-lined faces. (It was well known even in the Dales that the Old Race of Estcarp evidenced little sign of aging until death was but a handful of seasons away.)

Seeing the folk of Es City reminded Eydryth vividly—and painfully—of her mother. It was strange to think that she might be distantly related to some of these people. Elys had often told her daughter that her own parents had fled from Estcarp, for reasons they had never discussed.

A guard in mended, serviceable mail barred her way at the gate leading into a central courtyard. "Your business . . ." He cast a sharp glance at the symbol she wore. ". . . songsmith?"

"I seek audience with one of the witches," she said, stiffen-ing her spine to meet his flat, uncaring eyes. "A few minutes, no more."

His gaze traveled over her. "On what matter?"

"A matter of healing," Eydryth said, after a second's hesita-tion, trying to curb her impatience. *I've come so far! Blessed Gunnora, lend me strength!* "I was told any might consult with a witch on a matter of healing."

"Your name?"

"Eydryth."

"Wait here." The guardsman turned and disappeared into the huge, time-blackened portal, returning in a few minutes. "Tomorrow morn," he told her. "Before the sun tops the city wall."

"Many thanks," she said, resisting the grin of relief that wanted to spread over her face. "I will be here."

Her singing that night at The Silver Horseshoe consisted mostly of lightsome ballads, tales of wonder, good magic and love. It was hard to tone herself down when a dour old farmer

requested the lugubrious "Soldier's Lament." She sang, and
when her voice tired, she played her flute. By the time the
Horseshoe's patrons had departed for their beds, the young
minstrel had earned enough to replenish the coins she'd spent
during her four days on the road.

Dawn barely silvered the east when she awoke, unable to
sleep longer. After breaking her fast with porridge and goat's
milk, Eydryth shouldered her pack, then footed a quick way
through the twisting streets toward the Citadel. The sun had
only cleared the distant horizon when she sat down to wait,
half-concealed in a doorway across from the guard's post.

Her two hours' vigil stretched like an overwound harpstring, but finally she arose, brushing her cloak and breeches
off, then picked her way across the now-crowded street.

There was a different guardsman on duty, but, after consult-
ing a list, he ordered her to leave her quarterstaff with him,
then waved her toward the darkened portal. Eydryth tugged
open a massive, leather-bound door, to find herself in a long
stone corridor. A young woman faced her, garbed in a shrouding robe of misty silver, with the heavy weight of her night-
dark hair coiled into a silver net. Without a word, her dark
grey eyes downcast, she motioned to the songsmith to follow
her.

Eydryth strode after the girl—for a glance at the rounded
face had convinced the minstrel that the witch was several
years younger than herself—down the first corridor, then into
a second, and then, finally, a third. Each hall was featureless,
made of age-darkened stone, and illuminated only by a series
of palely lit globes suspended in metal baskets.

When she first saw those globes, Eydryth barely repressed a
gasp of surprise. She had seen similar lights before, but only
once. They hung from the walls and ceilings of her home, the
ancient Citadel of Kar Garudwyn. Knowing something of the
age of that stronghold, she looked about her with even greater
awe. This place was *old.*

The young witch stopped before another, smaller door.
Opening it, she silently waved Eydryth through, then followed
her.

A woman sat at a desk in the scroll-lined study beyond, a woman whose hawklike features (in the way of the Old Race) betrayed little age, but whose eyes made the younger woman flinch as she faced that unswerving gaze. The woman went gowned the same as Eydryth's guide, but with the addition of a cloudy, moon-colored jewel hanging from a chain about her neck.

The witch pushed back her chair a little and sat for a long moment in silent study. Her voice, when she finally spoke, bore a country accent, but her air of command argued that any peasant upbringing had long been put behind her. She did not introduce herself, but that did not surprise the minstrel; to give another one's true Name was to open a chink in one's armor of Power. "The songsmith Eydryth," she commented, finally. "You seek healing. For whom? Yourself? You appear healthy enough to me."

"No, not for me," Eydryth said, forcing her eyes to continue meeting the witch's uncompromising stare. "It is for someone else in my family."

"And you have come from far away, haven't you?" The woman rose to her feet, paced deliberately across the flagged floor to front the bard directly. She lacked half a head of Eydryth's height, but the aura of command surrounding her more than made up for the physical difference. "There is the smell of sea about you, and your boots have seen much walking. Are there no healers in your own province?"

"We have our Wise Women, true enough," Eydryth admitted. "But none so far have been able to help, for this illness is of the mind and spirit, not the body."

The witch's head moved in a tiny shake. "Not good, songsmith. Few indeed are the healers who can treat such. Who is so afflicted, and how did it happen?"

Eydryth took a deep breath as memory seared her. "It happened six years ago, when I was little more than a child. We were on a . . . quest . . . when we came across a place of the old Power. It was said to be a kind of oracle that could allow one to farsee the object of one's greatest desire. But when Jervon peered through it, it struck him down. Since then he has been as a small child, one who eats when fed, follows when led around—"

"He?" The witch's eyes held a faint, angry spark. "Do you mean to tell me a *man* sought to use a source of the Power? You seek my help for one who meddled in things those of his sex cannot hope to comprehend?"

"For my father, Jervon, yes," Eydryth stammered, wondering how she'd erred. "I was told you had ways of healing—"

She broke off as the witch's hand snaked up to grab her chin and turn it from side to side, consideringly. "Your eyes . . . ," the woman muttered to herself, "blue . . . and the jaw is wider . . . but still, the color of hair, the chin—" She glared up at the younger woman. "You are a child of the Old Race—in part. Yet your mother surely betrayed her calling by choosing to marry, when we needed every bit of Power we could summon! Do you think I would help a *man* who lay with one of my sisters, thus depriving her of her witchhood?"

But she didn't lose her Power! She wasn't even born in Estcarp! Eydryth silently protested. The undisguised hatred in the witch's eyes unnerved her; she knew that the women of Power deemed union with the males of their race as but a poor second to the holding of that Power, but nothing had prepared her for this irrational anger and hatred.

The woman's strong, short fingers tightened on the songsmith's chin. "And what about you?" she murmured, in a lower voice. "Did you escape the testing given all girl children? Do you hold the Power? If you do, we shall see—" Breaking off with a hiss, she held the cloudy jewel she wore up before the bewildered minstrel's face. "Touch it!" she commanded.

Will clashed with will as Eydryth tried to step back, away from those pale grey eyes glittering with a light that was not wholly rational. "No!"

"Touch it!"

Compelled, the younger woman blindly reached out a hesitant fingertip, felt it brush the witch's hand, then the cool slickness of the jewel's crystal. The witch broke their eye-hold, glancing down, and Eydryth watched the eagerness slowly fade from her expression. "Nothing . . . ," the woman murmured, her eyes fixed once more on the minstrel's face. "Nothing, the jewel remains dead. But I was so sure. . . ."

Perversely angered by yet another demonstration of her lack of Power, Eydryth glanced down at the jewel as she pulled her hand away and stared, suddenly arrested. Had she seen a tiny spark flicker deep within the heart of the cloudy gem? *You're imagining it,* she thought angrily. *Be grateful this time that you have no Power—otherwise, this half-crazed woman might well try to hold you here!*

The songsmith stepped back, away from the witch. "So you cannot help me," she said. "Or *will* not—which is it, Lady?"

The grey-clad, bowed shoulders shrugged; the woman's voice was naught but the thinnest thread of sound. "Once, perhaps, before the Turning . . . I do not know. But now . . ." The witch shook her head, putting out a hand to grip the carven back of the chair as though she might fall without the support. She made a gesture of dismissal. "Go now, songsmith. . . ."

"If you cannot help me, do you know of any who can?" Eydryth demanded, feeling the hope that had sustained her for the past months draining away, leaching the life and color from the entire world. "I *must* find someone to heal him, I *must!* You see, the fault for his illness lies with me. . . . We were searching for my mother, whom he loved more than . . ." Sobs choked her then, and she turned away, shamed that the witch had seen her so undone.

But the woman no longer seemed aware of her presence at all. Stumbling, shoulders sagging, Eydryth blindly followed the young witch out of the room.

They threaded the dim corridors, their feet whispering against the stone flags. Slowly, the songsmith regained her control, blinking back the tears that had threatened . . . but her pack seemed doubly heavy, and the harp within its case made a sad, muted sound as it brushed the wall. *What shall I do?* Eydryth wondered numbly. *Where can I go?* The thought of returning home to Kar Garudwyn empty-handed was intolerable, yet her mind envisioned as an alternate naught but years of hollow wandering in alien lands.

She rounded the last corner before the entrance portal, only to nearly trip over the girl who had been guiding her. "Quietly!" the witch whispered, glancing fearfully around. "In here, we needs must talk."

A chill hand came out of the silver-grey robe to grab Eydryth's sleeve, drawing her into a darkened room. After a moment, the songsmith made out dusty barrels and boxes surrounding them. *Some kind of a storeroom.*

The minstrel watched as the young witch peered carefully out of the entrance, making sure they had gone unobserved. Then the girl shut the door and touched finger to a candle she produced from the sleeve of her robe. A spark flared; then the taper was alight. In the flickering dimness, they stared at each other.

"What's to do?" Eydryth began, only to have the girl lay finger to her lips in a signal for whispers.

"Quiet!" the witch cautioned. "Listen a moment. I know of a place where you may find help in your quest, songsmith."

Two

*E*ydryth stared down into the witch's face, scarcely daring to believe that here might be one who could actually guide her in finding what she sought. "Where?" she demanded, finally. "Where can I find help for one who has been mind-blasted by ancient Power?"

"There is a place of learning," the girl said. "Old . . . perhaps older than Es Citadel itself. There are ancient records there, and some of them deal with healing. I have heard of legends that speak of healing stones, and a red mud that conquers even the gravest of injuries. Perhaps you can find the location of such cures in those records."

"Where?" The songsmith's question came with sharp impatience. "Where lies this stone? Where rests this mud?"

"I know not. Escore, perhaps . . . Much that we thought legend only has been proven real since the Tregarths discovered that ancient land from which the Old Race once fled, if the tales be true. At this place of ancient learning, you may well find answers."

"I am no scholar," Eydryth murmured doubtfully.

"But the ones who live there are, and they will aid you; they have little else to do. There is a chance you may find a mention of a cure written there, on some tattered scroll."

"A chance," Eydryth repeated, her mind racing. "A bare chance, seemingly."

"You do not appear to me to be one who can afford to overlook any possibility, no matter how small," the witch retorted.

Eydryth sighed. "You are right. What is this place?"

The other raised a cautioning hand. "Not so fast. If you aid me, I will tell you when we reach our destination. Will you swear by Blessed Gunnora, whose amulet you wear, that you will keep faith if I help you?"

Eydryth started, her hand going to the breast of her jerkin, where the amulet lay hidden. "How do you know what I wear concealed?" she asked, eyeing the younger woman suspiciously, striving to read her features in the dim light.

"My Power may be small, but it is sufficient to sense that you wear Gunnora's symbol on your breast," the witch snapped impatiently. "But that is not the important thing, here. Will you swear to aid me, in return for my help?"

"What aid do you seek?"

"Your assistance in escaping from the Citadel, then from Es City, and returning to Kastryn, the village of my birth. When we reach there, I will reveal to you the name of the place of ancient learning, and tell you how to reach it. Kastryn, you will find, is on the road to your eventual destination."

Eydryth gazed at the young woman, her eyes searching that narrow, pointed-chinned face. There was beauty there, though it appeared worn, fined-down, as if, despite the girl's youth, she had suffered much. "I might be able to discover the whereabouts of this 'place of ancient learning' without your aid," she said, slowly, "now that I know what manner of place to inquire about. If people live there, someone, somewhere, will know of it."

The witch bit her lip, her control slipping. "I have been a fool," she whispered, in a voice edged with desperation. "I was not brought up to be a mistress of intrigue and am blunt-spoken by nature. You are right. If you ask long enough among the learned scholars of Es, you will find one who knows of the existence of Lormt, and where it lies. Go, then. I wish you success on your quest."

She turned away, her slight shoulders drooping beneath the grey robe.

The songsmith felt sympathy stir within her, as she remembered her own despair at the thought of being kept here in this ancient stronghold by these hungry, hollow-eyed women. She reached out to put a gentle hand on the girl's shoulder. "Wait. Tell me more. You are one of them—why do you wish to leave?"

The witch did not turn or look up. "I am one who was forced to the test, just as you were, today," she said, dully. "But for me the stone glowed—only a spark, but the witches are desperate."

"I could see that. Why are they so?"

"They have been forced to watch their control of this land slowly slip from them into the hands of others—Koris and his Lady Loyse, Simon Tregarth (whom they have hated ever since he took one of their number to wife) and his lady, Ja-elithe. So any girl-child showing a trace of the Power, they take, in an attempt to rebuild their numbers."

The young woman's voice trembled. "I'd escaped the testing for two years, because I was sole support and nurse for my widowed mother. Then she died, so the next time the witch came to Kastryn, I needs must lay finger to her stone. It sparked, so they took me, brought me here . . . began to teach me."

"Magic?"

"As much as I could learn, which was little enough. I am not a dullard, but my heart and will are drawn elsewhere—I possess neither the desire nor the gift to become mistress of more than a few minor illusions, plus some healcraft and herb-lore! However, these other women, to them Power is all—meat, bread, drink and breath itself! I cannot expect you to understand, songsmith, but I can never be as they are—never!"

Eydryth recalled her own childhood, spent in a stronghold steeped in sorcery. . . . It had permeated the very air she breathed, and to the others around her, using magic was as natural as that breathing itself. Only she had possessed none of the ability—she, who had taken after her father. Her father, racked by the backlash of near-forgotten Power . . .

A surge of sympathy for the young woman before her made Eydryth's throat tighten. "I understand," she told the witch softly, "more than you can know."

The girl's voice broke. "And the worst of it all is, they took me without even leaving me time to send a message to Logar!"

"Logar?"

The girl turned back to face her questioner. In the candlelit dimness, her eyes sparkled, as if she were struggling to hold back tears. "Logar is my betrothed. He rides with the Borderers. The fangs of the Hounds have been partially drawn, but Alizon is still a dagger that pricks Estcarp's side. Their remaining Hounds are wilier than ever as they slink forth to harry our northern border. Thus, each young man who is whole and able must serve with those who patrol that border for a space of three years. Logar's time was up last month—by now he must be home, only to find me gone!"

Her mouth quivered, then tightened grimly. "We swore that when he returned, we would be wed. And I want nothing more from life than to be with him! But Logar cannot free me—for him to dare the Citadel would mean his death. But I am afraid that he might try such a foolhardy move . . . so I must escape, before he can!"

"I see . . . ," Eydryth said. "But if we journey to Kastryn—"

The young witch clutched the songsmith's sleeve. "We? Do you mean that you will still help me escape? Even though I have no way to pay or reward you?"

"Yes," said Eydryth, as solemnly as if she took oath, "I will aid you, sister."

The girl clasped Eydryth's hand with both her own. "My gratitude forever! May Gunnora's Blessings follow you—" she began, fervently.

But the minstrel shook her head, cutting off the outpouring of gratitude. "I will merit thanks only if we succeed, sister."

"Avris," the witch introduced herself, a little shyly. Eydryth's eyed widened. The girl nodded defiantly, acknowledging the songsmith's surprise that she had revealed her name. "My name is Avris," she repeated, as if proud to openly defy the rules of the Citadel. "And you?"

"Eydryth. Now, as I was saying, if we journey to Kastryn, will those of the Citadel not know immediately where you have gone, and seek us there?"

"They may seek me, but by the time they find me, I will be of no more use to them," Avris replied. "Logar and I will be wed in the same hour of seeing each other, and"—she grinned wryly—"once a wedded, bedded wife, my small trace of Power will vanish from me."

Do not be too sure of that, the songsmith thought, with a wry smile of her own, as she remembered her mother, the Lady Elys, and her foster-mother, the Lady Joisan. They were women of Power, had lain with their husbands and borne children to them, just as the Lady Jaelithe had. And they, also, had retained their Power. *Still, knowing the witches' hatred of men*, Eydryth concluded, *Avris is probably right. They will not want her among their numbers after she has been, to their minds, "tainted" by union with a male. They will let her go.*

"Besides," the young witch was continuing, "Logar and I will not tarry to face their ire. I will convince him that we must flee immediately—perhaps make our way eastward, to that land overmountain, Escore. The Tregarth brothers and sister found refuge there—why not Logar and I?"

"You have schemed long on this," Eydryth observed. "This is not just some idle impulse."

"Ever since they took me, I have thought of little else!" Avris's voice dropped to a fierce whisper. "Outwardly, I became resigned, applied myself to learning as best I might, so as to lull their suspicions. But all the time I was planning how to escape. Now there is no more time left—next week, I travel again to the Place of Wisdom for a final retreat, then they will lay the Witch Oath on me. I *must* get away before they can thus seal me to them!"

"Have you a plan for escaping the Citadel itself?"

The girl hesitated. "I have thought of one, but I am loath to suggest it, because it holds great danger for you. Have you no trace of the Power?"

"None," Eydryth said flatly. "But tell me your plan anyway."

"As I told you, my Power is weak," Avris said. "But I believe that I can manage to cloak my features with illusion for long enough to get past that guard out there. I will take on your image. He will be expecting you to leave, and thus will not regard you too closely. But a full-body Seeming is beyond me, so I must have your clothes, your pack and harp case."

"So you will take on my features with my garments, long enough to just walk out . . .," the bard mused. "An ingenuous plan, but my soldier father taught me much of stealth and tactics, and it is ofttimes the simplest scheme that holds the greatest chance of success. But then what happens to me?"

"That is the flaw," the girl said grimly. "They will question you, and if you give them any slightest reason to doubt your word, they can compel truth from you, using the Power."

"I can say that you ensorcelled me, held me helpless with your magic," Eydryth said, her words coming faster as she thought. "To lend credence to that, you must leave me bound, wearing only my drawers and underbodice. Perhaps it would also be wise for you to knock me unconscious."

"I could not hurt you!" Avris protested.

"I will show you where and how to strike the blow," the minstrel said. "One that will knock me out, but not injure me much beyond an aching head for a few hours."

"But—"

"You will do as you must," Eydryth said, firmly. "Remember, there is no better excuse for not raising the alarm than to be discovered bound and unconscious, with a lump behind one ear. I doubt very much that the witches will ever suspect us of conspiracy under those circumstances."

"But what if they *do* suspect you? Compel the truth from you?"

The songsmith considered. "I cannot believe that they will do much to me simply for allowing my clothes and pack to be stolen. That is hardly a hanging offense, especially considering that you have Power, and I have none. They will readily believe that you compelled me to do your will. And there is also this: I am not a citizen of Estcarp . . . I can truthfully plead ignorance of local laws. The fact that I asked one of the witches to aid a despised male proves that."

"Yes," the witch agreed, thoughtfully. "Any man or woman living within the boundaries of this land for long cannot remain ignorant of the ways of the witches." Her brows drew together in a worried frown. "But to strike you down . . . I cannot! We must find some other way."

Eydryth gripped the girl's shoulders, her strong fingers deliberately bringing pain. "You want to see your betrothed again, do you not?"

"Yes . . . ," Avris whispered.

"Then you will do as I say. You must! Every moment we delay means a greater chance of discovery!"

The girl's shoulders sagged. "Very well. But they will still question you. What of that?"

Eydryth smiled humorlessly. "Do not forget that I am a bard. One in my trade must be an accomplished actor or actress, remember? They will believe me." *At least, I hope they will*, she added, silently.

"One more question," the other said. *"Why*? I can see you aiding me if there was no risk to you, but this way, there is great danger. The anger of the witches is not a thing to risk lightly. So why are you moved to help me?"

Eydryth hesitated. "I am also one who has lived surrounded by those who have control over forces I cannot even discern," she said, finally. "I would not wish such a fate on another. And if you truly can set me on the road to this place of learning, this Lormt, a place where I may find some clue that will help me in my search . . ." She shrugged. "Nothing in all the world could mean more to me than that."

Avris held out her hand, and, after a moment, Eydryth took it. The small fingers felt cold in hers, but the witch's grasp was firm. "I thank you . . . sister."

While Eydryth remained concealed in the little storeroom, Avris hurriedly went in search of the items she would require to work the illusion. When she returned, carrying a small case filled with herbs and simples, they began.

It took only moments for Avris to assume Eydryth's outer clothing; then the songsmith stood shivering as the witch stared up into her face, intently, as if memorizing every feature. "I can do it . . . ," she whispered, almost to herself.

"Then by all means, begin," the bard said, trying to keep her teeth from chattering. "This floor is c-cold."

"Very well." Avris rooted through her bag, emerging finally with a dried leaf, which she handed to the songsmith. "I will need your spittle for the Seeming, and several of your hairs— living ones, drawn from their roots. Place all here."

Eydryth, long used to the principles of magic, though she could not apply them, knew better than to question or argue. She spat on the leaf, rubbing the moisture into its brownish-green surface, then plucked several hairs and placed them in the middle of it. "Here," she said.

The witch did not reply, only took the leaf, her eyes closed as she concentrated. Raising the leaf to her lips, she blew upon it, then rolled it into a ball. Slowly, she began tracing the contours of her own face, lightly rubbing them with the leaf-ball. As she did so, she sang softly, a monotonous, minor tune, its words so ancient that Eydryth recognized them as a form of the Old Tongue, the ancient language of Power, still spoken sometimes in distant, sorcery-shrouded Arvon.

As the music called to her, Eydryth took out her hand-harp and instinctively began plucking the strings. She sang, her voice harmonizing with the witch's, until, between them, the girls produced a faint, eerie, hair-prickling melody.

Avris stopped abruptly on a half-wail, and Eydryth started,

jerked out of the reverie she had fallen into. She looked over at the witch and gasped.

Her own face stared back at her—long, oval, with a traveler's sun-browned skin. Avris now seemed to have bright blue eyes, a straight nose, a strong, stubborn jaw, all beneath a wind-tossed cap of soft black curls. "It worked?" the girl demanded.

"Completely," Eydryth told her, amazed. "Except that you are still shorter than I, I do not believe even your Logar could tell us apart. It is as perfect a Seeming as any I have witnessed. Your Power must be greater than you think."

The witch shrugged. "Perhaps it is just that I am desperate. What I could not do *for* them, I will do to *escape* them. And the guard, I think, will not notice the difference in height. I will just roll up the sleeves and breeches a turn, so."

When she was finished ordering her borrowed clothing, Avris reached into the bag again, this time withdrawing a bundle of twigs, bound with red thread. Eydryth pulled back as the girl made to brush the bard's forehead with the twig-bundle. "What is that?" she demanded.

"Rowan," Avris replied. "Magic cannot work within its bounds, either of the Dark or Light. Its touch will help you resist the questioning of the witches."

Eydryth's mouth twisted into a hard, ugly shape. "I thought I recognized it, and I want none of it! I can endure the interrogation myself, with no aid from an ill-fortuned handful of wood!"

Avris stared up at her in shock, but recovered herself quickly. "It is a foolish soldier who throws away even his smallest blade on the eve of the battle," she pointed out. "I have trusted you, will you not trust me? I would do nothing to harm you, Eydryth."

The songsmith dropped her eyes, shamed, feeling the color rise hot to her cheeks. "I am sorry. You are right. Go ahead."

But despite her resolve, she could not keep from flinching as the twig-bundle swept across her forehead—once, twice, thrice.

"Tie me as soon as I am unconscious," Eydryth ordered,

then had to demonstrate to Avris how to weave knots that
would hold against a prisoner's struggles.

At last, nothing remained except the blow. "*Here,*" the
songsmith said, pointing to a spot just behind her ear. "And
you must strike with sufficient force to make them believe my
story. You do me no favor if you hold back. Have you a
weapon?"

"This," the girl said, and withdrew a dagger in a sheath
from the folds of her discarded grey robe. "Will it do?"

Eydryth ran a finger over the rounded steel pommel. "It
should. Grasp it by the sheath, so as to use the blunt end.
Strike using *this* much force—" Eydryth wadded the witch's
discarded robe and demonstrated swinging the weapon, sending it thudding into the wall, the sound of the blow muffled by
the fabric. "Now you try."

On her fourth attempt, the witch's arm swung with the
proper force. "Good. That is just the way of it. Can you do
it?"

The witch needs must run a tongue-tip over dry lips before
she could reply, but her voice was steady. "I can. I will."

"Good," Eydryth said. "I will meet you outside the walls,
in that first grove of trees to the south of the city. Hide yourself
well, and do not appear until you hear me whistle, so—" She
produced a few bars of an old marching song from High
Hallack. "And do not forget to pick up my gryphon-headed
quarterstaff from the guard on your way out. He will be
expecting you to ask for it."

"I understand."

"Good." Deliberately, the songsmith turned her back, trying not to tense, forcing herself to stand still and not anticipate
the blow. "Strike when you are ready," she said. "But I would
prefer not to have to wait much long—"

Pain and darkness crashed against her skull from behind.
Eydryth felt her knees buckle, felt herself begin to fall. She let
the blackness gulp her down, swallow her, like one of the
sea-leviathans in the Sulcar tales. . . .

* * *

The songsmith's memories were blurred after that. She half-roused to a ringing head and the sound of voices, then the touch of hands on her half-bare body. Then the hands lifted her, and she was careful to stay limp, let herself flop like a boneless doll stuffed with river sand, such as the little Kioga children cuddled.

Light met her closed eyelids then, and soon she was placed on a soft surface. Someone covered her chilled body with a blanket. "You may bring in the guard now," she heard a cold, passionless voice say.

"Yes, sister," came the response, followed by the sound of the door.

"Lady?" a gruff voice said, one tinged with fear and defiance. "Th' sister said you wished t' see me?"

"So I do, Jarulf. Look at this girl, here. Do you recognize her?"

A gasp. "But . . . Lady, that be th' same young woman who left before m' shift ended! The very same!"

"I see." The cold voice was even colder now, but still calm. "That will be all, Jarulf."

"Aye, Lady."

I ought to be coming around by now, Eydryth cautioned herself, and, accordingly, she moaned and tried to open her eyes. She did not have to feign the swift stab of pain the light brought her, or her squint. "What—what—"

The witch (for Eydryth could now see her silver-grey robe) moved back to look down at her, her face as blank as the stones of the walls enclosing them. She was older than the woman the songsmith had seen before, her features fine-drawn and aristocratic, her eyes hooded and remote in her oval face.

"You were found unconscious in a little-used storeroom," she said. "It seems that one of our sisterhood is missing—our search found no trace of her. Tell me, who are you, and how did you come there?"

The songsmith moistened her lips. "Water?" she whispered, hopefully. "Please, water?"

"On the table. You may help yourself."

With a groan that had nothing false about it, the bard

pushed herself upright, clutching the blanket against her chest. When she saw the younger woman's shaking hands, the witch grudgingly poured the water into a goblet for her.

The minstrel sipped, then put the cup down. "I am Eydryth, a wandering songsmith from a distant land," she said, hoarsely. "I had an audience with one of your number, but she told me that she could not help me, since I was seeking healing for my father. She said that you granted no boons to men. So I took my leave of her. I remember following the young witch who had been sent to guide me down the corridor, my heart heavy . . . and that is all I remember."

"Nothing more?"

The songsmith winced as she gingerly explored the lump behind her ear. "Naught . . . save that she turned back as if to speak to me, and there was something in her hand . . . something . . ." She frowned. "I know not what, save that it was bright, and my eyes were caught by it. . . ."

"Ah," the witch said, her grey eyes raking the young woman's face with the sharpness of fingernails. "What do you *think* happened then?"

Eydryth started to shake her head, but stopped with a grimace of pain. "I know not, Lady. Obviously, someone hit me, and took my clothes . . . my clothes!" She glanced around her, wildly, as if just realizing they were truly gone. "My pack . . . my harp! My purse! I've been robbed!"

"Indeed," the witch said, her eyes never leaving the bard's.

"My hand-harp . . . my mouth-flute! My instruments . . . all stolen! How will I earn my living?" The minstrel ran her hands through her hair, distractedly, being careful not to overplay her distress. "I have naught left to me—naught!"

The witch hesitated. "Since you were robbed on our premises, it is our duty, I suppose, to alleviate your situation as much as possible. We will provide you with clothing, food, and sufficient coin for two nights' lodging. *If* you are telling the truth, and were indeed the victim of thievery."

Eydryth hesitated, betraying confusion. "The truth? Of course I am! Why should I speak aught but the truth, Lady?"

"That is what I am wondering . . . ," the witch said, studying the younger woman as though she had suddenly sprouted feathers or fur. "Why should you?"

"I am no liar." Eydryth let some of her very genuine irritation and fear creep into her voice. It would have been unnatural not to react to the witch's implied accusation. "You have no right to name me one, either."

The witch raised a mocking eyebrow. "Really? We shall see, songsmith. We shall see."

Without another word, the witch cupped her milky jewel in her hand and stared down into it. As Eydryth watched, light began to emanate from the stone, all in one direction, until a luminescent beam shone full onto the minstrel's face.

Even as she realized what the witch was doing, Eydryth summoned all her will to project honesty, sincerity. . . . She banished all thought of Avris waiting in the grove of trees, concentrating instead on the story she had told, filling her mind with it. The false images as she had described them unfolded vividly before her eyes. . . .

"What is that you're humming?" the witch demanded, her voice sharp with anger.

Eydryth felt the blood rush to her cheeks. "I beg your pardon, Lady," she muttered. "An old habit of mine, and I fear an annoying one. Since I was little, whenever I grow frightened, I begin humming an old lullaby my mother sang to me whilst I was in my cradle."

The lullaby . . . her only heritage from the fishing village of Wark, where her mother had grown up. Always it had been her defense against fear, and concentrating on its music and words had enabled her, occasionally, to keep out the pryings of other minds when she was a child, growing up in a land rife with sorcery, where even those who shared the nursery with her had been gifted with Power.

The witch gave her a scornful glance. "I see. And are you frightened now?"

"The reputation of the witches is one to inspire both awe and fear," Eydryth equivocated. "I regret that I annoyed you. I have lived a very solitary life for the past several years, and solitary people ofttimes fall into the habit of speaking to themselves. But in my case, I hum, or sing. It keeps my voice limber, also."

"Well, be silent," the witch snapped. "I must concentrate."

Again the witch's mind brushed her own, darting and prob-ing, testing the surface for any trace of falsehood. The young woman felt a chill, dank sweat break out on her body as that questing Power sent out tendrils that would uncover falsehood as surely as a hound would uncover a fen-fox's burrow. She found that she was repeating the notes and music of the lull-aby in her mind, over and over, as a kind of litany against letting the truth slip through.

> Peace, peace little baby,
> Hear not the cruel storm
> Our boats have come safely,
> We're sheltered and warm.

The music filled her mind, growing more and more real:

> Be still, little darling
> And hark to the sound
> Of wind-song and wave-song
> So awesome and loud . . .

Eydryth lost herself within the web of music, as she had done ever since she had been hardly more than a babe able to toddle about, grasping her father's sword-callused fingers to stay upright. The chorus chimed sweetly throughout her being, driving out the fear.

> For wind-song shall free you
> And wave-song shall teach you
> And my song shall love you
> The good seasons round . . .
>
> So sleep, little seabird, sleep . . .

Without warning, the light from the witch's jewel died. "It seems that you are telling the truth, minstrel," the woman conceded, though there was no softening of her cold grey eyes. "I will see that clothes are brought to you, and food, and coppers for several nights' lodging."

"Thank you, Lady," Eydryth said humbly, schooling her face to reflect none of the triumph flaring within her. *Have I truly done it? Kept the truth from her?*

"Do you wish to leave now, songsmith?"

Eydryth stretched and sighed, with a deliberate show of weariness. "My head still aches, Lady," she said. "I will rest until midafternoon, if I may, then depart." *Don't appear to be too eager to rush out of here,* she cautioned herself, eyeing the witch covertly. *This may well be yet another test.* She resolved that she would exercise a scout's caution when she left the Citadel. *No doubt she will have me followed.*

The witch nodded, her hooded eyes expressionless. "As you wish, songsmith." She fixed a measuring gaze on the younger woman. "You say that you are from a faraway land," she said. "Do the women there have Power?"

"We have our village Wise Women," Eydryth replied, cautiously. "They doctor the sick with herbal potions, midwife the women and the animals . . ." She trailed off. "Why do you ask?"

"And have you ever been tested for the presence of the Power?" the witch demanded, deliberately ignoring the songsmith's question.

"Yes," Eydryth said, fighting the urge to swallow, her mouth suddenly dry. "I was tested today, by one of your number. I failed. I have no Power."

"What manner of testing?" the witch demanded.

"She compelled me to lay finger to the jewel she wore—such a jewel as yours, Lady."

The witch picked up her own jewel, fingered it thoughtfully. It glowed softly. For a moment the grey-robed woman closed her eyes; then she opened them again. "Mistakes have been made before," she murmured, staring speculatively at the younger woman. "Indeed, they have. . . ."

Eydryth knew she was in great danger. *What if she decides to hold me here, put me through more of their tests?* She remembered that brief flicker she'd thought she had glimpsed deep in the heart of the witch-jewel. *Avris said the jewel barely glowed for her. . . .*

As abruptly as a door opening, the witch's thoughts were as plain to the songsmith as though she *did* have the Power to see the unseen, hear the unheard. *Even now, she is thinking that I may be able to take Avris's place among them!*

A sharp rap at the door made both of them jump. The witch hastened to open it. Eydryth recognized the newcomer as the witch who had tested her earlier. "Sister?" she said. "You summoned me?"

"Yes," the older witch said. "This girl tells me that you tested her, today."

"I did. I thought that I sensed a trace of the Power . . . but the jewel stayed dark."

"You are sure?"

"Entirely."

"Very well. Thank you, sister."

The younger witch inclined her head, then departed. Eydryth's questioner smiled faintly. "Again it seems that you were speaking the truth, songsmith. Rest now, and I will have clothing brought to you so that you may depart when you awake."

The minstrel wet her lips. "Thank you, Lady," she said, holding her voice steady with an effort.

"You are welcome," the witch said. "Rest well, songsmith."

She left the room, closing the door behind her. Eydryth lay back upon the bed, but she did not close her eyes. *Tests within tests*, she thought, feeling the fear uncoil within her like a serpent. *I must guard my back when I leave. She intends to let me go, planning to have me lead her guardsmen to Avris. Then they will capture us both!*

Her fingers sought out Gunnora's amulet. Eydryth stroked the amber sheaf of grain, felt the small amethyst points that made up the fruit upon the heavy-laden grapevine binding it at its base. *Amber Lady*, she thought. *Aid me in escaping this trap. Please, Lady! I must be free, so I can find a cure for my father!*

Three

"*A*nd they simply allowed you to depart? Without following you?" Avris, arms wrapped around her knees, was still crouched in her hiding place, a hollow beneath the roots of a long-overturned oak. She gave her companion a skeptical glance. "I cannot believe it!"

Eydryth, who was sitting on the slope above her, pulling on her tall brown boots, grinned cheerfully at her companion. "When I said I wasn't followed here, it wasn't for lack of their trying. I had three shadows, sure enough, when I left the Citadel, and only one of them was my own. But I lost both of my tails in the marketplace without overmuch trouble. They were expecting to trail someone who knew nothing of their presence, and thus they were careless."

The songsmith slipped her battered brown leather jerkin on over her full-sleeved green tunic. "It is good to get my own clothes back," she said, busy with front lacings. "I refused a skirt, and the only guardsman small enough so I could fit his off-duty garments made but an indifferent habit of bathing." She wrinkled her nose as she rolled the cast-off clothing into a bundle. "Tomorrow, when we can move about freely, we must wash these, and oil the boots, so we may sell them in some town far from here. How do those things I bought you fit?"

Avris gave her a mock glare of impatience as she smoothed the front of her faded red tunic. "As you can plainly see, they are fine! Now, by the Mercy of Gunnora, finish your story!"

The minstrel shrugged. "There is little more to relate. Just to be safe, I holed up to wait out the night, and left the city when the gates opened at dawn. There were guards looking for me there, too, but I used the last of the witch's coppers to bribe an old man to let me hide under a blanket in the back of his farm wagon. He balanced two crates of pullets atop me, and, next to me, tied his newly weaned bull calf. The poor thing was bellowing loudly enough to rouse a dead man from his grave, so the guards were not very thorough in their check—they waved us through as quickly as possible." Eydryth dug a finger in her ear with a grimace. "I am still half-deafened!"

"So we are safe?"

"For the moment, yes."

Avris laughed aloud exultantly as she scrambled out from beneath the root-shadowed "cave" to stretch her arms wide beneath the green-gold spring leaves. "Free!" She whirled around in sheer exuberance. "I was so worried about you . . . that I have only just realized—I am free! *Free!*"

Eydryth smiled at her. "The feeling of being free, with the open road before one, is indeed a heady emotion. But curb yourself, sister. The hunt for both of us is undoubtedly up, and we must not allow ourselves to be recaptured. They would go very hard with us, I think."

The witch stopped, then nodded, some of the light fading from her eyes. "You are right. I am fortunate that you have some experience in these matters. How best should we do this?''

"I think it would be wisest for us to travel by night, until we are at least two days' ride from Es City. And we will not head directly for Kastryn, for that is what they will be expecting us to do. Instead, we will circle around Es City, cross the river, and travel northwest for a day or two.''

"But how will we reach Kastryn?"

"Then we will circle to the northeast, and come on Kastryn from the north, instead of the south. It will add many days to our journey, to be sure, but it is the wisest course.''

"If only we had horses.''

Eydryth grimaced, thinking of her mare, Vyar. "If only we did. But horses would also make us more conspicuous, and without them, we can hide more easily. Have you money?"

"A few coins. We lived a monastic life in the Citadel, and seldom needed it.''

"Well, can you sing?"

Avris grinned. "I can try.'' She raised her voice in a few measures of "The Riving of the Border.'' She had a clear, if thin, soprano.

"You will do well enough.'' Eydryth nodded. "We will practice before we must earn our supper.'' The songsmith yawned suddenly, widely, until her jaws nearly cracked. "And now, while I can, I must sleep, since I dared not close my eyes last night. We will eat and rest by turns, standing watches, and set out after sunset. Are we agreed?"

"Agreed.''

It was afternoon before the witch touched Eydryth's shoulder to rouse her. The songsmith awoke immediately, as her father had trained her, sitting upright in her cloak with a seasoned warrior's alertness. "You let me sleep too long!'' she exclaimed, seeing that the sun's rays were already slanting from the west.

"I was not tired, and you needed your rest,'' Avris said. "I slept last night, for I was too weary from my spelling to stay awake, even if the Guardian and all the other witches had been ranged around this grove.'' She smiled. "Fortunately, they were not.''

"Well, sleep now," Eydryth said, taking food from her pack and breaking off a chunk of journeybread. "I will guard."

"No, I am not tired. Now that I am breathing free air, I feel as though I will never be weary again." The two girls shared food in companionable silence, until Avris spoke again: "May I ask you something, Eydryth?"

"Ask away," the songsmith said, after swallowing a bite of dried apple.

"Why do you hate the rowan so?"

Eydryth could feel her body stiffen; her face become a hard, expressionless mask. "That is a long story," she said, finally.

"One that you would prefer not to tell? If so, I will understand," Avris said, her gaze holding nothing but friendship, sympathy. "But we have an hour or more yet to wait, and I do not ask from idle curiosity, believe me, sister. I sense a great hurt within you . . . and sometimes, such hurts may be eased in the speaking of them to another, one who truly cares."

Eydryth sat in silence for several minutes, forgetting the food in her hand, lost in memory. Finally, she stirred. "It happened years ago," she whispered. "And it is something I have never spoken of, except to those who shared those days with me. And you may not want to call me 'sister' after you hear what I did."

"I doubt that," Avris said, steadily. "You could never do anything truly wrong, Eydryth. I *know* that."

"Not so," the songsmith said, her voice grown husky. She cleared her throat. "You must understand that I grew up in a far land . . . across the sea. You have probably never even heard of Arvon."

"No, I never have," the witch conceded. "Does it lie near that land of many Dales, the one the captured soldiers of Alizon spoke of?"

"It lies west of High Hallack," Eydryth agreed, nodding. "Beyond the Waste. Arvon, like this Escore you speak of, is a very, very old land, unlike the others settled by humankind. It abounds with uncanny places, and strange beings. Creatures out of legend, many of them. Such as the demons called Keplians, shaped like beautiful horses . . . and the web-riders, those fell creatures with many-jointed legs, that weave webs, then cast them onto the wind and ride them, in search of prey. . . ."

"I have heard of such in Escore," Avris told her. "And do you also have the Flannan, the mosswives, the Scaled Ones, and the water-people, the Krogan?"

"No, I have not heard of them," Eydryth said. "But there are the Winged Ones, who have the heads of birds and the bodies of men or women, whose blood means death if spilled on living flesh, and who will fight even when beheaded or dismembered. . . ."

Avris shuddered. "Praise Gunnora, I have never heard of such in Escore! If I had, that land would prove no refuge at all!"

"Fortunately, their numbers are small, and appear to be dwindling," the songsmith said. "But not so for the Thas. They are a constant danger."

"Thas?"

"Dwellers below ground who tunnel as naturally as some creatures walk. They are ugly—" Eydryth shuddered at the memory. "Small, wiry bodies, with bloated stomachs, covered with scraggly, rootlike hair. But the worst thing is . . ." She trailed off, then swallowed hard. ". . . their faces . . . from their faces, you can tell that they . . . they used to be of humankind."

"How dreadful!" Avris cried. "Yes, I have heard of such, now that I hear them described. Lately they have been seen—and smelled—lurking around the fringes of towns near the mountains. Logar reported in one of his letters that they were attacked by several of the things, as they slept. One man was pulled down into the earth, never to be seen again."

The songsmith shook her head. "Your people had best ward their borders well," she said. "The Thas are cowards, who prefer such tactics to open battle, but they are deadly."

"Go on with your story," the witch urged.

Eydryth grimaced at the reminder. "I was hoping you would forget."

"If you do not wish to tell me—"

"No, it is just that it is difficult to speak of. . . ." The minstrel shrugged. "So. I grew up in Arvon, in an ancient citadel called

Kar Garudwyn. Time out of mind ago, an Adept lived there; its very walls are still steeped with sorcery. I was born of a strange union: my mother, Elys, was the daughter of a woman from overseas—Estcarp—and my father, Jervon, was a soldier, one accustomed to the command of men, not magic."

"An odd mix," Avris commented. "But they loved each other?"

"More than life itself," Eydryth said, matter-of-factly. "They defended each other's backs through many a battle, against human enemies, as well as those born of sorcery. They were comrades and friends long before they knew each other as man and woman."

Eydryth took a final bite of the journeybread, then passed the cake over to Avris. "We shared Kar Garudwyn with my parents' closest friends, the Lord Kerovan and the Lady Joisan. They were as father and mother to me also, and I loved them dearly. Also, there was Sylvya, who was our friend and teacher. She was from the Old Times, and had powers such as had not been seen since the very ancient days."

"Sylvya," Avris repeated, trying the alien sound of the name on her tongue. "Was she of the Old Race, too?"

"Partly, but also in her was another, nonhuman heritage. But she loved all of us children as though we were her own."

"Children?"

"Joisan and Kerovan had—have—two children. Hyana, their daughter, is nigh unto a year my elder. She is a quiet, deep-eyed girl, possessed of such innate Power that I doubt many of the witches in your Citadel could equal her, even when she was naught but a girl-child. But she makes no show of such strength, only uses it to help others. She can farsee, and her foretellings are such that no one can afford to ignore them." Eydryth's face darkened, and she lapsed into a brooding silence.

"And the other child?" the young witch prompted, when the songsmith showed no signs of continuing.

"Firdun is five years younger than I. He also has Power, but there is nothing quiet about Firdun! He was one of those children whose life one constantly fears for—you may know the kind. If there was but one apple tree in the entire orchard with a rotten limb, *that* is the tree Firdun must climb, and *that* would be the limb he chose to rest upon."

Avris chuckled. "I know very well. I have a cousin who has such a daughter. Have you brothers or sisters, Eydryth?"

The songsmith shook her head. "I know not," she whispered. "My mother vanished nine years ago, when I was but ten years old."

The witch was puzzled. " 'Vanished'? You mean, she left you and your father? Does she still live?"

"I know not," Eydryth repeated. "She did not leave us willingly, she was taken. Some Power from the Left-Hand Path swept her from our very midst, even as she lay resting in her chamber one afternoon."

"How did it happen?" the witch asked, her grey eyes intent on Eydryth's. The songsmith could feel her compassion, as tangible as a warm hand laid upon her shoulder.

"It was my fault," the bard said, past the tightness in her throat. "My fault. You see, when my mother discovered she was again with child, Hyana, who was eleven, did a foreseeing for her, because she sensed a troubling in the land.

"During her foreseeing, she saw that the child—she told us it would be a boy—would be a final link in a chain that would unite those of the Right-Hand Path in Arvon against the forces of the Dark. The outcome of that conflict, Hyana told us, was not clear, but she knew that my unborn little brother was to be a crucial piece in a very deadly game whose first move had not yet been made."

Avris nodded, wide-eyed.

"So we took all care that my mother would be protected. She stopped walking outside the citadel without escort, and never descended the ramp leading to the valley alone. She even gave up her rides on her smoke-colored mare. Unless she was in her chamber, Jervon, my father, or Lord Kerovan always accompanied her, armed and ready.

"And for those times when she needed to rest alone, Sylvya and the Lady Joisan devised a protective spell to surround her chamber. They braided a rope, using twigs from the rowan tree, lacing it with scarlet yarn, the color of protection. They rolled it in valerian, pennyroyal and mullein, chanting as they did so. Finally, they placed the rope around the ceiling inside the chamber, then bound the two ends together with a strip of scarlet silk, above the outside of the door. Within that room, no spell would work, no Power could enter."

"But something did enter," Avris guessed. "How?"

"Because I have no Power," Eydryth said, "and I was too proud to admit that I could not manage without it. With his mother and father so worried about my mother, I was set to watch over little Firdun. Born of a father and mother who both have Power, the gift was strong in him almost from babyhood. He played tricks on me, the kind of tricks such a child would play. He could cloud my mind, so that I could look full at him sometimes, and not see him. Once I went to wake him from his nap, only to find an adder coiled on his pillow, fangs dripping venom—but even as I gasped, it vanished, and he sat up, giggling. . . ." She shook her head, remembering.

"If only I had admitted that the boy was too much for me! But I was five years his elder, and I was ashamed to say that I could not control him. One day, as I sat there, telling him the tale of the Hungry Well—which he loved, as it was a true one, and his father was the hero—I turned, only to find that he had left my side."

Eydryth pounded a fist against her knee. "If I had gone for his parents, or Hyana, or even my father, somebody he would have listened to—! But, instead, I searched for him myself, only to find him before the door to my mother's chamber. He was staring up at the rowan."

" 'Don't touch it, Firdun!' I shouted. He gave me an impish grin, then his little hands clenched, and his chubby face grew taut with effort. Even as I watched in horror, the ribbon came untied, the rowan rope fell apart. The protective spell was broken."

"And your mother?"

"I screamed, because I knew how vital that rowan rope was. In moments my father was there, and Lady Joisan. They burst into the room, only to find my mother gone. . . . She had disappeared without a trace." She took a deep breath, controlling her voice with an effort. "There was only a stench left behind. The scent of evil. Have you ever smelled it?"

Avris shook her head.

"It is an odor of such foulness, I cannot even describe it. No one who ever once whiffs such a stench can mistake it for anything else. . . ."

"You searched for her?"

"Of course. My father nearly went mad with grief—he rode for weeks, barely stopping to rest his horse, sleeping in the saddle, forgetting to eat for days at a time. Lord Kerovan and Lady Joisan rode with him, leaving Sylvya to watch over me and Firdun. Hyana retired into her room and spent much of her time in trance, searching, emerging gaunt-eyed and thin . . . but there was nothing. Nothing. For more than a year we searched, and found nothing."

"But what happened was not your fault!"

"So my father told me," Eydryth said, bitterly, "but if not my fault, whose? You cannot blame a mischievous child of five for such a happening. And even Firdun, young as he was, understood that he had done something terrible. From that day he changed, becoming much quieter, more biddable. He never gave me another moment's trouble. . . ." Her mouth twisted in an ironic grimace. "But the damage had already been done. And it was my fault."

"I do not agree," Avris said. "You were naught but a child yourself."

"A proud child, who was so ashamed to have none of the gift the others had, that I did not admit my fault, did not summon aid," Eydryth maintained, stubbornly.

"But that cannot be the end of your tale," Avris said, crumbling a rotted acorn shell in her fingers. "You said that your father was hurt."

"That happened when I was thirteen," Eydryth said, nodding wearily. "We would go out and search in good weather, riding to villages, asking, looking for any Wise Man or Woman, or any Summoner, who might have heard rumors, felt a troubling . . . any who might scry for a vision of my mother." She caught Avris's questioning glance and explained, "Scrying is a means of seeing the past, the future, or things far away."

"I have heard of such," Avris said. "How is it done in your land?"

"By gazing into a bowl filled with liquid . . . water, ink, wine . . ."

"Did scrying work?" Avris asked.

"No more than anything else," Eydryth said wearily, resting her forearms on her upraised knees. "Arvon is a wide land, but we searched for a week's ride and more in each direction. Once we even dared the Grey Towers, and asked the Pack Leader of the Weres, Hyron, if he had heard aught of Elys."

The songsmith shivered at the memory. "And, let me assure you, there are few in Arvon who would even venture to ride within the shadow of that grim fortress's walls, let alone pass through its front gate. Especially to ask the whereabouts of a witch. The Weres hate women of Power, and have for time out of mind."

"Why?"

"Only they know the reason behind their prejudice." She stared unseeing through the trunks of the oak trees, out at the road they would soon be following. "But my father asked them, and they answered. Even the Weres, with all their strange powers—they who tread the border between the Light and the Dark, between humankind and beast—even they could tell us nothing of my mother's fate."

The songsmith lapsed into silence again, memories crowding her mind. "It sounds a hard life," Avris ventured, finally.

The bard shrugged. "I suppose it was, but at the time, it did not seem so. My father taught me much as we companied together, even as he and my mother had done . . . swordplay, and scout-lore, the planning and execution of battle. How to hunt, fish, and live off the land. If it had not been for the reason of our search, those would have been happy days, sleeping beneath the naked sky, riding my good Kioga mare every day. . . ."

Eydryth smiled wryly. "In the winters, when we were forced to shelter in Kar Garudwyn, I returned to the schoolroom. There, I learned dutifully enough, but the space within four walls was never my favorite place to be. I loved traveling. A fortunate thing, I suppose, since I've had to do so much of it."

Her smile faded; then she sighed. "But the journeying with my father ended, too. One day, he came to me as I sat playing the hand-harp Lord Kerovan had given me (after he had discovered it in an ancient storeroom in Kar Garudwyn). Jervon was excited—more hopeful than I had seen him for months. He told me that he had learned of an ancient 'Seeing Stone' located in the north. It was said that any who had the courage to climb up the cliff to peer into this Stone would behold his or her most-desired sight. We set out that very afternoon.

"It was a long ride. We passed several villages, but as our way took us further and further north, they became fewer and fewer. The country was nigh, and, save where rivers and streams ran, grew steadily more arid—my father told me it was beginning to resemble the Waste in High Hallack, the land he and my mother had originally come from. Finally, there was but one more settlement, a small town surrounding the old, old sanctum of sorcery called Garth Howell. A place where those with the Gift of Power journey to learn how to harness and develop their innate talents."

"Like our Place of Wisdom."

"Yes. Except that in Arvon it is an accepted fact that men as well as women may hold the Power. Both sexes are accepted as students. We asked directions at Garth Howell, and they pointed us to the northwest. But the lay sister who kept the gate secretly warned Jervon, saying that the Stone could be dangerous."

"But he did not heed her," Avris guessed.

"No, he did not. We rode, and two days later, we reached the Seeing Stone . . . a great cliff of crumbling ocher rock. When we reached there, late in the afternoon, it seemed to loom like something alive and malevolent. And it was strange . . ."

"How so?"

"One moment I was gazing at an ordinary cliff, but then, when the shadows began stealing across the scree, I made out hollows, and protrusions . . . and I realized that the entire cliff-face had, at one time, been one giant form. Possibly a female form, for I thought I glimpsed the mounds of pendulous breasts, but the face . . . that was not a woman's."

"What did the face look like?"

"I don't know," Eydryth admitted, softly. "Wide, too wide to be human. Lipless, I believe. There was still the hint of teeth visible, as though she . . . whatever she was . . . as though she smiled. Not such a smile as I would like to see on a living countenance, Avris. But her most distinctive feature was her Eye. There was only one. A wide, dark pit above what might have been a nose.

"My father was off his horse almost before I could bring Vyar to a halt, and heading for the cliff. I flung myself down, and ran after him, calling to him to wait . . . wait. But his face was as set as a man who has received a mortal wound, his teeth clenched within the stubble of his beard. He thrust me aside, ordering me to wait . . . and then, he was climbing."

Eydryth drew a long, shaky breath. "How he found finger and toe holds on the cliff, I know not. But he moved as steadily as a spider may on a stone wall. In moments, it seemed, he had reached the Eye. I saw him lean forward, his head and shoulders almost disappearing into the opening. A moment only he remained so, then—" She shook her head. "He screamed my mother's name once . . ." She swallowed. ". . . in a voice I can still hear in the worst of my dreams. Then his grasp loosened, and he fell."

"Down the entire cliff?" Avris gasped.

"No. His body caught on the tiniest of ledges, near the figure's shoulder. He lay there, unmoving."

"What did you do?"

"Climbed the cliff myself, anchored our ropes with spikes, then lowered him in a sort of harness I fashioned from his swordbelt and mine." Eydryth looked away. "He had a lump on the back of his head, but I do not believe it was that which caused the problem. It was that cursed Eye—the backlash of that ancient Power. When Jervon awoke, he was as he is now, mind-crippled.

"He eats when food is placed before him, stands and walks when tugged by the hand, sleeps when led to his bed. He never speaks, never smiles . . . except faintly, sometimes, when I played and sang for him. And so he has been, for the past six years."

"How dreadful!" Avris whispered. "Oh, Eydryth, I pray that Lormt will hold some answer for you." She put out her hand, squeezed the older girl's fingers. "But I cannot see that you are responsible for any of what happened. To climb that cliff and rescue him all by yourself—! You were brave, and more than brave, sister."

The songsmith gave her a somber glance. "If I was, it availed little," she said. "Many times I have thought that my father would have been better off if he had fallen to his death, that day. He was a proud man, a capable man. He would have hated what he has become. To see him as he is now, day after day, became such torture . . ."

Eydryth shook her head. "Eventually, I could stand it no more. I had to go looking for someone who might be able to make him whole again. And, truly, Avris, if I can find no means of healing him, I have promised myself that I will return home long enough to grant him a merciful death."

The journey to Kastryn, although long and wearying, proved uneventful. After many days of walking the roads, of searching out taverns where they might sing for their supper and a bed in the stable, and, occasionally, if none such were to be found, bedding down on the edges of new-turned fields, the two young women arrived in Kastryn.

Eydryth glanced around the sleeping village as they threaded a silent way through backyards in the chill grey light of predawn. "It is larger than I thought," she whispered. "Which house is Logar's?"

"His father is the town smith," Avris said. "It is that stone one, there, with the smithy beside." She pointed.

"Stay here. Let me scout," the songsmith ordered. "I think

it has been long enough for all pursuit to have been given up, but better safe than sorry, yes?"

Avris bit her lip; she was trembling with eagerness, but she nodded. "If it is safe for me to come, whistle," she said.

Eydryth shed her pack and slid through the shadows, over a fence, through a chicken yard, over another fence. She glanced both ways before crossing the wagon-rutted road, listening with all her being for the slithery clink of chain mail, the creak of leather as a dart gun was unholstered.

Nothing.

She scurried to the silent house, scouted the deserted smithy, then peered in the windows of the bottom floor. All the rooms were deserted. She waited, listening, until the dark grey had lightened sufficiently that her eyes began to discern the colors of the early-spring flowers planted in the window boxes.

Then, rising, she made her way to the front doorstep and whistled.

In a moment, Avris was there, shivering with relief and excitement. She knocked, softly but insistently, upon the door.

Finally, they heard a sleepy exclamation within, then the sound of feet. A young man, black hair tousled, his well-muscled body bare to the waist, swung the door open.

"Logar?" Avris breathed, pushing back her hood with trembling hands. "It is I. . . ."

"Avris!" the young man gasped. "They came looking for you a fortnight ago! When you did not come, I thought you must be dead!" He stood staring at her as though wondering if she could possibly be real.

Avris smiled diffidently. "Aren't you glad to see me?"

Logar came out of his daze with an inarticulate cry. *"Glad?"* he gasped. "Glad—!" With sudden, fierce joy, he pulled her into his arms.

Eydryth turned away, leaving them alone in their happiness. She swallowed, feeling an odd pain within her, a loneliness different from any she had experienced before. *You have a task to do,* she reminded herself, fiercely. *And you must do it alone. . . .*

As she had promised, Avris and Logar were married within

the hour. Eydryth stood by the former witch's side as Kastryn's alderwoman joined the couple's hands, then offered them sips from the same goblet, bites of cake from the same plate. Long before noon the couple had loaded their belongings into an ox-drawn wagon, and prepared to set their faces eastward, toward the mountains and distant Escore.

"Eydryth . . . sister . . ." Avris smiled tearfully as she embraced her friend. "How can I ever thank you for what you have done?"

"No need," the songsmith said, returning the younger woman's hug. "You have set me on the road to Lormt, and you know how much that hope means to me."

"At least take this," Avris said, pushing a small bag into the songsmith's hand. "My share of our earnings. I will have little need of money where I am going, I believe. It should be sufficient for you to buy a mount, so you may travel more swiftly."

"I cannot!" Eydryth protested. "You earned your share, just as I did."

"Take it," the girl said, closing the songsmith's fingers tightly over the leather pouch. "I insist. Logar's father tells me that there is a horse fair being held in Rylon Corners, the next town to the north of this one. A half-day's good walk should see you there."

"Well . . ." Eydryth smiled. "It would be good to travel astride once more. I thank you, Avris."

"We must be going, dear heart," Logar said, sliding an arm around his bride's shoulders. "We will name our first girl-child for you, Lady Eydryth," he promised, clasping the songsmith's shoulder with a sword-roughened hand. Then he swung his new wife up onto the wagonseat.

The entire village stood waving as the oxcart slowly creaked out onto the northeast road.

Eydryth refused Logar's mother's offer of a bed, but accepted the goodwife's bag of provisions. She headed out of Kastryn, taking the north road, toward Rylon Corners, and, beyond that, Lormt.

* * *

It was afternoon before the songsmith reached the town, but
the bustle of the horse fair was still in full swing. She threaded
her way through booths offering harness and saddles, brushes
and tonics, charms and hoof-gloss . . . all products imaginable
for the health, riding and beautification of horses. Eydryth
sniffed the air, smiling. *It almost smells like home, here*, she
thought. If she closed her eyes, she could nearly imagine that
she was back in the Kioga camp in the Valley of the Gryphon,
"talking horse" with Obred and Guret. She thought of Vyar's
glossy coat.

None of these animals, she thought, eyeing the horses
around her, *are the equal of the Kioga mounts . . . but I should
be able to find something to bear me on my journey.*

Eydryth wandered through the bustling crowd, running her
hand over a flank here, lifting a forefoot there, occasionally
opening an animal's mouth to examine its teeth.

Her small hoard of coins would not permit her to purchase
one of the fine, blooded animals, so she was forced to wander
among the culls, scowling more and more deeply as she examined the mounts she could afford.

She had just finished examining the teeth of a rangy grey
gelding while his owner, a whip-thin trader with most of his
front teeth gone (*Kicked out, most likely*, Eydryth thought),
smiled ingratiatingly at her. "You like him, bard? Seven years
old, and sound as yon stone wall."

The songsmith smiled grimly. "You mean, despite that curb
on his near hock?"

"That little bump?" the man demanded indignantly. "Call
that a curb? Why, I'll eat his saddle if that ever gives him a
moment's shortness, by Volt's Axe, I will."

Eydryth sniffed inquiringly at the gelding's nostrils. "Oh,
I'll wager he'll go perfectly sound, all right—at least until that
infusion you gave him wears off. What did you use? Black
willow bark?"

The trader eyed her angrily. "You can't prove that!"

"No, but I *can* show someone the file marks on his teeth.
Not a very expert job, you know . . . anyone with half a brain

will see right through it, and realize what you've done. Seven, hah! This horse is at least twice that!"

Without another word, the little man dragged the grey gelding's head around and hustled rapidly off into the press of the fair.

Eydryth glared angrily after him for a moment, then shrugged. The fair was due to continue through tomorrow. Perhaps she should seek out some of the local farmers, ask to see their stock, rather than taking her chances with traders. There was always the possibility that she'd run into one of them who knew a trick she didn't—and then she'd be burdened with a sick or crippled animal.

Still considering the livestock around her, the songsmith took out her hand-harp, then opened its case on the ground at her feet. While she decided what to do, she'd try earning a few more coins. Better to spend a little more, in order to get a far better bargain. Obred's words ran through her mind: *"Remember, girl, it takes just as many coins to feed a bad horse as it does a good one—so buy the best you can."*

She tuned the harp, running her fingers over the strings, humming under her breath to test her voice. *Something suitable to the locale and the day*, she thought, reviewing the songs she knew. *Ah, I have it! "Lord Faral's Race" will do nicely.*

Eydryth softly began to sing:

> Along the midnight road they ran
> Along the broad and gleaming span
> Five gallant steeds of noble pride,
> Not gold, but life, hung on their ride.

A few heads turned, a few footsteps slowed, and several passersby halted to listen. Encouraged, Eydryth took a breath and swung into the refrain:

> Beneath Gunnora's golden light
> Six horses raced into the night
> Against the dark and fearsome knight
> The Dark Light!

The black knight!
At midnight . . .

More listeners. The songsmith's flying fingers picked up the
tempo, strumming hard as she sang louder, more ringingly:

> For he had come, with helm drawn down
> Into the center of the town
> He challenged them with haughty voice
> And dared them to make another choice.
>
> "If you do win, I'll go my way,
> But if I win, then you will pay
> A bondage through eternity
> In servitude to mine and me."
>
> Then came Lord Faral, tall and proud,
> And raised his whip to hush the crowd;
> "So let it be! Then let us race
> For this is a protected place.
>
> Within Gunnora's smile we dwell
> Our horses drink from Lady's Well,
> Strive with us, if you so choose;
> Race with me, and surely lose!"
>
> "I will not race with one," said he,
> "Five noble lords must race with me."
> "Then I will my four brothers call,
> That none born here become your thrall!"

A coin spun into the case; another . . . then a third. Eydryth
continued:

> They raced along an ancient way,
> Through misty moonlight, silver-grey
> But dark seeks darkness for its boon
> And mortal flesh meets mortal doom.
>
> The one horse fell, and there were four
> and one heart burst and could no more—

> So three ran on into the dark
> Then from that black whip came a spark
> Of poison light; and there were two
> And Miroch's gelding threw a shoe—

By now she had collected a small crowd, and the music of her harp was augmented by hand-clapping and foot-stamping. Occasional coins thudded into the case, providing an irregular counterpoint. The minstrel swung into the final verses, playing as though her fingers were charmed:

> And Faral then the Black Lord paced,
> Step for step a time they raced
> But oh, the mists grew cold and dread
> And Faral's stallion tossed his head.

> "Abandon now," the Dark knight said,
> "For see, your brothers all are dead."
> "Far better here I make my grave,
> Then let my people be your slave!

> "I service to Gunnora vow,
> Both hand and heart, both foot and brow,
> And I shall never be forsworn
> Though life from me and mine be torn!"

> Then came a radiant, golden light
> And lifted Faral into flight
> His steed's feet did not touch the ground
> While the Dark horse tried to pound

> Itself into the glittering stone
> The Dark knight from its back was thrown
> Crying out in agony,
> The Dark did meet its destiny;

> For they had come to Lady's Well,
> That holy place of which tales tell
> For there, the Lady had prepared
> A trap from which no Dark was spared!

As she finished with a final sweeping chord, her watchers pelted the harp case with coins. "Another, minstrel!"

A little old man waved his battered straw hat at her. "You sing as sweetly as a brown wren, songsmith! Tell me, d'you know 'Hathor's Ghost Stallion'?"

Eydryth hesitated. "I think so . . . it goes like this?" she strummed a few chords, hummed a tune.

"That's it!" the old man cried. "Haven't heard that in—"

He broke off with a squawk of terror at the sudden drum of galloping hooves. The crowd scattered as a big black horse burst into their midst, heading for the field visible between two wagons. The grandsire tried to scuttle away, but tripped and fell.

As the horse swept toward them, Eydryth, without thinking, leaped forward so she was between the charging animal and the fallen man. The horse, a stallion, slid to a halt so violently that it half-reared.

"Steady, fellow!" Eydryth called, in a low, soothing voice. "Steady!"

The stallion's ears flattened even further against its head; its eyes sparked red in the light of the westering sun. With an enraged scream it reared again, its deadly hooves slashing the air just above Eydryth's head.

Four

*M*oving with the speed of desperation, Eydryth threw herself
away from the stallion's pawing hooves. She nearly tripped
over the old man, who lay frozen with fear, mouth open in a
soundless scream. Grabbing the grandsire by the shoulders of
his homespun jerkin, the songsmith dragged him over to the
perimeter of the gathering crowd. Only then did she turn back
to confront the horse.

The beast stood scant paces away, its eyes white-rimmed,
snorting as it dug a sharp forefoot into the trampled earth. Its
hide was lathered with sweat; the rank smell of it reached her
nostrils. Eydryth realized that anger was not the only reason
for the creature's attack—this animal was frightened as well as
enraged.

A broken halter hung from the runaway's neck, and its black coat was patched with tufts of thick winter hair, like a bearskin invaded by moths. An untidy bristle of upstanding mane crested the thick neck. Eydryth ran her eyes over its conformation, noting the powerful legs, broad, muscled hindquarters, and sloping shoulders. *Not tall or slender-legged enough for a sprinter*, she concluded, *but he looks as though he could run all day. I wonder what breed he is?*

The songsmith's blue eyes narrowed as she frowned. Something about this creature was familiar—disturbingly familiar.

The animal snorted nervously, then rolled its eyes at the milling crowd of onlookers now surrounding them. It sniffed the spring breeze, as though searching for something—or someone.

"I'll snare his forefeet and throw him. Bring a rope!" a burly man in the crowd called.

Eydryth saw muscles tense beneath that ebon hide as the stud sidled, muscles tensing. "Ho, son . . . easy now," she whispered, extending one hand as she stepped forward. "If you jump into the crowd, you'll surely hurt someone, so . . . whoa, now. Easy . . . easy . . ."

Black ears swiveled sharply forward to catch the crooning sound of her voice, but as Eydryth ventured another step, the horse flattened his ears, snorting an unmistakable warning. The onlookers gasped. The girl halted; then, remembering how she had soothed her own Kioga mare, Vyar, she began humming softly. The tune was the one the old man had requested only minutes ago.

Slowly, the black's ears moved forward as it listened. Gradually, its shivering eased. The muttering of the crowd faded into silence as Eydryth began singing, the words floating liquid and eerie in the still air:

> Lord Hathor and his horse were slain
> By the traitor's hand
> Now in moon-dark, mist and rain
> His stallion strides the land.
>
> His soul is filled with vengeance
> His eyes are filled with fire,

> And he has promised treachery
> Full venting of his ire.

Slowly, the songsmith stepped toward the creature . . . one step . . . two . . . a third . . .

Finally, she was at the animal's side. Eydryth held out her hand, feeling the warm puffs of breath as the horse scented her. She had to force herself to hold steady, knowing only too well the size of the teeth that were barely a handspan from her flesh. But he made no offer to snap.

> Lord Hathor, he was first to die,
> All in his youthful bloom
> But e'er death glazed the stallion's eyes
> The beast swore fearful doom.

The girl raised a hand to stroke the horse's neck.

"No! Lady, touch him not! He will kill you!"

The frantic shout came from some distance away. Eydryth's voice wavered, and the black ears flattened. Hastily, the songsmith resumed her soothing music. She did not turn around, but out of the corner of her eye the young woman glimpsed a running figure bursting out from between the farrier's forge and the saddlemaker's display. The newcomer began shoving a passage through the crowd.

Bending her head, Eydryth breathed gently into the red-rimmed, distended nostrils. They fluttered, but the animal did not move. She laid hand to the hot, sweaty neck, then began to stroke it gently, still singing.

> Of moonlight is the horse's mane
> His blood is formed from death
> His teeth are now a traitor's bane
> And fury now his breath.

When the stone-hard muscles beneath her fingers finally relaxed, the songsmith dared to grasp the broken halter. Reaching into the pocket of her jerkin, she took out a length of rawhide, using it to lace the leather straps together. All the while, she hummed softly.

Only when Eydryth was able to grasp the runaway by the now-repaired halter did she turn to regard the man who had shouted such a dire warning.

"Were you speaking to me, good sir?" she asked mildly.

The newcomer frankly gaped at her as she stood beside the now-placid horse, still humming. Of medium height and whip-slender, he gave the impression of a wiry toughness and strength. His hair was as black as the stallion's mane, his eyes dark grey. By the cast of his features he was young, but there was something ageless about him. Plainly, he was of the Old Race . . . and yet—

—yet—

For a moment Eydryth sensed something *different* about the newcomer . . . something that set him apart from the towns-people and farmers milling around him. Somehow, he seemed more *distinct* than the others. The songsmith blinked, startled; then the fleeting impression was gone. Facing her was naught but a young man, dressed simply in an unbleached linen shirt with a leather overjerkin, tan buckskin breeches, and battered, knee-high riding boots.

The stranger gave her a wry grin accompanied by a con-gratulatory bow. "I said, 'Thank you for capturing my horse, minstrel.' " His voice was a low, pleasant baritone, and his accent was that of an educated man, at variance with his rough clothing. A ripple of laughter went through the crowd, which then began dispersing, seeing that the excitement was now over.

Eydryth smiled, still patting the horse. "You are welcome, sir. Tell me, how did he come to be loose?"

The young man rubbed the back of his neck as though it pained him. "It was my fault," he admitted, unwrapping a leather lead-shank from about his waist and fastening it to the runaway's halter. The beast rumbled a low greeting deep in its throat. "I was careless. I took him to graze along the river-bank, and two ruffians evidently decided that it was easier to steal a mount than to acquire one honestly."

"They attacked you?"

"They were upon me before I knew they were there! One moment I was turning, thinking I heard a sound, the next I returned to my senses stretched out on the ground, with my horse nowhere to be seen. One of the brigands lay an arm's length away, trampled and dead, while the other was just disappearing into the forest, cradling an arm that will require splinting, if I'm any judge."

The man shook his head ruefully as he scratched behind the horse's ears, causing it to rub its head against him, nearly knocking him over. "This fellow has been trained to let no one else touch him. I was certain that you were about to share his would-be thieves' fate. But I was wrong." The newcomer gave Eydryth a searching look that made her cheeks grow warm. "Such lovely singing was too much for even Monso to resist."

Monso. Eydryth stared at the newcomer in shock. *That means "wind-swift" in the Old Tongue. But . . . how does this man come to know the Old Tongue?*

Her mind racing, Eydryth walked over to pick up her harp where it lay on the ground. After running her fingers over the wood and strings, she returned it to her pack.

"Is your harp damaged, Lady . . . Lady Songsmith?" the man asked worriedly.

She shook her head. "It is fine. I am Eydryth . . . and you are?"

He hesitated for a bare second, then bowed again. "I am called Dakar, Lady Eydryth."

Again the bard was careful not to betray any outward reaction to his words. *Dakar means "shadow" in the Old Tongue. Who is this man? Could he be from Arvon?*

Dakar ran a hand down Monso's neck, then across the broad chest. "He's still sweating. . . . I should walk him, lest his muscles cramp or stiffen. Will you . . . will you walk with us for a moment, Lady? I have scarcely thanked you."

"It was nothing," Eydryth demurred, but she slung her pack over her shoulders, then followed him as he led the stallion away from the fair booths toward an open meadow lying near the racecourse.

It was late afternoon now; the sun was dropping toward the dark shadow of the surrounding forest. The tiny white-and-gold lover's knots dotting the turf were beginning to close their petals. The bustle of the fair faded to a faint murmur far behind them as they walked.

Dakar glanced over at the racecourse, where the track was being smoothed by a heavy stone block dragged behind two oxen. "Soon it will be time for the day's race," he muttered, resting a hand on Monso's neck. He felt between the animal's forelegs, then, satisfied that the horse was now cool, halted him, allowing his mount to crop eagerly at the spring-green grass.

The youth rested an arm across his horse's back, leaning comfortably against the animal's barrel. He was not tall; his eyes and Eydryth's were nearly on a level as they stood together. "What brings you to the horse fair, Lady?" he asked.

Eydryth briefly explained her desire for a mount to carry her on her journeying, but admitted ruefully that her taste in horseflesh exceeded the wealth of her purse. Dakar nodded sympathetically. "There is fine stock to be had here, Lady, but only for those with the silver to purchase it. True bargains when buying horseflesh are rare."

Eydryth sighed. "You are right. I had just decided I would be better off earning yet another night's worth of silver, then trying again on the morrow. But I am anxious to proceed to Lormt—even a day's delay seems an eternity!"

"Lormt?" he gave her a sharp, sidelong glance. Plainly, he had heard of the ancient stronghold of knowledge.

"You know of Lormt?" she asked, eagerly. "Have you ever been there?"

"Never within its walls, Lady. But I worked with a mountain guide for nearly a year, leading parties into Escore, and we were accustomed to camp outside Lormt's walls on each trip. We watered our horses at the village well. The master chronicler, Duratan, gave my partner permission to do so."

"Have you met any of the scholars there? Any who might know aught of ancient scrolls having to do with healing?"

Dakar shook his head. "No, always I remained with the

party while Jon—" He broke off in midname, his mouth tightening, then continued, not looking at her. "—while my partner consulted with the scholars."

"But still, you know the way there. Is the overland route by way of South Wending the most direct road?"

He nodded. "It is. Except that there is an old forest trail after you pass South Wending that will save you half a day's journey. The entrance is nearly overgrown, but the path itself is clear. Look for it on your left just past a tall bank of red clay with a stream running at its foot."

"Thank you," Eydryth said.

"You are most welcome. I only wish I could be of more help. I can tell that your journey is . . . important."

The songsmith glanced away. "You *have* aided me. Anything that will hasten my journeying is all to the good. I am in your debt."

"Nonsense, my lady. I owe you far more than that, for catching Monso. Doubtless you kept him from injuring someone, or, at the least, damaging property." Dakar stopped to gaze thoughtfully over at the oval of beaten earth where soon the races would be run. A moment later, he turned back to catch the songsmith's gaze, hold it with his own.

"If I had coin of my own, I'd give it to you, Lady," he said, his pleasant voice suddenly low and intense. "Regrettably, races have been few and far between here in the south of Estcarp, and at the moment I have barely enough to pay my entry fee. But if you will trust me enough to risk some of your own silver, I swear that it will profit you."

Dakar took a brush from a pocket in his jerkin and began grooming his horse. Dried sweat rose in a dusty, salty cloud. "My beast may not be as tall, or as sleek and well groomed as these local beauties, Lady—but over a course this length, nothing can stay with him, much less pass him. Wager on us, and you'll not lose."

"But it's a long way from the riverbank to the fairgrounds," Eydryth pointed out. "He's run himself into a lather once already today. I saw some of the racers earlier—they are fine, blooded animals, and fresh, as Monso is not. How can you defeat them?"

Monso snorted explosively, then curled his upper lip, almost as though he were laughing. Dakar grinned as he curried his mount's back. "I admit it sounds unlikely, but I know what I know. Wager on us, Lady Eydryth, and you'll not have to sing tonight to earn extra silver."

The minstrel gazed at both horse and master for a long moment, then nodded. "May you race as fast as ever Lord Faral did, Dakar. I will go and place my wager."

Monso snorted again, then bobbed his head as though he understood and agreed perfectly.

An hour later, Eydryth jostled for position along the hedges dividing the racecourse from the fairground. Tucked safely into her coin purse was a flat chip of wood, marked with the amount of her wager and the odds. As she had suspected, Monso was not among those favored to win the race—too many people had seen the runaway's mad flight across the fairgrounds. Any horse that had already spent itself so greatly was regarded as too leg-weary to prove a dangerous challenger.

The songsmith squinted, trying to make out the field against the reddish glare from the westering sun.

There! One spot of dull brown and black, contrasting vividly with the colorful caps, sashes and saddlecloths of the other entries. Dakar rode Monso onto the course, his saddle one of the light ones used by battle-couriers. Unlike the other riders with their long-legged, secure seats, he rode with his stirrups short, almost perched atop, rather than astride, his mount.

Eydryth smiled inwardly. The Kioga rode like that when they raced . . . short-stirruped, crouching over their horses' withers, rather than sitting heavily on their backs. The young woman knew from experience that Dakar's position in the saddle would permit his horse maximum freedom of stride, while greatly lessening wind resistance.

Around her, the townspeople of Rylon Corners also noticed the stranger's odd seat. Several rough-looking rogues that she'd seen in the wagering tent pointed and laughed, predicting that the young man would find his brains spattered on the packed earth as soon as the race began.

As the horses milled behind a rope stretched across the track, the official starter took her place. She was the mayor's wife, a greying, buxom woman who stood beside the judges on the inside of the racecourse. In her hand was a red scarf that fluttered in the wind.

Minutes went by as the horses wheeled and sidled, their riders urging them into their appointed positions on the starting line. Eydryth noticed that none of the other animals would stand within a length of Monso. As though he had expected no less, Dakar, without being told, took up position on the far outside, where he would have the greatest distance to run—an additional handicap. Eydryth bit her lip, thinking of the silver coins she had wagered . . . thinking how ill she could afford to lose them.

A moment later, the line of horses momentarily steadied; then suddenly the strip of red silk fluttered free.

The rope barrier dropped.

A roar of excitement erupted from the watching crowd as the racers lunged forward, trying to gain a position next to the inside hedge. Great clumps of dried mud pelted the crowd, thrown up by the thundering hooves.

Monso! Where is he?

Eydryth craned her neck, trying desperately to see, but many of the men in the crowd were taller than she. She ducked between a goodwife carrying two hens in a cage, and a blank-shield whose breath proclaimed his afternoon in an alehouse. On tiptoe, fists clenched, she squinted at the course. Slowly, she was able to pick out the individual horses.

The grey in the lead, then the red chestnut . . . third was the dun . . . the golden bay was neck-and-neck with the liver chestnut, then came the dark bay with the blaze face. But no black!

Fear tightened like a fist on Eydryth's throat. *Monso! Dakar! Where are you?*

Anxiously, the bard looked back along the length of the track, fearing to see a downed horse and rider. But the hoof-scarred clay was clear. Puzzled, she turned back to the race.

The horses, still closely bunched, were approaching the far turn. But as they reached the opposite side of the oval track, Eydryth made out a smaller, black shadow clinging like a sticktight to the side of the second-running chestnut!

"Go!" Eydryth whispered, not even hearing herself amid the din of the crowd. "Run, Monso!"

As if he had indeed heard her, Dakar guided the black horse perilously closer to the inside hedge; then there was free track before them! Eydryth gasped as Monso leaped forward so swiftly that it seemed as though he had only now begun to run. In the space of a heartbeat he was beside the grey leader. Then he was past—a length in front—two lengths—

Eydryth clapped a hand to her mouth, seeing that Dakar was holding his mount tight-reined, not allowing him to run full-out. His hands moved, pulling hard, working the steel bit against the corners of the horse's mouth. And still the black, moving with the speed of an advancing tempest, continued to gain!

Monso was a full four lengths in the lead when he swept past the finish pole. There was no cheering from the crowd, only a stunned silence.

" 'Tis unnatural!" the woman with the hens exclaimed finally. "That creature ran past Hawrel's Grey Arrow as though the beast was hitched to a plow—and that grey is the fastest horse the town's seen in a score o' years!"

"Aye," the blank-shield muttered, disgustedly snapping his wagering chip in two. "No horse should have been able t' run like that, after that chase cross the fairground today. No *normal* horse, that is."

No normal horse.

Sudden realization made Eydryth fasten her teeth in her lower lip to avoid crying out in recognition. *Now* she knew where she'd seen Monso's like before. That spark of red in the beast's eyes had been no reflection of the sun! *That creature is no more a mortal horse than Hathor's Ghost Stallion!* she thought. But . . . *how?* How could anyone catch and master a *Keplian?*

The songsmith vividly remembered the time she had seen one of the demon horse-spirits sent by the Dark to lure unwary travelers. It had been shortly after her mother disappeared. She, Jervon and Lord Kerovan had been out searching, and had camped for the night near a stream in a seemingly deserted valley.

Eydryth had rolled out of her blankets in the silver dimness before dawn, only to see the creature standing just outside their camp. The Keplian had the seeming of a tall, perfect black stallion as it had stood cropping the dew-heavy grass. Both she and Jervon had cried out with pleasure at the sheer beauty of its delicate head, its straight, clean-boned legs . . . the flowing lines of its arched neck and straight-backed body.

Both she and her father had started toward it, enthralled by the creature's unearthly beauty. Both of them might well have been ensnared past all saving, but suddenly, Kerovan stepped into their path, the wristband that he wore glowing brightly. As its light bathed their eyes, they staggered back, returning to their senses, for the ancient talisman possessed the ability to warn and guard against the presence of any evil.

Kerovan had raised his arm in a warding gesture. "Get you gone, fell thing! Do not return!" As the wristlet's light struck the Keplian, it had snorted with pain, then raced away.

So Monso is a Keplian. That explains much, Eydryth thought, standing bemused, hardly hearing the disappointed grumblings of the departing onlookers. *And yet . . . he does not have that unnatural perfection of form that the creature I saw possessed. Could he be a crossbred? Is it possible that Keplians can mate with mortal horses?*

Her speculations continued without answer as the songsmith turned to make her way through the thinning crowd, her goal the wagering tent and the claiming of her winnings.

The race had been the last event of the horse fair; all around her horse traders and merchants were feeding their stock and closing up their pavilions until the morrow, when the fair would reopen. The sun was setting rapidly now, and by the time she emerged from the wagering tent, blue twilight was stealing across the land like a thief, robbing the place of color and life.

Eydryth smiled as she walked, feeling the heavy purse

weighing down the belt she wore inside her jerkin. *Enough, and more than enough to purchase a fine mount. I'll be in Lormt ere I thought possible!*

As she set off across the nearly deserted tangle of tents and booths, Eydryth saw Dakar walking Monso not far from where they had first met. Shrugging her pack a little higher on her shoulders, the songsmith veered aside from her chosen path with the intention of thanking the youth.

Torchlight sputtered in the night breeze that had sprung up, its reflection again awakening that disturbing scarlet spark in the black stallion's eyes. Eydryth halted, staring at the unlikely pair. After all, what did she know of Dakar? He rode a Keplian. It was therefore entirely possible—nay, probable—that he himself was of the Left-Hand Path, one of the Dark Ones. Legend held that they were often handsome, or beautiful . . . as fair outside as they were foul within.

As she wavered, on the verge of turning away, Dakar looked up, then waved cheerfully. "Lady Eydryth!" he called, as she came toward him. "Did you see the race?"

The minstrel nodded. "I did. Lord Faral's horse could not have run more swiftly!" As she reached him, she added, in a lower tone, "Now I will be able to reach Lormt in only a few days, thanks to my wager. I am indeed in your debt."

The young man shook his head. "Nonsense. We would have raced for the winner's purse whether or not you were wagering on us, my lady. I am just glad that you will be able to continue your journeying well-mounted."

Eydryth hesitated, tempted to ask where he and Monso would be going, now that the race day was over, but what was the sense in that? She would never see him—or his strange mount—again. The songsmith sighed, resolutely straightening her shoulders beneath the heavy pack. "Farewell, then, Dakar, and a safe journey to you on the morrow," she said.

He appeared to hesitate in his turn, then finally nodded. "A safe journey to you . . . and may you find what you are seeking." He held out his hand.

Eydryth clasped hands with him in a warrior's grip, feeling the leather-callused roughness of his palm against her own harpstring-toughened fingers. She saw his eyes widen slightly at the strength of her grip; then he smiled, his clasp shifted, and he bowed formally over her hand in courtly fashion. "Fare you well, Lady Eyd—"

"Spawn of the Dark!"

"You cheated! That's no ordinary horse!"

"Cheater! You witched my Grey Arrow!"

Eydryth and Dakar started, whirling to see a group of men approaching them, their shadowy forms huge and wavering in the wind-whipped torchlight.

Monso's rider put up his hands in a conciliatory fashion as the figures ranged themselves around them, hemming them in past all escape. "Gently, goodmen, gently! If any of you feel that my horse did not win fairly, you should have spoken to the judges before Monso was officially declared the winner. There was no such protest entered."

"That's because we were all bespelled!" Grey Arrow's owner, Hawrel, a tall, rawboned farmer with the fair hair of a Sulcarman, stepped forward. "You made fools of us all, but we've come to our senses now, and we demand you make right our losses!"

Monso lowered his head, snorting. One sharp hoof pawed in unmistakable challenge. Dakar grabbed the Keplian's halter, whispering to him, and slowly the black calmed. "Very well," his master said. "I want no trouble—for your sakes, as much as my own. I will give you what I have."

Eydryth made a small motion of protest, but did not speak, as Dakar slowly withdrew his winner's purse from within his jerkin. *Five . . . six . . .* She counted the figures in that grim circle, noting that several were armed with cudgels and one with a sword. *Too many to fight. And Dakar* did *cheat . . . racing a Keplian against mortal horses is hardly fair—*

—but neither is this! she thought angrily, watching the young man grimly weigh the purse in his hand, then toss it at Hawrel's feet. "Take it, then, and leave us in peace," he said, his shoulders sagging with sudden weariness. "I will leave your town, and nothing could induce me to return, I assure you."

The protesters did not miss the bitter mockery in his words.

Stung, they surged forward until Eydryth could recognize other faces—Grey Arrow's bowlegged little rider . . . the broad-shouldered blank-shield who had been standing near her in the crowd, the palm-polished grip of his sword gleaming faintly . . . the village blacksmith . . . the horse trader whose animal she'd rejected. The sixth man wore a muffling hood that hid his features.

"We'll not stand here and be mocked by a cheating rascal of a boy!" the smith snarled, slapping the rasp he carried against his callused palm. "You and that unnatural beast both deserve a beating, and that is what you're going to receive!"

"Wait!" Dakar held up both hands, genuinely alarmed now. "You must not! You could be killed! I want no bloodshed, please! At least allow the songsmith to—"

"At them, then, lads!" Hawrel shouted, and in deadly silence, the men rushed them. The songsmith dodged the one wearing the hood, her quarterstaff sweeping the ground, sending her attacker thudding heavily to the ground.

As he lay there, winded, Eydryth gave him a carefully calculated rap on the back of the head that stretched him out, unconscious; then she turned back to aid her companion. Dakar was holding onto his horse, shouting commands, while the heavyset blacksmith brandished his rasp at the young man's head, all the while trying to pull Monso's lead-shank away.

Hawrel grabbed the youth from behind, one hand clamping brutally over his mouth, his other arm tightening over his throat. The smith yanked the horse toward him, aiming a blow at the creature's head with the rasp.

The Keplian went up on his hind legs with a piercing scream of fury, forehooves slashing. His eyes flashed bloodred in the torchlight as the demon-horse struck like a snake. He grabbed the smith's arm, hoisting the man clean up into the air, his bared teeth ripping through heavy clothing and skin alike to lay the brawny forearm open to the bone. The injured man dangled, shrieking.

"Monso!" Dakar shouted, tearing his mouth free of Hawrel's grip. "No! Touch them not!"

Monso shook the smith as though he were a rat, then dropped him.

The bronze-sheathed butt of Eydryth's quarterstaff came down on the Sulcar farmer's head, sending him staggering, freeing Dakar, who ran to his horse, drawing his belt knife. The blank-shield rushed at him, his own knife out. Dakar struck out, trying to fend off his attacker, but it was clear to the songsmith that the youth was far from an experienced fighter. Even as Eydryth leaped to defend him, the mercenary flicked the knife out of the youth's grasp. Kicking it away, the big man advanced, his own blade weaving expertly before him.

Eydryth swung at his arm, but Hawrel's cudgel struck her shoulder, deflecting her stroke and sending a lance of pain down her arm. Gasping from the hurt, she lashed out at him; then trained muscles took over, and she was in the thick of the fight, automatically dodging, parrying, rapping the four remaining attackers sharply with the staff every time they left her an opening.

Cursing, the townsmen staggered back, out of range, wary now. One of them stumbled over the hooded man; then they dragged him with him. The smith was gone. Panting, Eydryth spoke to Dakar without taking her eyes off their foes. "Are you hurt?"

For answer, something large brushed her shoulder, sending her staggering.

Monso!

The stallion sprang forward, Dakar clinging to his mane; then, with a snort and a drum of hooves, mount and rider were through and away, leaving Eydryth to face their attackers alone.

With a bitter grimace—*When will I ever learn to keep from barging into fights that aren't mine?*—the bard braced herself for the next rush.

"So, songsmith," the blank-shield chuckled, drawing his sword, "looks as though you've been stuck with the burnt end of the stick, don't it? Yer sweetheart just left ye t' fend for yourself."

Grey Arrow's rider frowned uncertainly. "I dunno," he

muttered. "I don't hold with fightin' a bard. 'Tis said t' be bad luck. Some of uns can curse ye with a song, 'tis said. 'Sides," he pointed out, "she's a woman."

"The Dark Ones take her, she hits like a man, I say treat her like one," Hawrel said, rubbing his head and glaring at Eydryth. " 'Tis a wonder my skull ain't cracked, sure enough!"

"That's a big purse she's carrying," the hooded man whispered, climbing slowly to his feet. His concealing garment fell back, revealing skin darkened by sun to the color of an ancient bronze shield, and grizzled hair. "I watched Norden count out her winnin's, and they was enough t' choke a donkey. We can get the rest o' our losses back from her."

The wiry little rider shook his head. "Not me, I'm not risking any curse-songs. And I don't hold with stealing. Count me out, lads."

He turned and walked away into the night. The other men hesitated. "Give us the purse, songsmith," Hawrel said. "And we might let you off with only a few bruises to make up for those you gave us."

Gunnora, aid me, Eydryth prayed. *Let me take two of them with me.* She shook her head, not speaking.

"Your decision, then," the Sulcarman growled.

Eydryth grasped the slender barrel of the gryphon's body, the metal cool and comforting to her staff-chafed hand, and pulled. A blade of shining steel emerged from where it had been fitted into the length of the quarterstaff.

Eydryth saluted her opponents with the now-revealed sword, smiling grimly at their unconcealed surprise.

"She knows how t' use that blade," the hooded man observed, uneasily. He was still not steady on his feet.

"And if she does?" the blank-shield said. "There's still three of us, and I'm no stranger to swordplay. I'll keep her busy, and you take her from behind."

Slowly they began spreading out to do his bidding. Eydryth braced herself as they gathered themselves for a charge—

The thunder of racing hoofbeats suddenly filled the night!

"Songsmith! Be ready!" Dakar shouted, as he galloped toward her on Monso. The hooded man grabbed a lit torch and swiped at the Keplian. He screamed shrilly as the stallion lashed out with a forefoot; then they burst through, knocking Hawrel sprawling. The blank-shield fell back before the Keplian's bared teeth.

Eydryth had already resheathed her sword. She handed up her quarterstaff; then, grabbing the hand Dakar extended, she vaulted up behind him onto the dancing, plunging horse. She had barely enough time to snatch her weapon and grasp Dakar's belt one-handed before Monso's haunches bunched beneath her.

The Keplian sprang forward with a leap that nearly unseated her; then they were off, racing away from the torchlight, into the dark.

Five

*E*ydryth waited for Monso to slow once they left the fairground, but the stallion thundered on, his speed never slacken-
ing. He was running much faster than he had during the race;
she could feel Dakar fighting to bring him under control, but
to no avail.

Eydryth had heard tales, sung songs, of wanderers lured
into mounting Keplians, then being borne off to a fate best not
envisioned. She had always wondered why the hapless riders
did not simply leap from the demon-horse's back.

Now she knew; such a plunge from the back of a Keplian
galloping at full stride would mean almost certain death.

The girl knew herself to be a good—nay, an expert—rider,

but even so, she was in grave danger of being unseated. The moonless night was so dark that she could not see the horse's head past Dakar's shoulder, and thus she was caught unawares whenever the beast swerved sharply, or, in several cases, hurdled obstacles lying in their path.

Eydryth's left hand was locked in a death-grip on her companion's belt, but she dared not clamp her lower legs around her mount's sensitive flanks—to do so would have set Monso bucking and plunging like an unbroken colt. Instead she tightened her thigh muscles, struggling to keep her balance on the swaying, heaving creature she bestrode.

They hurtled down a slope at breakneck speed, and the songsmith shut her eyes, tempted to abandon her quarterstaff so that she might hold on with both hands. She felt Dakar lean forward; then the black wind of their passage carried his gasped warning. "Hold tight! There's a stream!"

Eydryth flattened herself against him, her arm clutching him round the waist. Muscles bunched beneath her; then for a breathless instant they hung suspended, creatures of air, not earth.

With a neck-snapping jar, they landed. One hind foot skimmed the water; icy droplets spattered both riders. Dakar was fighting the Keplian again; Eydryth could feel the muscles in his back tense as he exerted all his skill to gain mastery. But the runaway snorted, shaking his head, refusing to yield to the bit.

The songsmith closed her eyes, knowing that she could not hold on much longer. She heard Dakar muttering, but could not make out what he was saying. They lunged up a slope, and Eydryth felt herself slipping . . . *slipping.* . . .

With a suddenness that caused her to lose her seat entirely, Monso halted on the crest of a hill.

The girl was thrown forward, banging her nose painfully against Dakar's shoulder, then flung just as abruptly backward. She slid off over the Keplian's rump, landing in an undignified huddle directly behind the demon-horse.

Eydryth gasped for breath, but her wind was knocked out. Monso sidled nervously, switching his tail, and the harsh strands whipped across her face. The resulting sting revived the songsmith sufficiently to make her aware of her danger, and she managed to roll over, out of range, lest Monso should kick. But the Keplian made no further move, only stood head-down, blowing, seeming all at once like an ordinary horse silhouetted against the starry expanse of night sky.

"Lady Eydryth, are you hurt? Lady?" Dakar swung off, his movements stiff, lacking his usual grace. Eydryth heard a muttered curse as he stumbled, nearly falling in his turn. Then he was crouching beside her. "Lady Eydryth?"

The songsmith struggled again for breath, and this time succeeded in drawing a lungful of clean air. "Wind . . . knocked out," she panted.

He aided her into a sitting position, steadying her against his raised knee. "I am sorry that was such a rough ride, Lady. He had the bit in his teeth, and I could not stop him until now."

She nodded, then shivered, feeling suddenly weak and wobbly as a newborn foal. *Reaction to tonight's danger*, she realized, trying to breathe slowly, evenly, in order to slow the racing of her heart. "I thought you had left me to those ruffians," she whispered, finally.

"What else could you think?" he asked, in a bitter tone that she realized was directed at himself. "For that I am sorry, too. But I had to fetch my saddle and supplies . . . and, even more, I had to get Monso away before he could do any further harm. He would have killed those men, and such could have . . . awakened . . . something in him that must never be unleashed. There is . . . a darker side to his nature."

"Naturally." Eydryth spoke tartly as she tentatively moved her limbs, exploring bruises sustained in the fight and her fall. "He *is* a Keplian, after all."

Moonrise was yet hours off; the night was too dark to allow her to see his expression, but she felt him start and heard his quick, indrawn breath. "How did you know?"

"Do not think to deny it," she said. "I have seen a horse-demon before. And even those farmers recognized that Monso is not a normal creature. Hawrel was right—you *were* cheating, to race him against ordinary horses. I am surprised that the people of Rylon Corners were the first ones to realize that and object."

"I won the other races in a far less . . . spectacular . . . fashion," Dakar told her, dryly. "But today, Monso was so excited after the thieves tried to steal him that he would not be held back."

"The word will be out, now." Eydryth ran searching fingers anxiously over her harp, finding it—*Fortune be praised!*—undamaged. Then, sore muscles protesting, she climbed to her feet. The wind on the hillside tugged at her cropped curls as she turned her head, trying to discern her surroundings. She could see little, except short-turfed hillside occasionally studded with darker clumps that must be bushes. "You and your Keplian had both best find another method of earning your way here in Estcarp," she muttered absently. "Next time you are so beset, I will not be there to aid you."

Dakar also rose, standing close beside her. He peered at her face as though he could see her, though she knew he must be as night-blind as she. "Why did you aid me this time?" he asked, quietly. "If you had left before it began, they would doubtless have let you go."

"Because it was obvious that you could not aid yourself," Eydryth replied. "Did no one ever teach you to fight?"

"No," he answered, a rueful note in his voice. "Before this night I never had need to defend myself physically."

And yet, from his speech and manners, he was raised in a noble household, the songsmith thought with a frown. *Which should have included lessoning from an arms-master. Truly this Dakar is a cipher!* It was on the tip of her tongue to ask him why he had never been taught swordplay, but Eydryth repressed the urge. She had no wish to know why, she told herself, because she could ill afford to become caught up in another's problems . . . she had a quest of her own that was challenge enough.

"I must walk Monso," her companion said, stripping saddle and saddlebags from the Keplian's back.

"I suppose we should camp here," Eydryth said, reluctantly. "It is too dark to find our way back to the road to-night."

She saw the pale oval of his face as he nodded. "There seem to be several trees and large boulders over there," he said, pointing. "They would break the wind. The night is chilly already, and will be colder yet before dawn."

"Dare we kindle a fire?" she wondered aloud.

"I doubt that Hawrel and his supporters will risk further injury by following us," he said. "And there is no one else with any reason to seek *me* out." There was an ironic note in his voice. "If you can say the same, Lady, then by all means let us have a fire."

Eydryth thought of the witches as she shouldered her pack and Dakar's saddlebags; then she shook her head. She and Avris had been nearly a full moon on the road; surely any search the witches had ordered had been given up long ago. Cautiously, she began picking her way across the hilltop.

Her night-sight was complete, now, and she could dimly make out the grove of trees Dakar had mentioned. The hilltop was large and fairly level. *The grass is so short, it must be used for grazing . . . probably sheep or goats*, she decided. *We must be careful to be away by dawn, lest we encounter an angry shepherd.*

The lights of Rylon Corners sparkled in the distance, seeming almost farther away than the stars overhead.

Eydryth set up camp in the grove, kindling a pocket of fire behind a huge boulder that would conceal the small blaze from anyone in the town. Wrapping her cloak around her shoulders, she sat down on a log, rubbing her hands before the flames, grateful for their warmth.

A short while later, Dakar returned to feed, water and rub down Monso. Only when his mount was comfortable and settled for the night did the young man rest. He nodded silent thanks for the hunks of journeybread and venison jerky that Eydryth passed him from her pack. Silent with weariness, the two travelers ate, sharing a flask of rather sour wine Dakar produced.

Monso finished his oats, then ambled away to graze.

"You can leave him loose?" Eydryth asked, in surprise.

"Always he has stayed with me," Dakar said. "We are . . . companions, more than mount and master."

The songsmith tugged her cloak closer around her shoulders. "Before today, I would have sworn that no one could capture—much less tame—a Keplian. How did you do it?"

"Monso is not a full-blooded Keplian," her companion explained. "His sire was a Torgian stallion that was my first horse, his dam a Keplian mare. We found her, newly foaled, the morning after a battle in Escore. A Grey One had killed her mother. The filly was so young that she had not yet been corrupted by the Dark Adepts who breed the demon-horses."

"And you were able to mate her with your Torgian?" Eydryth had seen animals of the much-valued Torgian breed, steeds bred near the Fens of Tormarsh to possess both swiftness and great stamina. "But none of the horses in the race today would even approach Monso."

"There are many who live in Escore who use magic as naturally as breathing," Dakar said. "One such Adept was able to use his Power to accomplish the breeding."

"I see," Eydryth said. "Did you know him well, this Adept, this sorcerer?"

Dakar was silent for a long moment, head bowed. The songsmith studied his face, the angles of brow, cheekbones and jaw touched with firelight, the rest a mask sculpted by shadows. Finally he nodded. "Hilarion was the closest I ever came to having a father. He and his lady, the sorceress Kaththea, opened their ancient citadel to me when I naught but a boy, wandering a war-riven land with no companion but my Torgian. In a very real sense, theirs was the first true home I had ever known."

"Kaththea?" Eydryth's eyes widened. "I have heard that name. Is she not the daughter of Lord Simon Tregarth and the former witch, the Lady Jaelithe?"

"The very same."

"They say all three of their children were born at one birth—and that each has the Power."

"That is true," Dakar said. "When there is need, the three

of them unite and become One in shared power. However, each also possesses his or her own abilities. Lord Kyllan with animals, Lord Kemoc with ancient lore and Words of Power, and the Lady Kaththea with sorcery. She has always been the most powerful of the three."

"So you grew to manhood in a household surrounded by these magic-wielders?"

"Each of the Tregarths now has his or her own household in Escore," Alon replied. "But they stay very close—they can speak without words when there is need."

Eydryth, having seen similar closeness among her own family members, could well believe such. She nodded, memories crowding her mind. "I know what it is like to live among those with Power," she admitted.

"You lived in such a household also?" Dakar's eyes were intent on her face. "In Escore?"

"No, in another place. A land called Arvon, across the sea from Estcarp."

"Arvon . . . ," he whispered. "I have heard of it. Hilarion told me that when he first lived in Escore, before the Old Race crossed the mountains bordering Estcarp on the east, that there was a legend telling of two lands that had once been one land. Escore . . . and Arvon."

Eydryth blinked in surprise. "This Hilarion must be *old*," she said, startled into bluntness. "Time-out-of-mind old. There are ancient runes and scrolls in the Citadel of Kar Garudwyn, even some maps, and they show naught but wasteland lying to the far west of my land, wasteland that becomes a death-haunted desert."

"And what lies beyond the desert?"

"No one seemed certain. That land was blighted, poisonous to all life, and none dared traverse it. One Adept wrote that he had scryed far to the west, and that the land became ever more seared, until it ended on the melted, glassy shores of an uncanny sea inhabited by strange creatures."

"Which fits the legends Hilarion remembers." Dakar smiled a little. "My lord is not the greybeard you envision, my lady. He spent considerable time imprisoned beyond a Gate where

Time ran differently than it does on this world. Have you ever heard of such?"

"Yes, I know of the Gates."

Her companion hesitated. "You seem to know much about the uses of Power, my lady. Are you a Wise Woman, then?"

"No."

"A witch or sorceress?" he persisted.

She laughed, but the sound held a bitter note. "No, no, and no! I am no more a Holder of Power than you are, friend Dakar. Of all those who reside in Kar Garudwyn, only my father and I lack the Gift."

"I, too, know what it is like to be set apart," Dakar said, his eyes holding hers. "But . . . Lady . . . do not be too sure that possession of Power is always a Gift. I have been assured by those who know that it can also be a curse, a . . . shadow . . . over the life of the person who has it."

"So have I also been told," Eydryth admitted. "But still, it seemed to me when I was growing up that I was as lacking as a child born without eyes, or ears. My foster-sister, Hyana, told me time and again that was not so, but still . . ." She shrugged. "But you know what it is like, I need not remind you."

Her companion regarded her steadily, compassionately. Embarrassed, the young woman glanced away, feeling her cheeks grow warm. "Moonrise is not far off," she observed, seeing a faint glow in the east. "We had best sleep, so we can be up and away with first light. The first of us to wake must call the other." She hesitated, then said in a rush, "I neglected to thank you for risking everything to come back for me. Please . . . accept my gratitude, Dakar."

"Only if you will accept mine," he said, his eyes holding hers. "Both Monso and I owe you our lives."

She smiled. "We are all of us well thanked, then. Rest well, Dakar."

After pulling off her boots, Eydryth crawled into her bedroll, pillowing her head on her harp case. Determined to sleep, she closed her eyes.

Lulled by the fire's warmth, she had nearly drifted off when the other spoke again. "Lady Eydryth . . . about tomorrow. You will be going on to Lormt?"

"Yes," she murmured, gazing at him in the dimness, her eyes heavy-lidded with the great weariness that had descended upon her. "I *must* go on."

"But they may be searching for us," he pointed out.

Eydryth thought again of the witches. "They have your purse," she said. "That may satisfy them."

"Perhaps it would be best if we stayed hidden in these hills until we discover whether there is any pursuit. . . ."

"I cannot rest, nor turn back," she said, with a stubborn head-shake. "The life of someone I hold very dear depends on me."

"I see," he said thoughtfully. "Well, since it is my fault that you cannot return to Rylon Corners to buy a mount, I would be pleased to take you to Lormt. I know the way. We can make good time. Monso will not mind a double load." He spoke with a sort of wary eagerness, as though he were bracing himself to have her refuse his aid.

Eydryth pushed herself up on one elbow to stare at him across the dying fire. "You would do that for me? Why?"

"It is the least I can do. The saving of one's life is no small thing. Had it not been for you, that blank-shield would have sheathed his blade in my vitals."

She nodded slowly. "I had forgotten that. Very well . . . I would be pleased to company with you, Dakar."

He poked a twig into the coals, watched it smolder, smolder, then burst into flame. "And another thing," he continued, slowly. "My name is not 'Dakar.' I used that name because . . . because I did not want to use my rightful one among those who might have cause to . . . grow angry with me." He gave her a rueful half-smile. "For cheating, as you pointed out. It seemed prudent. But I would not want to deceive a . . . comrade-in-arms." His eyes met hers across the dying fire. "I am Alon."

The first rays of dawn slanted across Eydryth's closed eyelids. . . . Frowning, she stirred restlessly, dreaming. . . .

In her dream she saw her mother, Elys, looking not a day older than the last time Eydryth had seen her. The witch lay upon a pallet draped in grey silk, asleep or entranced. Only the slightest rise and fall of her breast proved that she still lived. Leaden-colored vapor swirled around her still figure, alternately obscuring, then revealing, her face.

"Mother!" Eydryth tried to shout, but no sound issued from her lips.

She managed a step forward, then another, but it was akin to walking beneath the surface of a lake or ocean; she could make but little progress. Peering down, the girl saw that her feet were weighed down, trapped within one of the coiling grey fingers of mist.

"Mother!"

Still no sound, and now the girl could move no farther; her groping hands encountered bars that she could feel but not see.

"Mother! Mother, I am here!"

As she struggled desperately, wildly, Elys, hands folded across the mound of her unborn child, faded away into the shrouding mist. . . .

Eydryth awoke with tears in her eyes, only to see a face peering into hers—a huge, golden-eyed, inhuman face, dominated by a cruelly hooked beak!

The songsmith jerked upright with a startled gasp, her heart slamming painfully. A moment later, she regained her sense of perspective, realizing that what she was seeing was no enormous monster, but a falcon. The bird was perched on the edge of the harp case that had pillowed her head; it had been eyeing her so closely that its beak had nearly brushed her nose.

The creature was large and black-feathered, save for a white V on its breast. Eydryth had seen its like before; several of the marines serving aboard the *Osprey* had been Falconers. But its yellow feet bore none of the scarlet thongs a Falconer's companion customarily wore—so from whence had it come? Surely a creature out of the wild would not behave so!

"Who are you?" Eydryth whispered, as though she might indeed be answered. "How did you come here?" *From Rylon*

Corners? Surely not! I have heard of no Falconer villages within the boundaries of Estcarp!

Still, the bird-helmed warriors' stronghold, the Eyrie, had been destroyed during the Turning. Perhaps some of those exiles were now living among the people of Estcarp. But she had heard in her travels that this strange race of warriors who hated their women and loved only their falcons were currently trying to establish a foothold at Seakeep in High Hallack.

None of which speculation helped her account for the presence of this bird, eyeing her so measuringly, first with one eye, then the other. Its head bobbed up and down with the motion.

"He calls himself Steel Talon," said a voice from behind her.

Eydryth whirled to find Alon, fully dressed, carrying a hide bag full of water. "Is . . . is he yours? You are no Falconer!"

"You speak truth," he agreed readily. "Steel Talon belongs to no one but himself. His master, Jonthal, was my friend and partner. He . . . was killed. Murdered. Instead of willing himself to join his master in death, as is customary for these birds, Steel Talon has chosen instead to live for the day in which he will find his master's slayer . . . and on that day, he will wreak a terrible vengeance."

"I see," Eydryth said, studying the bird, who stared back at her with hot golden eyes, eyes that held intelligence in their aurulent depths—a nonhuman kind of intelligence, but none the less for all that. "So he travels with you?"

"After a fashion," Alon replied. "He comes and goes as he pleases." He stepped forward to stand beside her, so they both faced the bird. "Steel Talon, this is the Lady Eydryth," he said, introducing her so solemnly that they might have been at some noble gathering, rather than in a misty, dew-wet pasture dotted with sheep dung. "Monso and I are taking her to Lormt, to aid her in her journey, so she will be companying with us today and on the morrow."

The songsmith inclined her head as she would have to a human. "Well-met, Steel Talon."

For a moment those fierce eyes met hers again, then the bird gave a piercing cry. He rose from the boulder in a blur of ebon wings and sailed away, out of sight. Eydryth turned to Alon. "Well? Did he approve?"

Her companion smiled at her. "How could he not? He is an extremely discerning creature."

The girl felt again that warmth of cheek and hoped that the light was still so dim that Alon could not make out her blush. Confused, she summoned words almost at random. "You were supposed to wake me at first light. We must hurry, or the shepherds will find us here."

Quickly they broke camp, not stopping to break their fast, only pocketing rounds of journeybread to chew as they rode.

Monso carried his double load seemingly effortlessly, though Alon constrained him to a far slower speed than that of the night before—much to Eydryth's relief. The Keplian's paces were uncannily smooth as her companion varied their speed according to the terrain: jog, canter, working trot, walk. Once they reached the road leading to South Wending, he kept the stallion to a slow, ground-covering canter.

Eydryth was amazed at the creature's endurance. The damp clay of the road flowed from beneath the Keplian's tireless legs like water running downstream. By the time they halted for their midday meal, she estimated that they had covered nearly ten leagues.

Standing beside Monso as he grazed, the songsmith dared to caress the muscled black shoulder. "He is truly amazing. Few mounts could have traveled the distance he did this morning carrying *one* rider—let alone two." The black raised his head, green tufts protruding from his lips, and blew gustily down the front of her jerkin, making the girl laugh.

"What I find amazing is that he has accepted *you* so completely." Alon spoke up from where he lay resting in the shade of a tall beech growing on the bank of a stream. "Before yesterday, he welcomed no one's touch but mine . . . he would barely suffer Hilarion's."

She walked over to drop down beside him, enjoying the feel of the new spring grass beneath her. "How long have you had him? How old is Monso?"

"He was born in the Year of the Werewolf," he replied. "When I was thirteen."

Then Alon was born in the Year of the Hippogriff, even as I was, she reflected. Before she thought, she found herself asking, "What month were you born, Alon?"

He rolled over on his side to look at her, his expression suddenly somber. "I know not," he said. "And when I said that I was thirteen in the Year of the Werewolf, that was my best guess, not something I know for truth."

"Because you are an orphan?" she guessed, remembering his words of last night, when he had spoke of finding his first home as Kaththea and Hilarion's fosterling.

He nodded. "I believe that I am nineteen, but I could be older. I will never know."

Eydryth thought about the warmth and love that had surrounded her while she was growing up in Kar Garudwyn, in the years before her mother's disappearance. *Perhaps*, she found herself thinking, *there are worse things than growing up without the Gift. Much worse . . .*

For a moment she was tempted to ask Alon to tell her the story of his life, but, again, she repressed that urge. *I must avoid . . . entanglements. I have a duty to fulfill, and nothing must be allowed to alter that. . . .*

"How old are you?" Alon asked quietly.

"I was born in the Month of the Gyrfalcon . . . nineteen years ago," she responded.

"And why . . . ," he began, then hesitated, as though he had changed his mind about voicing the question. A moment later he glanced up, then grinned. "Steel Talon is back . . . with an offering. We shall dine in style this evening!"

Eydryth sat up, watching as Alon went over to where the bird sat perched on a low limb of a nearby tree. A brown and white, blood-streaked ball of feathers lay on the grass beneath it. The young man picked up the chicken, shaking his head. "Raiding hen yards again? I told you how dangerous that is! What if the farmer had possessed a dart gun?"

The bird cocked its head, uttering a cry that, even to Eydryth's ears, sounded distinctly scornful.

"We can make do just as well with rabbit," Alon insisted. Glancing more closely at the falcon's prize, he scowled. "No wonder you caught her so easily. This one has seen many springs.''

The falcon ignored him as it began to preen its feathers.

The man sighed audibly, then looked back at Eydryth and shrugged. "I might as well be speaking with the voice of the wind, for all he attends."

Eydryth scrambled up to stand beside him as he began plucking the hen. "You two really speak together?"

"Not the way the birds can communicate with their Falconer comrades," he replied. "Steel Talon knows and understands much of what I say to him, that I know, but ours is a very one-sided conversation. I cannot talk with him as Jonthal could."

The songsmith eyed the falcon, remembering tales she had heard of how Falconers and their birds were inextricably linked, mind-to-mind, and that the death of one partner would almost certainly bring about the death of the other, even when no wound or illness was present. She had heard, once or twice, of Falconer men living after the demise of their winged comrades, but never had she known of a falcon surviving after its human companion died.

Vengeance . . ., she thought. *Alon said he was living to avenge himself on Jonthal's murderer. . . .* It was on the tip of her tongue to ask if Alon knew who had caused the death of his partner, but, again, she restrained herself.

We will reach Lormt soon, she thought, sternly. *And then we will part forever. Save your energy for your search!*

After allowing Monso to graze for another hour, Alon resaddled the half-bred and they continued on their way. Several times that afternoon Eydryth caught glimpses of Steel Talon, flying so high that he was little more than a soaring black dot against the puffy white clouds shouldering their way across the spring blue sky.

The sun was past its zenith by the time they saw the fork in the road with its signpost indicating the way to South Wending. They did not pass through the town, but skirted it through pastures dotted by cattle, sheep and horses. Several miles past the village, they reached the landmark Alon had mentioned—

the vivid red-clay bank with the small trickle of a creek running along its foot.

The turnoff was small and overgrown, but as they ducked beneath branches, Eydryth noticed that several of the tree's bright emerald leaves lay upon the ground. Bending lower, she observed that the track was scarred by the prints of many shod mounts.

"Look," she said to Alon, pointing. "At least seven or eight mounts passed this way . . . probably no later than this morning. Are there outlaws in this region?"

"Some," he replied uneasily. "But Koris the Seneschal, while he is a good ruler where honest folk are concerned, has little sympathy for those who prey upon others." He sat staring at the hoof-trodden earth for a moment, then straightened in his saddle, brightening visibly. "It is far more likely, though, that this is simply a party from some great lord's household, traveling to Lormt to seek out old family records. Many noble families have been doing so since the time of the Turning."

"I see," Eydryth murmured, still studying the tracks. There were no signs of wheel marks . . . or the lighter prints that would indicate a horse-drawn litter. *That only means that this party does not include the very old or very young*, she reminded herself. *It is likely that Alon's surmise is true.*

"Why now, since the Turning?" she asked.

"Estcarp has been at peace—more or less—since the witches reshaped the mountains. During peacetime, people have time to pursue such studies, and the study of family branchings has become increasingly popular."

Alon urged Monso forward; they went on.

For nearly an hour they traversed open fields, broken by stands of closely grown woods. Both travelers were forced to ward off branches continually, for this area, having been much stirred about during the aftershocks of the Turning, was covered with younger trees sprouted since the forest giants had fallen, thirty years before.

"How much farther, Alon?" Eydryth asked, batting a protruding branch away from her ribs. "It will soon be dark. Can we reach Lormt by then?"

"No, but it is not too far. We are less than a day's journey from the ancient stronghold of learning now," he replied. "Tomorrow at noon should see us there, even at an easy pace." He bent low in the saddle to avoid yet another gauntlet of low-hanging limbs. Eydryth flattened herself against his back, and as she did so, she distinctly heard a loud rumble from the region of his midsection. She chuckled. "Hungry, my lord? I am, too."

Alon laughed ruefully. "I am famished, my lady. And I regret to remind you that that hen Steel Talon stole for our dinner was a granddam many times over, and will need slow cooking. However, it will not be too bad. I have several rather withered potatoes and a clove of garlic in my saddlebag. With a few wild onions and some of those tubers, we should have the makings for a tasty—"

He broke off as Monso halted abruptly. The Keplian snorted a warning, pawing nervously at the ground. Like shadows come to life, the shapes of mounted men slid into view from where they had been concealed behind the trees.

They were surrounded.

The ambush had been well planned, Eydryth recognized that, even as her mind frantically sought, then discarded, possibilities for escape.

The underbrush was too thick to allow them to turn off the trail and use the Keplian's superior speed to outrun their would-be captors. Eydryth glanced back, only to note that the way back was also blocked.

Outlaws, she thought, and mentally prepared to sell her life dearly. A bard's traditional impunity would not hold with brigands; Eydryth knew she would not only be stripped of her possessions, but probably forced to submit to her attackers' attentions as well.

Then the lead rider moved forward, out of the shadows, and the girl recognized him as one of the guards of Estcarp. An officer, judging by the markings of rank on his sleeves and helmet. She felt immensely relieved, an emotion that Alon evidently shared, for she felt him relax. "Greetings, Lieutenant," he said. "For a moment we took you for ruffians. We are none such, I assure you; only two travelers bound to Lormt to request aid of the master chronicler, Duratan, and the lore-mistress, Nolar."

The officer did not return the young man's greeting, nor did his tight-drawn expression ease. He spoke without turning his head. "Lady, is this the girl you seek?"

Another figure urged a mount forward. Although mailed and helmed like the guards, the newcomer was not of them, for she was female. With a stab of fear, Eydryth recognized the witch who had interrogated her within the Citadel.

"This is indeed the girl we have been seeking," the woman spoke curtly. "Her name is Eydryth."

"So it is," the minstrel acknowledged, trying for a measure of bravado. "But knowing my name gives you no right to detain me!"

"You are under arrest," the witch said flatly. "You have broken our law."

The girl stiffened. "There is some mistake. I have committed no crime. Rather"—she allowed a measure of indignation to enter her voice—"*I* am the one who has been wronged; first, in your Citadel when one of your number ensorcelled me and stole my belongings, and now, by this wrongful charge of lawbreaking!"

"You aided a fugitive," the witch said, implacably. "Where is she? Where is the girl who companied with you?"

The minstrel considered swiftly, then decided that there was no point in lying about Avris's fate. "She is gone, Lady. By now she is deep in the mountains bordering Estcarp . . . a bride, she is, traveling in the company of her new husband." Eydryth smiled thinly. "I doubt that by now she would do you overmuch good, if marriage truly robs your sisterhood of their powers."

"So you admit that you aided her in her escape."

"I admit only that I was compelled to do so, but it is common knowledge that you witches can compel others to your will!" She fenced with words, using a version of the truth to lend her voice conviction.

The witch gazed at her, her grey eyes like shards of winter

ice, probing the songsmith's face to determine if she spoke truthfully. Finally she gave a faint, mocking smile that made the fear in Eydryth's heart congeal into a hard, painful lump within her breast. "I see . . . ," the older woman said, finally. "Well, that one will be but a small loss. We were after a bigger prize, and it seems we have found it."

The mail-clad woman regarded the bard measuringly. "You have led us quite a chase, girl. The Guardian wishes you to appear before her for testing. It seems that you have Power, after all. Only one with the Power could have quenched the light of a witch-jewel."

"No!" Eydryth cried, fighting panic. "I have no Power, Lady! I am naught but a wandering songsmith, I swear it to whatever gods may hold sway in this land! I *must* get to Lormt—the life of my father depends upon it!"

"See here," Alon spoke up, "Eydryth is not under your jurisdiction—she is not even from this land! She—"

"Quiet, lad," the officer commanded. "You will anger the lady."

The witch did not even glance at Alon as she said, "Bring the youth, also. I was advised last night that the sheriff of Rylon Corners has issued a warrant for his arrest."

Eydryth slid off Monso's back, then drew her sword from its place of concealment. "I will not let you stop me, Lady," she said, dropping into fighting stance. She smiled grimly. "Even if I had Power within me—which I do not—I cannot imagine that it will do you much good if the mortal vessel that holds it lies dead. I *must* reach Lormt, and if you wish to stop me, you must kill me."

Six

*H*earing the cold determination in Eydryth's voice, the witch and her troops halted. There came a rustle, then the sound of booted feet as Alon dismounted and walked over to stand with the songsmith, his shoulder brushing hers as they confronted the forces from Estcarp. "Here," the young woman said, passing her quarterstaff to her ally, "unless you wish to surrender yourself to them, you must fight with me, I fear. Guard my back."

He obeyed her, moving until they stood pressed back-to-back. Then she heard him whisper, in a voice so soft only she could hear: "You must have bade farewell to your wits, Lady! There are seven of them against our two!"

But he made no move to put down the weapon she had given him, holding it awkwardly, as though it were naught but a stick. Inwardly, the girl sighed. *If we ever are free again, I must teach him to fight. How could he have survived so long as a wanderer without such lessoning?*

"Well?" she demanded of their captors. "Which will it be, Lady Witch? Will you kill us, or let us depart in peace?"

"You speak with great conviction, songsmith," the older woman replied, breathing upon the cloudy jewel she now wore set into a silver wristlet. "But it remains to be seen whether you also speak the truth."

Above the witch-gem, their gazes locked, chill grey holding vivid blue, and Eydryth was suddenly conscious of the silence. Around them, the forest lay still—no bird sang, no insect hummed. Even the horses stood unmoving.

As the moments passed, she could feel the witch's will testing hers, pushing and probing at her mind, measuring, sifting. She attempted to summon her old defense of her mother's lullaby. The words . . . yes, the words were there:

> For wind-song shall free you
> And wave-song shall teach you
> And my song shall love you
> The good seasons round . . .
>
> So sleep, little seabird, sleep . . .

But, try as she might, the songsmith could not make the accompanying tune come to life in her mind. She could remember the notes, visualize the movement of her fingers as they formed the chords on her harpstrings, but she could not *hear* the music.

The girl's eyes wavered; she broke that locked gaze, no longer able to resist. When she looked back up, the witch was smiling again, a mocking twist of the lips that had nothing of good humor about it. "It is as I thought, Lieutenant," she addressed the officer in command of the guardsmen, "her mind does not reflect the conviction of her words. We are seven against two; no experienced fighter would sell her life cheaply by tackling such overwhelming odds. You may take her."

Eydryth closed her eyes, sick with despair. *Father, I am sorry*, she thought. *I have failed you—and we were so close to Lormt!* Her shoulders sagged, and she swayed, suddenly so exhausted that her head spun. Alon slid an arm around her, steadying her. "All is not lost," he whispered. "Wait. Tonight—"

"No talking, you two!" the officer commanded, pushing them apart. "Girl, hand over that sword, and let's have no trickery about the way you do it." He held out his hand.

Numbly, Eydryth relinquished her sword. The gryphon's blue quan-iron eyes flashed in the sunlight, as though the beast were protesting such treatment.

One of the guards seized Alon's arms, wrenching them behind the young man's back so cruelly that he grunted with pain. Eydryth received like treatment as her wrists were also bound securely. "Gently!" admonished the witch, when the girl gasped at a sharp tug of the leathern thongs. "She must not be hurt, is that understood?"

Hearing a shrill scream from overhead, the songsmith looked up, just as Steel Talon stooped, sharp talons ready to tear. With a yell of dismay, the lieutenant of the guards threw up an arm to cover his eyes and flung himself down on the mossy earth.

As the falcon swooped low, then mounted into the air, circling, several of the guards raised their dart guns and fired. "No!" Eydryth shouted, struggling against her bindings.

But none of the darts even came close, and while the guards' attention was distracted, Monso seemed to choose his moment. Without warning the stallion reared, teeth bared, then bounded forward, straight toward two of the guards' mounts.

The mortal horses scattered, squealing in fear, before the Keplian's charge. Within a heartbeat, the black was gone, crashing a path through the deep underbrush. The falcon had also vanished.

At least Monso and Steel Talon are still free, Eydryth

thought, dully, as her guard propelled her roughly across the
meadow, toward the campsite where the witch awaited them.
The sun was almost gone behind the trees now; darkness crept
across the soft spring turf.

She and Alon were allowed to wrap themselves in their
cloaks; then one of the men produced portions of journeybread and dried fruit, as well as a water bottle. Despite her
aching misery, Eydryth forced herself to chew and swallow.
Food meant strength—the strength, perhaps to escape. She
could not forget Alon's words of hope.

When the captives were finished eating, the guards bound
them hand and foot. Then, on the lieutenant's order, they
fastened their wrist-bindings to the trees behind them, tether-
ing them past all hope of working free. Alon was tied too far
away to speak to Eydryth, but when the guards finally left
them to get their own rations, he turned his head and his eyes
met hers. One eyelid closed in a quick wink; then he deliberately looked away.

As the camp settled down to its routine of night patrols and
the off-duty guards crawled into their bedrolls, the girl continued to covertly watch Alon. In the darkness, she could
barely discern the shape of his body against the trees, for
twilight was long past, and moonrise still hours away. As she
watched, he wriggled backward, clumsy because of his bound
wrists and ankles, until he was braced against the trunk of the
oak where his rope was secured. She could make out his profile
now, outlined by the campfire.

She watched the pale blur of his face turn toward hers, as
though to make sure she was watching; then, exaggeratedly, he
yawned. His shoulders sagged as he settled his chin on his
chest, obviously preparing for sleep.

Her heart thumping excitedly, Eydryth mimicked his actions. As the time dragged by, she found herself wondering
what her companion had meant by those final words. Did
Alon have some way of getting free? A blade, perhaps, sewn
into the bottom of his tunic, the hem of his cloak—or, perhaps, the sole of his boot? She had heard her father speak of
such places for concealing small weapons.

But Alon did not seem to be moving at all.

Eydryth listened with part of her mind to the lieutenant's voice as he inspected the watches, then the soft sounds of the sentries pacing, all mingled with the snorts and whufflings from the horses on the picket line. She was tired; all too soon, her feigned drowsiness became genuine.

The girl tried to hold her eyes open, but they felt as weighted as a Sulcar ship's anchor. Despite her struggles, she fell deeply asleep—

—only to jerk herself out of slumber with a gasp when something heavy landed on her booted legs. Frightened, she jerked her knees up, staring with horror at the formless black shape before her. With an offended squawk, it rose into the air, flapped to a nearby branch, then regarded her. The songsmith could see the gleam of its eyes and the white V on its breast in the moonlight.

"Steel Talon!" she whispered. "What are you doing here?"

Reflexively, she glanced over at Alon, seeing that he sat bolt upright, obviously awake. He whistled softly, the call of a night-swallow, and Steel Talon silently winged his way over to him. As Alon bent forward, the falcon landed behind him.

Eydryth watched as the young man's body jerked involuntarily, his face grimacing with pain in the moon's glow. She bit her lip in sympathy, realizing that the bird's cruelly hooked beak was now tearing at the leather thongs binding Alon to the tree.

Is this what he had planned? she wondered. *Is he controlling the falcon's actions somehow? Or do Falconers train their warbirds to free their masters in case of capture?* She did not know.

Minutes later, Alon's arms suddenly snapped forward, as he gave a last tug on his bonds and they parted. Eydryth watched him rub his hands together, trying to ease their numbness. Then he raised his knees, and his stiff fingers began tugging clumsily at the fastenings on his ankles.

The songsmith kept listening for the sounds of the sentries, fearing that they would be discovered, but there was nothing stirring in the dimness.

When he was free of his bonds, Alon crept cautiously over

the grass toward her, raising one finger to his lips in the signal for silence.

But to Eydryth's surprise, he did not begin working away at the thongs binding her. Instead, he put his hand on her brow and hissed in her ear, "Be patient. I will set you free in a moment."

When she tried to frame one of the questions whirling in her mind like chaff before a thunderstorm, he shook his head, laying a finger against her lips. "Wait," he whispered, still touching her brow. "Watch. . . ."

The songsmith heard the sound of trotting hooves, then a snort. A black shape trotted into view, stirrups flapping loose from an empty saddle. Then a dark shape winged its way over to land on the cantle of the saddle, balancing there.

Monso! Monso and Steel Talon, together!

As Eydryth watched, the Keplian and the falcon circled the camp, still moving at that deliberate pace.

Circled once . . .

Twice . . .

Thrice . . .

Magic, she realized, feeling a prickle run up her spine that she remembered from times when she had seen Joisan or Kerovan use the Power. *The animals are bespelling the camp!*

For a moment fear clutched at her; then she realized that the beasts were circling from right to left, deasil—not widdershins, not contrary to the path the sun followed in the sky. Eydryth relaxed. Nothing that followed the Left-Hand Path could move so.

When the third circle was completed, the Keplian halted, then gave a blasting snort. None of the sleeping figures around the faintly glowing campfire so much as stirred.

"Good," Alon muttered, then rose and walked over to the nearest guardsman. A moment later he was back, in his hand a knife. With a few tugs, he severed Eydryth's bonds. "We must go quickly," he said, not troubling to lower his voice. "The thrice-circle will not hold past first light."

The songsmith stared from the sleeping forms to the beasts standing a few paces away. *"They* did this?" she whispered, in awe. "How could a horse and a falcon cast a sleeping-spell?"

"Beasts have their own magic," he told her. "And neither Monso nor Steel Talon is an ordinary animal, do not forget."

"What about the sentries? And the witch?"

"Asleep, too." He took her hands in his, began chafing them briskly. She was shocked to feel how swollen his own fingers were. When she made a sound of distress, he glanced down at them, flexing them gingerly. "The guard was not gentle," he agreed ruefully. "They made it only too plain that I was not the favored prisoner."

A moment later, he stood up, then reached down a hand to pull her to her feet. Both of them stamped, wriggling their toes, wincing at the pinpricks of pain as the blood flowed freely once more.

Finally, he caught up her cloak, draped it around her shoulders. "Come," he said. "We must hurry."

Eydryth followed him into the camp, marveling at the peacefully sleeping faces that never altered as they searched for their belongings. In the moonlight even the witch appeared different, her stern countenance rendered relaxed and vulnerable with sleep. *So great was the Power of the beasts' thrice-circle that she did not even have time to grow alarmed,* Eydryth thought with awe.

"Find your weapons," Alon called, from across the camp. "I am gathering a few supplies. We must travel fast and light."

The songsmith located her sword and staff, then, on impulse, took the lieutenant's blade and swordbelt from where they lay beside his slumbering form. "Here," she said, holding the sheathed blade out to her companion, "put this on."

He took it, then hesitantly did as she bade.

"Not like that! Lower, so it rests down on your hip . . . so." She slid the leathern strap into place around his lean middle. "I will begin teaching you to use this, when we have time."

In the moonglow she saw him smile wryly. "You think it necessary for me to learn a soldier's skills?"

"I do," she nodded firmly, hands on hips as she surveyed him. "If we are to company together, even for the space of a day, I want you armed. I cannot go on protecting you!"

He laughed as he picked up the bag of food he had garnered. "No, I suppose you can't—though last night you did it very well." He glanced down at the sword at his side. "I can hardly wait."

After losing the tethered horses, the freed prisoners waved torches and blankets, sending the mounts racing away, snorting and kicking, into the darkness. Then Alon swung up on Monso's back and aided Eydryth up behind him.

"To Lormt," he said, turning the Keplian's nose to the east.

Eydryth nodded. "To Lormt," she echoed. "And may woe betide any who attempt to delay us further!"

Riding through the late-night darkness was frustrating, because they could not take advantage of their mount's superior speed. Much of the way the woods were too thick, and in the open, the chance of Monso sinking a foot in some ground-dweller's burrow and breaking a leg was too great. The travelers were forced to keep to a walk or a jog trot, when everything urged them to run—run!

Still exhausted by the events of the day, Eydryth found her eyes closing again as she perched on the Keplian's rhythmically swaying rump. In the waning moonlight, the landscape surrounding them appeared spectral, unreal. Her eyelids closed. . . .

She jerked awake when Monso stopped, realizing that she had been dozing with her cheek pressed against Alon's shoulder. Warmth flooded her cheeks as she hastily straightened. "Are we there?"

"No, we are still perhaps an hour's journey away," he said.

The darkness was fading; a rosy glow tinged the east. Dawn was not far off.

The songsmith narrowed her eyes as she surveyed the shadowed land ahead of them, seeing upthrust ridges of grey rock and growths of new timber. In the far distance she could make out a cottage with a thatched roof. The entire countryside had a curiously raw, jumbled look to it. "What happened here to stir the land so? The Turning?"

"Yes," Alon replied. "Lormt itself was protected, though.

The Ancients who constructed its walls and towers embedded spheres of quan-iron—the blue metal like that found in the eyes of your gryphon—in the foundations of the towers. The base of one tower had crumbled, causing its sphere to be lost over the ages, so, when the ground heaved, that tower fell, taking part of another tower and the connecting wall with it. But the other two stood fast."

They allowed Monso to crop the grass for a few minutes while they stretched their legs, shared a few bites of food, then laved their faces at a swift-running stream. The water had obviously flowed down from the mountains that now smudged the eastern horizon, for it was so chill it made Eydryth's teeth ache.

She could barely keep her eyes from searching their trail, her ears from straining for the sound of hoofbeats, though she knew that their captors would only now be awakening. The skin at the nape of her neck prickled as she envisioned the witch's fury at discovering that her quarry had escaped once again. "The thrice-circle spell the beasts set will be wearing off by now," she said. "We must not tarry, Alon."

He remained unworried. "We have several hours' start on them, and when we set off again, Monso can move at speed."

"But they know our destination." She remembered the witch's cold grey eyes and swallowed anxiously. "And the witch . . . she will not give up easily."

He tightened Monso's girth, his expression sobering. "Then we must continue to elude them. I have no wish to spend my days rotting in some jail in Rylon Corners."

Once they were astride again, he loosened the reins slightly and bent forward. "Go," he whispered, and the Keplian, with a snort, plunged forward eagerly.

The land around Eydryth blurred as her wind-whipped eyes watered. She clung to Alon's belt grimly, using every bit of her riding skill and balance to stay on as Monso galloped, trying to spot obstacles and changes of direction so they would not catch her unawares.

The sun was nearly a handspan past the horizon when Alon drew rein, bringing their mount to a plunging halt. "Lormt," he announced, breathing hard from the effort of curbing the sidling, wheeling Keplian.

Eydryth peered out from behind his shoulder to see a river that ran past a cluster of half-timbered cottages and a larger building that might have been an inn. Just beyond them lay a high stone wall, and the outlines of massive stone towers. As Alon had mentioned, one corner of the structure was naught but a tumbled pile of rubble, while the outlines of another tower could still be seen, though it was perhaps half-demolished.

The travelers jogged slowly down the rutted track that served the small village as a main thoroughfare. Eydryth was conscious of eyes peering out at them from behind curtains and cracks in doorways, but the only inhabitants brave enough to venture forth were several barefoot children, still too young to be working in the fields, or aiding with the spinning.

Eydryth wondered whether they would beg, but they did not; two, a boy and a girl, accompanied them, while a fourth child, older, pelted off through one of the many gaps in the crumbled wall, evidently to warn of their arrival.

The metal-bound gate stood permanently ajar and askew, and they rode through that into a stone and dirt courtyard. On the doorstep of one of the intact towers, two people were waiting to meet them, a man and a woman.

The man held himself with the upright carriage of those who have borne arms and marched to battle. He was slightly above middle height, plainly of the Old Race, and went clean-shaven. Instead of the scholar's robe Eydryth had expected, he wore a rust-colored tunic and leather jerkin, a horsehide belt with the hair left on, and breeches and boots.

The woman at his side wore a simple robe of rich autumn brown, with a light green shawl flung over her shoulders against the early-morning chill. Her hair was drawn back from her face and caught up in a loose knot at the back of her neck. Her features were strong and well cut, but a reddish birthmark spread over one cheek, marring her appearance.

Eydryth had to force herself to meet the woman's eyes

directly; it was hard to keep her eyes from fixing on that ugly mark. Compassion stirred within her, as she imagined all the cruel taunts children were wont to hurl at one whose difference was so plain to the eye.

But after a moment's measuring glance, Eydryth realized that this woman had come to terms with herself long ago; pity was something she neither needed or wanted. As she hesitated, wondering how to begin, Alon cleared his throat and sketched a half-bow. "Fair fortune to this holding, and good morning to you both. I am Alon, and this is the songsmith Eydryth."

The man nodded acknowledgment, his grey eyes never leaving the younger man's face. "You are well-come to Lormt, Alon and Eydryth. I am Master Duratan, and this is my lady, the lore-mistress, Nolar. How may we aid you?"

"The Lady Eydryth wishes to consult with you on a matter of healing."

"Healing? That is a subject I know well." Nolar spoke for the first time in a soft, melodious voice. "Enter, please. We can speak in my study."

Duratan waved the travelers past him with a courtly gesture. "I will have one of the stable lads attend to your mount."

But Alon did not move as he shook his head. "It is better that I care for the stallion myself, Master Duratan. His temper can be . . . uncertain. I will join you in a few minutes."

"Very well. I will show you to the stables." He walked over to join Alon, and the songsmith saw that, though he held himself as straight as possible, and there was good breadth to his shoulders, Duratan moved with a distinct limp.

Eydryth followed the lore-mistress into the ancient building, and found herself reminded of the Citadel in Es City. The same aura of age pervaded the stones—nay, if anything, this place seemed to be even older. The two women passed room after room filled with shelves, each shelf holding hundreds of books, or, even more ancient, rune-scrolls in metal and leather containers. Robed scholars, both male and female, moved soft-footed through the corridors, carrying armloads of blank parchment, and fresh quills.

They climbed the stairs into one of the towers; then Nolar

stopped before a door and opened it. The room within was large, with a window that looked out upon the eastern hills. Pots of herbs grew on the stone windowsill, and faded hangings gave a hint of soft color to the walls, though any pictures or stories they bore were nearly impossible to make out. The whitewashed walls were lined with chests, each holding many record-scrolls in bronze-reinforced or carved-wood cases.

Eydryth took a deep breath of the musty, vellum-scented air and thought that here, if any place in the world, there might be some scrap of healing-lore that would aid her father.

Nolar carefully moved some tattered scrolls she had evidently been studying, then waved the girl to a seat. "Tell me why you have come, Eydryth."

Taking a deep breath, the songsmith launched into her story. She was halfway through when Duratan and Alon entered the room. As she recounted the events of the past, she noticed that the master chronicler's eyes seldom left Alon's face; he avoided staring openly, but he watched the younger man as avidly as Steel Talon might have eyed a rabbit that had ventured too far from its burrow.

Why is the master chronicler so interested in Alon? she wondered; then a likely reason occurred to her. *Duratan has probably read of the Keplians in Escore, and recognized Monso for one. He would naturally be curious about one who could master such a creature.*

"... and so Jervon has remained, these past years," Eydryth concluded. "Much like a very small child . . . biddable, but needing help in even the simplest things; eating, bathing or dressing." She fixed the lore-mistress with a pleading gaze. "Lady Nolar . . . can you think of aught that might help him? I cannot let him continue to live thus!"

"And you say there is no scar, nor any depression in the bone of his skull where he hit his head?"

"None. The Lady Joisan, who fostered me when my own mother disappeared, is a Wise Woman and Healer of no little ability. She has said that my father's problem was not caused by injury to the body, but rather to the mind, and perhaps the spirit. Like . . ." She groped for an example. ". . . like a river during floodtime, where the channel can no longer contain the rush of water, and thus overflows its banks. So also with the pathways in Jervon's mind."

"I see . . . ," the lore-mistress murmured. She glanced at her lord. "Much like Elgaret's case, it seems to me. Perhaps the Stone . . ."

"The Stone?" Eydryth demanded. "What Stone?"

"The Stone of Konnard," Duratan said. "It is a healing stone of great power that lies within a cave in the mountains far from here. A shard from it healed my lady's aunt after her mind had been overpowered during the Turning. She was once one of the witches."

"Shard? May we obtain one? Or borrow yours?" Eydryth's heart was beating wildly, like a snared bird trying to escape capture.

"Alas, the shard is no longer mine," Nolar said.

"Soon after Elgaret's healing, the shard drew me back to the Stone, and cleaved again to it," Nolar added. "Thus, that piece is no longer in my possession. And I do not think another shard will be found, after all these years. Could you perhaps take your father here?"

"The Stone of Konnard . . . ," Eydryth whispered, now feeling her heart sink as she pictured traveling all those weary months to reach Kar Garudwyn again, then of trying to bring her father back to Estcarp, first over the mountains and through the Waste bordering Arvon, then across the Dales of High Hallack, over the sea, and traversing the entire land of Estcarp—!!

Eydryth did not see any way that such a journey could be accomplished. Jervon could and did walk every day, but only when taken by the hand and guided so that he would not stray off the path. He rode, but could not manage his own mount, and must needs be led. A companion or nurse had perforce to sleep in his chamber each night, to prevent him from wandering off. . . .

The songsmith swallowed, forcing back the tightness in her throat. *There must be another way*, she thought. *The gods would not be so cruel as to demand that my father make a journey that would be so perilous for him!*

Not to mention that the thought of so exposing her father's

mental infirmities to all and sundry was intolerable. The thought of pitying or scornful gazes staring at Jervon's slack-mouthed, vacant face and stumbling form made her wince.

"Bringing him would be exceedingly difficult, I know," the lore-mistress said, echoing the girl's thoughts. "And I must caution you that the journey to reach the Stone's resting place is long and dangerous. Strange creatures have come out of the mountains since the Turning, and they can pose a grave threat to travelers."

The songsmith wanted to bow her head and weep, but she forced herself to square her shoulders, meet Duratan's and Nolar's eyes straightly. "What I must do, I shall," she said. *Perhaps he could travel in a covered litter . . .* she thought wearily.

"But to undertake such a journey by yourself . . . ," the Lady Nolar began, then trailed off, shaking her head.

"I am sure that Lord Kerovan and Lady Joisan will aid me in bringing my father to be healed," Eydryth told her, before adding, with bitter frankness, "but one thing makes me hesitate: what if we make such a journey and the Stone does *not* heal Jervon? Or what if he is killed on the way there?"

Both chronicler and lore-mistress nodded back at her, obviously comprehending the reasons for her hesitation and distress.

Suddenly Alon, whom she had almost forgotten was present, stirred beside her, clearing his throat. "Mistress Nolar," he said, indicating one of the rune-scrolls in the stack on the table, "may I examine that scroll? The runes on its case remind me of one that my master Hilarion had in his collection. That one dealt with healing, and if this is a copy . . ."

Duratan sat up even straighter, raising his heavy eyebrows in surprise. "Hilarion? I have heard that name, from my friend Kemoc Tregarth."

"You know Kemoc?" Alon asked, equally surprised.

"We fought together on the Border, and became friends as well as comrades-in-arms. After Kemoc was wounded, he came to Lormt and I saw him again there, not long before the Turning. Since the exodus to resettle Escore by those of the

Old Race, we have corresponded by means of travelers and carrier birds." The master chronicler's eyes narrowed thoughtfully. "Kemoc told me much of this Hilarion, the man who wed his sister. And you say you were his apprentice?"

Alon hesitated. "Not really. Rather, Hilarion and his lady fostered me when I was left kinless and clanless in Karsten, then found my way into Escore as a child. He taught me many things . . . to read and write, to cipher, and also the lore of ancient lands."

Duratan's glance was sharp, but before he could speak again, Alon turned back to Nolar. "Please, Lady . . . may I examine the scroll?"

The lore-mistress gave the young man a searching look, then nodded. "Certainly," she said. "However, please be careful. As you no doubt know, such records are very fragile."

"I will take the greatest care," he promised, drawing the cylindrical metal casing toward him. With slow, cautious movements, he extracted the fragile record from the case, then began to unroll it.

Eydryth leaned over his shoulder to gaze at the revealed text. The script was faded almost to illegibility, and the runic symbols implied a form of the Old Tongue more ancient than any she had ever seen. The songsmith could make out only a word here and there.

"Ah . . . ," Alon muttered, scanning the ancient writing. "Yes, this is indeed a copy of the one I saw. And here"—he pointed a long forefinger to a page near the end—"is the reference I recalled—"

The young man broke off as his finger touched the smudged, faded runes, and they suddenly flared into dazzling clarity, glowing violet in the dusty sunlight of the study.

Duratan and Nolar both gasped, then leaped up and circled the table to stare incredulously at the scroll. "What did you do?" Nolar demanded, finding her voice first. "That light was violet, the color of great Power!"

"Great Power?" Eydryth stared wide-eyed at Alon. "You—"

His headshake silenced her. "It was nothing I did," he

stated. "There was a spell laid on that page." His face was suddenly drawn with weariness, as though that touch had taken something out of him. "I have heard Hilarion speak of such. This was an old spell of clarification so that the words therein could be read even after the ink that formed them was gone . . . providing the reader's need is great. The runes would have done so had any of you touched them. Thus—"

With a quick motion, he grasped Eydryth's fingers, moving them to brush against the ancient scroll. Again the runes flared brilliantly—but this time they blazed blue-green.

Eydryth felt something almost tangible run through her body at the touch of that ancient parchment—a tingling warmth. Alon released her fingers, staring at her as if startled, even though he had predicted that the scroll would react to the touch of any with great need to know its contents.

"So it deals with healing!" Eydryth exclaimed, returning to what was, for her, the most important thing. "What does it say? Can we translate it?"

"It is a very ancient form of the Old Tongue," the lore-mistress said slowly, studying the writing. "Older by far than any I have seen."

"I can read it," Alon said. "Hilarion was born into a time before the First Turning that sealed off Estcarp from Escore. This scroll dates from that time."

Duratan shook his head in wonderment. "*That* long ago? It is hardly to be believed!"

"My foster-father had scrolls in his holding that were even older than this one," the younger man muttered abstractedly, as he studied the page. Long moments later, he announced: "I was correct. This scroll mentions a place of healing on the outskirts of the Valley of the Green Silences."

Duratan nodded. "Morquant's Valley! Kemoc told me of it. His brother, Kyllan, is wedded to the Lady of the Green Silences."

"In Escore," Alon said, "she is called Dahaun."

"She has many names," Duratan agreed. "But it is part of the lore surrounding her that she has methods of healing in her valley that are greater even than that of the Stone of Konnard, powerful though that may be. If a wounded creature can but reach her healing place, death loses its power over flesh and bone there."

"But can her healing methods mend shattered minds and spirits as well as bodies?" Eydryth cried, scarcely daring to hope. "And is her secret of healing something that can be transported?"

Alon shook his head. "The scroll does not say. It is worth seeking out and asking, though."

"If only I could discover some healing potion or tisane that I could take back to my father!" the girl cried, daring, for the first time in hours, to think that her quest might succeed.

Nolar looked thoughtful. "Perhaps the Lady of the Green Silences knows of such."

"Perhaps she does," Alon said. "I have heard that there is little that she does *not* know."

"But how would I get there?" Eydryth wondered aloud, remembering the shadows of the eastern mountains against the sky. "It would be a journey of many days, just to climb the heights separating Escore and Estcarp." She considered for a moment, then asked, "Alon, do you know whether there is a trail or a road that leads across the mountains?"

When he did not reply to her question, she looked up, alerted by his silence, to find Alon staring expressionlessly back at Duratan. The master chronicler was again regarding the younger man with that measuring, avid gaze she had noted earlier.

"I would like to talk to you about this Hilarion," Duratan said, slowly. "And about yourself, Alon. We do not often encounter—"

"Those who have lived in Escore," the younger man broke in. "Yes, I know. But I am afraid that there is no time for such conversation at the moment, sir. If I am to guide the Lady Eydryth to the Valley of the Green Silences—" Eydryth's heart leaped as she took in his words. "—then we must needs leave immediately."

"Why so quickly?" Duratan demanded, with a touch of grim humor, as though he already suspected the answer.

Alon smiled crookedly. "There are . . . complications . . . that could keep us from reaching Escore. Complications that are even now following our trail."

"I see . . . ," Duratan said, still holding the younger man's eyes with his own. "You must make haste, then, of course. But should you ever return . . ."

"I will be happy to speak to you at length," Alon promised.

Rising, the young man looked down at the songsmith, then extended his hand to help her up. "We must hasten," he said. "Unless you do not wish to go?"

Eydryth grasped his fingers and rose, albeit a little unsteadily. "Do you really mean that you will take me over the mountains to Escore?" she whispered. "Oh, Alon . . . I . . . I can never repay you!"

"I am doing this as much for my own sake as for your father's," he reminded her. "There is an arrest warrant out for me in Rylon Corners, remember?"

"Yes, but—"

"In Escore, I can hide out until the witch and the townspeople have forgotten me completely. Then Monso and I can reappear on the tracks in the north of Estcarp, with none the wiser!"

Eydryth smiled knowingly. "You are only saying that because you want no one to know what a kind thing you are doing, aiding me. You'd rather play the rogue, concerned only with saving his own hide." Her expression sobered and her eyes held his. "But I know the truth. Accept my thanks, Alon."

"Do you need supplies for your journey?" the lore-mistress asked.

At her words, Eydryth let go of Alon's hand, and both travelers turned to her. "Perhaps a round or two of journeybread, should you have it," she said, as they headed for the door. "And . . . Mistress Nolar . . . thank you. Both of you."

Scant minutes later found them in the courtyard, while Alon packed the provisions the lore-mistress had provided into Monso's saddlebags. Just as he finished, the master chronicler reappeared, leading a bay mare. Duratan was carrying a handful of rags and twine.

"What size shoes does he wear?" the chronicler demanded without preamble, nodding at the Keplian half-bred.

Alon eyed the rags, twine and the bay horse's feet; then he smiled gratefully. "Size aught," he said. "You chose correctly."

"Like most Borderers, I did my share of makeshift smithing," the master chronicler commented, handing the younger man the cloths.

Taking the string, Eydryth aided Alon in tying the rags around the Keplian's hooves, so he would leave no prints.

When they were finished, Duratan swung himself up into the bay's saddle, then held out a hand to Nolar. "My lady," he said, with a smile touching his deep-set grey eyes, "it occurs to me that it has been long since we visited the southernmost farms to see if any are in need of your healing skills. Perhaps today would be a good day to do that."

Nolar chuckled. "Let me get my bag of simples," she said, and ran to fetch them. When she returned, she caught her lord's hand; then, with a swirl of russet skirts, she scrambled up onto the bay mare's rump.

Very canny, Eydryth thought approvingly. *Now the bay's hoofprints will sink deep enough to match the ones Monso has been leaving.*

"What will you say when they find you?" Alon asked worriedly.

"I will say, truthfully, that all our other mounts are in use," Duratan replied serenely, "and so my lady and I must needs ride double." He smiled at Alon. "Remember your promise, lad. I will be waiting for the day when we can have that long talk."

Alon nodded. "I will not forget."

"Well, then . . ." The master chronicler raised a hand in a half-salute. "A good journey to you both. May you find what you are seeking." Nolar nodded farewell as Duratan turned the horse and sent the animal trotting out of the courtyard.

Eydryth and Alon watched them go; then they, too, set off, leading the stallion, so as to further confound their pursuers. Only when the ground beneath their boots was hard-packed soil broken by the thrusts of rock outcrops did they take the muffling rags off Monso's hooves and mount.

Perched once more behind her escort, Eydryth looked ahead of them, to the nearby slopes of the foothills, then beyond to the mountains, many with their peaks still snow-splotched. Uneasily she turned to regard their back trail. "Do you think the witch and her guards will be fooled by Duratan's and Nolar's trick?"

Alon sighed. "For another hour or so, perhaps. But as soon as they see Nolar and Duratan, they will know the truth."

"Then the witch will scry, or farsee, and so discover which trail we have taken," Eydryth agreed. She indicated the rock-strewn countryside surrounding them. "And Monso's speed will be of little use to us when the ground is this broken."

He nodded silently. After a moment, she wet her lips. "Do you think the mountains will stop her?"

Alon shook his head. "Have they stopped you?" he asked, simply. "That lady is as determined to capture you as you are to see your father healed."

Eydryth knew that he spoke the truth; her fingers tightened convulsively on the leather of his belt. "Are you sure, Alon, that you wish to continue companying with me? You could let me off here and tell me where to find the mountain trail and the pass into—"

"*No*," he said, turning in the saddle to look at her. There was no mistaking the gleam of determination in his eyes. "We go together, or not at all. Do not forget that they want me, too."

But Eydryth knew better; if Alon would only abandon her, the guards of Estcarp would not not bother pursuing a mis-creant wanted only for a bit of racetrack chicanery. *She* was the one the witch wanted. The hunt was well and truly up, and she was the quarry.

I must make him leave me, she resolved, ignoring the pang that struck her at the thought. *No matter what it takes.*

Seven

*T*hey rode the sun down that day, not halting to make camp until the stars glimmered against the deep purple of the late-evening sky. For most of their hours in the saddle Alon held Monso to a ground-covering jog, but whenever they reached stretches of high moorland where the footing was good, he let the Keplian run. When they finally stopped, they were high in the foothills, with the true mountains looming over them like fortresses of ragged stone.

After they dismounted, Eydryth moved around their camp-site in a stumbling, dreamlike state, helping Alon rub the stallion down, then forcing herself to eat, knowing her body needed the food. Sleep claimed her the moment she crawled into her bedroll.

The travelers awoke before dawn to a drizzling rain. Heads ducked beneath the hoods of their cloaks, they hastily swallowed mouthfuls of damp journeybread, breaking camp while it was still dark.

Leading the Keplian, they started out. As they reached the crest of the nearest hillock, breathing heavily and slipping in the mud, Alon halted, turning to look back along their trail. After a moment he nudged Eydryth and pointed.

The girl squinted in the misty rain, narrowing her eyes until she made out what her companion was indicating—the dull red glow of several campfires, far behind them.

"We have nearly a full day's start on them," she said, but the aching lump of fear was back in her throat, nearly choking her.

"They will gain on us today," Alon said grimly. "They will be covering gentle slopes, while we will be climbing in earnest before the day is out."

"Is there another pass we could take?"

"Not that Monso could traverse . . . not for many leagues," he replied. "However . . . there is a chance that the witch will not be able to climb these eastern mountains. There is a mind-block set upon those of the Old Race, concerning these mountains and Escore. Lord Kemoc Tregarth was the first to discover it. But now that everyone knows of Escore, it may also be that the witch can overcome the effects of that ancient sorcery, since she knows that the spell exists."

Remembering her resolve that he and Monso should leave her before they risked being recaptured, Eydryth gave her companion a sidelong glance. "If there is a nearby pass that is only accessible to those traveling on foot, perhaps it would be best if you directed me to it. Then you could go on to the other pass with Monso."

A muscle in his jaw tightened, and he did not look at her. "Why?"

She took a deep breath. "Because from this point on, Monso will only slow us down. I know you will not abandon him, but I have no wish to be caught because I have held back to stay with you two."

The wan light of early dawn made Alon's unshaven face appear even more drawn and haggard as he gave her a long, measuring glance. "Do not concern yourself unduly," he said finally, in a tone that held the barest touch of sarcasm. "When we begin to hold you back, then it will be time enough for you to go on alone, Lady."

Fighting back an urge to apologize, to blurt out that she was only doing this for his own good, Eydryth nodded, no longer meeting his eyes. "Very well," she said, keeping her voice cold and hard with an effort. "But I shall be the judge."

"And jury-of-peers, and no doubt executioner, too," he said, giving her a crooked, mocking smile. "But for now, we must go."

They went on, afoot much of the time, stumbling upward over rocky slopes dotted with scrubby firs and prickly gorse. The songsmith walked blindly, barely noticing her surroundings enough to pick her path. Alon's last remark had disturbed her greatly. She had heard beneath the mockery a note of bitter pain; her words had hurt him more than he would ever reveal.

He is lonely, she thought, remembering how pleased he had been to have someone to talk with about Monso and Steel Talon. At the thought of the falcon, she glanced around, but saw no black speck outlined against the sky.

"Where is Steel Talon?" she asked, struggling not to gasp out the words. "I have not seen him since he and Monso made the thrice-circle."

"When I awoke this morning, I saw him perched in a grove of these scrub firs," Alon replied. "He seldom flies when it is wet, preferring to catch me up later. He will find us, never fear."

Eydryth nodded, wishing that *she* had such a choice available to her. A trickle of chill water found its way down the back of her neck, through the soaked hood of her cloak, making her shiver.

Finally, about an hour before sunset, the rain slackened, then stopped, and the sun came out. Alon promptly halted in his tracks, beside one of the stunted scrub oaks. Pulling off his cloak, he hastily shook the water off a limb and spread the garment to dry.

The bard considered urging him to continue on, but her feet and her muscles hurt so from all the climbing that she said nothing, only sought out another tree to hang her cloak.

"Dare we build a fire?" she wondered aloud. "All the wood is so wet it will surely smoke."

Alon shrugged. "The witch will know our whereabouts whether we have a fire or not. And I for one"—he pulled off his sodden leather jerkin—"would rather have the warmth." He rubbed his jaw, then grimaced. "Not to mention hot water for shaving."

Once the fire was kindled, reluctant and smoky even as Eydryth had predicted, the songsmith pulled off her own jerkin so her tunic could dry; then she drew her sword from its place of concealment. "Time for your first lesson," she announced solemnly.

At the look of astonishment on Alon's now smooth-skinned features, she smiled thinly, pointing with the tip of her blade to the one he wore. "Go on, draw it. Learning the basic stance and one or two moves will warm you up and loosen muscles stiff from walking in the rain."

"But . . ." He hesitated, then shrugged and obeyed.

Eydryth surveyed his drawn weapon with a practiced eye. "A general-issue sword, but the Estcarpian smiths know their craft. Double-edged and pointed . . . you will learn to use either point or edge. First of all, hold it out in front of you . . . so."

When he obeyed, she inspected his hand, touching the back of his wrist lightly, running her fingers up the length of his bared arm. "Good strength," she said. "I am not surprised, seeing that you can rein in Monso. Now place your feet like this. . . ." She moved into position, right foot ahead of left, crouching slightly. "Yes, that's correct, now bend your knees a little, thus. . . ."

Brow furrowed with concentration, he obeyed. "Good," she said. "Shoulders a bit forward, right more than left, eyes front, good . . ." She faced him, her own blade out. "You must learn to let your body think for you, while keeping your mind calm and detached so it can plan your next move.

"Look not at any one area, but rather let your eyes take in the entire form of your opponent. Not only his blade, but also the movement of head, shoulders—the entire torso. Eventually you will learn to note the placing of his body without having to think about it, and then you can begin to anticipate an opponent's moves from small shifts in his carriage, or from the way his eyes move. The eyes often reveal the next tactic even before the wrist or body knows what it will be."

"What do I do with my left hand?" Alon asked, concentrating grimly on holding the sword in the correct position.

"For now, just hold it so," she demonstrated. "It will help you balance. In time I will teach you to use your left hand, with a cloak wrapped around it, or with a dagger, to parry strokes."

"Is that how you fight? With a sword and dagger?"

"That is my preferred style, yes," she said. "Now put your blade back in its sheath."

Her student looked rather relieved to have gotten off so easily. "Are we done?"

"Hardly. But I have no desire to have you cut me should I miss a parry. The scabbard will make a good protector." When he'd obeyed, she said, "Good. Now . . . back into position."

Alon did so, grunting a little. "My legs will be stiff from this."

"No doubt," she agreed. "Now let me demonstrate a basic lunge and a basic parry for you to practice tonight. . . ."

Quickly she shifted her weight forward, her sword driving before her like a steel wind. The point halted just touching the fabric of the tunic covering Alon's midsection. With a startled gasp, he leaped back, wide-eyed. "Have a little caution, I beg you!" he sputtered. "You . . . you could have spitted me!"

"Certainly," Eydryth agreed calmly. "But I did not. Watch me again." She demonstrated the lunge while he looked on. "You must learn to feel the force and direction of the blade as though it were a part of your body, controlling it precisely.

Your blade moves first, propelled by your wrist and arm. Your body follows, and then, last of all, let yourself step forward. Now, you try it. . . ."

His first attempt made her shake her head reprovingly. "*Concentrate*, Alon. The steel is an extra length of arm for you now, and you must treat it so. Again."

Again.

And yet again.

Finally, on the young man's dozenth try, his teacher nodded, satisfied. "Better! Now try to touch point to this." She suspended Monso's feed bag over a branch. "Aim for the center buckle."

It took him nine attempts to touch blade to the target.

"Good! Much better!"

Alon's tight-jawed concentration broke into a wide grin. "The next time we are accosted by soldiers, my lady, you will not stand alone!"

Eydryth smiled tolerantly at his enthusiasm. "Now for the first of the parties. Cross swords with me, so."

Once in position, the songsmith made a small twisting motion with her wrist, and Alon's hand was suddenly empty. He stared from it to his sword, lying on the ground, and sighed. "I see that I have much yet to learn."

She nodded. "But you are doing well, for the first time. Now . . . again for the parry. This time, keep your wrist flexible, not stiff, so you can follow the motion of your blade and keep hold of it. Then it will be your turn to try. . . ."

By the time the lesson was over, the light was fading rapidly, and Alon's tunic was wet now with sweat, rather than rain. He hung it up to dry, then pulled on another shirt. "I will be back presently," he told Eydryth and started back down their trail, out of sight.

The songsmith began making camp, shaking her head over the dampness that had invaded her bedroll, even through its tallow-soaked covering. Unfastening the saddlebag, she took out the meat jerky and her small cooking pot. Simmered in water with crumbled journeybread to thicken it, the jerky would make a hot, though tasteless, meal.

It was full dark by the time Alon returned. Eydryth had let

the fire die down to coals, so she could make out his form only as a dark blot against the yellow stars that marked the campfires of their pursuers.

"They are closer," she said, eyeing the distance between them measuringly as Alon sat down with a weary sigh. He murmured a quick thanks for the plate she offered him.

"If they can keep up their pace, by this time tomorrow they will be almost upon us," the bard observed as she spooned up the last of her own meal. Hesitantly she bit her lip, then declared, "Tomorrow morning we had best go our separate ways, Alon."

"No," her companion said flatly. "They cannot possibly catch us tomorrow. The rocks will slow them, as today they slowed us."

"If not tomorrow, then surely the day after. We must part, so that I can go on faster alone!"

He turned his head to regard her, but she could not read his features in the faint light of the campfire. "If they are closer tomorrow night," he said evenly, "I will do as you say. Fair enough?"

"Yes," Eydryth said, feeling her throat grow tight as a harpstring. "Alon . . . I . . . I am grateful to you, for trying to aid me. I . . . I wish you well."

He made no reply.

They reached the first slope of the mountain pass by the next evening, but Eydryth took no joy in their accomplishment. On the morrow they would be fortunate to make half the distance they had covered today, and a detachment of guardsmen, with no horses to lead over the thin, stony soil, would have no trouble catching them.

Turning to scan the rocky hills over which they had so laboriously toiled, Eydryth frowned, puzzled. There was no sign of the witch and her troop. When she pointed this out to Alon, her companion suggested that perhaps their pursuers had lost the trail.

"But she can follow us by her witch-jewel," Eydryth argued. "You said so yourself."

"The use of the Power wears hardly upon the user," he said.

"She may have weakened, finally. Or, it may be that she could not force herself to travel this far east."

The songsmith shook her head slowly, remembering the Estcarpian woman's determined expression. "If she had to be tied upon her mount and led, she would not give up. It is more likely that they are camped tonight in one of the valleys instead of on top of a ridge where we could see them."

"We have lost them," Alon insisted. "I scanned our path frequently today, and there was no sign of them. I believe that tonight we may rest without fear." He turned away from her, calling back over his shoulder, "I will be back presently."

Steel Talon had brought them a rabbit earlier that day, so Eydryth busied herself skinning it and putting it into their cooking pot with several handfuls of vegetables and a few pinches of herbs. Then she took her sword out of the quarterstaff and practiced with it, lunging and parrying with an imaginary opponent. At last, sweating and panting, she halted, only to see last rays of the setting sun hang over the mountain peak towering above her, then vanish.

Still Alon did not return. *He must be delaying deliberately,* she thought with mounting irritation. *It is grown too dark now for a lesson.*

Scowling, she strode off down the slope, determined to give her errant pupil a lecture on the importance of daily practice if he wished to achieve any proficiency.

As she walked, however, she was struck by a sudden thought. *What if he has been captured, and I am now marching into a trap?*

The songsmith began moving with a scout's caution, shifting her weight with care on the stony ground lest she send a pebble skittering, taking advantage of every boulder, every scrap of concealment her rugged surroundings had to offer.

It was thus that she came upon her companion as he knelt on the stony ground, chanting softly. In one hand he held a swatch of black horsehair, which he was sweeping over a distinct hoofprint in a patch of loamy soil. Straining her ears, Eydryth caught snatches of what he was chanting, and realized it was that arcane form of the Old Tongue.

As she watched, tight-lipped with angry realization, Alon fell silent. He rose to his feet, arms held high, and suddenly the hoofprint, a scrape on a rock caused by a horse's metal shoe, and a mound of horse droppings all glowed violet—
—and vanished.

Mist rose out of the ground and began coiling down the hillside, snaking along their back trail. The songsmith knew instinctively that it would erase all traces of their passage as it flowed over the earth.

Alon stood for a moment more, arms raised; then he sighed audibly and his shoulders sagged. *Magic does indeed wear hardly upon the user*, Eydryth thought bitterly, her cheeks hot with fury and shame, remembering how she had confided in him about growing up in Kar Garudwyn. *How could I have been such a fool as to not realize the truth?*

Only a moment did the young man allow himself to rest; then he trudged back up the slope, obviously hurrying as fast as his tired legs would take him.

Eydryth let him draw even with her hiding place, then stepped out, barring his path. "I see now why you were so confident that the witch could no longer trail us," she said, her voice pitched low despite her anger.

He halted and stood staring at her for a long moment, his face a pale oval in the last glow of twilight. Finally he said, "I am sorry. You are right to be angry."

"By the Sword Arm of Karthen the Fair, I certainly am!" Eydryth hissed, so furious that she found she was trembling. "I *trusted* you, and all the while you were doubtless laughing at me up your sleeve! The great Adept—for you are no simple village Wise Man, or one who merely dabbles in arcane lore, that much even I can tell—the Adept, companying with the poor Powerless songsmith, using his magic to protect her—" She swallowed, the taste of anger like bile in her mouth. "Well, I can protect myself from now on! I don't need you!"

"I know that," he said, quietly.

His ready admission took her aback.

"You assumed without asking that I had no Power," he reminded her. "I did not lie outright."

"You allowed me to believe what was not true," Eydryth flared. "That is the same thing!"

"You have the right of it," he agreed, wearily. "But . . . Lady . . . by the time I realized what a mistake I had made, I was in too deep to extricate myself gracefully. I knew you would be angry, and I did not want to hurt you." He hesitated, then continued, in a low voice. "And yesterday, when you began saying that we must part, I knew that if you were to learn the truth, then you would indeed go your separate way— and I did not want that to happen."

As he spoke, Eydryth heard a note in his voice that broke through her ire. Her face flushed again, but not from anger, and she could feel her heart pounding, as though she had been sprinting. "I did not want you to risk falling into the witch's hands again on my behalf," she said awkwardly. "That would be poor repayment indeed for your aid."

"And my lack of truthfulness was poor exchange for your candor," he said. He stepped closer to her in the darkness. "I can only say that I am sorry. I was wrong, but the thought of never seeing you again was . . ." He hesitated. ". . . not something I wished to contemplate."

Eydryth backed away in confusion, half of her struggling to find words to answer him, half not wanting to hear any more.

"Shall I go, then?" he asked, with an undercurrent of sadness in his calm tones. "Must we indeed part?"

Mastering her conflicting emotions, Eydryth managed to say, levelly enough, "If you are certain that the witch has been foiled in her hopes of finding us, then I see no reason why we cannot continue on to the Valley of the Green Silences."

Silently he nodded, and they walked together back to the place where they had made camp.

The smell of stew tantalized the travelers when they reached the place where Monso waited, cropping determinedly at the scrubby clumps of grass nestled between the rocks. Alon fed the Keplian, then they sat down to their own meal.

When they finished, Eydryth gazed at her companion across their campfire and said, quietly, "You know my story, Alon. I feel I have the right now to know yours. How came you to be in Rylon Corners, racing Monso? A man with your abilities . . ."

She saw lines appear around his mouth as he grimaced, then he said bitterly, "It is true, most Adepts spend their days in other pursuits than cheating at horse racing. But believe me when I tell you that until I encountered you, and we were captured, I had not used magic in more than a year."

"So *you* put the guards and the witch to sleep?"

"I directed my Power through the beasts, yes."

"I should have guessed," Eydryth said, then in a burst of honesty admitted, "Perhaps I *did* guess—but I did not want to let myself see what lay plainly before my eyes. Duratan and Nolar . . . they knew, didn't they?"

"I believe so."

The songsmith stirred the dying fire with a branch until it blazed up, then tossed the stick into the glowing red heart of the coals. "From living in Kar Garudwyn, I know that it is no small thing to ignore one's Power. The Gift will out, no matter what. Why had you given up using your magic?"

"Because I killed my best friend with it," Alon replied.

She stared at him, shocked. Silence held between them for a little while; then Alon sighed and said, "It is a long story. I know not who I truly am, or what my parentage is. I was fostered by a Lord Parlan, for he believed me to be the son of a slain kinsman of his. Whether that story was the truth, I know not."

He paused, and Eydryth asked, "Why do you doubt that tale?"

"Because Yachne told Lord Parlan that I was born to his kinsman, but there was no other evidence to support that tale. And Yachne . . ." He hesitated. "I never trusted her, though she cared for me and raised me for my first dozen years."

"Who was this Yachne?"

"A Wise Woman, of that I am sure. She appeared at Lord Parlan's keep with me as a babe in arms, telling him the story of who I was and how I had been born. She claimed to have been my lady mother's servant."

"And she had the Power?"

"Yes. In many ways, I believe, she lessoned me subtly in its use from the time I could walk and talk. But I do not believe that she ever had any warmth or liking for me—only for what she thought I might be able to do for her."

Eydryth thought of what a barren existence he had evidently led—without true kin, or caring—and felt her heart tighten within her. "Perhaps," she ventured awkwardly, "this . . . Yachne . . . felt true affection for you, but had difficulty showing it. That is often the case with certain people."

Alon shook his head decisively. "Even by the time I was a lad of twelve, I knew better. She never acted like a mother, or an aunt, or even a fond teacher. She taught me as though she had a use for me, and I feared the day I would be put to that use." He stared bleakly at her across the yellow flames. "I learned from her, but I did not love her—though she never abused me or treated me with anything but a rather aloof kindness. She took very good care of me, but always I feared her more than a little."

"Did you worry that she meant you harm?"

"No . . ." He hesitated. "But I never wanted to be a dagger for her honing." Alon smiled wryly, but there was pain in his eyes. "However, I know with certainty that that is what I was to Yachne. That is *all* I was to her."

"So what set you free of the Wise Woman and Lord Parlan?"

"There was a raid by one who was in league with a powerful Dark One. Everyone in Lord Parlan's keep was killed, save for me. I managed to conceal myself from the raiders."

"By sorcerous means," Eydryth guessed, and was not surprised when he nodded assent. *"Everyone* was killed?" she continued. "Yachne too?"

He sighed, shaking his head. "I never saw her body, but I have no reason to believe she was spared. If she had still lived, it seemed to me, she would have come to my rescue. I was valuable to her, after all," he finished, with a bitter grimace.

"And then?" Eydryth prompted, when he fell silent once more. "What did you do then?"

"I made my way to Escore, and, as I told you, I was fostered there by Hilarion and Kaththea. But several years after I came to live with them, they had a child of their own . . . then, two years later, another.

"By that time I was near-grown, and Hilarion had taught me much of what he knew. They would have had me stay, but I was restless to see the land where I had been born—if Karsten was indeed that place, since I have no way of knowing. And I felt that my foster-parents should be able to raise their children without distraction. So I set off with Monso."

Resting his elbows on his knees, he leaned his chin in his hands, staring intently into the dwindling fire, as though he saw events from the past pictured there. "Once on the other side of the mountains, I encountered Jonthal, Steel Talon's master. I'd had a Falconer friend, Nirel, when I was a child, so I spoke to him, where I was cautious in speaking to other men. We became friends, and soon we were leading parties over the mountains from Karsten and Estcarp into Escore. Jonthal handled the business, and I rode with the travelers to protect them from the dangers that had been unleashed following the Turning . . . the Thas and the Grey Ones, mostly."

"I can see how a party could travel safely under your protection," Eydryth agreed. "No wonder you never needed to learn swordplay!"

"You have convinced me otherwise," he said. "Now that we have no further fear of Estcarpian pursuit, I will practice daily."

"Good," she said. "But pray continue your account."

"Jonthal always warned me that I was overconfident," Alon resumed his story with a tired sigh. "But I laughed at his fears. One night in Kars, we were dining in a tap-house, when a boy delivered a message, saying that a prospective client wished to see us. Jonthal did not wish to go, as the summons had come from a part of Kars City where even the City Guards did not venture, save in force, but I insisted. We needed the money, and what was there to fear, I said? My Power would protect us."

He laughed softly, bitterly, with such pain in the sound that Eydryth's heart ached to hear him. "And it did not?" she prompted, when he sat in silence, head bowed.

"You have the right of it. We walked into an alley, peering

at the doorways for the third one on the right, and they were upon us before we knew what had happened. Something kept me from sensing them, though my magic should have warned me. Hired toughs, four of them, armed with swords. Jonthal drew and engaged one, and I forced sleep upon the minds of two others. The fourth took to his heels. When I turned back to my friend, it was in time to see the cutthroat's blade driving straight for his throat.

"With every bit of Will I possessed, I lashed out—and the Power went awry. I . . .." For the first time his voice faltered. "I will never know the reason why, but I must have made . . . a mistake. The force I unleashed struck Jonthal, while the assassin stood unscathed. My friend was dead before he struck the stinking cobbles of that thrice-cursed alley." Alon stared fixedly at his hands. "I killed him."

"You were trying to save him," Eydryth pointed out. "If you had not struck, he would have died by the assassin's steel."

"Perhaps . . . or perhaps he might have parried it at the last moment. He was a good swordsman."

"You did not harm him intentionally," she continued earnestly. "It is not unknown in battle for a man to be slain accidentally by a comrade's sword-thrust. Mistakes happen. What occurred was not your fault, and you should forgive yourself for it." She sighed. "Guilt is a very crippling burden."

He stared at her intently in the waning firelight. "You above all others should know, Lady. You are still blaming yourself for something that was in no way your fault." Alon considered silently for a moment. "I will make a bargain with you, Eydryth."

"What kind of bargain?" the songsmith asked warily.

"I will endeavor to forgive myself, if you will do likewise. You are not to blame for your mother's disappearance, your father's mind-clouding. You are, if anything, far less culpable than I."

She bit her lip; then, slowly, she nodded. "Very well. I will try not to hold myself responsible, if you will do likewise."

"Done," he said, and held out his hand to seal their pact.

Eydryth reached out across the coals of the campfire, feeling the heat of them on her skin, to grasp his fingers tightly.

Since the travelers were no longer troubled by worries of pursuit, they climbed at a much more leisurely pace the next day. The snowcapped peaks towered above them, but the pass toward which they toiled was no more than a half-day's journey away. As they climbed higher, frost rimed the rocks underfoot, and the last of the underbrush was left behind. Now only grey-green lichens grew. Monso could find no forage at all.

Gasping from the thin air, Alon and Eydryth halted long before sunset to camp when they found a nearly level ledge that Alon reported as the only campsite this side of the pass. After they had rested and eaten, Alon insisted on taking on his sword and practicing a few lunges and parries. Huddled into her cloak, Eydryth watched, now and then correcting his stance or movements. But the young Adept was making praiseworthy progress, and she told him so.

Finally Alon halted, sweating despite the chill air, and sank down onto his bedroll, gasping. "Enough for tonight, teacher?"

"Indeed yes," she said. "Tomorrow—if either of us has the strength after making the final pull through the pass—I will demonstrate another kind of parry for you to practice."

"When will I be ready to match blades with a live opponent as opposed to a brave feed sack?"

She smiled. "At your current rate of progress? Oh . . . perhaps another month."

His face fell, and she hastily amended, "But you are learning faster than most, Alon! You must cultivate patience, if you hope to succeed."

He scowled. "Patience has never been one of my virtues." With a sigh, he reached for a piece of journeybread. Since there was no wood to be had above the treeline, they were making a cold supper.

Later, as they sat together companionably, watching the shadows of evening close in around them, he suddenly asked, "What song is that? It has a lovely tune."

Eydryth started, not realizing she had been humming aloud. "I don't know," she said, feeling foolish. "What did it sound like?"

Alon produced a few off-key snatches of melody. Hearing him, the songsmith felt herself coloring and was grateful for the encroaching darkness. The words that accompanied the tune came unbidden to her mind:

> Golden the sunlight on the hill,
> Silver the moonlight on the sea:
> Though fair these things are to see, still,
> No fairer than my love to me!
>
> Though merry the glint of dancing brook,
> Though sweet the carol when birds rejoice,
> No merrier than my sweetheart's look,
> No sweeter than my sweetheart's voice.
>
> Not gold nor silver, brook nor bird,
> Nor sun nor moon, though wondrous all
> Can touch my heart as does his word
> Nor gladden me as does his call!

"It is an old song from High Hallack," she said, reluctantly.

"Hearing you hum it just now reminded me that I haven't heard you sing since that day at the fairground when you serenaded Monso. Your voice is so fair . . . can you sing it for me?"

Eydryth shook her head. "I have forgotten the words," she lied, crossing her fingers behind her back in a gesture suddenly recalled from childhood.

"That's a pity. Please . . . hum it again, so I can remember the melody."

Eydryth complied, grateful that he could not see her blush. *You have no time for entanglements!* she reminded herself fiercely.

That night, they bedded down side by side, sharing their blankets, as was customary between companions on the trail when camping fireless in cold weather. Alon slung his cloak over Monso's back, then commanded the stallion to fold his legs beneath him so they could huddle together in the windbreak created by the Keplian's body. Tired from the day's journey, both travelers fell asleep quickly.

Eydryth awakened late that night to find the waning moon shining on her face and Alon snuggled close against her beneath their blankets. In his sleep he had flung an arm across her waist. The warmth of his breath stirred the curls at the back of her neck.

The young woman bit her lip, wondering how to extricate herself gracefully before he could awaken. She was acutely conscious of his body pressed against hers, his hand so close to her breast, even beneath the bulky layers of her clothing. Each breath he drew seemed to echo inside her own body.

As she hesitated, strangely reluctant to move, a glimmer of light caught her eye from a nearby mountain slope. Eydryth squinted, certain that she had been mistaken, but as the quarter-moon emerged from behind a bank of racing clouds, it was there again, shining brightly. The light beckoned to the bard, beckoned with a pure white light in the darkness.

What is it? she wondered, feeling it tug at her with an almost physical pull. She seemed to hear a strange music, high-pitched, uncanny—nothing that could be produced by any instrument or throat that she knew.

Wriggling gently out of Alon's hold, she sat up, her teeth chattering in the cold as the chill struck her like a blow. The Adept mumbled something inarticulate as his fingers quested blindly, seeking after her vanished warmth.

The glow softened, waned, then went out as another cloud covered the moon. The songsmith stared, hardly daring to blink lest she lose the spot where it had been. Long heartbeats later, as the rag of cloud gusted past, it was there once more, shining . . . beckoning.

The songsmith heard a soft snort, then turned to see Monso's head, an inky shadow against the light-colored rocks. The creature's ears were pricked up. The glow of the unknown beacon reflected eerily in the Keplian's eyes.

Hearing that high, eldritch music again, Eydryth turned to

her companion and shook his arm impatiently. "Alon! Rouse you! Waken, please!"

He came to alertness quickly, as any wayfarer must learn to do if he is to survive long on the trail. "What is it?" he demanded, sitting up, then cursing softly in the cold and pulling the blankets up around his shoulders.

"I know not," the bard said, pointing at the light and trying to repress her shivering. "Could it be some trap set by the witch?"

Alon handed over her cloak. "No . . . I would sense that one's presence. This is . . . greater. Much greater. Not living, but still . . . it is of the Power."

"What kind of Power? Surely not the Dark!" Eydryth protested. The light was so clean, so bright!

"I cannot be sure," Alon said. "I can sense little about it. But if it is activated by the moon, then it must be of the Light. And . . . it is drawing me . . . it has the power to . . . to summon."

"I know," she said. "It has been calling to me, also. Alon, this is important, I know it is! We must go there—quickly, before the moon sets!"

Eight

*I*t was a perilous journey they made by the light of the waning moon, stumbling and skidding over frozen, frost-rimed ground. As they ascended the mountainside, their way grew rougher, more broken, until they were picking a path between rocks and boulders streaked with glistening trails of ice. Eydryth led the way, her strides quick and impatient despite the poor footing. She gasped when a stone turned beneath her heel; only her companion's quick grasp on her arm saved her from a precipitous fall. "Slowly," he cautioned.

"But the moon's light will soon be gone. . . ."

"True, but if by moonset we are all resting at the bottom of yon gorge with broken necks, it will matter but little to us whether it shines or not." Monso snorted, as if in agreement. "Perhaps we should stop," Alon suggested, surveying the rugged path before them. "We could wait for daylight."

"No," she replied. "Without the moon's glow to guide us, we will never find that beacon. It does not shine by the sun's light, I am certain of that. Can you see in the dark?" she asked, remembering that her mother had always been able to do so, claiming that the ability was held by many with the kinship of Power.

"Not as well as Monso," he said. "But perhaps better than you can."

"Then you lead."

Slowly, he edged past her on the narrow ledge. "Hook your fingers in my belt," he instructed.

Eydryth obeyed. *"Hurry, Alon!"*

As they went on, an overhanging thrust of rock darkened their path even further. The songsmith clung to her companion's belt, prepared to follow blindly, but she heard the Adept mutter beneath his breath; then light shone from his right hand, each finger outlined in the white-violet glow. Spreading his fingers, he held them palm-down, so the light illuminated the path beneath their feet.

How long can he maintain that? she wondered worriedly. *Will keeping such a spell going draw so much energy from him that he cannot complete our climb? Should we stop and try again on the morrow? The moon will rise again. . . .*

She nearly voiced her concerns aloud, but then she shook her head and remained silent. Eydryth could not explain the urgency building within her, but it drove her across the mountain's flank with grim purpose. The high-pitched notes reverberated inside her head with a siren summons, making chills not born of the cold trace themselves down her spine. Alon, by his own admission, could not hear them.

But it was clear that Monso could. The Keplian pricked his ears and turned his head with each uncanny repetition.

The songsmith narrowed her eyes, using her gryphon-headed staff to test each step before trusting her full weight to the treacherous path. Slowly, the travelers picked their way across the loose rocks of the final slope. Finally, gasping and shivering, they halted, staring up at their destination. It was close, but to attain the ledge from whence the glow emanated, they would have to scramble up a trail so steep that it made the songsmith's head swim to contemplate it.

"How can we climb that?" she asked, despairingly.

"Monso can," Alon said after a moment. "Grab hold of the stirrup; use it to steady yourself." He took up position on the other side of the Keplian. "Ready?" he asked.

"Yes," she replied, her mouth dry from fear and anticipation.

"Monso, *hup!*" Alon cried, and the black surged forward, scrambling, powerful hindquarters thrusting, steel-shod forehooves clawing a purchase in the crusted, frozen earth. Eydryth launched herself beside the Keplian, endeavoring not to drag the creature off balance. Using her quarterstaff, she pulled herself up, the frigid air tearing her throat with each sobbing breath.

With a final gasp and heave, the three travelers were over the side of the ledge.

The feeble moonlight shone down full upon a huge sheet of crystal embedded in the mountainside. Eydryth stared at it, so exhausted that she could do naught but gasp, the air stabbing her lungs. She leaned against Monso's heaving side, feeling her knees buckle. Finally her legs steadied; only then was she able to walk over to gaze into the reflective surface.

"What is it?" she whispered, feeling a strange reluctance to speak aloud.

"A thing of Power," Alon said, coming up behind her, his voice equally quiet. Their own outlines swam before them, eerily limned by the moonglow. "For some reason we have been summoned here . . . by what power or agency I cannot guess."

"The moon is so bright on the crystal," Eydryth breathed, "that surely this thing is of the Light."

"I believe so," her companion agreed. "But often Light and Dark are balanced precariously in this world . . . and many things of the Light have their Dark shadows."

"What do you—," the songsmith began, only to break off as a cloud eclipsed the moon, and their own reflections dissolved like snowflakes encountering water. But the crystal surface did not stay blank; rather, it glowed darkly, as though a fire made from shadows had been kindled within it. Shapes slowly coalesced into recognizability . . . a large, rocky cave, its walls sheeted with water that glinted dully in the light of a single torch that smoldered sullenly.

"What . . . what are we seeing?" Eydryth cried.

"I cannot be sure," Alon said, "but I think this . . . mirror . . . is actually a Gate, one of those that lead to other places— perhaps even other worlds. We are seeing what lies on the other side of this Gate, I believe."

The songsmith caught her breath sharply, for even as Alon finished speaking, a figure shuffled into view, leaning on a short walking staff, and stood silhouetted against the dark mouth of the cave. At first they could make out nothing except that it was alive, and human, for the light was so wan and its clothing so shapeless and drab that age or features—even its sex—were impossible to discern.

It stopped; then they heard its voice, low and commanding, causing the first torch to flare into life and causing another to ignite with a reluctant sputter.

Eydryth squinted against the sudden light. In a moment her eyes adjusted and she could see again. The newcomer was a woman, clothed in a tattered grey hooded robe. Her features were shadowed by her hood, but from the appearance of her hands, and the presence of the walking staff, the songsmith thought she must be well past middle years. But she moved spryly enough as she bustled around the cave, humming tunelessly as she set out candles, then traced a design upon the stony floor with a wand she produced from her sleeve.

The lines she drew glowed blue as they formed a distinct shape. "A pentagram," Eydryth breathed, recognizing the age-old symbol that was prerequisite to a spell of summoning. "Is she a witch of Estcarp?"

"She wears no jewel," Alon pointed out, "but the color of her Power is correct. The witches deal in theurgy, the harnessing of will, faith and emotion to work their magic. Blue is the color of theurgy."

The woman stared at her pentagram, gave a satisfied nod, then raised a hand. The dark candles she had placed at the points of the star-shape burst into flame. She stepped out of her watchers' line of vision for a moment, but soon returned, carrying a net that writhed as the creature tangled within struggled vainly to escape, uttering small, piercing shrieks of fear.

Beside her, Alon stiffened with horrified recognition. "A Flannan!" he whispered.

Eydryth had heard of the small creatures that could take on the guise of either bird or small, winged mannikin. In Arvon and High Hallack they were naught more than legend, but the people of Estcarp told of how they had been seen in Escore near Dahaun's Valley of the Green Silences.

Flannan made flighty, unreliable allies, due to their capricious nature, but never had they been allied with the Dark. Snapping out a few short words that made Alon draw in his breath with a hiss, the woman thrust her hand into the net bag. Then the witch (for so Eydryth now thought of her) withdrew the small creature, clutching the Flannan by the scruff of its scrawny neck. It was not in its bird-form . . . its body bore arms and legs in addition to the wings that trailed limply down its back. The creature halted its struggles and now dangled bonelessly from the woman's hand, either drugged or bespelled into calmness.

The songsmith watched in shock as the witch reached into a sheath at her belt and withdrew a black-hilted athame. "No!" Eydryth whispered, in an agony of helplessness. She grasped Alon's arm, her fingers digging in painfully as the woman brought the blade up to the Flannan's throat, and, with a quick, ruthless thrust, pricked it deeply. Red flowed in a steady stream.

Eydryth had seen death dealt before, but always in clean and open battle—never like this. She pressed a hand to her mouth to stifle a cry, as the witch, chanting softly, began to encircle the pentagram, dribbling the weakly spasming Flannan's blood onto the stone floor of the cave.

As the blood of the dying creature congealed upon the cold rock, the blue light darkened, taking on a sickly purplish tinge. The yellow flames atop the dark candles blackened, until they were the same color as the wax. As she neared the end of her obscene task, grasping the limp and now plainly dead mannikin, the witch's chanting grew louder.

"What is she doing?" Eydryth whispered, fighting the urge to cower, hands over her ears, to shut out the sound. The witch's chanting was growing physically painful to hear.

"Some kind of summoning," Alon replied in a strained whisper. Eydryth glanced at his face in the moonlight and saw that he looked as sickened as she felt. "And a powerful one. She is invoking the Name of one of the most deadly of the Dark Adepts."

Circle complete, the witch's voice rose still higher as she gestured with her wand, raising her arms so high that her sleeves fell back from her flabby flesh and bony wrists. A blackish purple mist coiled upward out of the circle, hiding the pentagram from their view.

With a last, high-pitched cry of triumph, a sound that made Eydryth gasp and clap her hands over her ears, the witch fell silent. For long moments she stood poised; then she began to laugh delightedly. The skin at the back of the girl's neck crawled as though leeches had fastened there.

Within the smoky confines of the circle, trapped by the protective boundaries of the pentagram, something now moved, at first slowly, then thrashing wildly in frantic struggles. A deep male voice cried out in fear, then cursed foully.

Flashes of Power crackled within the boundary cast by the circle-spell. Power that bore the dark purple hue of the Shadow. With a low, crooning sound, the witch stretched out her arms toward the circle, and the lines of Power arced toward her, encircled her wrists, then flowed up her arms, writhing like serpents formed from the essence of the Darkness. They crossed the witch's breast, met over her heart, then pulsed, as though pumping their substance into her body. She gasped, transfixed with pain or pleasure, it was impossible to tell which.

But there was no doubt about the reaction of that dimly seen figure trapped within the circle. The man screamed in agony, as those lines of Power pulsed, feeding themselves into the witch. The prisoner's shriek rose higher and higher—

—abruptly, there was silence. The lines of Power disappeared into the witch's body, and slowly the mist faded away.

Eydryth saw that a man now stood within the pentagram, a tall man with a haughty, handsome face that bore the unmistakable stamp of the Old Race. He could have been Alon's father, or older brother, for the resemblance between them was strong. The stranger was wearing a hunter's or forester's garb . . . short cloak, leather jerkin, brown breeches and high, soft boots. An ornate jeweled dagger hung at his belt, and a more businesslike short sword rode his hip.

As the last wisps of mist vanished, he stared at the woman who fronted him in the darkened cave with horrified realization distorting his well-cut features.

"My Power—," he began in a choked voice.

"Is now *mine,* Lord Dinzil!" the witch crowed exultantly.

"But . . . why?" he asked dazedly.

The woman's features were still shadowed from Eydryth's view, but her voice bore a cruel smile. "You are a male, and for a male to have sorcerous abilities is a thing against nature." Her head lifted proudly. "Women are the only rightful vessels of Power. I lost most of mine, many years ago, but now . . ." She flexed her fingers and purple light outlined them for a moment. ". . . what I lost, I have regained . . . aye, all that, and more . . . more!"

"Dinzil!" Alon whispered softly. "I should have known. . . ."

"Who is he?" Eydryth asked, glancing up at him.

Her companion shook his head. "Later."

Suddenly the Dark Adept gave a low moan of distress and staggered. He put one hand to his head, then pulled it away with a cry of dismay, the fingers splayed widely. Eydryth could clearly make out the prominent veining and mottled skin of the elderly. As she watched, they crooked suddenly with the painful joint-rheum suffered by the aged. The Adept's features took on years as dry bread soaks up broth. Lines scored his cheeks; silver frosted his black hair. "My Power . . . ," the sorcerer whispered, "my Power . . ."

"Was all that was keeping you young, I fear, my lord," the witch told him calmly. "Now that it is gone, your years will come upon you . . . and those years are many, are they not?"

Dinzil did not answer her. Shudders racked his tall body, and with each spasm he seemed to shrink and wither apace. His hair grew white and sparse, wisping around a face that now resembled aged parchment crumpled by a careless hand. Then his lips parted in a gasp of agony and teeth cascaded out, rattling down onto the stone at his feet. Dinzil held out a now-withered claw to the witch, and they heard a voice, no longer strong and resonant, but shrill and breathless emerge from his near-toothless mouth. "I would curse you if I still could, witchwoman . . . curse you with my last breath."

The witch laughed.

"Ah, yes," the ancient man that had been Dinzil, the Dark Adept, wheezed, "laugh while you may, witchwoman. But even if my ill wishes have no teeth left to rend you, still you will find yourself cursed. The Left-Hand Path is a most demanding one. The Dark levies a heavy price on the spirits of its servants. You will realize before you die exactly what you have called into yourself, and therein lies my curse. May it fall soon!"

"*You* are the one who should worry about death, my lord," the witch mocked him. She raised a hand to push back her hood a little, and they saw that it had changed, was now firm-fleshed and slender. A lock of hair escaped from beneath the loosened hood, and that hair was now sable, as Dinzil's had been.

With a careless wave the witch caused the candles to snuff out; then she indicated the cave mouth. "And now, our business is done, my lord. You are no longer welcome here, so may I suggest that you take your leave? You will find the land without this cave to be a familiar one, I daresay . . . though the inhabitants hereabouts have little reason to love you, I believe."

With a courage and dignity that Eydryth had to admire, Dark Adept or no, Dinzil drew himself up as straight as he might, then tottered feebly toward the entrance. "Here, you will doubtless need this, grandsire," the witch said mockingly, handing him the walking staff that had been hers. For a moment Eydryth thought that he would fling the stick at his tormentor, but he did not speak or look back.

The witch quickly eradicated the traces of her spell with her wand; then she picked up a pack from the corner and slung it over her shoulder. "And now," she muttered, "to essay that mirror."

She turned to face her watchers, and for the first time they were able to discern her features clearly. Eydryth saw that she was plainly of the Old Race, a woman of early middle years, with strong, boldly marked features that were too thin and driven to hold any beauty.

Just then the songsmith heard Alon's soft gasp of recognition. *"Yachne!"* he whispered. "How—*why*—"

Eydryth's mouth dropped open. The Wise Woman who had taught him his first magic! Was it indeed she on the other side of this arcane mirror-portal, engaged in a Dark rite? She remembered Alon's face as he'd spoken of her, remembered his words: "But I never wanted to be a dagger for her honing."

The woman walked toward them, raised her wand, then muttered a few words. A purple glow awoke within the depths of the crystal mirror, painting her features with a sickly light. As she stared into her side of the crystal, her eyes abruptly widened. For the first time, she was aware of her watchers.

"Who—," she began; then she broke off, her gaze holding Alon's. "Why, it is my young charge, all grown up," she said after a moment, then smiled in a fashion that made Eydryth put hand to the hilt of the sword resting within her quarterstaff.

"Young Alon, well-met, well-met indeed! I was planning to seek you out, though perhaps not so soon. There are others I must visit first, before I will be ready to take on one who apprenticed with Hilarion."

"You know—" Alon broke off even before Eydryth could nudge him to silence. Power this woman might have, knowledge, also, no doubt, but they did not need to give her aught that she did not already know.

"Oh, I know . . . I know much, my fine young Adept. Much more than I did even a half-hour ago, as you no doubt witnessed. How did you happen by, Alon? Chance? That seems unlikely. Well, perhaps you were drawn by my spelling. After all, Power does call to Power, does it not?"

Alon remained silent, and the witch, for the first time, turned her attention to Eydryth. "And who is your fair companion, Alon? Your bride? Or is she something less . . . formal, perhaps? Your leman?"

The songsmith had heard battle-taunts before, and did not allow her face to change at Yachne's insult, but Alon stepped forward with an angry imprecation. "No, Alon," Eydryth said, softly, catching his arm, "that's what she wants."

"Perceptive girl," the witch said, amused. There was a wild glitter in her eyes that Eydryth thought was not wholly due to the purple glow from her side of the crystal. The younger woman swallowed, suddenly more frightened than she had been all night. "And what symbol it is that you bear on that staff of yours?" Yachne asked, her eyes narrowing with speculation. A moment later, she gave a shout of laughter. "Oh, very good! Very good indeed! The gryphon-lord! Landisl's vessel, Kerovan himself, gave that to you, did he not? Perhaps . . . yes, I shall visit *him* next!"

"Visit him for what?" Eydryth demanded, mostly to stall for time, for she had a sick feeling that she already knew whereof the witch spoke.

"I must visit them all, my dear," Yachne said, in a mock-confiding tone. "All the abominations, all the unnatural creatures that possess Power without any right to it. Males!" She spat. "They hold my sisters in bondage, subject to their disgusting lusts, their violence and greed. There are enough males with undeserved Power to make me the most powerful sorceress this world has ever seen. Lord Kerovan, that disgusting half-blooded monster, shall indeed be next. . . ."

A face appeared before them, one that Eydryth knew well, black-haired, with amber eyes that were slitted of pupil, like unto a goat's. "And also his son, Firdun." The image in the crystal altered to that of Eydryth's foster-brother. "He is young, but *they* told me that he will be one of the Seven, so he *must* be taken care of. . . ."

"Who is 'they'? And what are 'the Seven'?" Alon broke in, sharply, but Yachne ignored him. Her eyes were half-closed as she dreamily regarded the images she was conjuring. "And of course I must not forget Simon Tregarth, and his unnatural whelps. . . ." Three strongly marked faces, one older, the next two so alike in age and feature they could only be brothers, appeared in turn.

"And then *you*, my dear young Alon, I am afraid that you must be next. . . ." Alon's own features glimmered before them. "I will be quick, my dear, so fear not. You will not suffer, that I promise. And if you wish, I shall let you remain alive, so you can be with your young lady, here." She smiled at him gently. "Perhaps you could take up farming, since you will no longer be fitted for a life as a sorcerer!"

"You're mad," Alon said softly, and, for the first time since they had met, Eydryth heard fear in his voice.

"Certainly not!" she glared at him, shaken out of her reverie. "I have thought it through most carefully. The strongest of the abominations is Hilarion himself, and I shall need all of your combined Power before I can best him."

A last image formed on the crystal surface, that of a man who was still barely past youth in feature, but whose eyes bore the wisdom—much of it sad—of ages past.

"Yachne," Alon said, and Eydryth could tell that he was fighting to keep his voice even, "where did you learn that spell? When I knew you—before—you did not possess such abilities."

She smiled at him. "My abilities were not something you could measure, my dear. But you have the right of it . . . I did not know this spell until *they* taught it to me."

"Who?" he prodded.

But abruptly her urge to confide vanished, and she shook her head, her eyes as bright and cunning as those of a rasti run mad. "No, I think not, young Alon. That you must discover for yourself—if you dare. And now—" Her hand moved quickly over the surface of the crystal, and she chanted softly beneath her breath. "—I bid you farewell. . . ."

As the last syllable left her lips, she strode toward them. Eydryth gasped with terror. Fighting she knew, either with fists or steel, but Yachne was something far outside her experience, and instinct made her recoil. She ducked behind Alon, despising herself for such cowardice but unable to control her reaction.

When she dared to look again, expecting to find the witch before them on the ledge, there was only the view of the empty stone cave. "But . . . where did she go?" she asked, in blank astonishment. "I thought she would step through and be *here*."

"She activated her side of the crystal," Alon said absently, standing before the mirrored surface and studying it, head tilted to one side. "She went through it, to somewhere else. Probably to seek out this Kerovan she spoke of."

"*Kerovan!* No . . . oh, no!" Eydryth buried her face in her hands, trying by force of will to control her panic. Finally she was able to raise her head and say, tersely, "Do you remember my telling you of the lord and lady who raised me after my mother vanished and my father was mind-blasted? That was Lord Kerovan and his lady, Joisan! Alon, we *must* stop Yachne!"

"If she has all of Dinzil's abilities, she will make a formidable opponent," he said bleakly.

"Who is—or, rather, *was*—this Dinzil?"

"The strongest of the Dark Adepts from the days when Escore lay under the lash of the Shadow," he told her. "He kidnapped and nearly seduced Kaththea, my foster-mother, when she was but a maid. Seduced her, not in body, but in mind, so she turned from her family, and the Light, to the Darkness. It was only by the courage of her brother, Kemoc, who dared to enter the Dark Tower and seek her out, that she was saved. Dinzil disappeared after his forces were defeated. We always suspected that he had passed through some Gate of his own devising."

"Until Yachne summoned him."

"Yes. This Kerovan, he is a sorcerer also?"

"Kerovan has, in the past, wielded the magic of the ancient gryphon-lord, Landisl," Eydryth said. "But he cannot rely upon Landisl's Power. He has abilities of his own, true, but whether they would prove enough to best one like Yachne . . ." She shuddered. "She is mad, Alon."

"Yes."

"If we cannot stop her, we must at least warn Kerovan of his danger!"

"I agree," Alon said. "But for us to essay *this* Gate will take some doing. I have never opened one before."

"Did Hilarion teach you to do so?"

"He taught me the principles involved. But he warned me against such an action, reminding me of the time that he opened a Gate, entered another world, then found himself trapped and enslaved for thousands of our years."

Eydryth remembered that Alon had mentioned such before, and bit her lip. "But to be able to step from one place to another—one *land* to another, in a single heartbeat—we must chance it! We have no hope of catching her, else."

"I know," he said heavily. "Let me study how this can be accomplished, while you pack our gear and prepare as hearty as a meal as possible. Using the Power drains the energy . . . food will offset that loss by a small measure."

Eydryth nodded, and, in the grey light of predawn, went to do as he bade. She found that she was too upset to have much appetite, but forced herself to eat, not knowing when they would have the chance again. Alon chewed and swallowed mechanically, never taking his eyes from the portal, occasionally muttering snatches of arcane words beneath his breath, as if trying them out.

"Eydryth," he said, as the sun's rising flushed the snow-capped peaks that towered above them to the east with crimson, "lend me that talisman you bear, please."

"Talisman . . . ," she repeated uncertainly; then, following his gaze, she drew her gryphon-hilted sword with its two bits of quan-iron embedded for eyes. "Here."

"There are ways and ways to open Gates," the young Adept said, "but since this one is made of crystal, I believe that it may be activated by sound. Crystals give off musical notes when struck." So saying, he tapped the center of the mirrored surface with the gryphon's head. A clear, ringing tone filled the air—a note holding some of the same eeriness as the faintly heard sound that had awakened the songsmith last night.

"Mmmmmmm . . . ," Alon sang, trying, without notable success, to match that tone. Not only was his voice too deep, his sense of pitch and key were far off the mark. He frowned, then turned to his companion. "My lady, can you sing that note?"

"It is high," she said, consideringly, "and I am an alto. But perhaps . . . Strike it again, please."

He did so, and Eydryth raised her voice. She fell far short of her goal. "I have not sung in days," she said, "but perhaps if I warm up . . ."

"Try," he urged.

The songsmith attempted several scales, and then, in a few minutes, when her throat improved, sang several songs to exercise her range. Alon grinned as she finished with "The One-Spell Wizard." "Let us hope that I have more than one spell to my name," he said dryly.

"Strike the crystal again," the bard ordered, and when he did so, her voice soared up, matching the note perfectly.

As Eydryth's voice hung in the air, the crystal glowed violet, bathing Alon's face and hands in its light. Something flashed outward from its surface, and he exclaimed with surprise to find himself holding a perfectly formed crystal, clear on one end, amethyst on the other. And yet, Eydryth realized with amazement, as she let the sound die away, the surface of the mirror remained unmarred!

"What is it?" she asked, as he examined the mirror's gift, holding it up to the sunlight so that it made prisms across his features.

"Our key for unlocking this Gate," he said. "I only hope it

works. Monso!" he called, and the Keplian, snorting warily, came over to him.

Alon reached out and caught the creature's long, thick forelock, then quickly began twisting and twining the horsehair around the crystal to anchor it against the stallion's forehead. "What are you doing?" Eydryth asked curiously.

"I won't leave Monso behind," he said. "We will need him, if we are to catch up with Yachne, who is traveling afoot."

Finally he was done, and the mirror's gift rested within a little bag twined from horsehair that hung between Monso's eyes. Alon then swung up into the saddle, offering a hand to the songsmith. He still held her quarterstaff in his right hand.

"When I sound the note," he instructed, "you must sing it, holding it as long as possible—no matter what you may see or feel, do not, I entreat you, stop, or all our lives may be forfeit!"

"I understand," she said steadily.

Urging Monso forward with his legs, Alon reached out toward the mirror. But the Keplian shied back from the strange surface, snorting. "Easy, easy lad," he soothed the beast. "I know that this is passing strange, but you must stand steady while I strike!"

Twice more did Alon urge the stallion forward, only to have him shy away at the last moment. "Monso!" Alon commanded, a commanding ring to his voice. "Get *hup!*"

The half-bred took a final reluctant step forward, to stand so close to the crystal surface that his breath misted across it like a cloud. Alon struck the surface with the gryphon's head, and Eydryth matched the tone and held it—

—held it—

—then saw before her the mirror's surface change, glow, as it became misty . . . translucent. "Go!" yelled Alon, bending down and slapping the stallion's neck hard.

With a startled grunt the Keplian surged forward, his sudden leap nearly unseating Eydryth. Almost her voice faltered, but she forced herself not to waver.

Before her the Keplian's forehooves disappeared into the amethyst smoke, then his muzzle, neck, shoulders. . . . Eydryth closed her eyes as the mist struck her face, bringing with it a vast dizziness and disorientation.

But she held the note steady, despite it all, and a moment later felt beneath her the shock of Monso's hooves striking solid rock.

They were in the witch's cavern.

With a sobbing breath, the songsmith finally relinquished the crystal's note, and gazed around her in despair. "Where are we? I thought we would go where Yachne went!"

Alon turned Monso, careful of the surrounding stone walls, to gaze at the mirror within the cavern. "To do that, we must go through *that* mirror," he said, sounding so exhausted that Eydryth wondered how he managed to sit upright upon the Keplian.

"Then let us go!" she urged.

He shook his head grimly. "At the moment, I do not believe that would be the wisest course," he said quietly.

"Whyever not?" she demanded, wanting to shake him in her impatience to warn her foster-father of his danger. "We must save Kerovan! We can't afford to waste time!"

"Do not forget that she is walking, while we will be riding," he reminded her. "And after such a major feat of sorcery as opening not one, but *two* Gates, I feel sure that Yachne must needs rest for today." Alon sighed wearily. "But, my lady, those are not my two most pressing reasons for wanting to wait."

"Then what are they?"

"This is the first," Alon said, and, dropping Monso's reins, made a pass through the air with the quarterstaff and muttered beneath his breath. He was using, Eydryth thought, the same words as Yachne had voiced.

Obediently the mirror came to life, glowing with a sickly blackish-purple radiance that made Eydryth turn her head away with a cry of dismay. "This mirror represents the Darkside of the moon-crystal we leaped through. For us to use it to get to Arvon may be exceedingly dangerous."

"To our spirits," the songsmith agreed, through stiff lips. Seeing that eerie phosphorescent glow, she could well believe that he spoke truth.

"Even so."

"But Alon, we will have to risk it! Arvon is hundreds of leagues away, across the sea! We could never track Yachne in time, otherwise!"

"You may have the right of it," he agreed. "But do not forget that there is a second reason not to go immediately. . . ."

"Which is?" she asked, conscious suddenly of a great tiredness in her own body. It seemed all she could do to hold on to Alon's belt.

"I will show you." He reined Monso around and walked the Keplian out of the mouth of the cave, down a rocky trail, until they rounded a bend and stood upon a mountainside.

The sun was rising against the eastern horizon, with no mountains to block its rays. Alon indicated the surrounding countryside. "We are in Escore, my lady. If I am not mistaken, where we sit is not more than a half-day's ride from the Valley of the Green Silences."

"Dahaun's Valley!" Eydryth said, remembering their discussion with Nolar and Duratan. "The place of healing!"

"Yes. I have known about that Valley since I was a youth, of course, but I could not reveal my knowledge of such without giving myself away to you," he said ruefully. "So I made shift to 'discover' that scroll in Nolar's study."

"When all the time you knew!" she said, giving him a mock glare. "But is it true? Can the Lady Dahaun heal my father?"

"I cannot be sure. On one edge of the Valley lies a place of healing. There are pools of a red mud there that can overcome any injury or sickness. Death, if a victim can but reach that spot, has no power there. Whether Dahaun's red mud will work on an injury of the mind . . ." He shrugged. "I know not."

"But Kerovan . . . Yachne . . ." She made a helpless gesture. "She will destroy him if we do not stop her!"

"Are you prepared to give up your quest, sacrifice your father's chance to be healed in order to save this Lord Kerovan?"

Eydryth stared bleakly out over the rolling green hills of

Escore, feeling as though her heart had been ruthlessly seized by unseen hands and was being pulled apart within her breast. *Blessed Gunnora, what shall I do? I cannot choose between one and the other! I cannot! Amber Lady, help me!*

Nine

"*I* cannot choose between them," Eydryth said numbly. She gave him a despairing glance. "No one could make such a choice!"

"No one should have to," Alon agreed. "And I believe that there exists a way to save both of them. If we can reach the Valley of the Green Silences today, we can collect some of Dahaun's healing mud to carry with us, then go back through the gate tomorrow. With Monso's speed, we should be able to catch Yachne before she can harm your Kerovan."

"We do not know how much of Arvon she may have to cross before she reaches Kar Garudwyn," Eydryth said.

"She may not have to travel there," Alon warned. "I think

it more likely that she will seek out a place of the Shadow and work a summoning spell to draw him to her, as she did with Dinzil."

"Arvon has many such places," Eydryth whispered. "It is a gamble, Alon. If we are wrong, Kerovan's life may well be forfeit, and Yachne may well have such Power as to be nigh invincible."

"It is a gamble, yes," he agreed. "But I cannot leave Escore without warning my people. They are in terrible danger, too, never forget."

"Will the valley dwellers be able to carry the message to those the witch plans to harm?"

"Yes. Dahaun has birds that she trains to bear messages to Es City and all the different places in Escore, in case of any troubling in the land. Also, Kyllan is mind-linked with his brother, Kemoc, and his sister, Kaththea, and so may be able to warn them that way."

Eydryth straightened, feeling the muscles in her back and neck ache with the movement. "Let us go, then. We have no time to lose."

Alon nudged Monso with his heels and the Keplian began picking his way down the mountain slope. It was fortunate that the Gate on this side of the mountain range had deposited them far lower in the craggy heights than the one they had leaped through in Estcarp. Before they had gone a mile, they struck on a winding game trail that led downward to rolling hills. As they traveled, the songsmith kept a sharp lookout for any trace of Dinzil, but the suddenly aged sorcerer was nowhere to be seen.

Their last descent was a particularly precipitous scramble down a steep and muddy path, and, when they had negotiated it safely, Alon drew rein to allow Monso to breathe. Eydryth gazed around her, seeing no sign of anything living save a herd of pronghorns grazing on the spring turf of the next hillside. "What do you think happened to Dinzil?" she asked.

Alon hooked a leg up over the pommel of the saddle and turned sideways so he could regard her. "I do not believe that one such as Dinzil could face living as an ordinary man. If he truly was bereft of all his power, then I would wager that he lies now at the bottom of some cliff, free from his weak and aged body."

The songsmith nodded. "You are probably—"

She broke off with a startled cry, ducking as something black suddenly dived at them from the sky above. The creature gave a piercing scream as it glided by, turning toward them again, and Eydryth recognized the white V on its breast. "Steel Talon!" she cried. "He found us!"

Alon held out his arm, bracing himself, and, with another screech, the bird landed on that improvised perch. The Adept winced as the creature's talons dug into the leather of his sleeve. The falcon regarded each of the humans, first with one golden eye, then, cocking its head, with the other. Steel Talon cried out again, his wickedly hooked bill seeming suddenly far too close to Eydryth's eyes.

"We forgot him," she said, guiltily. "He is angry with us."

"I did not forget him," Alon said, as much to the falcon as to her. "I knew he would find us. He has been with me long enough so that he can sense my mind, even though I am not a Falconer. Those warriors can truly communicate mind-to-mind with their birds, but it does not require close contact for the bird simply to sense my whereabouts."

Eydryth spoke to the falcon as though the bird could understand her. "Winged warrior," she said, "I am sorry that we did not offer you the chance to travel through the Gate with us. But it was not a comfortable journey, I assure you. Doubtless flying over those mountains was much more to your liking."

"If he wishes to accompany us tomorrow, he will have to go through the Gate with us," Alon said. "He could not possibly follow us across two continents and an ocean—to the other side of the world."

"How can we manage to carry him?" she asked, dubiously eyeing the falcon's rending beak and sharp talons.

"With difficulty, I am sure," Alon said. "I will strive to communicate the problem to him tonight, with Dahaun to help me. She can mind-speak nearly any creature."

As he finished speaking, the falcon stretched out his wings, and, with a quick motion of his arm, Alon helped him launch himself skyward. Monso's breathing had slowed and calmed, so they set off again. Steel Talon wheeled in the sky above them, flying so high at times that he seemed naught but a pinprick of black against the blueness.

The slopes before them now were grassy and gently rolling, so Alon put the Keplian into a steady canter. They were headed due north, Eydryth realized, judging their direction from the position of the sun. She relaxed into the stallion's gait, balancing easily on those powerful haunches, feeling the rhythmic push and glide beneath her. Before long the steady motion had lulled her into a near-doze.

Finally, they struck on a dirt road, well-traveled by the looks of it. "Not far to go now," Alon said, and she straightened. "I am going to let him run a little," he warned. "So hold on!" He loosened the rein and Monso immediately surged into a full gallop—and then the Keplian, with a snort, fought to get a free head; his strides came faster and faster yet!

"Easy . . . easy, Monso . . . ," Alon said, but the horse only increased speed again.

"Can you hold him?" she cried, alarmed, only to have her words whipped away by the wind of their passage.

Eydryth clung to her companion's belt, resting her head against Alon's back and half-closing her eyes as the landscape flashed by them so fast it made her dizzy. This was the first time she had ridden Monso at a run in daylight, and the half-bred's speed both excited and frightened her. She could feel Alon's back muscles bunch against her cheek as he struggled to regain full control. He spoke softly to the beast, all the while striving with every bit of horsemanship he possessed to keep the Keplian from breaking loose and running totally free.

Finally, the creature's pace slackened slightly, and Alon again had full mastery. He turned his head slightly. "Are you still with me, lady songsmith?"

"Yes," Eydryth managed to gasp. "But when he goes like that . . . I cannot help but be frightened."

"You think I am not?" he retorted. "There is a wildness in his nature at such times that harkens back to the demon-

creature that foaled him. . . ." He was panting himself with the
effort to control the Keplian. "He sensed our urgency, also."

The Keplian's mad run had brought them a far distance, for
the mountains now were only craggy silhouettes behind them.
Before them lay a land where green fields sprouted their crops
and tidy farmsteads lay scattered. Eydryth had thought Escore
a very empty land in comparison to Arvon, and the sight of
those farms reassured her. She remembered Alon's saying that
the two lands had once been one. *That much have been long
and long ago, indeed,* she thought. Her mind reeled at the idea
of so many, many years.

The road led them toward two craggy ridges that did not
quite meet, forming a narrow pass in their midst. Alon slowed
Monso still more, until they were traveling at a slow, collected
canter.

As the travelers reached the shadowing heights of the pass,
Eydryth saw symbols etched deep into the ocher rockface of
each flanking cliff. Several of those incised markings were
close enough to runes from the Old Tongue that she recognized them. One of them she whispered softly as they passed
it, feeling relief and sense of peace steal over her, for it was a
powerful ward against the Dark.

"Euythayan . . . ," she breathed.

"Yes," Alon said, barely turning his head to make reply.
"Until the day that Dinzil betrayed the Valley by stealing
away Kaththea, none of the People of the Green Silences
thought that any harm could befall them here. It was a blow
to them to discover that their protections could be broken."

"Dinzil must have been a powerful Adept indeed," Eydryth
said, troubled exceedingly by this revelation.

"He was," Alon said, and then, evidently guessing her
thoughts, he added, "And now Yachne, if she has his Power,
might also be able to overcome the Valley's wards."

As they went on, the crags dropped away, and so did the
road. Then they rounded a gentle downward curve, and Eydryth found herself looking out across a vast valley.

It was so green! Lush with grass and flowers, shaded by
great trees, it seemed a dream of beauty that called out to her

weary spirit, as though she had come to a second home. The sight of the Valley of the Green Silences seemed to relieve and ease the songsmith's weary, anxious spirit, even as a healer's balm may ease a wound. Eydryth found herself running snatches of notes and words through her mind, in hopes that she could someday capture some of the loveliness of this place in a song.

Dwellings dotted the Valley, though they could not be termed "houses," for they grew out of the earth itself, their circular walls being formed of tree trunks or flowering bushes. Their peaked roofs were thatched with vivid blue-green feathers. As the travelers cantered slowly down the road, people came out of the houses. Many waved to Alon, and he returned their greeting, but he did not draw rein until they had reached the largest of the dwellings. As Monso halted, the doorway, which was curtained by flowering vines, moved aside, and a man came out, followed a moment later by a woman. *Lord Kyllan and Lady Dahaun*, Eydryth thought.

Both wore soft tunics and breeches of a spring green, with belts and wristlets of pale gold studded with blue-green gems. Kyllan was tall and broad-shouldered, with the air of one who has ridden to arms many times. In that way he reminded Eydryth of her father, Jervon; he had the same air of one who is accustomed to command. Physically, though, he was plainly of the Old Race, though his jaw was wider and his mouth held more than a touch of humor about it. Eydryth recalled that his father, Simon Tregarth, was reportedly an outlander, who had come from some distant world through one of the legendary Gates.

As the Lady of the Green Silences stepped forward, the girl's eyes widened in surprise. She gazed at her, blinked, then frankly stared. Never had she seen her like before!

Tall and slender, she seemed as graceful as a willow in her green tunic. Eydryth's eyes fastened on her face. Her hair was as pale gold as the metal of her wristlet . . . no, it was the color of new-smelted copper . . . no, it was as black as Eydryth's own . . . no, no, it was the green of the new spring leaves. . . .

The harder the songsmith stared, the more the woman's

coloring and features seemed to blur and change. She was many women . . . and all of them beautiful.

"Alon!" Dahaun exclaimed, stretching forth both her hands in warm and gracious greeting. "Oh, well-come indeed! You have returned to us!"

"Greetings, Lady . . . Kyllan," the Adept said. "I but wish that my visit were simply a visit, but, in truth, I come in haste, on a matter of great urgency." He turned in the saddle to give the songsmith a steadying grip as she slid off the Keplian, then swung down himself. Catching the minstrel's hand, he drew her forward. "But first, Dahaun, I must present my companion, the Lady Songsmith Eydryth."

With a gracious yet courtly air, the Lady inclined her head and reached to take the girl's hand in both of hers. "Be welcome to our home, Eydryth," she said warmly. "This is my lord, Kyllan." As the Lady of the Green Silences touched the girl's hand, her features steadied, until her face was oval, her eyes grey, her hair black. She now was as plainly of the Old Race as was her lord, Kyllan.

"Good fortune to your home, Lady Dahaun, now and evermore," Eydryth said, altering the traditional greeting a trifle. In no wise could one call this bower of living trees and vines a *house*.

The Lady released her guest's hand, and her features again took on that uncanny shifting, as her lord, Kyllan, also stepped forward to greet the songsmith. Then Tregarth turned back to Alon, who was standing with Monso's rein over his arm. He smiled with a touch of ruefulness. "If that were an ordinary mount you hold, Alon, I would offer to tend him for you, but perhaps that would not be wise of me."

Alon grinned. "My foster-mother has told me that you have no reason to love Keplians, having once almost been undone by one of Monso's breed. I will tend him myself."

Dahaun (once more her hair was as green as her garb) smiled mischievously at her lord. "Do not forget what a great gift the Keplian brought you that day so long ago, my lord. Had it not been for him, we two might never have met!"

He inclined his head. "For which I give heartfelt thanks

every day, my lady. Still, I have often thought that there must be easier ways for a man to first encounter his future bride than to have nearly every bone in his body smashed by a demon-horse!"

Turning back to her guest, the Lady said, "Take off your mount's saddle and bridle, Alon. Monso will be fine, here, will you not, my beauty?" She reached a slender hand toward the creature's forehead, then her eyes widened. "What is this?" she exclaimed.

Alon's fingers began separating the long strands of Monso's forelock. "The crystal I braided into his forelock, so we could open the Gate," he said. "I forgot all about it in our haste to reach you. But . . . but it has changed! What—?" he broke off in wonder as his questing fingers worked the amethyst-shaded crystal free of the Keplian's long forelock. "Look!" he cried, holding it out for all of them to see.

Instead of a netting of black horsehair, the shard from the mirror now lay encased in a delicate webbing of purest silver. "It must have transmuted when we leaped through," Alon whispered.

Dahaun put out a hand, but stopped short of actually laying finger to the crystal. "It is a powerful talisman," she said. Turning to her lord, she pulled free the silver cord that laced the top of his green tunic. Threading the cord through the net of silver, she formed a pendant from it. This she placed solemnly over Alon's head, so it hung down beneath the neck of his tunic. "Keep it always, and may it protect you from all manner of evil," she said quietly.

Then the Lady of the Green Silences turned back to the Keplian. "Leave Monso here," she repeated. "He will be fine." The black snorted, then bobbed his head up and down, exactly as if nodding agreement.

Quickly, Alon freed the stallion to graze, then the travelers followed their host and hostess into the dwelling.

Within, screens made of living vines or woven of feathers made rooms, and the floor was carpeted with soft living moss. Light filtered greenly through the roof and walls, making the interior pleasantly restful. When Alon would have launched immediately into their story, Dahaun stayed his words with a swift gesture. "Your story will wait a few minutes more," she said, waving Eydryth toward one alcove, while Kyllan took the young Adept's arm and steered him toward another. "You have been on the road for long and long, and need to rest, if only for a short while. Besides, we must summon the scouts to hear your tale firsthand, if they must needs carry it to others."

Alon nodded, albeit a bit reluctantly.

Eydryth followed the Lady into a room containing two pools, one holding water tinged red with mud, the other filled with clear water. Now that she was actually here, lack of sleep and food made her so weary she stumbled as she walked. Dahaun indicated the red-colored pool, and said, "This one first, Lady Eydryth."

Stripping off her travel-grimed clothes, the songsmith sank gratefully into the warm pool. Dahaun gathered up her stained breeches, tunic, and jerkin, promising to see that they were cleaned for use on the morrow, then left the girl to her bath. The red-tinged water was blissfully hot, and its touch revived her so completely that she felt all weariness and hunger vanishing. This pool, she thought, must share the restorative and healing abilities of the red mud pools Alon had spoken of earlier today.

Finishing off with a thorough rinse in the clear pool, she then donned the clothes her hostess had left, soft tunics, breeches and boots like unto the ones Dahaun and Kyllan wore.

When the girl emerged, feeling vastly more energetic, it was to find Alon, garbed like herself, sitting with a man of Dahaun's race, Ethutur, talking quietly. The Lord of the Green Silences also possessed the shape-shifting ability, though not as much as Dahaun. Two small, ivory horns rose from his forehead, nearly hidden by the loose curls of his ever-changing-hued hair.

No sooner had the songsmith been introduced and seated herself upon one of the moss-grown hummocks that served as cushions on the floor than the Lady herself returned. Dahaun was accompanied by two tall children who were carrying plat-

ters of food and drink, and by two men who wore the battered
boots and light mail of couriers or scouts. One of the men was
a giant who towered above the other.

Kyllan introduced the two men as the Valley's scouts,
Yonan and Urik. Yonan was of middle height, and evidently
descended from some Sulcar ancestor, if Eydryth guessed
aright. The giant was Urik.

The boy and girl (they appeared to be perhaps five years
younger than the songsmith herself) Kyllan identified as his
and Dahaun's twin children. Elona, the girl, had inherited
something of her mother's shape-changing ability, for whenever Eydryth gazed upon her, her features gradually took on
subtle shifts of shape, and her hair and eyes seemed to darken
and lighten, though not to the extent that Dahaun's did. Keris,
the boy, resembled his father, and his features did not change.
Nor did he have the horns of the Green Men.

Dahaun waved at the crisply baked rounds of thin bread,
wedges of cheese and an assortment of fruits and early vegetables. "Can you eat as you talk?"

Alon was already reaching for a piece of fruit. "If we cannot, we will take turns," he said. "I met this wandering songsmith while I was racing Monso in a village called Rylon
Corners. . . ."

He continued telling about how he had met Eydryth, while
the minstrel busied herself with the food. Then, when he came
to the reason for her quest, he nodded to his companion, and
she quickly explained about her search for a means to heal her
father. "Alon wondered whether the red mud that is to be
found within this Valley might not help," she concluded, giving the Lady an inquiring glance.

Dahaun's ever-shifting features were grave as she considered the girl's query. "I do not know," she said softly,
"whether the mud will heal ills of the mind and spirit as well
as those of the body. Never has it been so tested. But you are
welcome to take some with you and try."

"Thank you, Lady."

"But Eydryth's quest is but the half of it," Alon said, after
swallowing a last bite of food. "Last night, she was awakened
by a strange noise that I could not hear. . . ."

He continued, telling the strange tale of their journey to the ancient mirror-Gate, and of Yachne and her Power-stealing spell.

Kyllan's expression darkened when he heard the identity of the ancient sorcerer the witch had bested. "Dinzil!" he exclaimed. "I thought that one forever gone, or dead."

"Which he may well be, by now," Alon said, then he proceeded to tell Tregarth of the threat to all males possessing Power. "She called us things against nature, abominations," he finished, finally. "Yachne intends to make herself the most powerful sorceress the world has ever known."

"Where could she have come from?" Dahaun wondered aloud.

"From some of the things she said, I believe that she was once a witch of Estcarp," Eydryth said, and Alon nodded agreement. "One of the ones whose Power was broken when she made herself a vessel to channel the magic during the Turning."

"When she had the raising of you, did she ever refer to being a witch?" Kyllan asked Alon.

The younger man shook his head. "She was certainly a Wise Woman, but I would have sworn she had not the ability to perform such a summoning as we witnessed," he said thoughtfully. "Opening a Gate is, as I discovered for myself today, no easy task. The Yachne that I knew before could scry, and sense the presence of the Shadow, and heal, using herbs and such. Minor magics, at best. She was no sorceress."

"Where did she learn that spell, then?" Eydryth mused. "She said that someone had taught it to her. . . . but who?"

"Perhaps she lied, and actually uncovered it in some musty old scroll in Lormt," Alon speculated, then he sighed. "But however she learned it, it makes little difference. The danger to us is real."

"I will contact Kaththea and Kemoc immediately," Kyllan said. "And tomorrow morn my lady wife will release her messenger birds to carry the news across the mountains to my father, Simon, at Etsford."

"If only I had the Power," Eydryth murmured softly. "Then I might be able to warn Kerovan tonight."

"Tomorrow will be soon enough," Dahaun reassured her. "It is nearly sunset already . . . it will be dawn before you know it."

Eydryth nodded, knowing the Lady of the Green Silences strove only to comfort her, but she was restless. The restorative effects of the red pool had worked only too well. . . . She was too full of energy to sleep. Rising, she went outside, seeing Monso grazing on the lush grass, and Steel Talon perched in a tree not far from the stallion. A few minutes later, Alon followed her out, carrying both their swordbelts. "Time for my lesson," he reminded her.

Eydryth was only too glad to have something to take up her thoughts, and together they practiced his one lunge and parry. Adding to Alon's small store of knowledge, the songsmith then demonstrated a backhand parry, and they practiced that. Before they were done, Kyllan came out to tell them that Yonan and Urik had just set off, to ride with the warning to the settlement of the Old Race who had lived in Karsten before the Horning that had turned them into refugees. But now the former Karstenians were firmly established in this new—and, at the same time, ancient—land.

His news given, Tregarth lingered, observing the lesson. "You are a good teacher," Kyllan said to the bard when she and her student had parted, each to regain lost breath. "He has definitely mastered that lunge."

"Unfortunately, that is the only move I *have* mastered," Alon said ruefully, wiping sweat from his brow. "But one is better than none, I suppose."

Handing her sword to Kyllan, Eydryth encouraged Tregarth to coach her student. The older man readily did so, proving an able swordsman—probably, Eydryth thought, the equal of Jervon before his accident.

As if in response to her thought of her father and his plight, Dahaun appeared through the gathering dusk, holding out to the songsmith a small wood box that appeared to be sealed with wax or resin. This she put into Eydryth's hands. "Some of the healing mud," she said. "Be careful not to break the seal until you are ready to use it."

Clutching it, Eydryth ran trembling fingers over the top of the box. Could this really be the means to heal Jervon? "Lady," she said, her voice nigh to breaking, "I thank you. . . . I am so grateful. . . ."

"We are the ones who are in your debt," Dahaun assured her. "I only pray that the mud will work. You must smooth it over his brow and scalp, and allow it to dry before chipping it free."

"I will do so," the girl replied. "And thank you again, my lady."

Dahaun smiled at her. "It is I who owe you for the warning that may have saved my lord," she said. "Be very sure that we shall guard against this Yachne and her foul spells. Power rightfully belongs to whomever possesses it and wields it responsibly. It is not for her to say yea or nay as to who may work magic."

Eydryth nodded solemn agreement.

They left the Valley in the predawn darkness, with saddlebags replenished from Dahaun's larder. Monso snorted eagerly, seeming anxious to be on the way again, and they made a speedy return to Yachne's cave, arriving by midmorning.

"Do you remember how she opened the Gate?" Eydryth asked, as they dismounted outside the entrance. Steel Talon glided down from a nearby hillock to perch on the stallion's saddlebow. "Do you remember what she chanted?"

"I listened carefully," Alon replied, frowning, then he shrugged, as if unsure of his memory. "And last night I made notes of what I recalled and studied them. We can only hope that my efforts will serve. We cannot know until we make the attempt."

Once within the confines of the cavern, he drew forth a short wand from one of the saddlebags. "Elder," he said, holding it up for his companion's inspection. "Used for the darker and more powerful spells."

Quickly, he began sketching another pentagram on the floor of the cavern, in much the same manner as Yachne had. "But you are not going to summon anyone!" Eydryth protested.

"True, but I must follow the ritual exactly as she did. I know not what element will open the Gate," he told her. "She did no spell of opening, such as I did, only spoke the final words to the dark mirror. Therefore something in her spell to undo Dinzil must have awakened the Gate, tapped its power, then left it waiting to function."

Quickly, he set out candles Dahaun had supplied, lit them with a wave of his hand. "What will you use for blood?" the songsmith asked fearfully.

"My own," he said.

"But doing so may weaken you too much!" she protested. "Use mine, Alon."

Stubbornly, he shook his head. "I cannot use another living creature's blood to work spells. If I needs must work Dark spells, then I will work them as cleanly as I can . . . lest the very working blacken my spirit beyond redemption."

"Alon, do not be a fool! You need your strength to open that Gate! If you use my blood you will be taking from me only what I freely offer! That will not stain you!"

"No," he maintained, and she could glimpse the stubborn gleam in his eyes. "My own blood will I use, and no other."

Eydryth did not argue further, only drew her knife and deeply nicked her own wrist, then held it out to him. "Here."

He gave her an angry glare, but she shook her arm at him so that red spattered the rocky floor around them. "Don't waste it!"

Without further argument, he seized her wrist in his hands and began to chant softly, allowing the trickling blood to form an enclosing circle. Before many heartbeats had passed, Eydryth began to feel weak from the steady draining, but she forced herself to mask her dizziness. When they were about two-thirds of the way around the circle, though, she stumbled. In answer Alon's fingers clamped hard over the slash, and he muttered softly under his breath. The bleeding slowed and stopped.

"Go and bandage that," he ordered, "then get Steel Talon and Monso ready to go. Don't speak to me again until the spell is complete . . . I will need full concentration." Then,

drawing his own belt knife, he nicked his own wrist deeply and
set to completing the circle of blood.

As he finished, his chant grew louder. . . . Slowly, inexora-
bly, the candles began to darken. The words Alon was mouth-
ing now made Eydryth's head spin. She wanted to cover her
ears, just as she had before, hearing Yachne. The Adept's own
lips twisted as he spoke, as though the words he pronounced
tasted of bile.

The very air within the cavern grew as dark as the candles,
curdling with foulness, murky with unseen shapes. Horrors
seemed to gibber from the shadows, but every time Eydryth
turned to look, there was nothing there. Resolutely, she forced
herself to ignore them, and Alon, also.

Quickly she checked the fastenings of Monso's saddlebags,
fastened her quarterstaff into place beneath the stirrup on the
horse's off side; then she spread her cloak on the stony floor.
"It is time, Steel Talon," she said to the falcon still perched
atop the pommel of the saddle.

With a harsh screech, the bird glided down and stood upon
the cloak. Eydryth gathered up the edges, folding them up
around the bird, thus protecting her flesh from those raking
talons, that sharp beak. With the swathed falcon in her arms,
she straightened up, turning to regard the Adept, only to see
Alon, his head thrown back, a dark shadow half-obscuring his
features, voice a last, loud call that she recognized from
Yachne's attempt.

The sound of that terrifying summons coming from her
companion's throat was enough to send the girl stumbling
back against Monso's side. The Keplian rolled his eyes, trembling violently.

Slowly, the deep, shadow-shot purple expanse of the dark
mirror glowed foully to life. Their Gate was open.

Alon turned to regard his accomplishment with a look of
such revulsion stamped across his features that Eydryth cried
out in dismay. Then he staggered over into the corner of the
cave and was thoroughly sick, heaving as though he could
physically expel from his spirit the stain that Yachne's incan-
tation had left there. Finally, shaking, his features as waxy as

the candles he had used (candles, Eydryth noted with part of her mind, that were now as pitchy black as they had been white before), he straightened, wiping his mouth on his sleeve.

He spat one final time, then, obviously holding himself erect by force of will, walked over to Monso and mounted. Grimly, he held out his hand for the bundle that was Steel Talon, and, when the songsmith handed it to him, he hugged the falcon's shrouded form against his chest.

"Can you get up?" he asked. He smiled a shaky, apologetic smile. "I seem to be short of hands to aid you, at the moment."

"As long at Monso doesn't kick, I can," she said.

"No, he would not kick you," he assured her.

Stepping behind the stallion, the songsmith patted his rump. "Easy, boy." Then she backed away a few paces and came forward again at a run to vault neatly up over the Keplian's rump into her accustomed position behind Alon.

"Very nice," Alon said, admiration lightening the sick weariness that tinged his voice. "That is a feat I never learned."

"Obred, the Kioga herd-master, taught me," she said absently.

"And now for Arvon . . . I hope," he whispered. "Hold tight."

He urged the Keplian forward.

With a squeal of fear, the stallion plunged beneath them, back humping in protest. Alon shouted a harsh order, heels thumping against the creature's sides. Still the horse resisted, shaking his head and snorting with terror. The smell of his fear-sweat was rank in Eydryth's nostrils.

"Get *up!*" Alon shouted, then followed the order with a curse that made Eydryth gasp. His heels rammed his mount's sides again, even as he slashed the reins savagely across the black's neck, whipping him hard.

With a suddenness that sent Eydryth's head snapping painfully back, Monso launched himself at the Gate.

Their first such crossing had been disturbing enough, but this one was agony. A great shadow seemed to envelop them, and they hung suspended in a darkness so profound that Eydryth feared she had been blinded by it.

Her spirit quailed before the sense of evil, of *wrongness* that this Gate held. She found that her mouth was open as she tried desperately to scream, but no sound emerged. It was like the worst of nightmares, where the dreamer struggles vainly to awaken—except that she *knew* this was no dream.

How long that passage took—minutes, years, centuries—she could not tell. But at last she heard Monso's hooves strike hard ground with a thump, even as the world reappeared around them.

In the west, the sun was setting—and it had been well before noon in Escore! Eydryth stared around her, noting the colors and varieties of vegetation, the shapes of the distant mountains, then sniffed the air. "We did it," she said, softly. "This is Arvon."

"Good," Alon said, grim with exhaustion. He halted Monso, then slipped off him, murmuring apologies for having whipped him. "I am sorry, son," he whispered, then stooped to lay Eydryth's cloak on the ground. Steel Talon shook himself free, then flew to the branch of a nearby oak, screeching an ear-piercing protest against such a form of travel.

Numb, the songsmith slipped off the Keplian's back, then stood trembling, watching Alon repentently stroke his horse. Monso shoved his nose against him with a soft nicker.

"That was terrible," Eydryth whispered, when her voice was once more under her control—barely. "I could never do that again . . . *never.*"

"Nor could I," Alon agreed, soberly. His face was set in new, harsh lines, making him appear far older, far harder than he had only yesterday. "If it weren't for Yachne, we would never have had to take such a desperate route. When I catch up to her, she will pay for this."

"Will we able to capture her? And, if we do, is there some way she can be stripped of that terrible spell?" Eydryth asked, shivering as she remembered the witch's power.

"If there is, I don't know it," Alon said grimly. A cold, hating glint awakened in his eyes, disturbing Eydryth profoundly. His voice rang out suddenly with the strength of one taking a sacred vow. "But worry not. After I find her, I swear to every god that is and ever was that she will present no further threat to anyone!"

Eydryth stared at him in horror. "Surely you do not mean . . . ," she began, only to have him nod, his mouth naught but a grim slash.

"Oh, but I do," he said softly, in a cold voice so cruel that the songsmith backed away a step. "When I find her, I intend to kill her." He slanted a warning look at his companion. "And don't even think about trying to stop me, Lady Songsmith."

Ten

*T*he countryside around them was wild and empty of any sign of humankind. Steel Talon soared off into a sky shading into the purples of late evening, presumably searching for a place to sleep through the night. As the travelers rode across fields of tough, pale green grass, they saw no roads, no paths save game trails. This portion of Arvon seemed uninhabited, in contrast to the countryside Eydryth knew.

"We must be far to the northwest of Kar Garudwyn," she said, tilting back on the Keplian's rump to study the emerging stars, using them to gauge their relative location. "My father and I did not go far into the northwest because we were told that it was largely deserted, and such seems to be the case."

They passed no farmsteads, no villages, saw no distant lights. Herds of pronghorns and deer stared at them curiously, not particularly alarmed at their presence. "Man is not a predator they know," Alon observed. "We are indeed far from any villages or farmsteads. How far do you think we are from Kar Garudwyn?"

"Four days' ride—perhaps more—but that is only a guess," she replied. "If my reckoning is correct, we should strike the edge of Bluemantle lands late tomorrow or early the next day. Then we will make better time, traveling the roads."

"Perhaps we should not go to Kar Garudwyn immediately. Perhaps we should seek Yachne first," he suggested.

Eydryth shifted position, trying unsuccessfully to ease the sore muscles in her thighs and buttocks and sighed deeply. "No," she said, after a moment's consideration. "We must go to Kar Garudwyn first."

"Why?" he challenged. "Yachne is the threat. The sooner I deal with her, the sooner your foster-father will be safe."

Eydryth repressed a shudder as she remembered precisely *how* her companion proposed to "deal" with the renegade witch. But she forced herself to mask her feelings as she responded, evenly, "Because if we can but reach Kar Garudwyn, there is a Place of Power nearby, where Kerovan can seek refuge. It is called the Setting Up of the Kings. From what I know of the workings of magic, if Kerovan went there, Yachne's summoning spell could not pull him away; he would be protected."

"If it is a place of great Power, that could be true," Alon conceded reluctantly.

"Also," the songsmith added, "after Kerovan is safe, we would then have help in our search for Yachne."

"What kind of help?" he asked, skeptically.

"My foster-sister, Hyana, could probably scry out the witch's whereabouts. Then Joisan and Sylvya would ride with us to seek her. All of them are Wise Women to be reckoned with."

Alon's only reply was a noncommittal grunt. Eydryth bit her lip, concerned about him. This surly, brooding man seemed not at all the companion she had been coming to regard as a friend during the past six days. *Can it be only six days?* she wondered, dazedly. *It seems as though I have known him forever. . . .*

They halted for the night only when it grew so dark (the moon would not rise until long after midnight) that even Monso and Alon were having difficulty picking a path, and Eydryth had been riding blind for a long time. They camped in a meadow that was surrounded on three sides by forest some distance away. Tall growths of tangled wild rosebushes shielded them from the brisk northern breeze, their blossoming fragrance pervading the air, heady and sweet.

By the time they had unpacked and tended the Keplian, the travelers were almost too tired to eat, themselves. Hastily they swallowed a cold meal, since Eydryth advised against lighting a fire. "It would be best not to flaunt our presence," she cautioned Alon as they spread out their bedrolls.

"Why?" Alon said. "We have seen no sign of anyone but ourselves. Every land has its brigands, but would outlaws roam so far from homesteads and villages?"

"I know not," she said quietly. "My concern lies with the possible presence of other . . . dangers. Arvon, like Escore, holds perils for the unwary." She glanced cautiously around her. "Perhaps we should stand watches."

"Monso will warn if anyone comes," Alon pointed out. "If we are to make good time on the morrow, we will need a full night's sleep." Eydryth agreed, knowing that any animal's senses were far superior to her own.

But even though she was weary, snuggled warmly in her cloak and blankets, slumber eluded the songsmith, chased away by her uneasy thoughts, and questions that only time would answer. *Will Dahaun's red mud cure my father? Will we reach Kerovan in time to warn him? Will our warning be enough to save him, or will Yachne be able to summon him to her no matter where he may be, or how we try to protect him?*

And lastly, and most worrisome of all: *Alon is changing before my eyes. He is suspicious and morose . . . not himself.*

Why? And, more importantly, what can I do to halt what is happening?

Her eyelids were finally growing heavy. With a sigh, Eydryth let them close. . . .

She awakened with a start when Monso snorted loudly. It seemed that sleep had only claimed her for a moment, but the waning moon had risen, shedding a pallid light over the meadow. Eydryth lay in her blankets, every sense alert, listening. Monso snorted again. Last year's dead grass and bushes crackled as he pawed restlessly.

The songsmith turned her head on her arm, moving slowly, as if she still slept, but her eyes were open, scanning the distant woods, the field surrounding them. In the darkness, nothing moved. Nothing . . . for many heartbeats, nothing. . . .

Then, at the corner of her vision, something flickered. Alarmed now, Eydryth sat up, straining her eyes in the dim moonlight. Many faintly glowing shapes were drifting toward their campsite, borne on the night breeze. The songsmith reached for her companion's shoulder, nudged it. "Alon!" she whispered.

He awoke with a start, then sat up. "What . . . what is it?"

"Rouse you! Danger!"

As he rubbed blearily at his eyes, still groggy with sleep, Eydryth threw aside her blanket, pulled on her boots, then picked up the quarterstaff that lay beside her. With one swift movement, her sword was in her hand. She stood poised and ready.

Once more she attempted to discern what those wafting shapes were. They glowed a sickly greenish color against the distant blackness of the forest, a green shot through with streaks of pale purple. Eydryth had seen slime growths on the walls of caves glow eerily in just the same way. What could these floating creatures be?

Monso suddenly sounded a stallion's shrill battle-challenge, teeth bared to snap, forelegs ready to strike. The Keplian's nostrils flared widely; then he snorted again, as though he scented something noxious. Eydryth hastily fastened a lead-shank to the stallion's halter, then tied him to a scrubby tree beside their packs.

By the time she finished, Alon was on his feet—boots on, sword out and ready. As they stood together, his shoulder brushed Eydryth's; for a moment she fought the urge to lean against him, take his hand. Human comfort seemed very desirable in the face of the strange creatures bobbing ever closer to them. "What is it?" he whispered.

Eydryth pointed to those faintly luminous wind-riding shapes. "Look over there. Five . . . six . . . ten . . . at least a dozen of them, perhaps more."

"A dozen of *what?*" he demanded.

She shrugged, knowing he could see her clearly in the moonlight, even though his face was naught but a dim blur to her own eyes. "I cannot be sure . . . but I believe they may be web-riders."

He gave her a quick, incredulous glance. "But they are only tales . . . legends! I have traveled the length and breadth of Escore, and never have I heard of them as anything but stories to terrify children when told before a roaring fire in midwinter!"

"In Arvon, like Escore, many old tales prove to have all-too-real substance," she reminded him. "And if they are indeed web-riders . . . we may not live to see the morn, Alon."

Just then the minstrel caught a faint whiff of an odor that made her nose wrinkle. Rank it was, as though their visitors were long-dead and decayed. "Whatever they are, their smell tells me they come from the Left, not the Right-Hand Path."

Alon sniffed, too. Eydryth saw the white blur his hand made as he traced a glowing sign in the air. With a muttered curse, he jerked his fingers back, as if they had been burned. "You have the right of it," he agreed. "There is no doubt that they mean us harm."

"Could Yachne have sent them?"

"Possible. It is also possible that they are denizens of this land. Perhaps they are the reason that no one lives here."

The thought made Eydryth shudder as she watched those distant shapes drifting closer . . . closer. "Can you see them clearly?" she whispered to Alon.

"They appear to be greenish-white creatures riding atop those purple filaments," he said, his voice hardly more than a breath against her ear. "They are perhaps two handspans in width, with long, many-jointed legs. . . ."

"Like spiders?"

"More like some ugly cross between a spider and a crab," he said. "They seem half-transparent, as though they are so light that they wove those webs, then cast them adrift on the night breeze and leaped upon them to ride them here." He shuddered in his turn. "They are fanged, and have pincers, or claws. I would wager that they are poisonous, like spiders."

"You have just described a web-rider," she said grimly.

"I know."

Eydryth glanced around her, wondering whether they should make a stand here, or try to run. Her breath caught in her throat, and her fingers clamped onto Alon's forearm with a force that made him gasp. "More of them . . . many more . . . ," she whispered. "We are surrounded!"

As the fell creatures bobbed closer, Eydryth could make out what Alon had described. Their eyes gleamed tiny and reddish in the faint moonlight. Their pincers and fangs dripped with venom. Could they be intelligent? There was no way to know. One thing was certain . . . they were at a grave disadvantage trying to fight in the darkness. "Can you summon light?" she asked the Adept. "Enough so I can see to use my sword?"

"I can," he said, and made several gestures. A wan violet light flickered unevenly over the tramped-down grass marking their campsite. "But I do not believe that swordplay is the best way to fight them."

"Then what is?" she countered, edging around him until they stood back-to-back, her sword in her hand. By now the web-riders were so close that some of them were little more than a sword-length from the perimeter of their campsite. The creatures seemed to be at the mercy of the breeze, with little ability to direct their floating webs. *That is one small thing in our favor*, Eydryth thought.

"I may be able to—," Alon began; then he broke off as Monso screamed again and lunged toward the circling invaders. The lead-shank parted with a snap. "No, Monso!" Alon shouted, dashing up to catch the Keplian's halter. But the stallion reared violently, pulling his master clean off his feet, then, with a toss of his head, flung Alon down. Eydryth heard him land with a thud, heard him gasping, trying to regain the breath that had been driven from his lungs.

The songsmith started after the black half-bred as he plunged at the web-riders, shrieking his battle cry. A flashing forehoof struck, sending one of their attackers fluttering to the ground. Monso pounced like a cat, trampling the downed web-rider into the short turf.

Eydryth managed to grab Monso's halter, then halt him. She was surprised at his sudden docility, but the reason for it soon became clear. As he took a step backward, the stallion nearly fell when his right foreleg buckled beneath him. The songsmith glanced down at the leg, but the light was too dim for her to see clearly. Bending down, she ran an expert hand down the slim, sinewed length, discovering a rapidly swelling area above the knee. It was hot and throbbing. "Alon!" she cried. "He's been stung or bitten!"

The Adept was already hobbling toward them, still wheezing. He flung himself down beside the Keplian. "We'll have to get a poultice on it immediately, to draw out the poison," Eydryth gasped. "I have herbs and bandages in my—"

Alon shook his head, halting her words. "Just hold them off for a moment," he ordered. Eydryth straightened, her sword at the ready. The web-riders ringed them now, but none had crossed into the light Alon had summoned. The songsmith kept one eye on them, while stealing glances at her companion as he grasped the stallion's leg in both hands, all the while muttering under his breath. Violet light shimmered from between his fingers.

Catching a flash of motion in the corner of her eye, the bard whirled, raising sword into guard position. She was barely in time to duck and parry as a glowing shape swooped down at her head. Seen this close, the web-rider appeared more crab than insect as its pincers snapped viciously, barely a handspan from her eyes.

Repelled, she slashed upward, her sword catching the creature in its midsection, slicing it in two. It made a shrill noise that hurt her ears as the blade clove its body. Even as she winced back from that eerie sound, a glowing greenish ichor sprayed outward from the dying thing, sending a spray of droplets spattering across her right hand.

Eydryth screamed with pain as the web-rider's "blood" seared her hand. Her skin felt as though she had been doused with liquid fire. Clamping her teeth onto her lip, she quickly caught up her blanket and wiped the noxious slime off her flesh, but the ichor still burned fiercely; her vision blurred with the pain of it.

Swallowing, she forced herself to flex her fingers, pick up her dropped sword. Perhaps some virtue emanated from the quan-iron in its gryphon's-head hilt, for, as she touched it, the pain eased a little, though she still had to stifle a groan every time she moved her fingers.

The web-riders were now closing in on every side as the breeze picked up. Eydryth caught up the blanket, wrapped it around her left hand and forearm, using it as makeshift shield to buffet the drifting creatures away.

With her right hand, she wove intricate patterns with the point and edge of her sword, parrying and thrusting, trying to watch everywhere at once. Even as she strove, she recognized that her efforts could not save them for long; sooner or later an attacker would swoop at her from behind her back, and she would find herself stung or bitten.

For long moments Eydryth held them off, moving with a precision that she had never employed against a human opponent. Suddenly she sensed something behind her, nearly brushing her hair!

Stifling a shriek, she whirled, only to see Alon behind her, his hand sweeping in a blow aimed at her head. She ducked, wondering if he had gone mad, but a second later, with a muffled curse, he grabbed her shoulder, holding her steady, then knocked a web-rider off her head with his bare hand. Eydryth shrank back as he struck it to the earth with the songsmith's quarterstaff. Quickly he pounded the staff's steel-shod butt into the center of the creature's back. The web-rider squealed, convulsed and died.

"We have to get away!" the songsmith shouted, pointing to the east. "Into the woods, where the wind cannot carry them! How is Monso? Can he move?"

"I drew the poison out," he gasped, "but he'll need—" He broke off as he batted away another of their attackers.

"But can we get away?"

"We don't have to run," he promised grimly. "Just hold them off until I get my wand. . . ."

Quickly he upended the saddlebag, spilling its contents, then grabbed the branch of elder. Extending it before him, he began to hum, then thread the fingers of his free hand through the air, as though combing it, or gathering up something invisible. The breeze against Eydryth's face intensified, tossing her hair into her eyes, plucking at the loose sleeves of her shirt.

Even as he continued those gathering motions with one hand, Alon began to make circling motions in the air with the wand. The wind picked up, now blowing so hard that Eydryth staggered, then braced herself against it. Something long and dark lashed her face, stinging her eyes, and for a terror-stricken moment she thought one of the web-riders had landed there, but her attacker proved to be naught but Monso's tail. She brushed the clinging horsehair aside, realizing that the sudden gale must be Alon's doing. Blinking, she looked about her for the web-riders.

With that first gust, the noxious creatures had been blown away from their intended prey. Eydryth sighed with relief and lowered her sword, painfully loosing her swollen fingers from their tight clench about its hilt, holding it now with her left hand.

As the minstrel watched, fascinated, Alon began to make circling motions with the tip of the wand, just as if he were stirring soup. The wind began to swirl around the massed web-riders, blowing them against each other. Each glowing shape was caught up by that tiny maelstrom, caught past all escaping. Within moments their attackers resembled a small, sickly greenish cyclone.

"Good!" Eydryth raised her voice to be heard above the wind. "How far away can you be from that thing and still keep them so prisoned?" She wondered whether she could find some way to cut them down while they were helpless. Cold iron seemed to work against them . . . but the throbbing of her hand was a warning against close-quarters sword-wielding.

If we can get far enough away before his power over the web-riders fails, then we can surround ourselves with trees and a protective circle, so no menace can come at us again this night, she thought. Then she remembered the Keplian's injured leg. Monso could not carry them; they would be limited to the distance they could make afoot.

"I have other plans for these vermin," Alon told her, in a voice that was cold and even with suppressed rage. So saying, he closed his eyes, concentrating. After a moment, sweat sheened his forehead. The whirlwind with its spinning, squeaking inhabitants seemed to glow even brighter—

—and then, without warning, exploded into flame!

Even though she had been considering ways to kill the evil things herself, Eydryth bit back a cry of protest. Kill them, yes, but to burn them *alive*—!

For many heartbeats the trapped creatures struggled against the inferno that was consuming them, shrilling protests in high-pitched hisses and cries. Then, just when the songsmith thought she could stand the sounds no more, and must run gibbering away into the night, silence fell. Of their attackers, there remained naught but ash drifting on the soft breeze.

Eydryth clenched her teeth as the pain of her wounded hand reawakened, but it was not the pain that made her stomach turn over queasily. In the waning moonlight, she had caught a glimpse of Alon's face as he contemplated his victory.

The Adept was smiling.

It took the travelers until the first faint flush of dawn to tend each other's wounds (Alon had a livid welt along the side of his jaw where the venom from one of the creatures had sprayed). After poulticing and binding up each other's wounds, they turned their attention to the Keplian. The stallion's leg showed only a slight swelling now, but Alon worked again at drawing out any remaining vestiges of poison.

The stallion could not be ridden until the swelling was completely gone, but Alon decided that he would be able to carry their packs.

Finally, when all their tasks were over, Eydryth sat on her bedroll, regarding the pearl-touched sky with a listless indifference. She knew that she should climb to her feet and set off across those meadows again, but her body cried out for respite. She felt that she could not have been more wearied if she had walked every step from Escore to Arvon without halting.

"We ought to go," she murmured to Alon, who was sitting beside her, slumped over with his elbows resting on his drawn-up knees, head bowed with an exhaustion like unto her own.

He managed to raise his head, stared at her with dark-ringed eyes. "Monso needs a few hours to recover from any lingering effects of that creature's venom," he said. "And neither of us will get far afoot without rest. Sleep, Eydryth. I intend to."

Feeling like a traitor—*What if Yachne is even now closing in on Kerovan?*—Eydryth nevertheless realized that her companion had the right of it. She nodded at him, then tumbled over onto her blankets, pulled an edge of her battered cloak across her and knew no more.

Alon's nudge roused her midmorn, and, with a groan, she rolled over and sat up groggily. *A bath*, she thought longingly. *If only we had Dahaun's red pools hereabouts.* Her nostrils wrinkled at the smell of food, simmering in a pot over a small, nearly smokeless fire.

"Here," the Adept said, extending a cup filled with thick, hot gruel that was flavored with dried fruit. "Try this. You need to eat."

"I cannot . . . ," she protested, feeling her stomach lurch. "I don't feel as though I could ever eat again."

He gave her a level glance. "Food will aid your body in overcoming the effects of the web-rider's poison," he said. "If you do not eat, you'll be too weak to walk, and, remember, Monso goes unburdened today, save for our packs." The cup moved toward her again. "Try . . . please."

Dubiously, she took the thick stuff, sipped cautiously. As

soon as she had downed the first few swallows, the churning in her middle quieted. The world around her seemed to solidify, brighten; a measure of strength returned to her limbs.

When it was time to go, she was able to stand and walk unassisted. As the travelers set out, Steel Talon swooped toward them, alighting on a nearby branch. The falcon screamed excitedly, flapping his wings with agitation. Alon stopped to stare at the bird intently. "What was he trying to tell you?" Eydryth asked, when he began walking again.

"I cannot be sure," he said. "Contact between us is tenuous at best. But he believes that his quest may be coming to an end. He feels that soon he may be able to join his master."

Eydryth glanced over her shoulder at the bird, seeing him wing upward into the skies. "Poor Steel Talon . . ."

Alon's expression was grim. "We cannot help him. Best we concentrate on helping ourselves and those who are depending upon us."

They walked throughout the rest of the morning, trying to keep a steady, swift pace, chewing hunks of journeybread for their nooning without halting, then slogging determinedly into the afternoon. Eydryth thought longingly of the swiftness with which the Keplian had borne them as she forced herself to keep up with the others. Every muscle in her body seemed to be sprained or bruised.

Alon was quiet again, brooding, and she did not like the look in his eyes when she happened to meet them. His thoughts, she could tell, were far from lightsome. Something was growing in him, some darkness of spirit that she feared.

In the early afternoon they climbed a long, sloping hill, then halted on its summit to breathe and scan the countryside before them. The hill sloped downward to a raw gorge of boulder-strewn, earth-colored land that seemed to be filled with a faint haze, despite the sun's brightness overhead. The rift extended as far in either direction as the songsmith could see.

"Our path lies straight across yon gorge," she said, eyeing it dubiously. "But I like not the looks of it."

"Kar Garudwyn lies in that direction?" he asked, pointing.

"Yes. But that looks like very rough ground. Do you think we should turn aside, find a way around it?"

"Finding a way around would take us many extra hours of walking." Alon pointed out the truth. "The entire stretch is no more than half a mile wide. Despite its raw look, the ground appears solid. If we take it slowly over those rocks, there should be no danger."

Leading Monso, he started off down the hill. Eydryth followed, growing ever more repelled by this strange, narrow floor to this small divide. For a moment she wanted to shout to Alon not to venture onto this ground, but she forced herself to silence, remembering the urgency of their journey.

It will not take more than a half-hour to cross, she judged, eyeing the land before them, trying to find comfort in her thought. *Alon has the right of it . . . finding a way around would delay us by half a day or more. . . .*

Ahead of her, Alon stepped from the green verge of grass onto that churned earth. He waved at her. "It is solid. Come ahead!"

The songsmith nerved herself to step over that border. She took a few strides, then gasped as a section of ground that had seemed perfectly steady turned abruptly, twisting her ankle. She barely saved herself from a fall by quick use of her staff. Hobbling forward, she felt another chunk of earth turn beneath her heel. "Alon!" she cried. "Wait!"

He stumbled, nearly falling, catching himself on Monso's ragged mane, then halted and stood staring about him, his expression one of bewilderment and growing unease. Eydryth limped up to join him; then she, in turn, regarded the landscape surrounding them.

The green hillsides had vanished. Now the rock-strewn gorge seemed to stretch before them—and behind them—into infinity. Overhead, the sun had vanished, but a brassy, glaring sky made the land about them shimmer with heat. There was no living vegetation. Rather, dead trees seemed to have been cast down like a child's jackstraws, and the underbrush was withered to a spectral ashy grey. Shadowy vines looped and coiled, snaking across the broken, churned ground. They were not living, for they bore no hint of green, rather resembled long-dead serpents.

As they stood there, a tremor rippled through the soil beneath their feet, making them both cry out and clutch at Monso, who threw up his head and whinnied with terror. A long crevice opened in the rocky ground, even as they watched. Finally the shaking quieted and their feet were once more planted on steady footing.

"Alon . . ." Eydryth's words died on her lips, and she could only stand mute, knowing her fear must be written upon her features.

He nodded, shoulders sagging heavily. "I have been a fool. If only I weren't so tired I could have sensed it . . ." His mouth tightened grimly. "The entire place . . . ensorcelled. This is Yachne's doing. Her trap. And I marched us straight into it."

Eleven

"Where are we, then?" Eydryth asked, forcing her voice to remain steady. With one part of her mind she wanted to scream at Alon, curse him roundly for leading them into this trap, but what good would that do? With an effort that made her jaw muscles ache, she kept a tight rein on her tongue.

"I am not entirely sure," he said softly, and the bitterness in his voice told the songsmith that he was cursing himself far more vehemently than she could ever have done.

"Are we still in Arvon, do you think?" She gazed about them, seeing the eerily lit sky, the ravaged landscape stretching onward without discernible horizons. Fear surged within her. "Or did we come through some kind of Gate when we stepped into this blighted land?"

"I do not think so," he said, absently fingering the crystal talisman Dahaun had placed about his neck, as though touching it would help him think. "I believe rather that we are still within the confines of that mysterious gorge we entered only a few moments ago."

"But how can that be? There is no sun . . . and no horizon. We cannot see the hillsides that should surround us."

"I know. But much of what we are seeing in this place is illusion," he said. "Many of the false images I can dismiss by summoning true sight." He pointed at a jagged boulder in their path. A ghostly grey vine with shadow-colored blossoms crawled up it like a viper. "That, for instance. The reality is not a boulder, but a gaping crevice in the earth, half-covered in dead vines."

Eydryth stared at it, knowing that if she had continued onward, unwarned, she would have fallen over the edge. She licked dry lips. "Illusion . . . Can you break the spell, Alon?"

He gave a heartfelt sigh, leaning tiredly back against the Keplian's shoulder. "That I cannot," he said, sounding as if the admission cost him dearly. "Yachne's magic is too strong."

Her eyes widened in surprise. She had not expected him to admit defeat without even a trial. "How can you know unless you try?"

Bleak despair shadowed his face. "I *know*," he insisted quietly. "This is too powerful for me."

The songsmith opened her mouth to argue further, but after a moment she sighed softly and remained silent. *The spell is not only one of illusion*, she realized. *It is also one of hopelessness.* She could feel it affecting her, too . . . gnawing at the edges of her will, her determination, like a rasti chewing through a corncrib floor.

And without belief and faith, power is nothing, she thought, remembering snippets of magical lore that she had learned from her mother and Joisan. *Unless Alon believes that he can undo this ensorcellment, he cannot succeed.*

"Then what must we do?" she asked, trying not to let her fear show.

"We must cross the gorge," he replied. "Yachne cannot have bespelled the entire width of Arvon. If we can find the true path through the illusion, we will emerge from it into the reality. But it will not be easy." He shook his head, his uncertainty plain to read. "There are traps within traps here for the unwary. If we take a false step, we will surely be lost."

"But you can see past the falseness to the truth, can't you, Alon?" she asked. The panic that she had been holding back ever since they had walked blindly into this place was growing. What if they were trapped here, past all escape?

"The simpler, less complex illusions, yes. But Yachne's power is now . . . formidable." His mouth tightened grimly. "Simple illusion is an easy spell, but what surrounds us is far from simple . . . it is so detailed, so many-layered. Here there are illusions within illusions!"

"I understand . . . ," she whispered. Catching a movement in the corner of her eye, she whirled around, but, as before, all was still . . . as still as death. Even so, the songsmith could not rid herself of the conviction that, just out of her sight, something had spied, then skittered giggling from one hiding place to another. From somewhere she heard a faint whine, and a gust of hot air brushed her cheek.

The ghost of a wind? she wondered, putting out a wetted finger. As if reading her thoughts, Alon nodded. "Illusion," he said flatly. "This spell is not only complex, it is affecting more than just our vision. We will not only *see* what is not there, we will hear and feel it, also."

Having grown up with the simple illusions that Elys had sometimes conjured to amuse her child, Eydryth was taken aback. Most Seeming-spells could not stand up to investigation by touch; attempting to verify the reality of an illusion by laying hand to it was usually the surest way to make it dissolve. The songsmith shuddered. "We must indeed be cautious."

He nodded absently, gazing around them. "And there is one more thing," he added heavily. "My instincts tell me that this spell has somehow altered even time itself . . . or our perception of it, at least."

"How so?"

"It is seeming to draw time out, slow it down. Crossing this gorge will take us long enough—if we even make it—" His mouth twisted. "But however long it takes us, it will *seem* even longer."

"But . . ." Eydryth pressed her fingers against her left side, feeling her heartbeat, reassuring in its steady rhythm. "But my heart is beating, I am breathing . . . I feel no different!"

"*You* are not different, Lady, not physically. Illusion works within the mind, though its effects can be very real-seeming indeed." Alon glanced around them at the desolation of this violated, denuded land. "Somewhere around us lies the true path, masked by illusion, and that is what we must seek."

"And the finding of that path will be no easy task," Eydryth finished with what she believed to be the truth. He nodded.

"But you *can* find it . . . ," she said urgently, searching for reassurance in his grim expression—and not finding it. "You have the true sight!"

"I do," he agreed. "But constant use of the true sight is wearing . . . more wearying than fighting a score of armsmen. I only hope that my sight does not wane as I tire."

"I will do whatever I can to aid you," Eydryth promised. "We had better get started before another of those earth-tremors comes." She turned away, then gave him a sideways glance. "Or are they, too, illusion?"

"The ones we experienced before were real," Alon told her levelly. "If one of us were to fall into one of those crevasses as they open . . . death would be equally real." Only his eyes betrayed what he was feeling—a fear as great as her own.

Eydryth swallowed, resolutely fighting down the terror that wanted to possess her, make her run screaming in any direction, heedless of danger. "I understand. Now . . . which way? With no sun to guide us, all trails seem the same."

"There," Alon said, pointing to a opening between two towering reddish spires. "Walk directly behind me, and do not step off the path I hold to."

He handed Monso's lead to her, then turned to go. Suddenly he halted. "May I carry your staff?" he asked. "The

quan-iron in the gryphon's-head may aid in warning against a
false step."

Wordlessly, she handed him the quarterstaff, saw him re-
verse it in his hand so that the gryphon's-head pointed downward, toward the ground before him. He began walking.

Eydryth followed him, eyes on the ground, stepping in the
same places his feet had rested. She kept Monso snubbed close
on a short rein, forcing the Keplian to walk beside her. Fortunately the stallion's injury served to slow his naturally long
strides.

Even this extreme caution did not completely save her from
mishaps. The raw, rock-studded earth beneath her feet was
littered with stones that seemed almost to nudge their way
beneath her toes or heels so that they could then slip treacher-
ously out from underfoot, or turn sharply, wrenching her
ankles. The dead, greyed vegetation proved another hindrance, snagging her toes, slowing and tripping her no matter
how carefully she stepped. Eydryth nearly fell several times.
Once only her hold on Monso's lead saved her from a headlong plunge down a short, precipitous cliff.

Soon the songsmith was hobbling in earnest, wincing with
every step. Her eyes ached from the hot, brassy glare overhead; she blinked them only when they began to sting unbear-
ably, afraid that closing them even for an instant would cause
her to miss the true path.

Even with his true sight, Alon fared little better. His riding
boots were not intended for prolonged walking, even without
the hindrance of a bespelled land that seemed determined to
thwart every forward step. Soon he, too, was limping.

The young Adept alternated between picking out the path
a few stumbling steps ahead, then halting for endless moments
to scan the torn, churned vista before them, using the quarterstaff to sweep the ground before his boots.

Several times he muttered softly, extending a hand, and
Eydryth saw dark violet light flare from his fingertips, coalesce
into a slender arrow of brightness, then wind its way along the
ground before him, vanishing ten or fifteen paces farther on.

If he can thus mark the true path for us, then we will be able to escape this maze, she thought with relief.

But soon she realized that using his Power to indicate their direction was wearing dangerously upon her companion. Each time he called up the violet arrows of light, the lines around Alon's eyes and mouth deepened, the skin over his cheekbones grew tighter, until he seemed naught but a gaunt, greyed shadow of the man Eydryth had known. Sweat made runnels in the dust on his face; his thin shirt clung to his back, dark and soaked.

The songsmith fought back a surge of pity, reminding herself coldly that it was he who had led them into this peril in the first place. With a small, distant portion of her mind she was shocked by her own callousness, but she angrily hardened her heart as she placed one foot before the other, over and over again.

Onward they toiled, their pitifully slow progress made even more halting by their frequent stops while Alon determined the correct route. Overhead the sickly-hued sky never changed; heat pressed down on them like a muffling blanket. Thirst soon became a torment.

The travelers had three water flasks between them, hardly enough to last them even one day's hard journey, considering that Monso must needs share their supply. The only water they had encountered within Yachne's blighted land lay in muddy, scummed pools of such rankness that no creature could safely drink from them, or from springs that bubbled hot from the bowels of the earth, emitting eye- and throat-searing fumes.

After a time that went unmeasured except by Eydryth's increasing thirst, pain from her wrenched ankles, and general misery from the will-sapping spell lying over the ensorcelled land, Alon halted. "Rest awhile . . . ," he rasped. "Water . . ."

Slowly his knees folded and he sank to the ground, where he sat unmoving, shoulders bowed, head hanging with exhaustion.

The songsmith halted, too, then took out their packs of

food and water flasks. She held out the container to Alon, who stared at it, his eyes so reddened and dulled with weariness that he seemed scarcely aware of what it was. "Here," she said, steadying it as she removed the stopper. "Water. Drink, Alon."

Catching the scent of water, the Keplian whickered softly, nostrils flaring. The Adept looked down at the flask, then took a deep breath, awareness returning to his gaze. He shook his head, then handed the water back to Eydryth with the ghost of a courtly flourish in the gesture. "You first, my lady," he said, in that harsh, barely understandable whisper.

Unable to summon breath or wit to argue with him, she did as he bade, feeling the stale, warm liquid trickle down her throat like the finest of chilled wine from a High Lord's table. Running her tongue over cracked lips to catch the last drops, she handed the flask to her companion.

But still Alon did not drink.

"Here, fellow . . . ," he said, tugging the Keplian's lead so the stallion stood nearly atop him. "You must be thirsty, too. . . ."

Retrieving his leather jerkin, he spread it over his crossed knees so as to make a hollow. Then the Adept cautiously tipped half of the contents of the flask into the makeshift pail. Monso gulped the scant amount noisily. Only after the stallion had licked up all of the moisture did Alon raise the flask to his lips and drink sparingly.

The Adept shook the last drops from the now-empty flask into the jerkin for the stallion; then he crumbled journeybread for the Keplian to lip up from the garment's battered surface. Plainly forcing himself, Alon broke off pieces of journeybread, trying not to open his cracked and bloodied mouth any wider than necessary to eat. Grimly, he chewed and swallowed the morsels. But when he held out a chunk to the songsmith, she shook her head. "I cannot. The journeybread is too dry."

"Some fruit, then," he said, locating the packet Dahaun had packed for them. "You need the strength, Eydryth."

Too tired to argue, she mouthed and swallowed the over-whelming sweetness of the dried pulp. Eating did little to restore her blighted spirits, but slowly a measure of strength returned to her weary body.

She watched in dull surprise as Alon unstoppered their second flask and poured another generous measure for the horse. When Eydryth made a small, protesting movement, he shook his head. "I have traveled on short rations before. Rationing too severely does more harm than good, my lady. We are better off drinking now, attempting to keep our strength up while a measure of it still remains, rather than saving most of the water until we are too weak to go on."

Remembering that her father had once told her something of the same thing, the minstrel nodded, accepted the second flask, then drank. "But only if you take more, too," she said, handing it to her fellow-traveler. At her insistence, he took several more swallows, then stoppered the remainder carefully.

"How far have we come?" she whispered, trying not to move her parched lips more than necessary to make her voice heard. "How much farther to the end of this place?"

He shrugged grimly. "We have come farther than Yachne would ever have suspected we could," he said. "Of that I am sure. The way out should lie just over that hill." He pointed. Eydryth saw that his hand was shaking, despite his effort to steady it.

"What hill?" she whispered.

"You cannot see it?"

"Of course not." Old anger made her tone sharper than she had intended. "I see only a thicket of dead bushes laced with thorny vines, all of it so interwoven it might as well be a hanging in the great hall of a keep."

Alon gazed at her speculatively. "The thicket is illusion."

"I will take your word for it." The asperity was still there in her voice, though Eydryth was not sure precisely why she felt so nettled with him. Was it the witch's spell that was causing her to feel such frustration and hopelessness? Or her anger at Alon for leading them into this trap of Yachne's? She did not know. At his steady, measuring glance, her mouth tightened defiantly and she looked away, studying the vegetation that Alon insisted was not really there.

"Will we feel the vines and thorns?" she whispered, eyeing the sharp, greyish brambles apprehensively. "Or is this illusion one that confuses only the eye?"

"I fear that it is one of the more tangible ones," he said. "Monso I can blindfold and lead, but you . . ." He shook his head.

"If I try and make my way through that, I will be flayed alive . . . ," she muttered, staring at the vicious thorns. "Perhaps if my eyes were covered, also . . ." She trailed off with an inquiring glance.

Grimly, he shook his head again. "For you, the illusion is the reality. Whether you see it or not will make but little difference. As long as the false is real within your own mind, you will feel the results."

"Can we go around?" she glanced at both sides of the thicket.

"Hardly. There"—he pointed to the left of the thicket—"is a scattering of large boulders, crowded so close that a dog would be hard-pressed to thread a way between them, much less something of Monso's size. And there"—he indicated the right—"is one of the steaming pools. Can you not smell it?"

Eydryth's nostrils twitched, then wrinkled. She could definitely detect the noxious fumes that proclaimed the reality of his assertion.

"Is that the only way we can go?" Panic clutched at her mind. Perhaps if she muffled her face and hands with pieces of blanket, and moved very slowly, she could avoid serious injury. . . .

"That is the only true path," he said. "See for yourself." Rising to his feet, he muttered softly, then held out both hands. Purple light slowly outlined his fingers, dripped with painful slowness to the ground, where it gathered and coalesced into one of the sinuous arrow-shapes she had seen earlier. The light writhed forward, toward the center thicket, marking their path. But this time it waned quickly, fading almost before she fixed her eyes on it. Alon staggered, gasping, and had to brace himself against Monso's shoulder. "The marker . . . ," he muttered hoarsely. "Did you see it?"

"Yes, I saw where it pointed. I will just have to go slowly, I suppose."

Alon shook his head, teeth clamping onto his torn lower lip as he pushed himself upright. "No," he said. "That will not work."

"But I cannot—"

"Yes, you *can!*" His eyes held hers with a fierceness he had never shown before. "I have neither time nor strength to allow you to cling to your own comforting illusions, Lady," he rasped. "What you must needs do is break this Seeming for yourself."

She stared at him blankly. "But I have no Power! You know that!" she protested finally, her voice shrill.

"I know that you *believe* that you have no Power," he countered. "And I know also that that belief is what holds you back."

"Just as your belief that Yachne's spell is too powerful for you to break is holding *you* back?" she demanded coldly. "I never took you for a coward, Alon, until now. How dare you lead us into this trap, then blame me for not having abilities I have never possessed?" Her accusation was filled with venom that made him flinch away as though she had actually struck him.

His mouth tightened, his shoulders that had hunched before her bitter anger slowly straightened. "You possess 'the Gift,' as you call it, Eydryth. I have known that since the first night we met. I also saw that the truth was too frightening for you to face, so I let you hold to your mistaken belief. But now you must face the truth!"

"Don't be ridiculous," Eydryth snarled. "The heat has addled your wits!"

"No, it has not. Only your lack of belief in yourself keeps you from seeing through that illusion. Only your lack of belief in your own Power holds us prisoner. Why do you think the witch of Estcarp pursued you so single-mindedly? You have blinded yourself to the truth from fear—but now it is time to face truth—and use the Power within you!"

"No!" she choked, furious at him. "You lie!"

Blind with rage, she lurched to her feet and struck out at him, flailing, kicking, but he avoided her blows, seizing her shoulders in his hands. Whirling her around, he pulled her back against him, gripping her hard. Hands and arms that could curb Monso's headlong rushes tightened on her flesh and bone, holding her past any ability of hers to struggle free. Eydryth gasped with the pain. *"Look!"* he ordered, his mouth so close to her ear that she could hear him clearly, despite the harsh rasp that served him now for a voice. "That thicket is *not there!* That thicket is the lie! Look well, songsmith, and see past the falsehood to the truth, which is the hillside!"

Unable to break his grip, she subsided, then stared sullenly at the pale grey vegetation. "I see only the thicket," she muttered.

"You are not trying!" he said fiercely. "You must *try!* Concentrate! See the hillside!"

She fixed her eyes on the spot, feeling them throb and burn from the glare overhead. The outlines of the vegetation began to shimmer slightly—or was it her imagination?

"I cannot. . . ." She was shaking now, feeling a different sort of fear seize her.

"You must *believe!* You can, I swear it by my life, you can do it!"

She focused, stared until her vision blurred, tears of pain nearly blinding her as she forced herself not to blink. *See a hillside—there is a hillside*, she insisted to herself. Vegetation swam before her; then there was something . . . something reddish showing through. . . .

"I see . . ." She was forced to blink, then it was gone. She sagged back against his chest, limp with defeat. "I cannot, Alon!" she pleaded.

"You *can*," he insisted, supporting her, though she could feel him trembling with weariness. "Eydryth . . . try humming while you look."

She craned her neck to fix him with an incredulous glance, but he only nodded firmly. "Go on . . . try."

Eydryth turned back to the tangle of shadowy vines, then began to hum, scarcely aware of what tune she had chosen.

The greyness swam before her dazzled eyes, and she blinked to clear her vision, concentrating. . . .

As if it had always been there before her, she now saw a hill with a trail leading straight up it, narrow and precipitous between jagged boulders!

Eydryth gasped, and with the interruption of the music, the grey curtain of vines returned. "Alon!" she whispered. "I saw it!"

"Good," he said, not at all surprised, and released her. "Your gift must be linked to music, Eydryth. When you tamed Monso, you sang. When you fooled the witch back in Es City, you were humming, were you not?"

She cast her mind back to events that now seemed years—instead of mere days—ago. "Yes, I was," she said after a moment. "My mother's lullaby . . ." She regarded him, completely bewildered. "But . . . Alon . . . how can this be? I have never heard of such a talent!"

"Neither have I," he admitted. "But, now that I think of it, much of magic is dependent upon sounds—chants, incantations, even songs. Remember the crystal Gate? The spell to open it depended on the correct note being sung!"

She nodded, bemused. "This discovery explains . . . much," she said slowly.

"At the moment, our concern must be escaping from this place and tracing Yachne," he reminded her. Quickly, he stripped off his shirt, then used its sleeves to tie it snugly over Monso's eyes. "If he cannot see where he is going, I do not believe the illusion will prevail for him," he told the songsmith. "This would not work for one of us, for our minds are more complex, and thus not so easily fooled. Are you ready, my lady?"

Eydryth nodded firmly. "I am."

"Can you see the hillside?"

She summoned music, hummed between parched lips, then nodded as the trail took shape before her eyes. "Then . . . after you, my lady," Alon said, in his cracked, rasping voice. He bowed, waving her past with a courtly gesture. The contrast between his formal manner and his appearance made Eydryth

shake her head. His face, with its livid weal caused by the
web-rider's slash, was blistered and seared by the heat, and his
bare chest and shoulders were streaked with dust and muddy
sweat. For a moment she wondered if he had gone quite
mad—he certainly appeared demented.

But no, his eyes were sane. He believed in her. The least she
could do was to believe in herself. Taking a deep breath,
Eydryth hummed steadily, and they started up the long, rocky
trail. The songsmith concentrated on filling her mind with the
music. She was so intent upon her task that she did not feel the
earth-tremor until it struck, making her stagger, making her
gasp—

—whereupon, instantly, she was surrounded by bushes and
dead vines. A thousand thorns jabbed her. Only by the grace
of fortune were her eyes spared that assault.

"Concentrate!" she heard Alon's shout from behind her.

Already she was summoning the music again, and the feel
of the entangling growth was gone. She took a step forward,
felt no obstruction, took another, and only then dared open
her eyes. The hillside lay before her.

Eydryth slogged her way toward the top of the hill, alert for
more quakes, kicking loose stones from her path, humming
like an insect gone mad.

"You may stop now, and breathe," Alon's rasping whisper
reached her. "We are beyond the illusion-thicket."

The songsmith halted, regarding her arms with a silent
thanksgiving to Gunnora that she had not panicked. Dozens
of small pinpricks oozed a single droplet of scarlet apiece.
Cautiously, she explored her grimy face with even dirtier fingertips, discovering several more stabs.

"For an illusion," she said to Alon as he came up beside her,
"that was all too real." She held out her arm.

He nodded grimly. "At least we are past. You have learned
a valuable lesson today, Lady. When one is working any kind
of spell or counterspell, it can be disaster to let one's concentration break. The first year or so as an apprentice is spent
learning to focus and not to be distracted. You had to master
that lesson in the space of minutes."

"Be assured it is a lessoning I shall not soon forget."

He stepped up beside her, and together they made their way to the crest of the hillside. As weary as they were, it took them a long time, and they were gasping when they reached it. There they halted, gazing down at what now lay before them.

A short walk beyond, the blighted land ended abruptly in a chasm so deep and so black that Eydryth could not discern any bottom to it. A wall of thick grey mist seemed to rise out of the opening, roiling and drifting as though blown by a wind, though she could feel none. The mist extended before them, as high as she could see in each direction, blocking their sight of what, if anything, lay beyond.

They had reached the end of their road . . . they could go no farther.

Tears of despair filled the songsmith's eyes, and she sank weakly to her knees, pressing both hands to her broken lips. Sobs shook her, wrenched her shoulders. To have come all this way, only to have it end thus. To have come all this way for nothing!

Alon sighed, dropping to sit beside her. His bare shoulders bowed forward as he buried his face in his hands, obviously as shaken as she.

"We shall have to go back," Eydryth whispered, after a while. It was either that or die right here, and she wasn't . . . quite . . . ready to die. "Perhaps there is another way. . . ."

He shook his head, then, with an effort that was palpable, straightened his shoulders. Retrieving his shirt from Monso's head, he pulled it on, buttoning it with none-too-steady fingers. "We cannot," he said. "Our way out lies there." He pointed across the chasm. "That mist hides the real Arvon. We must find some way to cross over the chasm . . . to bridge that gap."

Eydryth stared at him, certain that he was now completely bereft of his wits. "But . . . how?"

"We must make a bridge."

"There is no way! We have nothing to build with—even if a bridge could span that void, which I do not for one moment believe!"

"It is the only way out," he maintained stubbornly. "Arvon—the real Arvon—is there." He pointed. "I can sense it. By the Sword Arm of Karthen the Fair, I can *smell* it! Cannot you?"

She gave him a sideways glance, then, as he regarded her steadily, ventured a sniff. "I smell . . . ," she whispered. "I smell flowers! And water! Is that another illusion?"

"No," he said. "It is real. The other hillside is there. We must cross the chasm to reach it, Eydryth. We must make a bridge."

"Out of what? We have nothing!"

He did not answer, only unfastened the last water flask from Monso's saddle. "Drink," he said, holding it and the packet of food out to her. "And eat. Force yourself. You will need all your strength for what is about to come."

Bewildered, she did as he bade. Scenting the water, Monso whickered pleadingly, but this time the Adept shook his head at the stallion. "I am sorry, old son," he said, giving the Keplian a comforting pat, "but if we succeed, your thirst will be eased very quickly."

"And if we fail?" asked Eydryth, giving him a sidelong glance. She could not imagine what he had in mind.

"If we fail," he said grimly, "then neither thirst nor hunger will torture us for much longer, so the result will be the same."

After they had eaten and drunk, emptying the third and last flask between them, they made their way down the raw rock of the hillside, then walked the short distance to the edge of the drop. Making sure both feet were planted as securely as possible, Eydryth took hold of Monso's right stirrup and leaned forward, gazing downward.

Sheer red rock for as far down as she could see, disappearing finally into the swirling grey mist.

Alon picked up a stone, held it suspended over the gorge, then released it. It fell . . .

and fell . . .

. . . and fell. They never heard it strike bottom.

Eydryth stared at the wall of mist before them. It was perhaps two of Monso's lengths distant. "You believe that if we can plunge into that mist, we shall be released from the spell and back in the real Arvon," she said finally.

Alon nodded.

"How shall we cross the gap?" she asked, keeping her voice level, as though they were discussing a problem with a solution, rather than quick and certain death.

"We must make a bridge," he repeated.

"Using what?"

"Ourselves," he said flatly. "Our Power. My blood. Your music."

She gazed at him wide-eyed. "You *are* mad," she whispered.

Alon shook his head at her warningly. "You have already learned the value of belief, Eydryth. You will need all of it you can summon. Do not let doubt intrude. I am sane, never doubt it. This"—he waved at the abyss—"is our way out. On the other side lies the Arvon we left."

She caught again that faint scent of flowers. Monso sniffed the air; then the Keplian's nostrils widened and he nickered, pawing. "He smells the water," Alon said.

Eydryth bit her lip, then took a deep breath. What choice, after all, did she have? "Very well," she said quietly. "I believe. How shall we do it?"

He gave her a quick, approving nod. "We will need to combine our Power," he said. "Create a Seeming of our own. One of the ones so strong that it has solidity, substance. It will not be easy," he finished, warningly. "But it can be done."

"I am ready," she said resolutely. "Tell me what to do."

"In the first place, you must concentrate," he told her. "If the earth trembles this time, you must not let it disturb you, do you understand?"

She nodded.

The Adept took his knife out of its sheath, handed it to her. "When I nod, you must cut," he said, tapping his wrist. "Cut deeply enough so that the blood flows freely, but not so deep that we cannot staunch the wound later." Eydryth hesitated, then took the knife he held out. "I would do it myself," Alon said, with a note of apology, "but we must link hands for this. Whatever happens, do *not* let go."

"I understand," she said, studying the blue veins running

along the inside of his forearm, planning the best place to do as he bade. "Then what?"

"You must sing. You will feel the Power leaving you, joining with the blood to create the bridge. Use your music to strengthen your Power—and our bridge. Sing, and stop for nothing! As soon as the bridge is solid, you must send Monso across, then lead me. I will have my eyes closed, holding the spell in my mind's eye, and I will not be able to see what I—we—have wrought."

He gazed at her intently. "If Gunnora smiles upon us, by the time I next see you, we will be back in Arvon."

Eydryth touched the symbol of the Amber Lady that she wore upon her neck. Then, quickly, she checked that all their supplies were securely lashed to Monso's saddle. "We are ready," she told Alon.

Solemnly, he unbuttoned his left sleeve, rolled it up so his arm was bared. The he held out both hands to her. Eydryth grasped his right hand tightly with her left, then raised the knife.

Alon closed his eyes, took several deep breaths, then nodded. "First, the music," he muttered.

Eydryth began to hum softly. . . . Choosing a tune nearly at random, she was taken aback to realize it was "Hathor's Ghost Stallion," the melody she had been singing when first they had met. As she began to sing the words, his fingers squeezed hers. "Now," he whispered.

Bracing herself, Eydryth brought the knife up to the flesh of his wrist. *It would be far easier to cut myself,* she thought, forcing herself to keep singing. *Amber Lady, aid me! Do not let me hurt him! Let us escape from this place, I beg of You!*

Touching the blade to skin, she resolutely drew it across and down. A tiny trickle of red followed, and she forced herself to cut deeper . . . deeper. The trickle strengthened, began to drip . . . then flow.

The songsmith had spilled blood before, but never like this. She felt darkness creeping up on the edges of her vision, and only the hard grasp on her fingers kept her from fainting or being sick. Still, she sang, never missing a note.

Alon began to mutter hoarsely, chanting in a language she

did not recognize, as blood splashed on the edge of the abyss. Eydryth was conscious of a sudden *pull* upon her inner strength. Alon's blood was only the outward sign of what was happening here. There was a draining, a flow from her to him, that made her almost falter. Summoning all her will, her determination, she stood firm, singing, and watched the abyss.

From that steady drip of scarlet, something was growing. Eydryth's eyes widened as she saw something taking shape . . . a bridge! An actual curved span, shadowy, but gaining substance! It was red . . . as red as blood, pulsing to the beat of both their hearts . . . and with each beat, it gained substance.

Alon's face was pale now, beneath his tan, but his chanting grew louder. Blood spattered. Eydryth was singing loudly now, forcing the words to ring out true and strong, forcing herself to *believe* in what she was seeing.

The bridge shimmered scarlet in the light, stretching across the chasm, into the grey mist. Careful not to loose her grip on Alon's hand, the songsmith raised her foot, touched it to the bridge. It was solid—it took her weight. *But will it hold the stallion's?*

"Come on, Monso," she sang, incorporating the order into one of the verses. One-handed, she grasped the Keplian's rein and pulled him so he fronted that span. She tugged at his lead, indicating she wanted him to cross. "Go on, boy!" she sang, her voice ringing out in a musical command. "Go!"

The stallion pawed at the bridge, obviously dubious, but the scent of water, and the solid feel of Alon's creation beneath his questing hoof, convinced him. With a snort, the half-bred plunged forward. His hooves clattered on the bridge, as he surged up onto it, then disappeared into the mist. A last flick of his black tail, then he was gone.

Did he fall? Eydryth wondered, but resolutely forced herself not to even consider that possibility. She guided Alon to step onto the span, nerving herself to place both feet on that crimson surface. Together, they edged along, the Adept chanting, Eydryth singing.

A moment later, the most wonderful music she had ever

heard reached the songsmith's ears, even above the sound of her own singing. It was the sound of a horse drinking, great, gulping slurps of water. "Thank you, Amber Lady!" Eydryth sang, careful not to look down. She pulled Alon faster, as they made a crablike progress.

They were slightly more than halfway across when Eydryth felt the Adept stagger. Casting an anxious glance at him, she saw that his face was grey. His eyes rolled back in his head; showing only the whites. Knees buckling, he swayed. The shining crimson surface beneath their feet began to quiver.

Eydryth slung her free arm around Alon's waist, holding him against her. The bridge shivered, fading. Resolutely squeezing her own eyes shut, Eydryth lunged forward, leaping into the mist, dragging Alon with her.

A heartbeat later she felt herself falling . . . falling. . . .

Twelve

*F*or what seemed endless seconds, Eydryth fell through the swirling greyness. A scream welled in her throat, trying to burst from her lips. But before any sound could emerge, she struck solid ground, landing so hard that the breath rushed from her lungs. She pitched over, rolling, the rich smell of growing turf filling her nostrils.

When the world finally stopped its dizzying spin, Eydryth found herself staring dazedly at a blue sky dotted with white clouds. The sun shone just past its zenith. Raising her head weakly, she saw Monso regarding her, ears pricked, muzzle still dripping water from the stream flowing past his hooves.

Someone groaned.

The pain in that sound brought her up onto hands and knees. "Alon?"

The Adept was lying behind her, on the hillside. His eyes were closed; the sound of his name did not rouse him. Bright scarlet splashed the green grass by his side, soaking into the ground. That sight made the songsmith scuttle forward to seize his wrist, squeezing hard to stop the blood flow.

Finally, it halted. Eydryth sat back on her heels, her scarlet-streaked hands shaking as she tried to summon the strength to do what she could to aid him. Alon still lay unconscious, so pale his skin was greyish and his lips blue. Despite the warmth of the sun, he was shivering beneath the thin fabric of his once-white linen shirt, now a rusty brown from drying blood.

Blankets . . . liquids . . . Healcraft that Joisan had taught her came slowly to mind. Pushing herself up onto legs that trembled at first from her own weakness, she walked slowly over to the Keplian and led him back to the Adept's side. Untying their packs, she then unsaddled the stallion, turning him loose to roll and graze, trusting that he would stay near his master.

Wrapping Alon snugly in both their cloaks, she gathered wood to build a small fire, then fetched water from the stream to heat. While she was waiting for the pot to simmer, she unpacked the small bag of simples Joisan had assembled for her so long ago. Snippets of lore gained from her foster-mother came back to her as the sometimes sweet, sometimes sharp scents of the powdered herbs made her nostrils twitch.

A restorative . . . verbena! A tea made with verbena . . .

Scenting the distinctive sharp, lemony scent, she opened the proper bag, dropping the dried leaves into the pot. When the tisane was ready, she strained it, then, propping Alon's head on her knee, urged him to drink. His eyelids fluttered, and he roused enough to swallow the tea, but he did not regain consciousness. His shivering eased, though, and for that the songsmith was grateful.

Before tackling the wound on his wrist, she drank a cup of the brew herself. The songsmith felt as emptied as if she had been awake and without food for days. Such weariness was normal after use of the Power, she knew that. The thought sparked a bittersweet memory.

I worked magic, she thought, scarcely able to believe it. Even though it had happened only a short while ago, the memory was already raveling and faded, as if it had happened to another person, not the Eydryth of here-and-now. She sighed, shaking her head as she visualized again that hillside thorn-walled by illusion, and how she had sung the falseness away to discover the truth beneath. *Did I truly do that? Or was it Alon's magic affecting me somehow? Is it possible that I truly do hold my own kind of Power?*

There were no certain answers to her questions, and no time to ponder them. Kneeling beside the fast-running water, Eydryth washed her face and hands, scrubbing her fingertips and nails with white sand from the stream bottom. Joisan maintained that keeping wounds clean was fully as important as using the proper herbs and spells for their treatment.

After washing the oozing slash with boiled water, into which she had dissolved generous pinches of saffron and yarrow, to promote healing, she frowned as she studied the extent of the cut. It needed stitching, such as she had seen her foster-mother do. But here in the wilds of Arvon, she had no needle, no boiled thread.

Eydryth considered simply bandaging the wound, but it was so deep that she thought it would take very little movement to reopen it and start the bleeding afresh. And in Alon's present condition, any further blood loss would be dangerous—quite possibly fatal.

As she hesitated, her eye was caught by Dahaun's small, sealed box containing the red mud from the Valley of the Green Silences. *No!* she thought, biting her lip. An idea had come to her, but it was not one she cared to contemplate. *Dahaun said not to open the box! That mud is for Jervon—his last chance to be healed!*

She glared down at Alon with sudden animosity. *I will not use Jervon's cure to heal* you. *I will NOT!* Anger waxed hot within her. One small portion of her mind argued that her fury was irrational, but she was too angry to listen to it.

"No!" she whispered fiercely. "Jervon is my father! You are nothing to me, nothing, do you hear?"

Her wrath had become a fire within her, raging out of control. *It would serve you right if I went on without you, after you plunged us into such a morass of sorcery!* she thought savagely. *I ought to leave you here—leave you to die!*

The young man stirred restlessly, as though even unconscious he sensed her sudden ire. Eydryth felt half-drunk with rage, with hate. For a moment her hand twitched toward her dagger; then she rose and walked straight away, not looking back.

Picking up her pack, she shouldered it, then started up the hillside. Monso whickered, pawing the ground anxiously, but she ignored the stallion. Furious, shaking, she remembered how they had escaped from Yachne's illusion-land. She *hated* Alon for what he had forced her to discover about herself. *I don't want Power!* she thought, incensed. *It carries too much danger, too much risk! He had no right to do what he did!*

Without warning, a blackness swooped out of the sky, heading straight for her eyes. A shrill scream rent the air. Eydryth ducked as it winged by her, its tailfeathers brushing the top of her head.

As she straightened up, the creature flung itself at her again, clawed talons nearly raking her face. The songsmith stumbled back, losing her footing on the hillside, then sat down so hard that lights flashed behind her eyes and a roaring filled her ears. Blinking, she stared wide-eyed at her surroundings. The creature that had swooped at her alighted on a dead tree nearby. It was a falcon, and, as she stared at it, it screamed again.

"Steel Talon!" Eydryth exclaimed, then, suddenly uncertain and shaken, she put a hand to her head. *What was I doing? Abandoning Alon? Leaving him to die?*

Incredulous horror filled her as she recalled the events of the past few minutes. If it had not been for Steel Talon, she might not have returned to her senses. *What is wrong with me?* she wondered. She remembered Alon's cruel smile as he had watched the web-riders burn to death. *Why are we behaving so? What is happening to us?*

Confused, fighting down panic, she ran back down the hill-side to where Alon lay. Steel Talon alighted on the cantle of the saddle, where he perched, regarding her curiously as the songsmith applied the edge of her knife to the seal on the box. Moments later, she had it open, revealing the rich, red mud. Scooping up a generous dollop, she spread it thickly across the wound. Quickly she closed the container tightly, then used a stub of candle to reseal the box with wax, hoping fervently that it would serve, and that the healing substance within would retain its potency.

Within moments after the red mud was patted into place on his wrist, the lines of pain on Alon's countenance smoothed out. His muscles relaxed, and he appeared to fall into a deep, natural sleep. With slow, careful movements, she managed to ease off his blood-soaked shirt, then wet a cloth with hot water and used it to cleanse as much of the dried dirt and caked blood from his face, arms and chest as possible.

By the time she was finished, the sun had warmed and dried him. Though still pale, his color was better. Tucking the cloaks up snugly beneath his chin, she sat back on her heels and had another cup of tea. Then, while she chewed on a piece of journeybread, she crumbled another piece into water to make a sort of porridge. Glancing up at Steel Talon, she spoke aloud, finding her own voice strange and harsh in her ears. "After losing so much blood he really needs fresh meat, Winged One. Can you find something?"

The falcon gave a soft, piercing cry, then, in a blur of blackness, launched himself upward, winging off over the hill. By the time Eydryth had washed her patient's tunic, then managed to gently ease him into his clean shirt, the falcon sailed into view again. Steel Talon circled low over her, some-thing clutched in his talons—something that he dropped, so it landed half a dozen paces away.

Rising, Eydryth went over to find a small burrower. Picking the limp creature up by its long ears, she called out, "Thank you, Steel Talon!"

After skinning the animal, then chopping the meat as fine as the heavy blade of her dagger would allow, she dropped the sticky handfuls into the pot. While she waited for the thick broth to cook, she busied herself tending the Keplian's leg.

Encouraged to find the swelling down and the wound almost completely closed, Eydryth left the pot to simmer and took her pack around the curve of the hillside, following the stream until she found a shallow pool. There she stripped and washed; her breath caught in her throat at the chill of the water, but being clean again refreshed her. Her own blood-streaked shirt and breeches she soaked to remove the stains, then scrubbed with sand and stretched over a bush in the sunlight. Pulling on clean clothing, Eydryth went back to Alon.

The broth was ready. Cooling it with a little water, she managed to rouse Alon enough to get him to swallow it. She drank a cup of the hearty—though tasteless—brew herself, wishing she had thought to season it with thyme or sage.

Then, knowing that she could do nothing more to aid Alon, and by now so weary that the hillside blurred around her, reminding her of Yachne's spell-land, Eydryth lifted a corner of the cloak and crawled under it, fitting herself against Alon's warmth, careful not to jar his injured arm. *Just for a few minutes,* she thought. *I'll just doze for . . .*

Monso's moist, hot breath in her face woke her hours later. The Keplian was nosing her hair, snuffling eagerly at the sack of grain she was using for a pillow. Rubbing her eyes and yawning until she thought her jaw would split in two, the songsmith sat up, seeing that the sun lay far to the west.

After feeding the stallion, Eydryth put a hand on Alon's forehead to check for fever. His skin was slightly overwarm, but his color was good. The red mud, she noted, was nearly dried out. Dahaun had warned her to let it dry and harden until it cracked, before stripping it away. The songsmith wound a length of bandage around her patient's wrist to hold it in place.

After heating the broth again, she prepared to feed the Adept as before, but this time, when she touched him, Alon's grey eyes opened. Though clouded by bewilderment, he seemed lucid enough. "How do you feel?" she asked him.

"We are . . . back?" he whispered hoarsely.

She nodded. "The bridge-spell worked."

"Yachne?"

"There has been no sign of her or of any further spells," she told him. "Steel Talon and Monso would have given warning, I believe. After tending you, I was so weary that I could not stay awake."

He tried to push himself up on his elbows, but she forestalled him with a hand on his chest. "Softly, Alon. You are still weak. You lost a great deal of blood."

The Adept subsided for the moment, but the expression on his face told Eydryth that he would not accept her edict for long. "We cannot linger here," he said, his voice strengthening a bit. "We must take up the search again."

"It will do us little good to find Yachne if you are too weak to face her," she countered. "Even if I possess a tiny measure of the Power myself, I am no match for a sorceress with her ability."

His mouth tightened grimly. "I am by no means sure that *I* can face her with any chance of winning," he admitted. "That spell she wove to trap us . . . I could not equal that."

"But her Power is stolen," the songsmith pointed out. "Mayhap her knowledge is lacking, even if her ability is not. Here . . . ," she urged, dipping into the pot over the fire, "take some more soup. It will strengthen you." Carefully she helped him sit up, then put the cup into his hands. The thick liquid sloshed; his hands were trembling. Silently the songsmith helped him steady the container. He sipped, cautiously at first, then with more assurance.

It took all of Alon's strength to drink the soup and nibble halfheartedly at a few bits of dried fruit. He was plainly dismayed at his own weakness. "How is Monso?" he asked.

"The wound is closed. He seems nearly well."

"He has always healed quickly," the Adept said. His voice took on a bitter note. "Would that I could do likewise!"

"You must give yourself time to recover," Eydryth said. "I was exhausted from the spell you worked, and I had only to back you." She shook her head. "Nor did I lose the amount of blood you did. You need rest, and food."

"What I *need*," he said curtly, "is to find Yachne, so that I may repay her for the trials she has caused us! But by now she could be anywhere!"

Steel Talon squawked suddenly, sharply, plainly demanding attention. Alon turned to regard the bird intently, as the two obviously shared some wordless communication. As he "listened," the Adept's taut shoulders abruptly relaxed. "What is it?" Eydryth demanded.

"If I understand Steel Talon aright, he is telling me that the one we followed through the Gate is perhaps a half-day's journey ahead of us, no more—and that she is not hurrying." His mouth twisted sardonically. "Which should not surprise me. After working the spell that created that massive illusion-land, it is no wonder the witch is wearied!" He gazed thoughtfully up at the falcon. "There is something more . . . something clouded by anger that I cannot understand clearly. Steel Talon feels great anger toward Yachne."

"Because she is the cause of your troubles here in Arvon?" Eydryth guessed aloud.

"Steel Talon does not feel that strongly for me," Alon said. "It was Jon that he loved. Falconers and their birds are bound together by ties of great loyalty and affection."

"But you have companied together for a long time," she countered. "Steel Talon has affection for you, I can tell. When I told him that you needed fresh meat to regain your strength, he returned with some as swiftly as he could."

"Perhaps . . . ," he said, his voice ending with a sigh.

"You are wearied," she told him. "Lie back and rest."

He turned to regard the sun, hovering only a handspan over the distant hills. Crimson and yellow splashed the western clouds. "I can rest atop Monso. He can bear my weight, I believe, if we do no more than walk."

Eydryth opened her mouth to protest, but halted as he shook his head. "I know what you are about to say, but I will not be able to rest while we are so close to Yachne's bespelled ground. What if somehow we became entrapped there again?"

Eydryth glanced back uneasily at that faintly shimmering, raw-cut gorge. "Could that happen?"

"I know not. The spell she used was beyond my ability . . .

I cannot judge. I only know that I will rest better on Monso's back, going away from this place, than I ever could so near to it."

The songsmith sighed and gave in. Truth to tell, now that Alon had brought up the possibility that the spell-land might ensnare them again, she would not be able to relax near it, either. "Very well," she said. "I will lead Monso, and we will walk—but only for an hour or so, understand?"

He nodded. "I can sleep on horseback. I have done it before."

Leaning on Eydryth for support, he managed to walk the short distance to the streamside, where he laved his hands and face with the chill water, afterward drinking deeply. Then, while Eydryth saddled the Keplian and repacked their supplies, Alon swallowed another measure of the strengthening tisane.

When they were ready to start, Eydryth led the Keplian to a position downhill from the Adept. With her aid, he was able to place foot to stirrup, then clamber into the saddle, grunting with the effort. When he settled into place, she saw that his teeth were fastened in his lower lip, and sweat beaded his forehead.

Clumsily, favoring his injured arm, he drew his cloak around him, and they started off, the setting sun at their backs.

Fortunately, their path lay across gently rolling meadows, and Eydryth could see well enough to continue until full dark, thus putting several hillsides between them and Yachne's trap. When she reached the crest of the third such hillside, she halted, breathing a bit heavily, but feeling her spirits lift to be moving once again in the direction of their goal. She refused to let herself contemplate what might lie at the end of their search.

Looking up at Alon in the growing darkness, she saw that his eyes were closed, and he was slumped in the saddle, dozing. *If only I could go on a little farther before halting*, she thought, glancing back at the faint line of reddish-orange that still marked the western sky. *Monso, like all horses, has good night vision and will not need much guidance. If only I had the Power to see in the dark as Alon can!*

An instant later that idly framed thought brought her up short. *But I do* have the Power! *Perhaps I can use it, even as he does!*

Taking a quick drink from her flask to ease the dryness of her throat after walking, she opened her eyes wide, imagining herself seeing in the dark; then, softly, she began to hum.

To her left . . . there, that was a bush. As Eydryth concentrated, its outlines sharpened. And there . . . that was a small gully gouged by the hard spring rains. Over to her right was an ancient limb, its bare branches seeming skeletal in the uncanny vision she was acquiring.

Picking up Monso's lead once again, humming steadily, the songsmith went on.

By midnight she was stumbling with weariness, and her throat was too raw to produce any more sound. She had discovered, however, that simply holding the melody firmly in mind, hearing it within the confines of her own head, sufficed to allow her to use this small magic she now owned.

However, there was a price. By the Amber Lady, there was a grim tax levied on anyone who would use magic. For the first time Eydryth truly understood, understood in every muscle, every sinew, why Joisan and Elys and Alon and Hyana always emerged from spell-casting sessions shaking with weariness and ravenously hungry. Several times she had halted to chew handfuls of dried fruit.

Finally, when she was beginning to weave with exhaustion and clutch Monso's scraggly mane to stay upright, the songsmith had to halt. Her legs folded beneath her without her leave; she sank down on the grass.

She must have dozed there for several minutes, but finally she was roused by Monso's nosing the back of her neck. Stiff muscles screamed silent protest as she hoisted herself wearily to her feet. Alon was still a-horse, though he lay slumped across Monso's neck.

When she tried to loosen his hands, she found them locked in a death-grip on the Keplian's mane. She had to pry his fingers up, one by one.

Then she tugged at his body until he toppled toward her. She groaned aloud as she caught his limp weight. Though not much taller than she was, he weighed more. Struggling, she managed to ease him to the ground unharmed. Hastily wrapping him in his cloak, she left him to sleep. Food and water could wait. It was all she could do to pull Monso's saddle off, so the Keplian could graze.

Then, rolling herself in her own cloak, Eydryth stretched out on the ground, and knew no more.

She awoke some time later to the sound of Monso snorting and pawing nervously. The night was far spent; the thinnest sliver of moon shed a faint light. *By tomorrow it will be moon-dark*, she thought absently, pushing herself up on one elbow, wondering what had awakened her from such a profound slumber. Her answer came quickly—Monso. The half-bred stood nearby, not grazing, clearly agitated and on sentry-go.

"What is it, fellow?" she asked softly.

For reply the Keplian snorted so loudly that she jumped—a noisy *houufff!* of expelled breath.

The songsmith summoned night-sight, mentally running a melody through her mind, and clearly saw Monso, spilled ink against the softer blackness of the spring night. He was staring northward, neck arched, ears pricked so far forward they nearly touched at the tips, his ebony tail flung straight up. He snorted again, then, without warning, screamed—the ringing challenge of one stallion to another.

An answer came out of the distance—a slurred, hissing call that sounded like no creature she had ever encountered!

Thoroughly alarmed, the songsmith scrambled free of her cloak, hand reaching for her staff. When she drew her sword, the bared steel glimmered faintly in the wan light of the dying moon.

Alon mumbled something in his sleep, but did not awaken. Eydryth considered trying to rouse him, but, remembering his weakness, decided to let him sleep, if possible. Perhaps Monso's challenge had been voiced at the leader of a band of wild horses. Such were known to roam Arvon in its remoter parts. Distance or rock formations could have distorted the sound, made it seem so eerie.

But, as she gained her feet and stared northward, that faint hope vanished. Three mounted figures were trotting toward them. The songsmith's heart contracted within her.

Quickly she found Alon's lead-shank, then tethered the Keplian to a stout bush. There were no trees nearby, but she thought the fastening would hold him for a lunge or two. If their callers came in peace—*Please, by Your blessing, Amber Lady, let them not mean us harm!*—she did not want a stallion-battle on her hands.

As their visitors approached, she strained to make out details. The one in the center was tall, and bestrode a huge black. Seeing the flash of red from the creature's eyes, Eydryth realized that the beast was a full-blooded Keplian. Any small hope she had held that their nocturnal callers came with friendly intentions now vanished.

The two beasts flanking the Keplian seemed, at first glance, to be light grey or white horses. But as they came closer, she saw that they were not like any creatures she had ever seen.

Their heads were long and narrow, as were their necks, bodies and legs. Instead of a true horse's short hair, they seemed to gleam faintly, as though their skins were not only smooth, but also scaled! Glimpses of sharp, curving teeth were revealed as their riders reined them down to a walk some distance away. Eydryth saw that they did not have hooves, but clawed talons, much like the falcon's.

Like some kind of unnatural cross between horses and lizards, she thought. *Like those beasts Sylvya told me of, the ones that Maleron and his hunters bestrode, when they rode as That Which Runs the Ridges . . .*

The two armsmen wore black armor, and their faces were overshadowed by their helms, so the songsmith could make out no features.

But the central rider, the one mounted on the Keplian, wore brightly burnished chain mail and a dark red surcoat over it, worked with a crest. The songsmith stared at that device, certain that she had seen its like before, somewhere . . . a snake—or, rather, the bare skull of a snake—crowned, with dark rays of Power emanating from it. . . .

Where had she seen such a crest? Eydryth's mind spun

frantically, searching, scrabbling through memory. She had been with Jervon . . . yes, he had been there, and that same device had been carved . . . yes, carved . . . into a gatepost!

She had it now! It had been a gatepost at Garth Howell, the school where those with the Power came to learn to use their magic!

The memory surged into Eydryth's mind with such force that she gasped. She remembered the day she and her father had gone to the place to inquire about the Seeing Stone. The abbot, a thin, dark man with pale, ascetic features had courteously given them directions to reach the farseeing Place of Power. But before they had ridden forth, a young lay sister had drawn them aside, then whispered a few hasty words of warning. "Beware the Stone." Eydryth could hear again that hoarse young voice in her mind. "It gives true sight, but it exacts a terrible price for it!"

And behind the girl's head had been the gatepost, and upon it, graven deep into the granite, the same design that now faced her. The inhabitants of Arvon feared the school as a place where Power-wielders gathered, much as they feared the Grey Towers of the Wereriders. The place did not give open allegiance to the Left-Hand Path, but, over the years, there had been tales . . .

Eydryth's hand itched to raise her sword, but she forced herself to stand motionless as the riders halted before her. The one mounted on the Keplian unhelmed, and she saw, with her augmented vision, that he was well-favored—even handsome, with a strong jaw and regular features. *"Fair can be foul,"* she remembered Sylvya telling her. *"My brother Maleron was handsome. . . ."*

And so was Dinzil, Eydryth suddenly remembered. She kept her head up, her sword pointed down, but her knees were bent, her body poised to assume fighting stance. The songsmith held her silence, forcing the newcomer to speak first.

He leaned on the pommel of his saddle, his eyes holding hers. "Fair meeting, minstrel," he said, his tones cultured and deliberately mild. "You and your companion are traveling through our lands."

Garth Howell's lands, she thought, but did not reveal that she had recognized the device on his surcoat. Since it did not appear on any of the publicly displayed banners flown from the towers, she assumed that this sigil was intended to remain secret. "If we have trespassed, sir, I beg forgiveness. It was done in ignorance," she replied, keeping her voice smooth and courteous. "We are bound for Redmantle lands and beyond."

"Few travelers pass this way," he said, and with her increased night vision she discerned the raking glance he gave her, the still-slumbering Adept, and Monso. "Our dominions lie rather off the known paths. How did you come to be here?"

He is baiting me, she thought, but kept her voice civil and noncommittal. "We have been traveling for days," she said, speaking perfect truth but deliberately twisting the meaning. "Most recently we traversed a great Waste lying to the west of these foothills, after which we found ourselves here."

Her inquisitor could not conceal a start of surprise. His eyes narrowed in unbelief . . . and well he might be skeptical. No one that Eydryth had ever heard of before could claim to have crossed the noxious Waste that lay to the far west of Arvon. She smiled at him tentatively, wondering all the while why he and his men-at-arms (*Are they indeed of humankind?* she found herself thinking. *Their hands seem oddly shaped. . . .*) had come here.

"Indeed," he said softly. "That is extraordinary hearing."

Monso rumbled a deep challenge, and the leader's mount raised its head. The creature was too well schooled to reply, but its eyes gleamed red. "And that is an extraordinary stallion you have been riding," the newcomer continued, with barely a pause.

"No more so than your own," Eydryth countered pleasantly.

He smiled; that stretch of lip and flash of teeth, instead of making him seem more human, made him seem far less. "My mount is of the pure blood, yours is . . . something different. A cross that I would have considered impossible."

"Obviously not," she pointed out, "since he stands before you."

He chuckled, and the sound made the songsmith's skin crawl, as though slimy hands had fingered her naked flesh. One of the outriders made a chortling sound, and she thought she glimpsed sharpened rows of teeth within his mouth. Or was there a muzzle beneath that helm? She could not be sure. . . .

"Excellent!" the Dark leader announced. "You are a most extraordinary—and amusing—creature yourself, my lady. Not to mention passing fair." He swept her a bow from his saddle.

"Thank you, sir," she managed through stiff lips. Her fear of this Dark Adept—for so she now believed him to be—was growing, making the assumed lightness of their discourse more and more difficult for her to maintain. "May I ask a boon, please?"

"Of course!" He appeared delighted, and the aura of *wrongness* surrounding him intensified with each passing moment.

"May we traverse your demesnes, just long enough to reach the road? Again, I offer my deepest apologies for our inadvertent blunder."

" 'Our' ?" he said, then deliberately, as if noticing for the first time, looked down at Alon, who lay huddled and still. "You have a companion! One that shares your bed, perhaps, as well as your road?"

Ignoring Eydryth's tight-lipped headshake, he went on, in tones of mock-grief, "Alas, it seems I have a rival . . . oh, my heart lies in ruins, songsmith," he said, gauntleted hand pressed to the breast of his surcoat, where that disturbing design was growing ever more distinct. Pearly light brightened the east now; sunrise was not far off. Eydryth wondered distractedly whether these creatures could stand to encounter the light of day—many Shadowed beings could not—but neither the leader nor his outriders seemed worried by dawn's nearness.

The Dark Adept looked down at Alon's wan, pinched features beneath his tumbled, none-too-clean hair, then sighed deeply. "I must say, my lady songsmith, that I fail to comprehend your taste. You could do better, I am certain."

Anger surged up in Eydryth, growing hotter by the moment, and with a toss of her head she abandoned this ridiculous facade of flirtation, this mockery of courtly conversation. "You did not answer my question, sir," she said bluntly.

"What question, fair lady?"

"About whether we have permission to cross your domain."

"That is correct, I did not." The Dark One studied her intently. "Remiss of me. My answer is thus. You will accompany me back to our stronghold to speak with the Lord Abbot, who is the one you must entreat. I am certain that he will grant your request to traverse our lands."

"And how far away is your stronghold?" she demanded.

"Barely a full day's ride," he replied lightly. "Such a small delay will not trouble you overmuch, will it, my lady?"

Eydryth felt anger building, until it pulsed behind her eyes, hot and vital. She recognized that strength of Will, that resolve, that gathering for what it was—*Power*. The songsmith did not allow herself to think about the abilities of the Adept she faced, his probable mastery of magic. Instead she merely smiled grimly. "I am afraid that it would be a great inconvenience. I regret that I must decline your kind invitation, sir."

His handsome face hardened, and he laid hand to the hilt of his sword, then drew it smoothly. "And I am afraid that I must insist."

She laughed outright, saw him start with surprise. "Then, sir, I must resist!" she cried, deliberately rhyming him. An idea was surging through her mind like Monso at full gallop, an idea built on generations of tradition—and on the Power she could feel herself becoming a vessel to hold. Lyrics and melody crowded her mind, pouring in without conscious thought.

"With that?" Recovering, he smiled grimly and pointed at her sword.

"No . . . ," Eydryth said, then slowly, deliberately, sheathed the blade. Picking up her hand-harp case, she took out the instrument, struck a ringing chord that seemed to swell and resound in the air, until it was nearly deafening. "With this!"

The Power filled her as she began to strum, then sing:

Would you then offend me, sir?
I'll stand on minstrel's right:

> May your bright blade blind you,
> That you see not where it falls,
> May your heartthrob fill your ears
> That you hear not succor's call.
> May every briar bind you,
> And fling you to your knees,
> May a loose-willed wench deny you,
> When you would seek her ease.

She saw the two unhuman outriders surreptitiously edge their mounts away from their overlord, watched his open consternation as her satire—filled with the Power she could feel emanating from her, thrumming forth from her harp—dominated the air. Ancient lore had it that one who offended a bard could be ill-wished, cursed, even unto death.

Eydryth poured into her song all her rage, all her frustration, all her anger at Yachne. *The witch is probably behind this*, she thought, feeling the words emerge from her mouth so poisoned that they might have been dipped in venom. *The forces of the Dark want to delay us, which will aid her. Well, we shall see about* that!

Her mind working fast, she fingered the harp in ringing chords, wishing for a fleeting moment that she had thought to put her finger picks on. The quan-iron strings stung her fingers. More words fell into place as she hastily composed the second verse of the satire. A rapid strum, then she continued, her voice rising with every note:

> Then would you draw sword on me?
> Why sir, so let this be!
> Now let the moon-mad guide you
> Down illusion's wandering ways,
> Now let you outlive your children,
> In an eternity of days:
> Let cowardice o'ertake you
> When you would be most brave;
> And let your rotted body lie
> In an unremembered grave!

The Keplian squealed, frightened, in response to a cruel jab from a spaded bit. The outriders backed their mounts away from their leader. Guttural, gobbling sounds broken with hisses emerged from the misshapen mouths the songsmith could glimpse beneath the creatures' helmets. Eydryth had never heard their language before, but, even so, she could not mistake the fear in their voices.

The Dark Adept's features writhed in pain and fear. Eydryth's fingers plucked the strings of her harp, sending forth the music, and her anger, directed straight at him. She knew beyond legend, beyond knowledge, beyond instinct . . . she knew in her bones that her words held Truth as well as Power. Her curse would come to pass. She was singing the Dark Adept's fate, sealing it with her own magic.

"Let your rotted body lie in an unremembered grave!" She flung the last line at him again, seeing it strike with the force of an actual blow. With a wordless snarl, the leader spun his mount on its haunches and spurred it back in the direction they had come. The two outriders followed, but slower, staying well away from their master's vicinity—as though they feared that the fate Eydryth had cursed him with might fall upon them, too, if they ventured too close.

Just as the flaming edge of the sun glimmered over the nearest hill, they vanished into the forested slope, heading north.

Eydryth stared after them, savoring her victory. She felt strong, triumphant, burning as though a fire of angry hatred blazed within her. As she remembered the Dark Adept's expression, and the fate she had called down upon him, the songsmith threw back her head and laughed—laughed long and loud . . . laughed until she had no breath left, and needs must gasp after it. Some small corner of her mind was shrieking at her that it was wrong to so exult in the downfall of another—even a Dark One—but she ignored that prickle of conscience.

"Let your rotted body lie in an unremembered grave," Eydryth whispered, smiling a death's-head grin as the dawnlight crept across her face.

Thirteen

*A*s Eydryth's laughter finally faded away into small wheezes of savage merriment, a voice reached her ears: "Well done, songsmith."

She whirled around, to find Alon sitting up, regarding her steadily. "How long have you been awake?" she demanded, feeling some of yesterday's anger at him surface again.

"Long enough," he made reply, "to see that you needed no aid in defeating that one." He nodded in the direction of the vanished Dark Adept. "Congratulations."

She scowled at him furiously. "Small help you were! I thought you too weak to even sit up without aid, else I would have tried to awaken you, so *you* could have dealt with our visitor." The rush of Power was ebbing, emptying her, leaving her body so weak that she was suddenly forced to sit down before she toppled over. Her head ached fiercely . . . her flesh seemed to shrivel on her bones.

Alon shrugged carelessly. "You did not need me. And now perhaps you will believe that you possess more than a touch of Power." He smiled without humor. "I would never have thought of using a satire. Those things will come to pass for him, you know," he said, slanting a curious glance at her, as if asking whether she minded.

The songsmith tossed her head. "I know they will," she said, then smiled, feeling a rush of satisfaction. Her own exultation at the defeat of the Dark One again struck her as wrong, shadowed, but she easily pushed that small, nagging prickle of conscience aside. "Now what?" she asked.

He dragged over the saddlebag containing their provisions. "First we eat and drink, then we depart," he said simply. "We must be gone from here as swiftly as may be. There may be more where *he* came from."

After they finished eating, Eydryth checked his wound. Beneath the scrap of bandage, the mud was hardened and cracking loose, so she chipped it away with a ragged fingernail. Where the gaping slash had been, there was naught but a thin, white scar. She stared at it wonderingly. *If only it can work such wonders on my father!* Her hope was shaken, though, when she remembered that she had broken the seal on Dahaun's box.

Monso's wound was much improved, and his master again chanted a healing-spell over it, while rubbing it with a paste he produced from his supplies. When Eydryth would have taken her accustomed place at the Keplian's head, the Adept pointed to the stirrup. "Today you ride," he said. "Such magic as you worked demands a cruel toll from the body. I will walk."

She studied his features, still pale beneath the weathering caused by their days in the sun. "You are not strong enough yet," she said, knowing she spoke truth.

"I slept most of yesterday," he reminded her. "Where you barely rested at all. Up you go," he ordered, pointing to the saddle.

Eydryth hesitated, but then, feeling her own weakness, she

placed foot to stirrup. Alon steadied her as she slowly swung up onto the Keplian's back, stifling a grunt of pain as sore muscles protested.

It seemed odd to sit in the middle of Monso's back, rather than on his rump. The half-bred shifted restlessly, rolling an eye back at her; then his ears flattened. She tensed as she felt the coiled strength in his hindquarters and shoulders. The Keplian snorted, pawing angrily.

"Am I the first person to bestride him other than you?" she asked, suppressing a catch in her voice. Memory of those terrifying rides when Monso had bolted made her swallow.

The Adept nodded. 'Keep your legs loose on his sides," he warned, reminding her curtly of what she already knew from her years of experience while riding with the Kioga, helping them break horses. "If you are tense, he will feel your unease." Quietly, he soothed his horse.

The songsmith nodded, forcing herself to relax in the saddle. Gradually, the hump in the Keplian's back eased. Alon started forward, leading the half-bred. Moments later, Steel Talon swooped by, screeching a hoarse greeting.

Within an hour, the lack of sleep and the previous day's exertions told on Eydryth; she fell into a light doze in the saddle, her body automatically swaying to the rhythm of Monso's walk.

She awoke with a gasp and a jerk when the black half-bred abruptly halted, flinging his head up as though he had been unexpectedly jabbed by the bit. Startled, Eydryth sat up, blinking, then rubbed sleep out of her gritty eyes. Her mouth was dry, filled with a taste that made her grimace. Hunger gnawed her vitals. By the look of the sun, it was well past noon.

Ahead of them stretched a road, the first such they had seen. Eydryth glanced down at Alon, saw him leaning heavily against Monso's shoulder, as though that support were the only thing keeping him up.

The bard swallowed, attempting to force words from the dry well that was now her throat. "Alon?" she croaked. "What chances? Are you hurt?"

He shook his head, but made no move to straighten up. Eydryth slid down out of the saddle, catching him by the arm and peering into his face. He was sweating and pale. "What happened?" she asked worriedly.

"Twisted my foot," he muttered. "Need a moment . . ."

"You have walked too far," she said, taking down the water flask and lifting it to her lips, first rinsing the vileness from her mouth, then drinking thirstily. She handed it to him, watched him drink, then said, "You ride now. I'll walk."

"No," he said, sealing the flask. His tone brooked no opposition. "Climb back on. I can walk."

"Walk?" She let her scorn at the idea fill her voice. "Oh, of a certainty! And run, too, no doubt! Don't be a fool!"

His grey eyes hardened until they appeared as light and flat as pebbles in a streambed. "I told you, *I* will walk." He jerked his head at the Keplian's empty saddle. "Climb back up. Now."

"You cannot order me," she stated, her voice cold and soft. "You will be an even greater fool if you attempt that."

The Adept flushed angrily. "Watch your tongue, songsmith. It is wagging too freely."

"What I say and where I go—and *how* I reach my destination"—her own anger was growing, and she clenched both fists—"are *my* concern, not yours!"

His mouth tightened to a grim slash, and around him the air seemed to shiver and glow. Fear touched the bard, and she took a hasty step backward before she could stop herself.

Alon opened his mouth to say something—and, from his expression, it was no pleasantry—but his words were never uttered. Without warning, Steel Talon screamed shrilly; then Monso thrust his big black head against his master's chest, nearly knocking him over. The Adept swore as his injured foot gave way beneath him. He barely managed to stay on his feet. By the time he had recovered his balance, Eydryth had regained control of her temper.

Pointing down at the Keplian's leg, she said, "He is nearly healed. If we go slowly, there is no reason we both cannot ride."

Her companion hesitated. She watched as he tried unobtrusively to rest his weight on his right foot, then repressed a wince. Finally, Alon nodded. "Very well," he snapped.

Limping, he went over to the stallion and climbed up; then, reluctantly, he turned in the saddle to offer a hand to the songsmith. Pointedly, she ignored his grudging offer of aid, managing instead to swing up behind him unassisted.

Scowling blackly, Alon signaled Monso forward, and the Keplian walked steadily toward the road. But when they reached that earthen track, Alon turned the stallion's head southeast. Eydryth nudged him. "Kar Garudwyn lies that way," she said urgently, pointing due east, to their left.

He ignored her.

Urgently, the songsmith tugged at his arm. "You are heading the wrong way!"

Stubbornly, he shook his head.

"Alon!" She struck him lightly on the shoulder. *"Halt!"*

His voice, when it finally came, was little more than a sullen growl. "No."

"Alon, we must go due east, not this way! What do you hope to gain by this?"

Finally he signaled the Keplian to stop, then turned to look at her. "Yachne's death," he said flatly. "The sorceress is that way," he added, pointing southeast.

"But . . . but . . . ," she stammered with indignation, feeling an anger that was being rapidly quenched by fear. *He truly means to do it!* "We have already decided that it would be best to go straight to Kar Garudwyn. We cannot turn aside from our path! Kerovan, remember? We must save Kerovan!"

"When Yachne is dead, she will prove no threat to anyone on this world," he said, and there was a vicious undertone to his voice that made Eydryth's breath catch in her throat. "Steel Talon tells me that she has headed this way, and is still little more than a half-day's journey ahead of us."

"I am not going!" Eydryth cried. "I will go on alone to warn Kerovan!"

"Go then," he snarled, "and take my curse!"

Fury surged hot within her, but something in Alon's eyes as

he stared at her made her swallow and remain silent. She shifted her weight so she could slide down the near side of Monso's rump. "I'll go," she whispered.

Steel Talon suddenly plunged out of the air, screaming shrilly. Monso shied. If the Keplian had leaped to the right, Eydryth would have been left hanging in midair, her destination the green meadow grass. But instead Monso moved to his left, dropping and lunging so that the songsmith found herself again in the middle of his rump.

Instinctively, she grabbed Alon around the waist, just as the stallion plunged forward with a heart-stopping buck. "No!" Alon yelled, struggling to regain control. The Adept's legs closed on the stallion's sides, trying to drive the half-bred forward, so his head would come up. He bent over, hands squeezing and releasing on the reins, trying to dislodge the bit from the Keplian's teeth—

—and succeeded only too well. Grunting, Monso flung his head up. His heavy stallion's crest with its crowning bristle of mane struck his rider full in the face. The Adept sagged, limp. He would have fallen were it not for Eydryth's enclosing arms.

Even the smallest crowhop would have unseated his riders by then, but Monso had apparently abandoned his efforts to rid himself of his passengers. Instead, the Keplian's strides began to lengthen. He broke into a swift canter, and then he was galloping.

Eydryth managed to grab the pommel of the saddle with both hands, then heaved herself up and over the cantle, until she was jammed into the seat with Alon. Groping for the reins, she snatched them from the Adept's lax fingers, and, peering past his shoulder, began sawing at the stallion's mouth.

Monso ignored her efforts. He was running now, moving with those long, swift strides that marked his fastest pace. "Monso!" she shouted into the whipping wind. Eydryth's surroundings blurred as tears filled her eyes. "Easy, boy! Ho, now!" One black ear turned back to catch her words, but there was no other reaction.

They were heading east now, in the direction of Kar Garudwyn, flashing down the soft-packed road with the headlong rush of a forest fire. Alon's weight swayed dangerously in the saddle, and the songsmith stiffened her arms to keep him from pitching headlong onto the verge. At the speed they were now traveling, such a fall could have been fatal.

Wedged into the saddle as she was, Eydryth herself was in little danger of falling, for Monso ran straight and leveled-out, his strides so smooth that very little motion was perceived by his rider. But as for control over the Keplian . . . she had none. The stallion might as well have had a halter on his head instead of a bridle, for all the attention he paid to the bit or her attempts to slow him.

Eydryth felt light-headed from fear. Monso was moving so fast that time itself seemed blurred. Had the Keplian been running for minutes? Hours? There was no way to know.

Summoning up all her strength, she attempted to sing soothingly, as she had done that day at the horse fair. But her words were blown away by the wind of their passage. Grimly, she tried putting pressure on only one rein, hoping she could so direct the Keplian into a slowly diminishing circle, but, again, her efforts were useless.

Alon stirred before her, then moaned, beginning to struggle feebly as consciousness returned. "Hold still!" Eydryth screamed in his ear. "Don't move, or we'll both fall!"

She knew he must have heard her, because, moments later, his hands closed over hers on the reins. Together they fought to slow Monso—still to no avail.

There was something ahead of them . . . to the left, off the road. A strange shape, like that of a giant, grey-stemmed mushroom with a spring-green cap, set on the crest of a hill. A black streak winged past them, stooping out of the air, and she heard Steel Talon's shrill shriek. Monso abruptly veered off the road, and, if anything, increased his pace as he headed up the hill toward the crest.

Eydryth closed her eyes, offering up a silent plea to Gunnora that the racing Keplian would not encounter a burrower's hole or a stoat's den—or the sunken remains of a fence—at this insane speed.

The steepness of the hillside did not slow the Keplian.

Monso was now moving so swiftly that Eydryth felt as though she were astride Steel Talon, flying, rather than riding a land-bound creature.

As they reached the top of the hill, Eydryth blinked, and suddenly the mushroom-shape before them sprang into clear view: it was a circular grove of mammoth trees with pale-grey trunks, topped with feathery green boughs that sprouted only from their uppermost heights. Monso slowed to a gallop as he began moving around the perimeter of the huge grove.

The trees stood so symmetrically in a circle that their planting must have been the work of some hand, not nature's happenstance. A loud, rasping sound now reached the song-smith's ears, and she realized that Monso was finally winded, his breath rasping like iron filings. White foam curded his neck.

"Can you stop him now?" she shouted into Alon's ear.

"I'm trying," came his grim reply.

But the Keplian galloped on, around the narrow trunks that almost formed a natural barrier, so close together did they grow. They were on the eastern side of the hill now, following the curve of the grove.

Eydryth glanced down at the thick green grass beneath them. "Should we jump?"

"You jump," Alon ordered, leaning back against the reins, his shoulders working. "But I stay with—"

He broke off as Steel Talon again flew past them, screaming his piercing cry. Immediately Monso planted his forehooves in the turf, tucked his hindquarters beneath him, and skidded to a halt. Both riders were thrown forward, slamming into him and each other with bruising force.

Alon began to curse the stallion, then, in a frenzy of anger, lashed the black's neck with the end of his reins. Eydryth was shocked by the savagery in his voice, the vicious snap of his blows against the sweating black hide.

Steel Talon screamed again.

Their mount lunged forward in a huge leap, bucking like a demon-horse possessed. Eydryth clung grimly through one leap—two—then felt herself slipping as the Keplian sunfished, flinging his hind legs up and out behind her head, then twisting in midair like a serpent writhing with a broken back.

The bard felt the wind of her own passage as she was hurled into the air. Following instinct learned from years of training horses with the Kioga, she curled into a ball, ducking her head to protect it. Monso was bellowing with fury, and she had one final moment to hope that he did not land on her during one of his frenzied leaps.

As she struck the ground, Eydryth managed to roll, absorbing most of the impact on the soft turf. Even so, she gasped, feeling as though a giant hand had wrung her chest and back.

Dazedly, she raised her head, saw Alon grimly clinging to the madly plunging stallion, but it was plain that the Adept was losing his battle. Blood was running freely from his nostrils; he had abandoned pride and was gripping the pommel of the saddle with one hand, even as he fought stubbornly to pull Monso's head up and drive the horse forward.

As she lay there, struggling to catch her breath, Eydryth felt a strange warmth tingling along her left arm. Fearing the worst, she turned her head, but her fingers curled at her command, there was no bleeding or break. The bard saw that Monso's buck had thrown her almost within the only opening in the giant circular grove of uncanny trees. Her left arm lay within the opening—and from it, a sensation was spreading.

Warmth . . . comfort . . . healing . . . light. It was all those things, and more. Much more. The light crept within her, spreading, filling her with peace, driving out the anger, the *wrongness* that had frightened her during the past days when she had felt it trying to possess her. The sensation of being *healed* of a dark sickness of the spirit was so compelling that she stared at her arm, transfixed, forgetting Alon, forgetting the battle between mount and master raging still behind her.

Cautiously, she levered herself up on her hands. Her head still spun from the fall, her ears rang with weakness, but the urge to drive out the Darkness that had been growing within her drove her onward. Eydryth crawled slowly, not halting until her entire body lay within the entrance to this strange place.

Light and warmth enveloped her, soothing body and spirit. Understanding grew as it did so, knowledge of what had been happening to her, the reason that both she and Alon had been reacting so strangely. Ever since they had jumped through that Dark Gate, a malignant Shadow had grown within them, a darkness of spirit that was now being driven out by the light and life of this hallowed Place of Power.

Healing . . . it was healing her, body and spirit.

After a time . . . she had no idea how long, though later she realized it could not have been more than a minute or two . . . Eydryth sighed, then levered herself up. Strength returned to her—not the black strength of raging hate and anger that had empowered her before, but a quiet healing strength that this Place of Power had bestowed upon her, a gift beyond price.

Her bruises had stopped aching, she felt renewed . . . refreshed.

Gazing back through the entrance, she was just in time to see Monso rear up. His front legs slashed the air as he towered like some ancient elemental horse-spirit, his eyes crimson with savage fury, strings of reddish foam dripping from his open mouth. Then, in a frenzy of rage, the stallion flung himself over backward. Helplessly Eydryth crouched, hands pressed against her mouth, certain that Alon would be killed.

But, at the last possible moment, the Adept leaped free of the saddle, landing halfway between the bard and his erstwhile steed. Monso rolled over and struggled to his feet, head hanging low, breathing in agonized gasps.

Slowly his master sat up. "Alon!" Eydryth cried, but he stared at her blankly, without recognition. Fresh horror filled her as she realized that Alon's grey eyes had gone a strange, dead silver.

As she flung herself toward him, he shook off her grasping arm, ignoring her, then climbed to his feet and headed back for the stallion, his expression a silent curse that boded no good for his hapless mount. Purple lightning—*Purple is the color of the Shadow*, Eydryth remembered with a sick feeling of horror—began to crackle from between his splayed fingers.

Eydryth realized that he meant to kill the Keplian. The Shadow that had been growing within her had possessed him completely. *And no wonder*, she realized, as she stumbled after him, *he not only went through the Dark Gate, he worked the black spell that caused it to open! That essence of the Shadow that was growing within me has affected him even more strongly. When he worked that Dark magic, Alon took the Shadow into himself, as surely as if he poisoned himself by eating rancid or rotting meat!*

"Run, Monso!" Eydryth screamed. She made a futile grab for the Adept, just as a bolt of purple flamed from Alon's fingers. It licked out, but the Keplian shied violently and it missed him. The stallion, obviously confused, the habit of obedience conflicting with his sudden fear of the master that he loved, backed slowly away. Alon stalked toward him, his bloody face dark with fury, eyes cold and sharp as argent blades. Both hands came up, fingers crooked, for another attempt.

Eydryth hit the Adept in the small of his back with her shoulder, driving him forward and down. Purple lightning crackled, snaking along the ground, leaving a blackened trail in the thick turf.

Alon rolled over, cursing aloud now. Seeing his face, the songsmith knew that now it was she who was in great danger. *I have to get him into the Place of Power*, she thought. *Mayhap it can heal him, too!*

Gritting her teeth, hating herself for what she was about to do, she clenched her fist and slammed it into his jaw, even as he struggled to regain his feet.

The Adept went down again, stunned, and she hastily grabbed his foot, began dragging him toward that haven of healing and light. "Please, Amber Lady," she whispered through dry lips. "Please, let him be—"

Alon's other foot, booted and heavy, smashed hard against her forearm, numbing it instantly. Eydryth cried out, dropping his leg, unable to hold on. He was already rolling away from her, coming up, turning to run—run away from the Place of Power. Fear was graven into every line of his features.

It's the Shadow within him . . ., she thought. *It will not give him up!*

"Alon, no!" she cried, bolting after him. He had nearly reached the heaving, spraddle-legged Keplian when she caught him, shoving him aside with a hard thrust of her good arm. He spun, fell, then was up again, moving with a quickness that bespoke desperation.

But already the songsmith's fingers had closed on her quarterstaff, which was fastened along the Keplian's side. She jerked it free with a frantic tug. "Alon . . . ," she gasped, trying to hold his eyes with her own, reach beyond the Darkness that had engulfed him, "you . . . have to come . . . with me."

He did not answer, only backed away. Purple light sparked from his hands, and she knew that he could kill her—kill her easily. "Don't—" she pleaded. "Remember Jonthal. . . ."

He blinked, confused, and for a moment his eyes were his own dark grey again. But then they hardened, brightened, and the bard knew that she had lost him.

With a sudden leap he was on her, kicking the staff. Her still-numbed fingers could not hold it, and it flew spinning from her hand. Alon's left fist slammed into her head, near her ear, just as the fingers of his right hand dug into her throat.

Red flashes went off behind her eyes, but she reacted as Jervon had trained her, going with her attacker's motion, giving way, using his superior strength against him. Eydryth let herself fall, rolling onto her back, spine curved, at the same moment bringing her knees up. They slammed hard into Alon's midsection, and she heard the breath go out of him in a great wheeze.

Quickly, she shoved him over, then swung her small, callused fist into his jaw. Once . . . twice . . . His eyes glazed over, and she saw the light go out of them. He sagged, barely conscious.

Breathing now as hard as Monso, she grabbed his arms, dragged them over his head, then began tugging him back toward the entrance. Halfway there, she glanced behind her, marking the gap in the tree trunks—and that proved her undoing.

Alon suddenly came to life again, twisting in her grasp, wrenching himself away. As he spun, one leg kicked out, cutting both feet out from under her.

Eydryth went down, landing hard; then he was up and away, running haltingly, not toward Monso, now, but west, back the way they had come. The songsmith's flailing hand closed on her quarterstaff, and, before she could even complete the idea in her mind, she was up on one knee, her good arm drawn back to its fullest extent. Her shoulder protested as she hurled the bronze-shod length after the limping man.

The gryphon-headed staff whirled through the air, low and parallel to the ground, to strike hard against Alon's booted legs. The Adept went down again, and this time he lay unmoving.

Sobs nearly overcame her for a second—*Amber Lady, what have I done?* Then the bard was up and running. *If I've killed him* . . .

Eydryth reached Alon's side. Dropping to her knees, she cautiously rolled him over. The man's face was a hideous mask of bruised flesh and bloody scratches, but his chest was moving. Eydryth touched fingers to his throat, felt the throb of the pulse there. She drew breath into her aching lungs; then tears again coursed down her face—but this time they were of relief.

Quickly, before Alon could regain consciousness, the songsmith began dragging him again toward the entrance, halting only when he lay completely within the gap in the trees. She sagged to her knees beside him, fingers gripping his cold hand, hardly daring to hope. For the first time, she glanced past the trunks of the entrance, to see what lay inside this tree-barriered enclosure.

The circular expanse of ground within was covered with soft turf, sprinkled liberally with wildflowers. Scarlet and indigo, amber and pale yellow, violet and dusky rose . . . never had she seen such a profusion. In the middle of them were tumbled rocks, and in the sudden silence of this Place, Eydryth could distinctly hear the bubbling of a spring.

Water . . . The thought made her tremble with sudden thirst. *Water to drink, water to wash Alon's wounds . . . water for Monso* . . .

Moving unsteadily, she made her way over to the Keplian, pulled off his saddle, then emptied all their water flasks, slinging them over her shoulder. With stumbling, eager strides she reentered the Place of Power. The heady scents of the wildflowers rose up around her like incense as she trod that many-hued carpet.

The spring welled into a hollow in the middle of the largest boulder. Eydryth rolled up her sleeves as she knelt on the edge of a sun-warmed boulder, looking down.

Clear, cold, seeming to gleam with an inner Light, the water from the spring bubbled up. She held out her hands, dipped them gratefully into the coldness, then cupped them, brought forth a sparkling handful, sipped.

The water coursed down her throat like a cool blessing. Eydryth drank her fill, then laved her face, her hands, washing away sweat and dirt, feeling more renewed with each passing moment. The pain from her bruises and strained muscles vanished.

Gazing around her, marveling at the effect of that water, the songsmith wondered yet again just what manner of place this was. Obviously a Place of Power . . . Then, suddenly, the knowledge surfaced in her mind, recalled from tales heard long ago.

The Fane of Neave.

It was said to lie in the northwestern portion of this ancient land. Dark sorcery could not enter the Fane, could not exist within it. Small wonder that that inner darkness that had been growing within her had utterly disappeared once she crossed the border of this place. Neave . . . Neave was one of the Oldest Ones. Neave was all things natural, and good, and fruitful.

Even now, when couples were wed in Arvon, they drank a toast, each in turn, invoking Neave with their bridal cup, asking Neave to bless their union, make it devoted and fruitful.

The Fane of Neave. It had to be.

"Thank you, O Neave," Eydryth breathed, her voice soft and earnest. "Thank you. . . ."

A sense of peace, quiet benediction, filled her. After a moment she bent to her task again, refilling the water flasks with the springwater.

Carrying them, she went back to the entrance, her step once more swift and assured. Glancing down at Alon as she passed, she saw that he still lay unmoving, but the lines of pain and fear had smoothed out on his bruised, battered countenance. He seemed now to be in a natural sleep.

Once outside the Fane, she whistled softly, then saw the Keplian some distance away, cropping desultorily at the grass. Eydryth walked over to Monso, checked first his wound, and was relieved to discover that he had not reopened it, fortune be praised. Scenting the water, he nudged her, rumbling low in his throat.

She dared not let him drink much so soon after running so hard, but she gave the stallion several carefully rationed sips from Neave's spring, using their small cooking pot. The thirsty creature lapped the cool liquid with his huge, pale-pink tongue, reminding her for all the world of a cat. Wetting down a corner of her cloak, she swiped and rinsed the sweat from the sable hide until the salty stiffness was gone.

By the time she had finished, Monso had begun to graze, tearing hungrily at the grass. Relieved that Neave's spring had worked its restorative effect again, and that the Keplian no longer was on the verge of foundering with exhaustion, she went back to the Adept.

Sitting down cross-legged beside him, she carefully lifted his head into her lap, then wiped his face and hands. At the touch of that cool water, she saw the bruises and swellings visibly lessen, until they seemed only shadows of the original injuries.

Then, steadying his head against her thigh, she held the flask to his lips, urging him softly to drink. Alon sipped a little, swallowed, sipped again. He sighed deeply as the last lines of pain smoothed away from his face; then, a moment later, he opened his eyes. Eydryth offered a silent invocation of thanks, for his eyes were his own again, dark grey, gentle, and, at the moment, bewildered.

"What happened?" he whispered.

She touched finger to his lips, cautioning him to be quiet.

"In a moment," she promised. "Drink some more, Alon. You must be very thirsty."

He sighed, nodding, never taking his eyes from her face as he drank again, this time deeply. "We are in a safe place," Eydryth told him, when he finished. "A Place of Power. Monso ran away . . . do you remember?"

Alon turned his head, and his eyes left hers to fasten on the Keplian, hungrily cropping grass. "He is fine," she reassured him. "I will give him more to drink in a little while. The water from this spring is very restoring. How do you feel?"

"Well . . . now. But I cannot remember how I came here. I remember walking an endless dead land . . . and you singing . . . and a bridge of blood. I remember a Dark One . . . that you vanquished. Or was I dreaming?" he whispered uncertainly.

"No dream," she replied, simply.

He turned his head as it lay pillowed in her lap, seeing the entrance to the Fane, the wildflower sward, the boulders surrounding the spring. "Where are we?" he whispered, finally.

"The Fane of Neave," she replied. "Or so I believe."

"A Place of Power . . . ," he said.

"Yes. How do you feel now?" she asked again.

"Well," he replied. "The pain is gone. I feel as though I may have been . . . ill. Was I sick?" he asked, almost childlike in his bemusement.

"Yes. But you are well now," she assured him. "We are safe here."

"I have been . . . cleansed," he said after a moment, as if just realizing it. His eyes held hers intently for a long moment. "So have we both," he added.

"Yes. Nothing of the Shadow can exist here. This is a protected place."

"The past days . . ." He put out a hand, grasped hers tightly, urgently, and Eydryth watched memory flood back. "I *was* . . . sick. Poisoned by the Shadow. I said things . . ." He halted, nearly choking, his eyes widening with alarm. "Eydryth . . . I was planning to . . . to kill Yachne!"

"I know," she said, gently. "But you were not yourself. Nor was I myself, when I drove away that Dark One."

"I could never harm her," he went on dully. "She raised me . . . cared for me. If she bore me no affection, that still does not lessen the debt I owe her for that. And remembering that I had planned to kill her makes me—" He broke off, and the songsmith could see more memories surface. The Adept drew a hard, sharp breath. "Eydryth—! I tried to kill Monso!"

"You did not harm him," she made swift reply.

He sat up with a lurch, his eyes wide with horror. She saw him begin to shake, as though with an ague. "But the Amber Lady, Eydryth, it all comes back . . . I did my best to kill *you!*"

"I am fine," she said, smiling, but she could not meet his gaze, suddenly afraid of the intensity she knew would be there. "As you can plainly see. Alon . . ." She swallowed, her throat tight. "Alon, you were not yourself. Neither of us remained untouched, but you— Working that spell to open the Dark Gate meant that you were more affected than I. If it were not for the Fane, we would both have been lost to ourselves."

His hands came up, closed on her shoulders with a grip that made her gasp. "Eydryth . . . look at me. *Look* at me." He waited, and after a moment she managed to raise her eyes to his, color rising hot into her cheeks at what she read there. "If anything happened to you . . ." He struggled for words, his voice grown thick and unsteady. "I would not . . . could not . . . without you . . . there is nothing . . ." He drew a deep, ragged breath. "Nothing, do you understand?"

She could summon no words of her own, could only stare at him, wide-eyed, feeling his breath touch her face, so close were they now.

Was it Alon who first leaned forward? Was it she? Or had they both moved at the same moment? Eydryth was never sure. She only knew that his hands had moved from her shoulders to gently cup her face; she only knew that their mouths met.

It was a gentle, tentative caress, a mere brushing of lips. Even though she had almost no experience at this herself, the songsmith realized immediately, instinctively, that Alon was no more lessoned in such matters than she—and found that knowledge pleased her, though why, she could not have told.

After a moment, he drew away, eyes searching her face, his fingers softly, hesitantly tracing her cheekbones, threading through the tumbled curls over her temples, pushing them back from her eyes. Eydryth struggled to speak, but Alon shook his head sternly, his fingers brushing her lips, halting any words.

Rising to his feet, he reached out a hand. As if spellbound (though this was a different magic from any she had yet encountered, if no less strong) she reached up, laid her fingers in his. He pulled her up to her feet, then into his arms, holding her tightly.

There was nothing tentative about this second kiss. Eydryth clung to him, shaken, as new feelings, desires, awoke within her, making her face honestly for the first time the knowledge that had been growing inside her ever since they had met. Until now she had pushed away her own longings, refused to acknowledge them, buried them as deeply as she could. But that was over now. Now there could be no denying, no going back . . . nor did she wish to.

Finally, he drew away slightly, stared down at her wordlessly. Eydryth rested her forehead against his shoulder, leaning against him as he stroked her tangled hair. The silence stretched between them, until finally he broke it. "Oh, my," she heard him whisper. She smiled, shaking her head, repressing a sudden urge to laugh.

"Is that all you can think of to say?" she murmured, gently mocking.

"I can think of a thousand things to say," he told her, his lips moving against her temple, her cheekbone. "But what I cannot decide is which of them to say *first.*" He chuckled softly. "Perhaps *you* should start."

She shook her head, smiling slightly, wistfully. "I cannot. There is too much to say." Eydryth raised her head, gazed at him, then laid her cheek against his, feeling the faint prickle of unshaven cheek against the softness of her own skin. "To even make a good beginning at saying what I want to say to you, would require the rest of the day . . . at least."

"You may have the day. I will take the *night*," he said, his tone still light, but the grey eyes held such intensity that her breath caught in her throat. Her heart was pounding so hard she wondered whether he could hear it. Confused, yet feeling such joy as she had never known, Eydryth glanced away from him, then froze.

The sun was already far to the west. The night that he spoke of would be here only too soon. Memory of the reason they were here rushed back, filling her, and, when Alon followed her gaze, she saw the same realization in his eyes.

"I wish . . . ," she said slowly. "Oh, Alon . . . I wish! But, my dear heart . . . we cannot linger here. Kerovan's life depends upon us."

His expression hardened; then he nodded. "Yachne must be stopped. I will think of a way to restrain her without harming her. Right now"—his glance turned tender for one final moment—"I feel strong enough to accomplish anything."

He sighed; then his arms tightened around her, and she returned the embrace. Then, slowly, formally, they both stepped back a pace, deliberately leaving the words unsaid, the caresses unmade.

As she heard a grunt from behind her, Eydryth glanced over her shoulder to see Monso, legs flailing the air as the stallion rolled. Alon went over to his mount, felt his chest and shoulders, then examined the healing wound on his leg.

"He can have water, now," he said, then, catching the Keplian's rein, led him toward the entrance, heading for the spring.

But as they neared that gap in the trees marking the entrance to the Fane, the half-bred halted, eyes rolling wildly, then backed away, ears flattened.

"What ails him?" Alon demanded, staring at the frightened creature. "Cannot beasts enter this place?"

Eydryth glanced inside the Fane, saw Steel Talon sitting perched on one of the rocks. "I think I know," she said. "Steel Talon can enter this place because he is a natural creature. Monso is a half-bred, created by sorcery, and no natural being. Nothing of the Shadow can exist within the Fane of Neave, which is where I believe we are."

"And Monso is part . . . part demon-horse," Alon said

slowly. "But . . . how then did he know where to bring us, so that we could be cleansed . . . healed?"

"I do not know," Eydryth said, with equal gravity. She glanced thoughtfully at the falcon. "Unless Steel Talon told him . . ."

They both fell silent, remembering the way the falcon's cries had seemingly triggered the Keplian's actions. Finally, Alon shook his head. "Even if poor Monso cannot enter this Fane," he said, "surely he can drink from the water?"

"He can," she assured him. "I gave him some earlier." Once again they rigged a makeshift trough from Alon's jerkin; then, flask by flask, the Adept allowed the horse to drink, slowly letting him swallow his fill.

Finally, the Keplian's thirst was satisfied. Alon fed him a measure of grain, and while he munched, both humans ministered to him, brushing him until the black coat shone once more in the red-tinged light of the westering sun.

Steel Talon winged over to sit on the cantle of the saddle, and, as he worked, Alon glanced frequently at the falcon, as if the bird were reporting to him. Having seen him do such before, Eydryth was not surprised to see Alon's expression darken with concern. "What is it?" she asked softly.

"Steel Talon has seen the witch. She is still heading southeast, toward a place that my winged friend thinks of as 'the dead place, the sick trees place, the Power-cage place,' which I take to mean that Yachne has discovered a place that is the opposite of this one." He nodded at the Fane. "It is my guess that she will use this evil place to focus her magic as she seeks to entrap Kerovan."

"How far away?"

"Several hours from here, on foot." He stared east, obviously thinking hard. "How far away is Kar Garudwyn, by your best estimate?"

Eydryth considered. "I believe that Kar Garudwyn lies perhaps twenty leagues distant," she said, pointing east. "That is, if I correctly remember the legends of where the Fane lies, in relation to Redmantle lands. My home is just beyond their boundaries."

He stepped forward, caught her hands in his. "Carrying

double, Monso would have no chance to make that distance tonight, Eydryth. And someone must go after Yachne."

She gazed at him, her breath catching in her throat. 'What . . . what are you suggesting?"

"We split up." His voice was low, urgent. "I will go after Yachne, afoot. I am young, and Neave's spring did its work well. My leg is healed. Steel Talon can lead me to the sorceress—I will do my best to catch her before she can harness the Power of that Shadowed place."

"And I?" she asked, feeling fear catch in her throat like a harsh crust of bread. "What would you have me do?"

He drew a deep breath. "Eydryth . . . you must ride Monso to Kar Garudwyn. You alone know the way . . . your family will listen to you, where they would distrust a stranger."

The songsmith stared past Alon's shoulder at the grazing stallion, placid enough now. She shivered. To ride the demon-horse alone, across leagues of countryside, racing wildly through a moonless night? What if Monso threw her, or turned against her? She remembered that terrifying speed, and her mouth went dry. "Alon . . . I do not think I can," she whispered.

He grabbed her shoulders, shaking her until she tore her eyes from the stallion and stared back up at him. "You must," he said. "There is naught else to be done, Eydryth! You *must* take Monso, and ride as if all the Shadows of this earth were on your trail—which may well be the case. But it is the only way to warn Kerovan in time!"

She bit her lip, then took a deep breath, nodding. "Help me saddle him," she said.

Fourteen

*T*he travelers abandoned their packs, except for Eydryth's harp, caching them in the branches of a beech tree on the edge of the meadow. As she helped to secure them aloft, Eydryth wondered silently whether such precautions were foolish. The chances were excellent that neither of them would ever return to claim their belongings.

When they had finished, she tied her staff atop the saddle-bags, then drew her gryphon-headed sword from its place of concealment. Slowly, the songsmith held it out to her companion. "I want you to take it," she said. "I cannot abandon my harp, but I will not burden Monso with the weight of both of them. Besides, you may need a weapon."

He hesitated, then reached out, fingers tracing the golden gryphon that formed the hilt. The creature's mouth gaped open, and in its jaws it grasped a heavy bluish crystal that served as a counterbalance. The creature's blue quan-iron eyes seemed to regard them knowingly.

Alon's fingers traced the sinuous body of the gryphon. Wrapped with silver wire to provide a secure grip, it formed the narrow portion of the hilt above the guard. Sliding his hand around the grip, the Adept hefted the sword, then swung it, hesitantly testing its balance.

Ripples of crimson ran down the blued steel as the setting sun's rays reflected off the blade. A tentative smile curved Alon's mouth as his sweeps and thrusts grew surer. "It has a sweet balance in my hand," he said wonderingly. "Almost as if it is alive, and responsive to my wishes."

"The best swords are forged so," she told him. "I want you to carry it, Alon. It will serve you far better than that other," she finished, a catch in her throat. Silently, she prayed to Gunnora that he would not have to use it. Alon was still far from being a swordsman, and the finest weapon in the world could not alter that.

He turned to regard her soberly, then shook his head and held out the sword. "My thanks, but I was planning on leaving my weapon with everything else," he said. "One cannot run with a sword in its sheath to hamper one's strides. And to catch Yachne, I must make all possible speed." He shrugged ruefully. "It would be different if I were able to use it effectively."

Eydryth gazed at him, pleading now. "We will rig a sling for it across your back, so you may carry it the way the Sulcar do their great broadswords," she told him; then, taking his swordbelt, she demonstrated by buckling it around his shoulders. After sheathing her sword in his old scabbard, she fastened the weapon into place securely. "See? Balanced thus, the weight is not much," she insisted.

Still he hesitated.

"Alon . . . ," she whispered, holding his eyes with her own. "Carry it, please. Carry it, and remember everything that I have taught you."

He smiled ruefully. "One lunge and two parries," he observed dryly. "I am indeed ready to take on all comers." Then, seeing the expression in her blue eyes, he nodded, sobering. "I will carry it, dear heart. And I will remember."

Eydryth breathed a profound sigh of relief. She could not have said why this was so important to her; she only knew that it was. The songsmith was as sure of it as if she could scry the future, the way her foster-sister, Hyana, could.

Together they returned to Monso, who stood saddled and ready before the entrance to the Fane. Eydryth's harp was wrapped in her stained, battered cloak and lashed to the back of the saddle. Songsmith and Adept had traded footgear, to better fit them for their appointed tasks. Eydryth now wore Alon's high, scarred riding boots . . . a trifle large, but she had padded the toes. The Adept had laced on a pair of her old trail buskins, loose on her now from much walking.

"Here," he said, pulling off his heavy leather jerkin, "you had best take this. It will protect you from underbrush."

She donned the leather garment, then pulled on her gloves. Measuring the stirrups against her arm, she shortened them several notches. Monso turned his head to sniff at her curiously while the songsmith fastened one of the flasks filled with Neave's springwater to the saddle. Eydryth patted the Keplian. "Now it will be just the two of us, son," she murmured. "If you allow me to stay aboard."

Finally, she thrust Dahaun's small box into the pocket of Alon's jerkin, fastening the flap down to secure it. "Ready," she announced.

Silently, Alon offered her his cupped hands for a leg up. Quickly, before she could change her mind, Eydryth gathered the reins in her left hand, then put her left foot into Alon's hands. A quick boost . . . she was up.

Monso snorted, pawed the ground restlessly as she gathered up the reins. "Twenty leagues, you said?" Alon asked, turning to regard the darkening east.

"Perhaps as much as twenty-five," she admitted. "At the last of it I will have to leave the road and go cross-country over the Kioga lands. There is only one entrance to Landisl's Valley."

He swung back to regard her earnestly, then put a hand atop her gloved ones as she held the reins. "At a steady gallop, you should be there by midnight," he said. "If you do not let Monso out, you should be able to rein him where you wish to go, control his speed. But you know for yourself what can happen if he's allowed to run all-out."

She knew only too well. "I will be careful," she assured him gravely. "Besides"—she forced a lighter tone—"this fellow is likely still tired from his race to the Fane today. Perhaps Neave's water has had the same pacifying effect on him as it did on us. From now on, he'll likely be as docile as a child's palfrey, won't you, Monso?" she asked, smoothing the restless Keplian's mane.

Alon ignored her feeble attempt at humor, only stared up at her steadily. His hand as it rested atop hers tightened around her fingers until his grip was almost painful. "May the Amber Lady watch over you, my love," he whispered. "I pray that we will see each other again. Until then . . . fare you well."

Eydryth's heart was too full for words, and she knew better than to trust her voice. Instead she leaned down, and managed to drop a kiss on his temple before Monso, uneasy with his new rider, sidled away.

Alon turned, sword across his back, then waved to summon Steel Talon. "Be my guide, winged warrior!" he shouted, then began trotting downslope as the bird circled overhead.

Monso, left behind, arched his neck and crab-stepped. Taking a deep breath, the songsmith loosened the reins a notch . . . then another. The Keplian paced forward, then he was trotting after his master, his strides lengthening.

Eydryth stood in her stirrups, her fingers working the reins, and through them the bit in the Keplian's mouth . . . squeeze, relax, squeeze, relax . . .

Cautiously, she loosened rein another notch; then Monso was cantering downhill, passing Alon in two strides. As they reached the spot where they had left the road, Eydryth's fingers tightened on the left rein as the muscles of her right leg squeezed her mount's barrel. The Keplian obediently bore left, turning back onto the road.

She glanced up, once, just before a screen of brush blocked

her view, to see Alon waving farewell as he reached the last of the downslope. Then the green branches eclipsed the Adept, and there was only the road, bare and red in the light of sunset, beckoning her east.

Still standing in her stirrups to keep her weight balanced over Monso's shoulders, Eydryth let out another bit of rein, and then the stallion was galloping.

Galloping . . . galloping . . .

The surface beneath them was perfect for a running horse—not so hard-packed that it would cause splints or sole bruises, nor dry enough yet to raise a choking dust. Seeing the empty road before him, Monso tugged hopefully at the bit, but obeyed Eydryth's hands when she held him back. The songsmith felt a sense of exultation fill her. To be in command of such speed, such power! It was a heady sensation as they glided along.

Twilight darkened around them, and still they encountered no one. Monso seemed content to gallop along at a speed most mortal steeds would have been hard-pressed to match.

Before long, Eydryth must needs summon her night vision, letting a thread of melody run through her mind. She hummed aloud, watching the landscape sharpen around her, saw one black ear turn back to catch her voice. She hummed louder, then found herself singing to the Keplian—a tune that, under the circumstances, seemed only too fitting:

> Along the midnight road they ran
> Along the broad and gleaming span
> Five gallant steeds of noble pride,
> Not gold, but life, hung on their ride.

She continued through all of "Lord Faral's Race," while Monso kept one ear pricked back, as though enjoying the song.

Time passed. . . . On a moonless night, such as this one was, it was hard to guess just how much, but Eydryth could now see farmlands and an occasional house as they flashed by. They had galloped into the more populated lands of Arvon.

Once they raced through a town. Monso's shoes struck

sparks from a cobbled street, and the sound of rapid hoofbeats doubled and redoubled as they echoed off the stone and timbered houses and shops. Hanging above the door of the townhall was a clan mantle; the songsmith's enhanced vision saw that it was blue.

"We're in Bluemantle lands, Monso," she sang, ignoring the tavern door that was flung open behind her, the shouts of inquiry from startled villagers that quickly faded and were gone. "We've come at least ten leagues already. If we stay on this road, we'll be crossing Redmantle lands soon. Are you wearied?"

The black half-bred snorted, almost as if in disdain at the idea. Eydryth laughed aloud, and they galloped on.

Farmlands stretched again to each side of them. A stone bridge flashed by beneath Monso's hooves. Eydryth heard the chuckling lap of the water as it splashed the pilings, and ran a dry tongue across wind-chapped lips. For a moment she thought of halting, taking a breather, sipping some of the water from Neave's spring, but she decided she could hold out a little longer.

Once we're on Redmantle lands, she promised herself. *The ford at the Deepwater. We'll rest a few minutes there. . . .*

By now her legs were aching from standing in the stirrups. Eydryth eased herself down into the saddle, though still she leaned forward, trying to rest lightly on the Keplian's back. They were galloping now toward what appeared to be a dark blot crouching over the road like some gigantic beast, ready to engulf them within its maw.

Eydryth strained her night vision, made out trees. *Of course*, she remembered. *The forest. We've reached the Bluemantle forest. We're almost to the border of Redmantle lands. . . .*

As the Keplian galloped into the forest, they plunged into a dark so complete that even Eydryth's night vision could scarcely pierce it. Monso snorted uneasily, slowing abruptly to an uncertain canter. Knowing that her mount's eyes must be adjusting to the increased darkness within the forest, the songsmith did not urge him faster.

The darkness beneath the trees was cavelike, nearly complete. Eydryth concentrated harder, humming loudly, and made out the road stretching before them like a black satin ribbon laid across a black velvet gown. Monso's strides steadied as the Keplian's eyes also adjusted to the absence of light beneath the trees. They cantered on, not daring to go faster.

Eydryth crouched over Monso's withers, shivering as a chill wind brushed the back of her neck like a long-dead finger. The breeze came again, harder, colder, pushing at her back, tossing her hair.

The songsmith stiffened, her nostrils flaring. That wind bore with it an odor . . . a rank, yet familiar, odor. Eydryth grimaced at the smell. Where had she scented its like before? She turned her head to glance behind her, seeking its source. A dank gust of wind struck her face like a foul breath.

Glowing spectrally with their own ghastly light, more than a score of web-riders were being borne along on that wind, heading straight for her and Monso!

The poisonous creatures were already so close that Eydryth could see their pincers. Their jaws dripped venom, spattering the surface of the barely seen road; gobs of sickly greenish light marked their path. Another blast of wind sent the web-riders hurtling toward the songsmith and her mount. In a moment they would be upon them!

Eydryth leaned forward with a terrified gasp, feeling that unnatural wind push again at her back. "Go, boy!" she cried, slamming her heels into Monso's sides. "Go!" She glanced back, glimpsed pincers only an arm's length from her eyes. *"Run!"* she screamed, lashing the Keplian's neck with the reins.

By that time Monso, too, had caught wind of their pursuers. The Keplian needed no further urging. Springing forward as though shot from a dart gun, he raced through the dark woods.

Darkness blurred in Eydryth's sight. She struggled to keep her night vision, every moment fearing that her brains would be dashed out against some low-hanging limb. But she feared the fell creatures behind them more than she feared a clean death, so she made no effort to slow Monso, only flattened herself as best she could along the Keplian's neck, clinging to his mane with both hands.

There were occasional gaps in the tree cover overhead now, and she could see a little better. Greatly daring, the songsmith glanced back, saw that they had gained on the web-riders. Still that unnatural gale assaulted her back.

Sorcery, she realized. *That wind was sent, as were these creatures. By whom? Yachne? The Adepts at Garth Howell?* There was no way to know. *We are not racing the web-riders,* she realized, *we are racing the wind! And if that wind grows stronger . . .*

By now they were passing trees so rapidly that their trunks blurred, seeming as close together as fence posts, so fast was Monso running.

Without warning, they were out of the forest, plunging steeply downhill toward the starlit gleam of a river. *The Deep-water!* Eydryth realized. She struggled to keep her balance as the Keplian hurtled down the road. *If he catches a foot and falls at this speed, I'll be crushed beneath him*, she thought.

Glancing back, she saw that the web-riders had scattered after leaving the narrow confines of the forest road. They were outdistancing the Shadow-creatures rapidly now.

Eydryth took hold of the Keplian's mouth. "Monso . . . easy, son . . . we can slow a bit, now. . . ."

Her pull on the stallion's mouth went unanswered. The half-bred raced down the hillside toward the river with the rush of a stooping falcon. Eydryth begged, sang, pulled until her arms seemed to loosen in their sockets—to no avail.

She was still trying to slow the Keplian when Monso, running blindly, plunged full-force into the spring-swollen waters of the ford. The Keplian half-reared, trying to leap through the water. His struggles sent him plunging sideways, away from the stone-paved bottom of the ford, into deeper water. The river now rose belly-high on him. He staggered, trying to keep his footing on the slick, muddy bottom. Water washed up over his shoulders.

Eydryth felt the stallion's hind feet slip out from under him; then Monso was falling. The black water rose up and engulfed horse and rider.

The songsmith kicked her feet loose from the stirrups as her mount rolled over, terrified lest she be dragged down beneath his body to drown. Her head went under as she flailed desperately. Choking and gasping, she swallowed and gagged on the cold water, but managed to fight her way back to the surface, then forced her arms to move, her legs to kick. Coughing, she trod water for a moment while she caught her breath, then she swam, feeling the current drag at her like a live thing. Eydryth blinked, vainly trying to shake the water from her eyes. Her night vision was gone, fled with her concentration on the melody.

Beside her, something large moved, snorted loudly. Monso! The Keplian had recovered himself and was striking out strongly for the opposite shore. Eydryth lunged toward him, felt something brush her hand, grabbed it, then realized that she had grasped one of the trailing reins.

Swiftly she pulled herself back to the stallion, hand over hand; then she was able to grasp the pommel of the saddle. Monso surged through the water, breasting the flood, towing the woman alongside him.

Eydryth knew that she would have only moments when the stallion struck solid footing to prevent him from breaking free and racing away from her into the night. Turning to glance back over her shoulder, she saw that the web-riders were no longer following. Their phosphorescent forms glimmered as they drifted aimlessly along the far bank of the Deepwater.

Of course, she thought. *Like most creatures of the Shadow, they cannot cross running water.*

Monso's steadily stroking forefeet suddenly struck land, then the Keplian was surging forward, snorting, water cascading off his powerful body. Eydryth swung herself forward, both hands closing on the horse's headstall and bit. "Monso, ho!" she commanded, leaning her full weight back, digging her heels into the mucky, reed-grown riverbank. "Ho, son!"

The half-bred shook his head, but after a moment he obeyed. Eydryth stumbled beside him as he struggled up, out of the water. The minstrel collapsed for a second on shore, pushing her soaked hair out of her eyes; then, wavering to her feet, she summoned up her night vision again, seeing with relief that her harp was still tied firmly in place. It would have to be dried carefully lest it warp. Then she scanned her surroundings for a place from which to mount.

The night wind cut through her sopping clothes like a sword blade as she stumbled along, making her shiver. Finding a small boulder with a flat top, Eydryth halted the trembling, sweating horse beside it. She stroked Monso, soothing him for a moment; then her foot found the stirrup and she swung back up, settling into the soaked saddle with an audible squish.

As she turned her mount and walked him up the bank, Eydryth felt exhaustion drag at her with a pull every bit as insistent as the Deepwater's current. She patted her pocket, feeling the hard lump that was Dahaun's box. *Did the make-shift seal I placed on it hold?* she wondered frantically. *Or is Jervon's cure now mingling with the mud on the bottom of the river?* She was afraid to look, and could not have spared the time anyway. Biting her lip, the minstrel urged the Keplian forward.

For the next few minutes she trotted until she was sure of her path, then, cautiously, eased her mount into a canter again. The time they had lost at the ford gnawed at her. . . . What if, even now, Yachne was setting her trap for Kerovan?

Eydryth let the soaked reins out a notch, until they were galloping again.

Redmantle lands. She knew the road well now, having accompanied her family to town many times as a girl. Only a league or so down this road, she would take a branching trail, then cut cross-country over Kioga territory.

Monso no longer needed to be held in, which worried Eydryth. She knew that swimming the Deepwater had taken a heavy toll of the stallion's endurance, if her own weariness was any indication. She wondered whether they would make it the rest of the way to Kar Garudwyn.

At least the web-riders were well and truly gone. She risked a final glance behind, seeing only darkness. Would those who had set them on their trail send another menace? She had no way of knowing.

Some distance farther on, the songsmith slowed Monso to

a canter, watching to her right as they splashed through a small stream. A moment later, she saw it—a faint trail leading away across a meadow. It might have almost been a game path, but Eydryth knew better. Reining right, she turned the Keplian onto it.

The Kioga were not a people to leave well-marked trails to their grazing grounds. Whenever trading parties ventured outside their territory, they used small, insignificant trails such as this one, careful not to allow them to become too well marked.

Eydryth galloped across the meadow, but when the trail began looping through a small wood, she needs must slow to a canter. As they came around a bend in the path, a puddle of darkness suddenly blocked their way.

It seemed to crouch before them, making the songsmith wonder for a moment whether it was some kind of wild beast. But no, it was only a washed-out gully filled with debris from the spring floods. Bending low on the Keplian's neck, the bard gave her mount free rein, urging him on.

Monso soared into the air, clearing the entire gap. For a moment Eydryth felt as though they were flying; then the Keplian's forehooves came back to earth with scarcely a jar.

"Good boy!" she cried, shakily. *Alon trained him well*, she thought, steadying him and increasing speed to a hand-gallop. She was fighting her own exhaustion and chill, now, and the continual drain of using her newfound Power to see in the darkness was wearing her down even faster than the exertion of the ride.

Twice more they leaped trees that had fallen across the path—the first was low, scarcely more than thigh-high had Eydryth been standing. The second came as they rounded a last turn on the woodland trail. At first it seemed to her aching eyes naught more than a small tree resting in a patch of shadow from the woods.

But, just as they drew too close to safely halt, the songsmith realized to her horror that her magically enhanced night vision had played tricks upon her. What she had taken for shadow was substance, and the tree trunk now looming before them would have been chin-high on even a tall man!

All Eydryth's instincts screamed out for her to sit back and drag the Keplian to a halt, but she realized immediately that it was too late. The stallion was headed straight for the tree, too fast to stop without crashing into the obstacle. Stifling a scream, Eydryth closed her legs on his sides, bent low over the black neck, and shut her eyes. The Keplian's leap as he soared into the air nearly unseated her.

Eydryth held her breath, expecting any moment to feel Monso smash into the trunk. But somehow, the stallion cleared it, though she heard bark scrape beneath them. They hung in midair for what seemed forever; then they were over, and falling . . . falling. Horse and rider landed hard and off-balance—but safe.

As the stallion recovered his stride, breathing now in hard, panting gasps, the minstrel clutched him around the neck, nearly sobbing with relief. "Thank you . . . thank you, Monso . . . ," she stammered.

A short distance later, they left the last of the trees to pound across a long, gradually sloping field. Monso's breathing was now labored. They had nearly reached the opposite side of the field when the challenge that Eydryth had been anticipating ever since they had turned off the road rang out. "You! Rider! Halt! You are on Kioga land! Halt and identify yourself and your business here!"

Knowing that the sentry was armed with a wickedly barbed lance, Eydryth sat back in the saddle, reining Monso to a quick halt. For once, the stallion seemed to welcome the chance to stand still and regain his wind.

After a moment, Monso's breathing eased; then, scenting the Kioga mount, the Keplian rumbled a deep challenge. The songsmith heard the mortal horse whicker with fear as it approached. Her night vision made out the shadow blot of a rider mounted upon a grey mare; then the Kioga tribesman lit a torch. Eydryth shielded her eyes from the sudden, dazzling light.

"It is I, Eydryth, Jervon's daughter," she called. "Who of the Kioga rides on sentry-go tonight?"

"Eydryth?" The tribesman's voice was sharp with suspicion. "If you are the Lady Eydryth, prove it. Tell me your dun gelding's name."

She laughed wearily, at last recognizing the speaker's weather-beaten, mustached features as her eyes adjusted to the light. "My *mare* is a red chestnut, Guret, as you well know. Her name is Vyar."

"Eydryth!" Guret gasped. "What are *you* doing here? You left so long ago! And now to return in the middle of the night . . ." He urged his grey closer, controlling her with firm legs, forcing her to hold steady despite her fear of Monso. "And astride such a mount! Wherever did you get him?"

The songsmith sighed, shaking her head. "It is a very long story, my friend, one that I have not time to tell. Let me only say that Lord Kerovan is in grave danger, and I ride to warn him. As soon as my warning is delivered, I, and possibly others from Kar Garudwyn, will ride forth from the valley this same night. I left a friend behind, possibly in great danger, to ride here tonight. I must return to aid him."

"A . . . friend," Guret said, evidently catching some inflection in Eydryth's voice that she had not been aware of herself.

"He is the one who bred and trained Monso, here," she said, stroking the panting Keplian's foam-drenched neck.

"Then he must be a master horseman," the Kioga man said. "To capture and train a Keplian."

"I will tell you the entire story—or Alon will—as soon as may be," Eydryth promised, "but not now. Guret, I have ridden across nigh half of Arvon tonight. I must make it to Kar Garudwyn as soon as possible!"

He nodded. "I will help you, Lady. But stay only a moment." One-handed, he pulled the gaudily embroidered blanket he wore as a protection against the night's chill over his head, shaking his long, dark braids to free them. "Here, wear this. You look like a half-drowned yearling," he said, extending the blanket.

Gratefully, the songsmith slipped it over her head, relishing the heat of Guret's body still trapped within its warm folds. The Kioga man jerked a thumb behind him. "You ride, Lady. I will call another for sentry duty, then go down-valley myself to catch up the castlefolk's mounts and have them saddled and ready."

She flashed him a grateful smile. "Bring Vyar, too," she

said. "This fellow deserves to rest for some time. I thank you for your aid, Guret."

Eydryth urged Monso onward. The stallion stumbled as he obeyed, and Guret gave her mount a measuring glance. "Will he make it? Do you want to take Takala here, in his stead?"

"No, Guret." She patted Monso's shoulder. "Even exhausted, this one could outrun your mare. Every moment counts. Thank you again for your help."

He raised the flickering torch in salute as she turned and left him.

Once past the circle cast by Guret's light, Eydryth was hard-pressed to regain her night-sight. She relied mostly on Monso's eyes to pick his way uphill at a slow canter.

Long minutes later, the songsmith caught sight of a familiar landmark—a huge granite outcropping. She slowed Monso to a walk, following the bulge of the gigantic thrust of rock. When it split in twain to become a narrow pass, she turned down it. Midway down that dark throat, two pillars of quan-iron stood, topped with winged globes.

The entrance to the valley. She was almost home.

With a gasp of thankfulness that sounded perilously akin to a sob of weariness, the songsmith urged Monso toward the entrance. The land beyond was filled with a swirling mist, part of the spell-laid protection that encompassed the valley where Landisl, the powerful gryphon-being, had once made his ancient home.

But as Monso tried to step past that barrier, the Keplian halted, tossing his head snorting. He sidled away, much as he had at the entrance to the Fane of Neave.

Of course, Eydryth thought. *The wards on the valley. Monso is part Shadow-creature, so he may not pass them. . . .*

But if she had to abandon the Keplian and run the rest of the way, it would take her an hour or more to reach the castle on the mountainside! Eydryth stared determinedly at the barrier, reaching within herself for the Power Alon had assured her she bore. She began to sing, raising her voice in a wordless appeal, concentrating on an image in her mind of portals giving way before them, allowing them free entrance.

Her voice filled the narrow cut, and, slowly the winged globes began to pulse in time to the rise and fall of her melody. Holding firm the image in her mind of portals opening, Eydryth urged Monso forward again.

Slowly, now favoring the foreleg the web-riders had injured, the Keplian walked between the pillars.

The glamourie that always surrounded one who rode into the valley began to make swirling images before Eydryth's eyes, but she continued to sing as she urged Monso forward, and a few strides farther on, it abruptly vanished. Eydryth looked to her right, and saw, glowing blue against the darkness, near the summit of the mountain, the spires of Kar Garudwyn—a name which meant, in the Old Tongue, "High Castle of the Gryphon."

Home. Her heart leaped within her.

"Just a little farther, Monso. Then you can rest," she muttered, stroking the Keplian. Summoning the dregs of her energy, she began to hum, and her night vision slowly crept back. As soon as she could see the path before her, Eydryth chirruped to Monso, then, when he did not respond, used her bootheels to goad the stallion into a canter.

She kept her legs and heels in his sides until the Keplian had increased speed to a hand-gallop along the trail. She felt ashamed doing it, knowing that she was abusing an animal that had already given his all, an animal now on the verge of total exhaustion and collapse, but they still had more than a league to go.

I'm tired, too, son, Eydryth thought, patting the Keplian's neck. "Come on, you can do it," she whispered, thinking it would be such a relief to stop . . . just to fall out of the saddle and lie on the ground and sleep . . . sleep. . . .

Kerovan's image filled her mind, making her stiffen her shoulders. *Just a little farther . . .*

The Keplian's strides now were labored; his breath rasped loud in her ears. He was clearly favoring his injured foreleg. Biting her lip, the songsmith forced him onward, slapping the reins lightly against his neck.

Her night-sight was gone; the darkness blurred around her.

Eydryth swayed in the saddle, then forced herself to grip the pommel. Where was she? How far had she come?

There! Off to her right . . . the entrance to the ramp that led up the mountainside! To one who had not lived here all her life, it would seem naught but a sheer wall of rock, but Kerovan had long ago adjusted the spell that held it concealed so that his foster-daughter could come and go as she pleased.

Crouching low on the Keplian's back, she turned him toward that opening in the mountainside, then lashed down hard with the reins, driving him forward and upward with her seat, heels and voice. "Almost there, Monso!" she gasped. "Go, boy! For Alon!"

The Keplian's steel-shod hooves clattered against the stone as they entered the stone tunnel that slanted up, round and round, leading to Kar Garudwyn. The walls and ceiling glowed faintly blue, as did all the stone from which the mountain citadel was constructed.

There was barely enough room within the ramped tunnel for the Keplian and his rider. Eydryth had to lie flat along his neck, and even then her shoulders and head brushed the stone walls and ceiling. Several times she bumped hard against the unyielding rock as the stallion turned and twisted, head ducked low, sides heaving like a smith's bellows, climbing . . . climbing.

"Almost there . . . ," Eydryth whispered, though no sound escaped her dry lips. "Almost there, Monso . . . keep going!"

Somehow, the Keplian climbed.

When horse and rider finally scrambled out of the enclosed rampway they were faced with the lighted glory that had been Landisl's ancient citadel. Kar Garudwyn was a towering structure with tall, strangely twisted spires and multitudes of narrow, arched windows and doorways. A muted blue light emanated from those openings.

Halting Monso on the stone-paved walkway, the songsmith took a deep breath, then shouted: "Rouse you! Kerovan! Joisan! Sylvya! There is danger! Wake!"

Her family must have realized as soon as someone entered the rampway that a newcomer was on the way, for she had scarcely finished her first summons before two fully-dressed figures appeared in the huge arched doorway.

Joisan and, at her side, Kerovan!

Eydryth felt a vast relief sweep her as she saw her foster-father unharmed. A moment later Firdun—*He's grown so tall!* she thought distractedly—then his sister, Hyana, appeared. Lastly, Sylvya was there. The halfling woman had a cap of downy feathers instead of hair, and round eyes much larger than any of full humankind heritage.

"Eydryth!" Joisan exclaimed, starting down the steps toward her foster-daughter. "My dear, what—"

Kerovan's lady halted and broke off as Monso swayed, then groaned loudly. The Keplian's head dropped forward until his nose touched the stones beneath his forefeet. His agonized, rasping breaths suddenly filled the night.

Before his dazed rider could leap off, the stallion quivered like an arrow driven deep into a target; then slowly, ponderously, his legs buckled and he sank down on his knees. Eydryth barely managed to get her right leg out of the way as the Keplian rolled over on his left side, then lay unmoving.

Slowly, stumbling, the songsmith stepped over and away from the still black form, its legs stiffly outthrust; then she gazed up at her family, tears streaming down her face. "I've killed him," she said, in a voice that even she could barely hear. "Oh, Alon . . . I'm so sorry. Monso . . . so sorry . . ."

"Eydryth . . ." Joisan was hastening down the steps toward her, arms held out.

The minstrel drew herself up, forced herself to speak clearly, despite the roaring sound that still made even her own voice difficult to hear. "I came to warn you. Kerovan . . . you are in great danger. It is the sorceress Yachne. She has great Power, and she plans to steal yours. She will try to take you with her spell . . . tonight. You must protect yourself. You must . . ."

Eydryth's words faltered, then trailed off. At first she thought the ground was moving beneath her; then she realized that it was she who was swaying back and forth. She tried to stiffen her knees, but she could not feel her legs. A high, thin note reverberated in her ears. Accompanying that monotonous shrilling was a wave of blackness even darker and colder than the depths of the Deepwater. The darkness rose up around her, drowning her, pulling her down.

Before her stunned family could reach her, Eydryth crumpled to the pavement beside Monso.

Fifteen

"*E*ydryth." A voice reached her ears . . . a familiar voice. "Eydryth . . . ," it called again. "Sister, awaken, please. . . ." Fingers stroked her aching head, easing the pain behind her temples. She was resting on something soft and warm. "Here," the voice said. "Some water . . . drink, Sister."

Cool liquid in her mouth, trickling down her throat, easing the dryness. The songsmith swallowed eagerly, then opened her eyes to see Hyana's face hovering above hers.

"Eydryth . . . Sister, how do you feel?" she asked, concerned. Hyana resembled her mother, with her light chestnut hair, green eyes and the fair complexion of a Daleswoman. Only her high cheekbones and pointed chin marked her as being Kerovan's daughter, also.

"Oh, Hyana," Eydryth whispered. "What of Kerovan? Is he safe?"

"He is," a new voice said, and the songsmith turned her head as Firdun appeared beside his sister. "Father is fine."

As her foster-brother smiled reassuringly at her, Eydryth was again reminded of how much he had grown. At fourteen, he was more youth now than lad, tall and leggy. He had his father's long, oval face, dark hair, and eyes that in some lights appeared yellowish brown, and in others pale grey.

"Where is Kerovan?" Eydryth asked. Her mind seemed to be filled with wool rather than thought. She could see from the expression on her foster-siblings' faces that they were barely holding themselves back from a thousand questions. "He is in danger. I rode from near Garth Howell to warn him. . . ."

"Have no fear for Father," Firdun assured her. "Even now he is sitting on Landisl's throne in the Great Hall, ringed about with enough charms and talismans to set up a booth at a fair." He flashed his irreverent grin. "And complaining loudly because Mother warned him not to leave the protections. He is demanding to know what chances out here. I told him I would do my best to find out."

"Where is Joisan? And Sylvya?" Eydryth demanded.

"They left me to tend you, while they are tending to your . . . mount," Hyana replied.

"Tending to him?" Eydryth repeated blankly. "But . . . Monso is dead. . . ."

Her foster-sister shook her head, her long braids, wrapped with colorful embroidered ribbons in the Kioga fashion, bouncing on her shoulders as she did so. "The creature lives," she said. "But for how long . . ." She trailed off, shaking her head.

"I thought I had ridden him to death," Eydryth murmured. Indeed, her brain was not working well . . . or was it her hearing that was lacking? It did not seem possible that Monso could still be alive, after the way the Keplian had collapsed.

"No, he lives," Hyana assured her. "But . . . he is very weak, Eydryth. Mother is using her healcraft, but she does not know whether he can be saved."

Memory rushed back, propelling Eydryth upward, off Hyana's lap. Ignoring Hyana's and Firdun's efforts to restrain her, the bard sat up. "The water!" she cried, looking wildly about her for Monso's tack. "The water in my flask. The water from Neave's spring—perhaps it can save him!"

Firdun held something up before her eyes. "This flask?"

"Yes!" Eagerly, the minstrel grabbed it. She hesitated, feeling her own weakness. She needed strength, too, or she would never be able to do what she must during the remainder of this night. Where was Alon by now? Confronting Yachne?

Determinedly, the girl unstoppered the flask, held it to her lips. Carefully, deliberately, she counted swallows, allowing herself only five.

She could feel the restorative effect of the blessed springwater working on her tired body almost immediately. After a minute, Eydryth was able to climb to her feet unaided, then walk steadily across the stone flags to where Joisan and Sylvya crouched beside the stricken Keplian.

As she neared them, the songsmith was horrified to see that the gaping wound on Monso's foreleg had opened. The leg was covered with both fresh and dried blood. The stallion must have run for leagues after the wound had opened, and she had not seen it in the darkness. "Monso . . . ," she whispered, sinking down beside him and stroking his neck. He lay unmoving, barely breathing. Eydryth felt tears well up again, and resolutely fought them back. Weeping would not help Monso, but Neave's springwater might!

"Joisan . . . Sylvya . . ." She clasped hands briefly with each of these women who had helped to raise her. There would be time later, after everything possible had been done for Monso, for embraces and loving greetings. "I have something that may help. We have to drench him with this," she said, holding up the flask. "He is too weak to swallow, so I will have to pour the water down his gullet while you hold his head up."

"Water?" Joisan asked. Eydryth saw that the Wise Woman had her bag of simples and her healcraft supplies arranged beside her. The wound was already cleansed. A curved needle and a length of pronghorn sinew were laid out on the clean cloth beside her foster-mother. "What kind of water? How can mere water aid him?"

"Not just any water," the minstrel explained. "This is water from Neave's spring. It has great restorative effects." She held out her own hands, palm up. "I just drank some, and see how it has aided me. Otherwise, I would not be on my feet any more than Monso is."

Joisan gave her a measuring glance, then nodded quickly. "Firdun! Hyana!" she called. "Come, help me hold this creature's head up so Eydryth can drench him!"

It took three of them to raise Monso's head so that his neck lay at the proper angle for him to swallow. Then Eydryth used both hands to pry open the unconscious stallion's jaws. Pulling his tongue out to one side of his mouth, she drew the stopper from the flask, then, cautiously, poured the water down the pale pink tunnel with its enormous teeth.

She poured . . . rubbed the Keplian's throat until he swallowed, reflexively, then poured another measure down.

This time Monso swallowed on his own. Eydryth replaced the stopper, saving the remaining water for a later dose. Gently, her helpers eased the big head back down onto the pavement.

Monso's eyelids lifted, then closed again. The stallion groaned, but did not awaken. His breathing grew stronger, more distinct, however, and Joisan, who kept one hand on his chest, behind his foreleg, looked up excitedly. "His heartbeat is strengthening!"

Sylvya laid her head against his shoulder, then glanced up at her friend, her enormous round eyes beneath her downy head-covering full of warning. "It is indeed! You had best do your stitchery while the beast remains unconscious, Joisan!"

Nodding agreement, the Wise Woman bent to her task, again cleansing the wound, then aligning the gaping edges, pulling them closed with careful, precise stitches, knotting and securing each one separately.

"Eydryth, I am anxious to know the whole of your story," Joisan said as she worked, not looking up from her task.

The songsmith sighed. "So much has happened that I

scarcely know where to start! Oh, Joisan . . . we must save
Monso, if that is possible. He is Alon's horse . . . and Alon may
even now be in terrible danger! We must help him!"

Joisan gave her a quick, sideways glance. "Who is Alon?"

Eydryth could not help it; she felt her cheeks grow hot.
Firdun and Hyana, who were crouching nearby, exchanged
speculative glances. "Alon . . . ," the girl muttered, still blush-
ing. "He is . . . Monso—this Keplian's—owner and master,"
she began. "He is my . . . friend . . ."

The Wise Woman smiled slightly, and gave her fosterling a
fond look. "Friend," she repeated blandly.

Eydryth grew very busy checking to see that the water flask
was indeed stoppered tightly. "He is an Adept who helped me
on my quest to find a way to heal Jervon." She patted the box
in Alon's jerkin pocket. "I have the cure with me. Praise
Gunnora it will—"

She broke off at the click of hooves upon the steps. They all
turned to see Kerovan descending. The Lord of Kar Garudwyn was of the heritage of the Old Ones, and was plainly not
of full humankind. His eyes were amber, with slitted, uncanny
pupils, and he stood upon cloven hooves rather than feet.
Otherwise he was human, with black hair and features typical
of the Old Race.

Eydryth's mouth fell open, then she leapt up. "Kerovan,
you must not leave your protections! Yachne may be trying to
bespell you even now!"

"I could no longer remain inside," her foster-father said
testily, even as he enveloped her in a tight embrace. His
strength and warmth felt wonderful after the perils of the
night. Eydryth felt tears threaten again as she leaned against
him for a moment; then he held her away, looking full into her
face. "Eydryth . . . Daughter . . . scold me if you must, but, by
the Nine Words of Min, tell me what chances tonight!"

Joisan carefully knotted the last stitch, then looked up at
her lord, her brows drawing together in a frown. "Kerovan,"
she said sternly. "Eydryth says that you are in danger. You
must not—"

He shook his head impatiently. "You cannot expect me to

sit in there and remain idle while there is a threat to my home and family, Joisan!" Kerovan turned to his foster-daughter, one hand going to the hilt of his sword. "Who is this Yachne you spoke of? How does she threaten us?" he demanded, all his years of soldiering coming to the fore.

The songsmith silently struggled to order the events of the past days into some kind of coherent account. As she hesitated, Joisan threw a blanket over the still-recumbent Keplian, then turned back to her lord. Suddenly the Wise Woman stiffened, then pointed at her husband's feet with a cry of dismay. "Kerovan! Look!" she exclaimed.

Eydryth stepped back and stared, wide-eyed. On the stone around Kerovan's hooves a dark mist—one that she well remembered from Yachne's cave—was slowly forming!

"Kerovan!" she gasped, pointing. "That is Yachne's spell! She means to draw you to her, then drain you of all Power! You must break the ensorcellment!"

Joisan bolted forward, hands going out to her lord, but he motioned her back, staring down at the dark purple mist now swirling around his legs. "No, my lady," he ordered, in a voice that brooked no argument. "Do not seek to touch me, lest you be taken also."

Eydryth felt as though she were trapped in a nightmare with no waking. She twisted her hands in impotent anguish. "Oh, Kerovan . . . can you stop it? Don't let it take you!"

He raised one hand into the air, slowly, formally, in a beckoning gesture that was not aimed at anyone present. "Yes," he said a moment later, calmly. "I can stop it." The lord's strange, inhuman eyes seemed to glow with an inner light as he began chanting in the Old Tongue.

The stunned onlookers watched as a glowing shape began forming around the heir to the gryphon-lord, encompassing him as he stood. Eydryth glimpsed a fierce head that reminded her of Steel Talon's, then a huge, raised paw. Tawny hindquarters like unto a lion's merged into an eagle's foreparts.

The unhuman shadow's eyes glowed golden-amber . . . and its eyes were Kerovan's eyes. But the rest of that uncanny, dimly glimpsed shape was that of Landisl's messenger, guardian and protector, the gryphon, Telpher. All her life Eydryth had heard the tales of how Landisl, the gryphon-lord, and Telpher, his servant, had protected both Joisan and Kerovan during their adventures . . . but never had she seen Landisl's heir summon the guardian spirit until now.

Slowly, almost contemptuously, Telpher's shadowy form raised a massive paw, then dragged it through the thickening mist, breaking the spell-circle.

Then both mist and shadowy gryphon-image abruptly vanished. Kerovan stood, hooves planted firmly upon the stone pavement, unharmed.

Eydryth staggered forward with a cry of gladness, flung her arms around her foster-father, clutching him tightly. The rest of his family crowded around, exclaiming with relief.

"You . . . you broke the spell!" Eydryth stammered finally, stepping back to look up at him. "And so easily . . . where Dinzil could not help himself." She frowned, thinking of how hard they had striven to reach Kerovan with the warning, remembering the Deepwater, Monso's collapse . . . and, most frightening of all, her abandonment of Alon. Had it all been for naught? "Perhaps . . ." Her voice faltered. "Perhaps my warning was not necessary. Perhaps I did not need to leave Alon. . . ."

Joisan by now was close-pressed against her lord's side, one arm around him, the other encircling her foster-daughter. The Wise Woman shook her head. "Not so, Eydryth," she said solemnly.

Kerovan echoed his wife's gesture. "My lady has the right of it, Eydryth," he said. "I was warned, and thus could defeat the spell when it attempted to ensnare me. But had you not come here tonight, this Yachne's ensorcellment would have found me asleep and unprepared. . . ." He shook his head grimly. "And I have no doubt that I would have been trapped."

"You have a long story to tell us, Sister," Hyana said. "And you spoke of an Alon who is in danger. . . ."

"There is so much to tell, and so little time!" Eydryth said. "I must see Jervon immediately—I may have found the means to heal him! And then we must all ride to aid Alon, because I fear that Yachne will try and take *him*, since she could not prey upon Kerovan. He went to seek her, but he is wearied, and was wounded yesterday. I fear greatly for him. . . ."

"Eydryth . . . dear one . . ." Sylvya was staring at the young woman in open amazement, as if she had never seen her before. "I sense so many changes . . . you are so different! You have been places, done things . . . changed . . ." Quickly, the woman from the ancient past of Arvon traced a symbol in the air, and it glowed blue, tinged with green.

The songsmith drew herself up. "You have the right of it, Aunt," she said, smiling faintly, proudly. Then, humming softly, she drew a sign of her own in the air—the shape of a musical note. It hung before them, outlined as if in a trail of turquoise fire. "I have discovered Power of my own kind," she said. "Through my music. Else I could not have gotten Monso past the valley's wards."

Amazement spread across their faces; then they all stepped forward, besieging the songsmith with questions. Kerovan had to shout to be heard above the excited inquiries. "We must have the entire story, sitting down!" he ordered, now very much the lord of the hold. "And I for one will be most interested to hear about this mysterious Alon!"

Eydryth felt warmth again reddening her cheeks. She cast about again for words to tell the group about Alon, but still could find none. She smiled at her family, feeling their love, their concern, enclose her like warm arms after a nightmare. "I will tell you everything," she promised, "as soon as may be. But first . . ." She took out Dahaun's box, then opened it to peer cautiously within. To her vast relief, the healing red mud still lay within, seeming as fresh as the time she had used it to treat the Adept's wrist. "First Jervon. I cannot sit still until I have seen my father."

"Is that the cure you have brought?" Kerovan asked, peering skeptically into the little box. "Mud?"

Joisan put out a finger, touched the moist earth tentatively, then drew back as if it had stung her. "Where did you find this?" she gasped.

"From the Lady of the Green Silences in Escore," Eydryth said. She glanced down at the sleeping horse, then picked up her harp from where it lay on the ground, still wrapped in her cloak. "If we are fortunate, there may be enough mud in Dahaun's box to help Monso's wound, also." She smiled at all of them. "But first, oh, first I must see my father!"

Joisan smiled warmly as her fosterling. "Go, by all means, my dear. In the meantime, Kerovan and I will prepare food—I believe we have all worked up an appetite, with all these midnight alarums and excursions. Firdun and Sylvya will watch over your mount."

"Come, Sister," Hyana said, taking the songsmith's arm, "I will accompany you."

Carrying her harp and the little box, Eydryth followed her foster-sister through the halls of Kar Garudwyn, along a corridor lit by the light-globes like unto those she had seen in Es city, in the witches' citadel. For a moment she found herself remembering Avris and wondered how her friend now fared. Then they came to Jervon's door, and paused outside, trembling suddenly.

What if Dahaun's mud does not work? she wondered, feeling her mouth go dry with fear. *I have traveled so long . . . it has been so many years . . . please, Amber Lady . . . please, Neave! I beg of you, give my father back to me!*

Hyana placed a steadying hand upon her arm. Eydryth nodded at her foster-sister, straightened her shoulders, then walked in.

Jervon was lying on his pallet. A Kioga girl sat in a chair, dozing. A servant or a member of the family always watched over the Power-blasted man, lest he wander away or harm himself inadvertently, like the very young child he now resembled.

The girl, whom Eydryth remembered was named Karlis, stared wide-eyed at the newcomer. "Eydryth!" she blurted. "Welcome home, Lady!"

The songsmith greeted the servant; then Hyana smiled reassuringly at the girl. "We will watch him for a while," she said, and Karlis took her leave.

Eydryth walked slowly over to her father's pallet. Even in his sleep, the slackness around his mouth, the vacant expression on his face, betrayed his malady. Sitting down beside him, his daughter took his hand gently. Beneath tumbled russet-brown curls, he opened blue eyes that had once been the same vivid color as his daughter's, but now were faded, empty of reason. "Father . . . ," the songsmith whispered, stroking his hair, "I've come home."

Jervon grinned, then babbled at her, mixing random words with nonsense syllables. *At least he still recognizes me*, the girl thought, wiping a smear of wetness from his chin when he had finished his greeting—if such it could be termed. "Just hold still, now," she whispered, then began to gently stroke Dahaun's healing mud across his forehead, covering it with a thin layer of the cool redness.

Jervon twitched, raised his hands to swipe fretfully at the healing substance. "No, don't wipe it off," Eydryth said, and together, she and Hyana held his hands down until he subsided, eyeing them both nervously.

"When he quiets," Eydryth said softly, "I want you to take the mud that is left to Joisan. Tell her to spread it over the Keplian's wound. Then have her rinse the container in a bucket of water, so that he may be offered that water to drink when he awakens and can stand again."

"I understand," her foster-sister said, softly.

Jervon gazed at them, then at the water jug that stood in its place on the bureau. He waved at it, babbling again. "He wants a drink," Eydryth said, recognizing the gesture and sounds.

But before she held the goblet Hyana filled to Jervon's lips, Eydryth, acting on impulse, dropped a dollop of the red mud into the liquid, then stirred it with a forefinger until it dissolved. "Here, Father," she said, aiding him as he sat up. Jervon drank thirstily, then smiled vacantly and lay back down. He tossed restlessly, still wanting to scratch at the mud now drying across his forehead. "No, no," Eydryth whispered. "Leave it where it is, Father. . . ."

Hyana was holding the container, eyeing the red mud still

within it. "Whoever this Lady of the Green Silences is, she is
someone with great Power," she said. "I can feel her magic
through this container."

"Dahaun has great Power, yes," Eydryth said. "That is part
of the story I have yet to tell you. Shhhh," she said, turning her
attention back to her father, "lie still, dear Father. Rest easy."

"Perhaps if you sang to him . . . ," Hyana suggested. "That
always used to quiet him, even on his worst days."

Eydryth nodded, then picked up her hand-harp. A moment
to tune it, then she began gently plucking the strings, humming as she searched in her mind for a song. Alon's face swam
before her eyes, and before she knew what she was about, she
was singing:

> When the hills were purple with heather
> And spring rode over the Dale
> When my love and I were together,
> I could dream of a bridal veil.
>
> Before the Hounds came to rend us,
> We did own the spring and the moor—
> Now war has become my love's mistress
> And my young heart is weary and sore.
>
> Still in dreams do I walk our fair valley
> Still in dreams I remember his voice,
> In that lost time still do we dally
> And still now is he my heart's choice.
> For a bond, once formed, is not broken
> And a promise, once having been spoken
> Must be kept, regardless of cost.

She sang the old song quietly, as tears filled her eyes and
slipped quietly down her face. When she was finished, Jervon
had fallen asleep again. The red mud had dried, and was now
hardening into its crust upon his forehead. Hyana placed a
hand on her sister's shoulder. "You love him, do you not?"
she murmured. "This . . . Alon."

"Yes, I love him," Eydryth whispered, leaning her face

against Hyana's shoulder, unable to meet the older girl's eyes. "I love him . . . more than I can say."

Hyana hugged her gently, stroking her foster-sister's curls. "Tell me, does he return your love?"

Silently, the songsmith nodded. "But I fear for him," she murmured. "He was heading into great danger."

"We will aid you, Sister," Hyana promised, drawing back and clasping Eydryth's hands in a reassuring grip. "I will tell Mother and Father to prepare to ride forth tomorrow."

Eydryth shook her head. "Tomorrow may be too late. We must go as soon as possible. Tonight. Alon went alone to track Yachne, to a Place of Power—Dark Power. I dare not delay until daylight."

Hyana looked grave. "There is no moon tonight," she said quietly. "The Power of the Shadow is at its strongest, now. Especially in one of the Dark Places."

The songsmith nodded. "I know. That is all the more reason to go before dawn."

Joisan and Kerovan's daughter nodded, then, quietly, slipped from the room, leaving Eydryth alone with her father.

The songsmith sat beside him, his hand clasped in hers, watching him sleep. Softly, she sang to him again, as memories ran through her mind like playful children. Jervon . . . carrying her on his shoulders when she was very small. Jervon, practicing swordplay in the courtyard with Kerovan, his face flushed and full of life. Jervon, teaching her to lunge and parry with her own wooden sword. Jervon, picking her up after her first hard fall from a horse, his face drawn with worry . . . Jervon, standing with his arm around his wife, the last time she had seen them together before Elys disappeared . . .

Eydryth's memories dissolved into dreams as she dozed, sitting on her father's bed, still holding his hand.

The songsmith started awake when the door opened to admit Joisan. Her foster-mother had changed her dress for riding trousers and thigh-high boots to protect her from underbrush. She wore a padded leather jerkin and heavy tunic, and her chestnut hair was braided tightly.

In her arms, she carried a bundle of clothing. "I brought

some of your clothes," she whispered. "So you can change out of those damp ones." She gazed down at Jervon. "How fares he?"

Eydryth tapped the mud with a testing forefinger. "It is dry, and cracking," she said. "Dahaun said to remove it when—"

She broke off as Jervon opened his eyes. His gaze traveled from Joisan to Eydryth; then he blinked, and it sharpened. "Joisan?" he whispered, staring at the Wise Woman.

Both women gasped in sudden hope and amazement. "Jervon!" Joisan exclaimed, her hand going out to clasp her friend's. "Jervon, you *know* me?"

"Of course I know you," he replied, obviously bewildered. "But . . . who is this?" He pointed at Eydryth.

The songsmith gulped, then raised the hand she still held to her cheek. Her tears splashed down, hot and salty. "Father . . ." she whispered. "Oh, Father! Thank you, Amber Lady! Thank you, Dahaun!"

Jervon stared at her, his eyes widening incredulously. He sat up, grasping her shoulders hard. "*Eydryth?*" he whispered. "Is that you? But . . . but . . ."

Joisan hugged her foster-daughter, who was now crying too hard to speak. "Yes, Jervon. It is Eydryth. You have been . . . ill . . . for a time. A long time. It was only tonight that your daughter brought home a cure for your malady, and it was thus that you have awakened at last!"

Jervon reached out to hug Eydryth, cradling her against his shoulder. Joy welled up in her, such joy as made all her struggles, her sacrifices, seem as nothing by comparison to the feeling of having her father's arms around her, hearing his voice speak her name.

After a moment, Jervon spoke again, his voice strained and still bewildered . . . but already he was beginning to grasp that there had been changes . . . vast changes . . . that he yet remained unaware of. "Time . . ." he whispered. "Joisan . . . how much time?"

The Wise Woman drew a deep breath. "Six years, Jervon," she said, steadily, giving him the truth.

"Oh, no . . . " Jervon whispered. "My child . . . grown into a woman. My wife . . ." Sudden hope brightened his voice. "What of Elys?"

"Still missing, Father," Eydryth said, pulling back a little to look at him, run her fingers over his dear, familiar face. Tenderly, she chipped away the last of the red mud. Now that his expression was animated, full of life again, it seemed that the intervening years had wrought but little change in him.

Her father stared at her. "You look so much like her," he said, wonderingly. "You have grown into a beauty, Daughter."

"What is the last thing you remember, Father?" she asked.

"The Seeing Stone," he said. "I climbed . . . I looked . . ." He drew a quick breath. "Eydryth, I saw her! I saw Elys that day! She lay within a Place of Power—one I would recognize if I saw it again. In my vision, she was lying upon a pallet, her hands folded upon her breast. Our son . . ." He drew a deep, ragged breath. "Our son was still within her. I could see the swell of her belly. Elys was surrounded by a mist, a glamourie of some kind, that shields her from view . . . but"—he grasped his daughter's hands tightly—"she is *alive*, Eydryth! Alive!"

"Oh, Father!" she whispered. "If only we can find her . . . save her!"

"We will," he promised, and his words bore the ring of a sacred vow. "We will."

Joisan stood up, one hand resting on each shoulder. "I must carry these happy tidings to my lord," she said. "And then . . . Eydryth, we are all still waiting for your story."

The songsmith smiled up at her foster-mother. "I will be with you shortly," she said.

"We will both be there," Jervon amended. "If there is a story to be told, I want to hear it, also." He smiled ruefully. "I have much catching up to do, it seems."

Less than an hour later, Eydryth, dressed in fresh clothing, her hunger truly satisfied for the first time in days, sat on one of the stone benches in the Great Hall, finishing her food, her tale (cut to the bare bones) told. "And so," she concluded, "Alon went to track the witch alone. I fear for him." She glanced at her family's faces. "So much so that I ride back out tonight. Guret must already be waiting with the horses saddled."

"I will ride with you, Sister!" Firdun was the first to speak. "I have no fear of a sorceress!"

"And that lack of fear is precisely why you will remain here," Kerovan told his impetuous son, grimly. *"I* will ride with Eydryth."

"And so will I," Hyana and Joisan said, together.

"And I." Jervon was only a heartbeat behind. The former invalid was dressed now in riding garb. Thanks to the walks and rides his companions had taken him on, he was not wasted, although he had complained bitterly at his own thinness and lost muscle tone.

Now he smiled at his daughter and squeezed her hand, his blue eyes sparkling with teasing laughter. "We must rescue this young sorcerer, if only so that I may inquire as to his intentions toward my daughter." He shook his head. "What a night! I have regained myself after years of lost time, only to discover that I now have a sorceress of no little power as a daughter, and an Adept as a prospective son. My head is spinning!"

Eydryth shook her head, willing herself not to blush again. She had said naught about what had happened in the Fane of Neave, beyond the bare fact that the Place of Power had cured both she and Alon of the Shadow-taint. And she knew that Hyana had not betrayed her confidence. But her family knew her well, and her voice had given her away every time she had spoken Alon's name, she feared.

"Father!" she said, mock-reprovingly. "I said nothing of . . . of . . ."

"You did not have to," Jervon said gently; then he sobered. "After so long unaware of anything, I see tonight as if I have been new-forged. My daughter is a woman, and a Wise Woman at that. All of this will take me some time."

"Thanks to the Lady of the Green Silences, we will all have that time," Joisan said. "But for now, I suggest that we ride!"

In the end, it was decided that Sylvya and Firdun would remain behind . . . over Firdun's bitter protests. Kerovan reminded his son that he could track his sister by mind-link, and thus keep those at Kar Garudwyn informed as to their progress. As soon as all was in readiness, Joisan, Kerovan, Eydryth, Hyana and Jervon left the Great Hall together.

Outside Kar Garudwyn, Monso stood, chewing a mouthful of hay, awaiting them. The Keplian's ordeal had left him thin and worn, but Dahaun's red mud had again worked its magic, and his leg was nearly healed. The stallion had finished the water from Neave's spring, and the water that Sylvya had given him after rinsing Dahaun's box in it. Looking at him, Eydryth could scarcely believe that only two hours had passed since they had arrived at Landisl's citadel.

She patted the Keplian, then swiftly saddled and bridled him. "Surely you do not intend to ride him?" Joisan said. "He needs rest, not more riding!"

Eydryth shook her head. "I will ride Vyar," she told her foster-mother. "But Alon will need a mount, if we find him. And Monso will not be content to wait here for his master's return. No stall or fence could hold him if he wishes to come with us . . . and he does," she said, smiling as the stallion whickered, then pawed, as if he understood her perfectly.

She removed the reins from the Keplian's bit, so he would run no risk of stepping on them, coiling them and tying them on the saddle. Even as she had predicted, Monso clattered after them as they descended the ramp to the valley.

Within minutes, the rescue party set out, trotting slowly in single file, with Jervon, who did not have the night-sight, riding in their midst.

By the time they had reached the road, and set out along it, Eydryth was barely able to hold herself back from galloping full speed along it. Her worry for Alon gnawed at her like some wild creature.

As they moved westward at a ground-eating trot, she chafed, realizing for the first time how slow a mortal horse's gaits were, in comparison to Monso's. The riderless stallion ranged ahead of them, scenting the air as though trying to trace his master that way.

Suddenly Monso shrilled his stallion's scream into the

night, then reared before them. Fearing that the half-bred had gone berserk, the riders drew rein, watching the Keplian anxiously as he stood pawing nervously in the middle of the road. The half-bred screamed yet again—

—and this time he was answered!

A shrill cry broke through the night air, and Eydryth suddenly discerned a blacker-than-black shape winging toward them. A shape that bore a white V on its breast.

"Steel Talon!" she gasped, as the falcon came to rest on the cantle of Monso's saddle. She knew that the falcon would not normally fly at night, and her heart began slamming within her.

"This is the falcon you spoke of?" Kerovan asked.

"Yes," Eydryth whispered, through dry lips. The bird looked straight at the songsmith and screamed again. "He has come to lead us to Alon," she said, suddenly sure that she spoke truth. "He is even now in terrible danger!"

Sixteen

Steel Talon led them, winging from tree to bush, alighting always a short distance away, then voicing his shrill cry. Monso cantered after the falcon, and Eydryth and her family followed the Keplian.

Roads stretched before them in the darkness of the waning, now-overcast night—first the broad, well-traveled highway Eydryth had taken to reach Kar Garudwyn, then another, narrower way that turned south off the main route somewhere in Bluemantle lands. This secondary road soon deteriorated to little more than an overgrown, cart-rutted track.

All of the party, except for Jervon, could summon night vision at need, so they took turns riding point. In that way, no one person had to bear that burden alone. When Kerovan rode at the head of the group, Jervon rode beside him. As they companied side by side, Eydryth could hear the soft rise and fall of Kerovan's voice, broken every so often by a quiet question or comment from her father. She guessed that Kerovan was attempting to fill in the missing years for his newly recovered friend.

Dawn was still more than an hour away when the little party reached the Place of Power that was Yachne's destination. For the past hour, the riders had crossed moorland and picked their way across marshy hallows, for the trail had deteriorated to a game path, then dwindled away completely. If it had not been for the Keplian and the falcon, they would have been completely lost.

As they rounded a stand of brush, Eydryth, who was riding in the fore with Hyana, saw Monso stop. The stallion snorted, then stuck out his upper lip, exposing his teeth, as if he scented something foul. Steel Talon alighted on the cantle of Alon's saddle a moment later. "Our destination lies just ahead," Eydryth's foster-sister said in a hushed voice. "I can sense that from the falcon."

Peering through the night, Eydryth concentrated her night vision, making out a faint light from somewhere ahead. It brightened the way ahead, seeming as strong as the glow of a forest fire Eydryth had once seen—a forest fire that had burned itself down to embers. But the bard knew instinctively that whatever caused this light had no kinship with honest fire or once-living wood. The glow that now rose ahead of them was *unclean.*

Vyar, Eydryth's Kioga mare, suddenly halted, ears pointing forward, then abruptly flattening as her nostrils flared. The songsmith felt her shiver; then, without warning, the horse ducked her head down to her chest and began backing away. If Eydryth had not driven her forward with her legs, she would have turned tail and bolted.

Hyana's gelding shied also. Even in the darkness the songsmith could see the ring of white encircling the terrified creature's eye. Kerovan's voice came from behind them, floating softly on the pitchy air. "What chances?"

"The horses," Eydryth kept her own voice soft. "They are

balking. They smell something ahead that they do not care to approach."

"Must we go on afoot?" Joisan asked.

"I do not know. Perhaps."

But, after a brief struggle (and a firm *smack* with the reins), the songsmith was able to force her mount onward. Vyar was trembling beneath her, but, having managed the Keplian, Eydryth found a mortal horse far easier to handle. Once he was given a lead to follow, Hyana's grey, Raney, fell in behind Vyar.

Stiff-legged, trembling, the mare followed Monso toward the source of that glow. It seemed to Eydryth to be a forest, one that had died—died so swiftly that the leaves had had no chance to drop from the branches. They shone white, a rank, phosphorescent white, like the lichens which grew in some caves. The branches and trunks which sprouted those eldritch leaves were dull black, as if they had turned in a trice to solid pillars of rot. And from many of those branches hung lengths of dead, silvery moss, veiling the depths of the forest from their eyes like concealing tapestries.

If it had not been for the stomach-wrenching reek that emanated from that strange wood, that eye-searing aura of total *wrongness,* the place might have been termed strangely beautiful. As they halted just outside of the strange wood, Eydryth looked over at Hyana. "What do you make of it, Sister?" she asked, knowing that the other had the gift of seeing beyond the ken of humankind, into the spirit and future of things.

"Truly, this is a case where fair is foul and foul, fair," Hyana replied. "If your Alon has followed the witch within, he has endangered not merely his body, but his innermost essence. To die in this place would leave one not only dead, but damned without hope of succor or mercy."

"A path." Jervon, ever the practical strategist, pointed to a distinct trail. "But there is no telling whether it leads to the right place."

"If there is a path, then it is that way we must go," Kerovan said. "Touching one of those 'trees'—if such they ever truly were—would be as poisonous as inviting the strike of an adder." Eydryth saw that the wristlet he always wore was softly glowing, warning, as was its nature, against evil.

"Will the horses take it?" Joisan asked, soothing her golden chestnut. "Varren is not happy even standing here, much less entering that place."

"Monso is already going," Eydryth cried, pointing to the Keplian, who was even now trotting up the trail. "Quickly, while he gives us a lead!" Her legs closed around Vyar's barrel, but it took another smack with the reins to force the mare after the stallion.

The rot-trees (or so Eydryth had come to think of them) closed in around her. The soil beneath the mare's hooves was grey, leached of life, sterile and powdery as talc. After a breath or two, Eydryth fumbled out her kerchief and tied it over her mouth and nose. She risked a swift glance back, and saw the others following her example. The horses were plainly not at ease in this "forest," but none had balked.

Eydryth was in a fever of impatience, wanting to urge Vyar into a gallop, but, after Kerovan's warning about the danger of touching the trees, she restrained herself . . . barely. Her conviction that Alon was in trouble grew until she was quivering like a plucked harpstring. She found herself remembering every moment, every passing touch between them since they had met, and was powerless to halt the images flowing through her mind.

The wood stretched away on either side of them, quiet and poisonous, but, somewhat to Eydryth's surprise, they met no one and nothing. She had half-expected another contingent of web-riders. If there ever existed a place more perfect to have been their spawning ground, she had never seen it.

Glancing back at the others, she saw Kerovan's wristlet glowing brilliant blue, as it had that day she and Jervon were nearly ensorcelled by the Keplian. But they did not need the talisman to warn them against the Shadow—or to tell them they were in grave peril. The rank stench surrounding them would not allow even a moment's forgetting.

Steel Talon sat hunched on the cantle of the Keplian's saddle, and Eydryth realized that the falcon was, rightfully, loath to perch on any of the limbs in this unnatural wood. She wondered how far this Place extended—they had already ridden for nearly a league.

Even as that thought crossed her mind, they came to the end of their trail. Suddenly the rot-trees ended, leaving a huge, roughly circular meadow in their midst. The "meadow" was covered in a short, sere turf, the color of ancient lichen. In its center rose an enormous rock, as large as a good-sized cottage.

Monso trotted swiftly into the meadow with a nicker of recognition. Eydryth followed the Keplian's direction, then saw, silhouetted against that massive boulder, two figures.

Violet light surrounded one, emanating from the crystal talisman he wore. His hands were up in a warding gesture, and a violet haze wreathed them, shaped almost like a warrior's shield. The other figure was undoubtedly Yachne, though she still wore a shapeless grey robe and hood, hiding her identity. Serpent-shaped trails of purple light shot through with dark-red streaks fell from the tip of her fingers, then launched themselves across the intervening space, aimed at the Adept's head.

"Alon!" Eydryth shouted, and was off Vyar and running toward him before the mare even came to a stop. "Alon!"

Monso bolted toward his master; then, with a suddenness that nearly knocked him off all four feet, the half-bred stopped dead, as though he had run into some invisible barrier.

Which indeed he had, as Eydryth discovered a heartbeat later, as she, too, slammed into something unyielding. She fell hard, then lay winded. A moment later Kerovan grabbed her arm, and aided her to her feet.

The songsmith saw with horror what was happening. Evidently Alon had lost his concentration on his spelling when he had heard her shout, because, even as Eydryth focused on him again, the Adept was struck by one of Yachne's snake-bolts of Power. He reeled, stumbled, then went down to his knees, plainly dazed.

"No!" Eydryth whispered in agony. Trapped behind the unseen wall, she was forced to watch helplessly. Seeing her and the other would-be rescuers, Yachne laughed aloud, gave the

newcomers a cheery "thank you!" wave, then bent to her task.
Horrified, Eydryth realized that she was completing the last
closing of the spell she had employed to steal Dinzil's Power.
A dead fawn lay on the "grass" not far from her, its throat
slashed. The blood-circle was nearly complete.

Eydryth pounded helplessly against the unseen barrier as
the witch scratched her skinny wrist with the blade of the
athame. In a trice she had completed the closing of her ghastly
circle; then she began to chant.

Alon slumped forward onto his hands and knees as the mist
began coalescing around him. "Alon!" Eydryth screamed.
"Stop her! You must stop her!"

After a moment the young man wavered to his feet, then
stared down in horror as the thickening mist suddenly bil-
lowed up, nearly waist-high. "No!" Eydryth sobbed. She was
scarcely aware of her father putting an arm around her, as she
turned to Hyana. "Does Yachne's wall extend all the way
around this clearing?" she gasped.

Her foster-sister nodded. "I can see it. A barrier of pale
light, nearly as tall as the tops of these loathsome trees."

"Can you break the spell?" the songsmith implored Joisan
and Kerovan.

The Wise Woman shook her head. "I have been trying to do
just that, ever since we came here, but this is no spell I have
ever encountered before."

Laughing delightedly, Yachne walked closer to Alon. The
Adept was struggling to force the mist back down into the
ground, using the glow given off by his crystal talisman. But,
slowly, a finger-width at a time, he was losing that battle. The
mist by now was up to his chest. Eydryth knew that if it
completely enclosed him, the Alon as she knew him now
would be forever lost—to himself as well as to her.

"Alon!" she screamed. "The sword! Remember the sword!"
Cold iron or steel, she knew, was ofttimes a powerful weapon
against evil magic. And the gryphon-sword had quan-iron,
that bane of all Darkness, embedded in its hilt. "The sword!"
she cupped her hands around her mouth to help her voice
carry. "Try the sword!"

Still obviously dazed from Yachne's Power-blast, Alon

shook his head, one hand still clutching his crystal talisman. Eydryth realized that he could no longer hear her—somehow Yachne's spell must also be muffling sound.

The sorceress came closer to her victim now, just as Monso screamed in rage and rose onto his hind legs. The stallion's powerful forefeet battered at the invisible barrier, but to no avail.

The mist was creeping up toward Alon's chin. Eydryth turned to Hyana, clutching the other woman's hands in both of hers desperately. "Can you mind-send?" she demanded.

Hyana hesitated. "I can with my mother and father . . . and Firdun. Sometimes with you."

"Try to mind-send to Alon, Hyana! Tell him to use the sword! Try, please!

The other frowned, but obediently closed her eyes, concentrating. *The sword*, Eydryth thought. *Alon, use the sword. It may break the mist! Use the sword!*

Yachne was standing before Alon, now, her hands weaving in the air as she continued her chant. The mist thickened even further. . . .

Alon fumbled at his back, as if in a dream. "Yes!" Eydryth whispered. "Yes, Alon! The sword . . . oh, please, use it!"

The Adept bent, disappearing from view behind the mist that by now nearly reached his eyes. Eydryth clenched her fists so hard that her hands ached, but she was hardly aware of the pain. *The sword! Is he unbuckling it, unsheathing it? What is he doing?*

Yachne gave a final, commanding cry, using a Word that made the air seem to curdle with darkness. Mist lapped over the top of the pillar enclosing Alon. Eydryth shut her eyes, unable to watch—then immediately opened them again. She could not look, but she swiftly discovered that she could not bear to look away.

Amber Lady, she prayed silently, tears slipping from her eyes, *help him!*

Purple light wreathed the sorceress's arms as she began to draw Alon's Power into herself, just as she had done with Dinzil.

Help him! Somebody help him!

A shrill scream rent the air, just as something small and black fell upon Yachne like a stone, wicked talons aiming for her eyes. The only one of them who could fly over the barrier—Steel Talon!

The witch ducked, barely missing the winged death stooping out of the skies. The purple light wreathing her arms faltered, halted completely as she threw up both arms. A lash of dark lightning crackled from her fingers, striking the small black shape with the white V on its chest—

—even as the blade of Eydryth's sword poked through the mist surrounding Alon, cutting it away as though it were a solid substance. It slashed an opening; then, before Yachne was more than half-aware that her captive was making a bid for escape, Eydryth saw Alon's dim form move within that pillar of deadly mist.

Weight balanced on the balls of his feet, knees flexed, arm extended—it was the one lunge she had taught him, and he did it perfectly. The length of shining steel licked out like a cleansing streak of blue-white fire, thrusting through the hole in the mist, burying its sharpness just below the breast of the woman's tattered grey robe, impaling the witch.

Yachne stiffened with a shriek of mingled pain and fury as Eydryth's gryphon-hilted sword, with all the strength of Alon's arm behind it, transfixed her.

The mist vanished as the witch toppled over backward—and lay unmoving.

At the same moment, Eydryth and the others staggered forward as the barrier that had kept them helpless on the outside of the meadow disappeared.

"Alon, oh, Alon!" The songsmith ran straight to the Adept, grabbing his shoulders, hugging him ecstatically, but only for a moment did he return her embrace. His face set, he gently put her aside, then walked forward to pick up a small, stricken form lying on the ground next to the dying sorceress.

Eydryth cried out softly with grief and pity. Steel Talon was not dead yet . . . but he soon would be, that was plain. "Oh, no!" she whispered.

Tears stood in the Adept's eyes as he cradled the dying falcon against him. "Steel Talon . . . ," he whispered brokenly. "You saved me. . . ."

Eydryth lifted a hand to gently touch that fierce beak, staring at those dimming eyes. She thought that she glimpsed a strange satisfaction deep in them. Alon glanced up at her, startled. "Steel Talon is . . . content," he whispered.

Eydryth nodded as understanding suddenly flooded through her. "Because he has fulfilled the quest that was the only thing keeping him alive, is that not so?" she asked. "He dies content, knowing that he has gained his revenge."

Alon nodded. "Yachne . . . it was Yachne that night, when Jonthal died. She set the trap . . . for me. But it was Jonthal who died. . . ."

Steel Talon's fierce eyes seemed to blaze even more fiercely; then the bird abruptly stiffened, jerked several times, and sagged, limp. Alon swallowed, then turned to walk away, toward Monso.

Eydryth started after him, but Jervon caught her arm. "No," her father said gently. "Give him a moment to grieve in private. He would wish it so."

The songsmith took a deep breath; then she nodded. They watched as Alon walked over to Monso, gave the stallion a quick pat, then carefully, tenderly, wrapped the falcon's body in his undertunic. He tied the small, wrapped form to the saddle. She knew, without being told, that the Adept intended to give the bird proper burial on clean ground.

Eydryth turned back to her family, and saw Joisan and Hyana crouched beside Yachne. The songsmith was faintly surprised to see that the sorceress still lived, though it was plain that no healcraft could aid her.

Dropping to her knees beside the witch, Eydryth stared down at her, thinking how suddenly small and shrunken she appeared. Yachne opened grey eyes to regard her, and the younger woman realized that the gleam of madness that had so frightened her before was gone. The witch struggled to draw breath. "Am . . . am I dying?" she whispered.

Joisan hesitated, then nodded. "Yes. If I could help you, I would, but your wound is beyond any ability of mine to heal."

Sweat stood out on the dying woman's face. "Yes . . . feel it. Hurts . . . hurts so . . ."

"I am sorry," Joisan said. "I can try to sing you into a painless state, if you so wish. That is all I can do to ease your passing."

The witch nodded. "Alon?" she whispered. "Where is Alon?"

Eydryth hastily beckoned the Adept, who was even now returning to them, to come quickly. When he reached the woman who had cared for him as a child, he dropped down beside her, took her hand. "I am sorry," he said quietly. "So sorry. I wish there had been some other way."

"Not . . . not your fault," she whispered. "I see clearly now . . . been so long since I could do that . . ."

"Hush," Alon said, fighting to keep his voice from breaking. "Don't try to talk."

"Must . . . must talk . . . ," she insisted. "It was the Turning . . . the Turning." She gasped for breath. "I was . . . witch of Estcarp before then. . . ."

"So we guessed," Eydryth said. "And you lost your powers after the Turning?"

The former witch nodded. "Angry. Wanted what should have been mine forever . . . wanted it back . . ." Joisan carefully wiped Yachne's dry lips with a cloth moistened in water. The old woman (for all her borrowed "youth" had vanished) sucked gratefully at the moisture. Joisan aided her as she swallowed a sip from a water flask. "Then I found out . . . about the ones who still had the Power . . . the males. They had what should have been mine. . . ."

After a moment she went on, "Wandered . . . long time. Garth Howell . . . they took me in. They were there, too, the males with the Power . . . the creatures against nature . . . but they offered me a way. . . ." She sucked in breath, then writhed for a moment. Finally, sweat pouring down her face, she subsided. "The spell. The abbot taught me . . . spell. As long as I would take the Power from you . . ." She gasped, staring at Alon. "That was the price . . . one I was willing to pay . . . and gladly. I am sorry for that, Alon. . . ."

"Me?" He was plainly startled. "Why? I have never encountered the denizens of Garth Howell, never harmed them. I was half the world away! Why me?"

"They fear you . . . ," she whispered. "You are one of the Seven." She stared then at Eydryth, and Hyana. "As are they. The Seven . . ."

"The Seven what?" Eydryth wondered.

"Defenders . . . defenders of this land . . . defenders of Arvon," Yachne replied. She was laboring now for breath, and it was pain to hear her. "There will be . . . Seven. Last has not yet . . . been born." Her gaze turned again to Eydryth. "Your brother," she muttered. "Will be the last. If he is ever born."

Eydryth grabbed the old woman's hand in both of hers. "What know you of my brother?" she demanded fiercely.

"Promise . . . promise you will ease my passing . . ." the sorceress said.

"I swear by Gunnora's amulet," she vowed. "Where is my brother, Yachne?"

"Here . . . and not-here. Within the stone that is not-stone. Beyond the cage, beneath the flesh . . . uhhhh . . ." With a rattling moan, she trailed off.

To Eydryth, the words had no meaning. She began to demand further explanation, but Joisan nudged her. "She is beyond speech, Daughter," she whispered. "Shall we fulfill our promise?"

Together, Joisan and Eydryth sang softly, and all of the group watched the lines of pain smooth away from the aged features. When Yachne died, minutes later, her countenance was almost peaceful.

They covered her face with a fold from her ragged mantle, then withdrew to the other side of the massive stone to speak together for the first time. Joisan looked up at the eastern side of the Shadow Place. "Dawn is breaking," she said softly. "We have lived through this night . . . something that I doubted, a few hours ago."

Alon stared around him at his rescuers. "I thank you for coming to my aid. Without your"—he nodded at Hyana—"mind-sending, I would never have remembered that sword."

"Alon, this is Hyana, my foster-sister," Eydryth said, remembering her manners. "And this is Lord Kerovan and Lady Joisan, my foster parents." Pride tinged her voice as she hooked her arm through Jervon's. "And this is my father, Jervon."

Alon had bowed in turn as each introduction was made, but when he heard this last, he blinked in surprise. "Dahaun's mud worked!" he cried. "This is . . . this is wonderful hearing! Sir," he added hastily.

Jervon smiled. "I owe you much, young sorcerer," he said. "And I gather from everything that my daughter has *not* said, that we have a great deal to discuss, you and I." He held out his hand. "Well-met, Alon!"

This time it was the Adept's turn to color, but he grasped the older man's hand with a strong grip, and met his eyes steadily. "You have the right of it . . . sir," he said. "Well-met, indeed, Jervon. You are a most fortunate man. We had no idea whether Dahaun's red mud would restore an injured mind."

"I am fortunate indeed," Jervon said. "To have a daughter such as mine. Although"—he gave Alon an equally level stare—"I have gained the impression that I must now resign myself to sharing her."

Alon's mouth quirked slightly. "Perceptive, as well as fortunate," he said.

Kerovan chuckled, then reached into his saddlebag and brought out hunks of journeybread and another water flask. "Here, Alon, you must be hungry."

The little group sat in a circle, sharing food and water, while dawn slowly brightened the eldritch woods around them. The events of the night weighed heavy upon the songsmith now, and she felt at once so tired that she could have lain down and slept next to Yachne's stiffening corpse, and so keyed up with frustration that she felt as though she must needs scream aloud.

Catching her father's eye upon her, she gave him a wan smile. "To come so close to finding her . . . and fail. Yachne knew where my mother is."

He nodded. "It is hard," he said. "But we will not give up."

"Here and not-here," Alon repeated, puzzling aloud. "Stone that is not-stone." He shook his head. "What can it mean?"

None of them could think of an answer. But Alon refused to give up, worrying at the riddle as though it were a bone and he a hound. "Here . . ." He glanced around the clearing. "What could be here, and yet not-here? Stone and not-stone? Stone . . . stone is rock, it is granite, it is limestone, and quartz . . ." He trailed off, staring down at the crystal he wore. "Crystal!" he exclaimed. "It is stone, yet not-stone. Could that be what Yachne meant?"

All of them turned to survey their surroundings in the growing light. "There is no stone except that one," Jervon said, finally, pointing to the monstrous boulder. "And that appears grey, not crystal."

The Adept rose and walked over to the stone. Eydryth walked beside him, and together they gazed upon it. "Here and not-here," Alon said. "Stone and not-stone. It sounds rather like those mirror Gates we used, does it not?"

It was obvious that he was having some insight that Eydryth could not follow. "But that stone is nothing like this one," she said, touching the crystal talisman he wore with her fingers, tapping it with a nail. It rang, ever so faintly, and Alon, who had been staring at the huge rock, gasped.

"Do that again!" he commanded, holding the crystal out to her. "And match the note with your voice, as you did once before!"

Puzzled, she obeyed him, making the crystal *ting*, then attempting to match the note.

"I see it!" Alon exclaimed, wide-eyed. "Eydryth, look at the stone as you do so!"

Again she sounded the crystal, echoed it with a sung note. And, before her eyes, the great stone grew translucent!

She could see within it . . . and, in the crystalline depths, there was a pallet, and upon the pallet, a human shape!

"It *is* a Gate!" she exclaimed in astonishment. By that time the others, arrested by their excited voices, had come over to discover what chanced.

Once more Alon performed his demonstration, and this time it was Jervon's turn to grow wide-eyed. "That is Elys!" he gasped. "That is what I saw in the Seeing Stone! I knew I would recognize it if I ever saw it again!"

"We must break the illusion that this is a solid boulder," Joisan said. "We must link and attempt to open the Gate."

"How?" Kerovan asked. "You and Alon seem to be the ones who have done so in the past."

"I believe we should link hands and Power," Joisan said. "Then pour our Power into Eydryth. The crystal responds to sound, and she is our singer. Her voice is the key that will unlock this Gate." The Wise Woman glanced at Alon, and he nodded agreement.

So it was that they linked hands, concentrated. Within moments Eydryth began to feel light-headed, as though she were some kind of rod that was being used to conduct a thunderbolt. Opening her mouth, she sang—and her voice rang out with greater volume and clarity than she had ever possessed before.

Slowly, the boulder cleared again . . . became crystal . . . then became mist. With Jervon close behind them, the group took a step forward, straight into that mist.

They were in a place, and it was filled with light—but it was a Dark light, as though Shadow had been turned to flame, and given substance. The place had no horizons, no boundaries. There was no sky . . . nothing. Their feet rested on something, but it was difficult to tell what. Eydryth swallowed as she was assailed by sudden vertigo. It was extremely disconcerting to have no reference points.

Except one. Before her was the pallet, and on it, Elys lay sleeping. Eydryth saw the gentle mound of her belly beneath her robe. "She has been here the entire time," Joisan whispered.

"But why?" Kerovan asked. "Why take her and confine her? If these Adepts at Garth Howell are so powerful, and yet evil enough to do this, then why not simply do away with her?"

"Because to murder a woman who is carrying is such a great transgression that even the masters and mistresses of Garth

Howell would not dare to do so," Hyana replied. "Gunnora is a powerful spirit who protects the unborn, and those who carry them. They dared not harm Elys outright. They feared Gunnora's reprisal too much."

Eydryth walked forward, and they followed her. The songsmith's eyes adjusted more to the strangeness of this Place, and she could see lines of Dark light arcing over her sleeping mother's form, as though she lay within a cage.

"Beyond the cage, beneath the flesh," Alon whispered. "The Seventh Defender of Arvon sleeps before us."

"How can we free her?" Hyana asked. "I know of no spell to undo this kind of sorcery."

"Nor do I," Joisan admitted.

"Landisl cannot help us here," Kerovan said. "This Place is outside our world, and not within any that he ever trod."

Eydryth scarcely heard her family's comments. She stared at those lines of Dark light. And the longer she stared at those lines of Dark light arcing over the pallet, the more they seemed to her to akin to harpstrings. As though they could be . . . plucked. Music. Music had been the key to so many of the spells they had encountered. . . .

"Alon . . . ," the minstrel whispered hoarsely, "lend me all your strength!"

"You have it," he replied, and a moment later his fingers tightened around hers. Power flooded her . . . poured into her in a wave of warmth.

Humming, the songsmith formed in her mind the image of a giant finger pick. Concentrating fiercely, she forced herself to *see* it, glimpse it hovering over those "strings."

Then, with an effort that made her break out in a sweat, she moved her giant mind-pick downward, made it pluck one of those "strings."

A sound so loud it staggered her boomed out. Eydryth waited, but the cage remained in place. She concentrated again, and "plucked" another string. Then another.

"That's three," Alon said. "One of the numbers of Power."

"What are the others?" she asked. "Three did not work, as you can see."

"Seven," he said. "And nine."

"Seven," she said. "Seven Defenders . . . and, Alon"—her voice grew more excited, as she swiftly counted—"there are seven 'strings'!"

"Try it," he urged.

Shaking with the effort it took, the songsmith plucked the strings steadily . . . until finally all seven had been sounded.

Nothing happened. Eydryth fought back tears of disappointment.

"Seven . . . it must be related to seven," Alon whispered. "It cannot be coincidence. Spells are often constructed with repetitions of certain numbers, words, sounds. . . ."

"Seven Defenders, seven strings . . . ," Eydryth whispered. "Seven sevens . . ."

"Try it," Alon urged again.

Eydryth began. Wielding the huge "mind-pick" was taking an increasing toll of her strength . . . and of the borrowed Power she was getting from Alon. The songsmith knew she was draining him every bit as surely as Yachne had planned to. His hand in hers began to tremble.

And still she sounded the notes. Seven different notes, in a complex pattern, choosing them nearly at random . . . but aware all the time that a melody was being shaped. A melody of love, of longing. A child's love for her mother, a husband's love for his wife . . . all of that and more she forged into that melody.

Fourteen . . . twenty-one . . . thirty-five . . . Blackness was nibbling at the edges of her vision, like a voracious rasti. Forty-two . . . forty-nine!

With a suddenness that made them all blink and stagger, the lines of Dark light vanished!

Alon and Eydryth stumbled forward; then Alon caught her arm, held her back. "Let your father go first," he whispered.

The songsmith hesitated, then halted, knowing the Adept was right.

Slowly, reverently, Elys's lord approached the pallet; then his fingers went out, stroked his sleeping wife's cheek. "Elys . . ." he whispered. "Oh, my heart . . . my lady . . ."

Gently, he kissed her forehead, her lips; then Jervon raised her hand, prisoned safely within his own, to his face. A tear broke free, ran down his stubbled cheek, to trickle at last over her finger. At that touch, the sleeping woman's eyelids fluttered, then lifted. She gazed up at him, bewildered. "Jervon . . . " she whispered. "My lord . . ."

"My lady," he murmured, in a hushed, ragged voice. "Oh, Elys!" Quickly, he scooped her up into his arms, and, when Kerovan would have aided him, unsure that his friend was up to bearing her weight, shook his head fiercely at the other.

Silently, the group trailed behind them as Jervon strode forward, carrying his precious burden, and vanished through the Gate, leaving that uncanny Place behind forever.

When they emerged back into the clearing, it was into full sunlight. Elys seemed to have suffered no ill effects from her long ensorcellment, and as soon as her husband set her on her feet, she held out a hand to her daughter. "Eydryth?" she whispered. "Can it be?"

"Mother!" the songsmith said, and then the two of them were hugging and weeping with joy. Eydryth felt as though her heart could hold no more happiness. To have both her parents returned to her in the space of a single day!

When, at length, Elys was able to relinquish her hold on her child (as though she were afraid one of them might be torn away again), she greeted her friends. "Tell me what has chanced," she begged, "for I remember naught."

Voices rose in an excited babble as each tried to render his or her own version of all the lost years. When their story was finished, the witch's lovely features were troubled, but Elys had been a warrior for years in a war-torn land, as well as a witch, so she did not cry out or rail when she discovered that the Adepts at Garth Howell had stolen nine years of her life from her.

Instead she shook her head, staring around her. "I remember nothing," she said simply. "As far as I know, I lay down to nap in Kar Garudwyn, then awoke here. It is you"—she gazed at her husband and grown daughter, her friends and shield-mates—"my loved ones, who have suffered, not I!" Her mouth tightened. "I swear by All the Powers That Be, there will be a reckoning." Her voice was quiet, but a note in it sent shivers down Eydryth's back.

In silent accord, the group turned to make their way across the clearing to where the horses were tethered. But scarcely had she taken more than a step when Elys suddenly gasped, putting a hand to the small of her back. "Elys?" Joisan was at her side immediately, her arm circling her friend, supporting her. "Is it the baby?"

Eydryth's mother nodded. "And none too soon, apparently," she said, with a grim attempt at humor, "since I have been carrying him, if what you tell me is true, for nine years!"

The single group quickly separated into three. Hyana and Joisan, both experienced healers and midwives, tended Elys as the hours passed. Jervon and Kerovan rode out of the clearing in quest of supplies and transportation for Elys, and returned some time later with their horses hitched to an ancient wagon they had managed to persuade a local farmer to lend them. They had left their swords with the man as a pledge of good faith in lieu of the future payment in gold they promised.

Eydryth and Alon worked together to bury Yachne, then spent their time talking, tending Monso and the other horses, catching each other up on the desperate hours of the past night. The songsmith learned that the Adept had been caught and tricked into entering Yachne's illusion-cloaked circle with a vision of herself, lying upon the ground with a broken leg.

The sun was slanting toward the west, far past noon, when a squalling yowl of indignation—sounding almost like a cat whose tail has been assaulted by an unwary foot—filled the clearing. Eydryth and Alon, hand in hand, went together to gaze upon where Jervon, grinning broadly, stood holding the Seventh Defender of Arvon.

He was much too small, the songsmith decided, to bear such a portentious title . . . and seemed almost too small to bear the name his fond parents had bestowed upon him. "Trevon," Elys whispered, from her nest of blankets in the wagon, as she regarded the squirming red morsel her lord held so proudly.

"Hope," Alon said. "In the Old Tongue, that means 'hope.'"

"I know," Eydryth told him, putting her arm around his waist and leaning wearily against him. "And hope is something we will need sorely in the coming years, if Hyana's foretelling about a great conflict here in Arvon comes to pass—a war like unto the one you finished fighting in Escore not so long ago."

The Adept nodded soberly, but there was a light in his grey eyes. "And apparently you and I have a role to play in that conflict," he whispered softly. "Hope. We will need it." He gazed intently at Trevon. "We will need *him.*"

Some hours later, the party left the clearing, leaving behind a mound of freshly turned earth where Yachne lay. Alon, astride Monso, suddenly pointed. "Look!"

Eydryth, beside him on Vyar, gasped. "The grass! It has turned green!"

Hyana's voice rose, also filled with wonderment. "Look! Look at the woods!"

The rot-trees were changing, altering, as they neared them. Oak, rowan, beech and maple and evergreen now stood, instead of those stark black-and-white ghosts of trees. "The wood!" Eydryth cried, staring amazed. "It is healing itself!"

Beside her, Alon smiled, then reached over to take her hand. They rode on together, side by side, and the new tide of living greenness went before them, swelling outward, like a wave upon the shore.

Epilogue

*E*ydryth's fingers swept a last, ringing chord, sending the note bounding around the Great Hall in Kar Garudwyn like a child on the morning of Midwinter Feast. "And so," she said softly, as that final note began to die away, "they returned to Kar Garudwyn, after cleansing and healing that Place of Power. And their joy was very great."

Clapping rang out as she bowed, applause from the assembled guests and family members. Even Trevon smiled toothlessly, gurgling in his mother's lap.

"A fine song, Eydryth!" Jervon said. " 'The Ballad of the Songsmith' is the best you've written so far!"

She smiled fondly at her father. "It is always best to write what you know," she said wryly.

Suddenly the bard was conscious of someone leaning over the back of her chair, and, turning her head, she saw (though she had known the newcomer's identity within her heart immediately) that it was Alon. He smiled at the assembled guests. "A great success, my lady. I liked it very much. Especially the requiem to Steel Talon."

Then, lowering his voice, he added, "But perhaps our visitors are wearied. It has been a long day of feasting, and evening is now upon us."

Laughter boomed out from Obred, the Kioga chieftain. "I heard that, Lord Alon!"

Eydryth and Alon both colored, and the Kioga leader laughed harder. "We can take a hint, Lord Alon, and you have the right of it—it is indeed time to go. But," Obred said, smiling, "you must expect such minor inconveniences if you would wed a songsmith. Especially one as good as the Lady Eydryth. Hearing her play and sing, one is loath to depart a gathering where she performs."

Alon grinned at the burly leader. "I well understand, Obred. It was hearing her voice that made me fall under her spell in the first place."

Eydryth put aside her hand-harp, then stood up, smoothing the skirt of her blue wedding gown. "You forget, my lord," she said, under her breath, as she put her hand on her new husband's arm, and made to follow him out of the hall, " 'twas *Monso* fell under my spell first! You merely followed his example!"

"And a very good example it was, too," Alon said, as he led her in the opposite direction from the departing guests, toward the stairs. They stopped, smiled and waved amid a last chorus of toasts and good-wishings.

Eydryth paused at the top landing to gaze back along the gallery, where they could see Kerovan and Joisan, Sylvya, Firdun, Hyana, and Elys and Jervon all bidding farewell to the wedding guests. The happiness of seeing them all together again filled her heart until it felt as though it would burst. "I will have to write a song about today," she said softly.

Alon slipped an arm around her, then gently brushed back

a wayward curl. "Cannot it wait until tomorrow?" he asked mock-plaintively. "Or will you forget it if you do not write it down immediately?"

Eydryth laid her head against her lord's shoulder. "It can wait," she promised, with a smile, then kissed him. "The best songs cannot be forgotten."